Snowflakes in the Sahara

Snowflakes in the Sahara

Alan A. Winter

Writer's Showcase
San Jose New York Lincoln Shanghai

Snowflakes in the Sahara

Writer's Showcase
an imprint of iUniverse.com, Inc.

For information address:
iUniverse.com, Inc.
620 North 48th Street, Suite 201
Lincoln, NE 68504-3467
www.iuniverse.com

Second Edition, January, 2001

ISBN: 0-595-10025-2

Printed in the United States of America

To my loving wife, Joy. Your unwavering spirit, support, and understanding has made this possible. This one's for you.

"We did not inherit the earth from our parents.

We are borrowing it from our children."

Native American saying

"*Snowflakes in the Sahara*" is a clever novel that you can't help but sink your literary teeth into, as Carly Mason does for forensic dentistry what Quincy did for medicine. Carly is a one-of-a-kind heroine who helps solve a multinational mystery by using her forensic bag of tricks. Winter is not only a skillful writer who knows how to weave a good tale, he makes *"Snowflakes..."* leap off the pages, because he's one of us. Move over Kay Scarpetta and Patricia Cornwell, Winter's Carly Mason just may be the new female super sleuth!"

Howard S. Glazer, DDS, FAAFS
Deputy Chief Forensic Dentist
Office of Chief Medical Examiner, City of New York

Acknowledgements

I could not have written this book without the tutelage and guidance of those who have affected me throughout my life. My warmest thanks to the history professors at Rutgers University who taught me to see the future by studying the past; to the faculty of NYU and Columbia dental schools who taught me to be a student every day of my life; and to the professional staff at the Armed Forces Institute of Pathology who taught me forensic dentistry, and that every body has a story.

Two pathologists gave unstintingly of their time. My gratitude to Dr. Sue Campbell, medical examiner for Bergen County, Paramus, New Jersey, who answered my many questions while she performed—and I watched—numerous autopsies, and Dr. Cindy Porterfield, medical examiner for Tucson, Arizona, who shared her knowledge and expertise while we studied forensic anthropology together at the University of New Mexico, and then was kind enough to check medical facts and jargon in the manuscript.

I owe a debt of thanks to Dr. Howard S. Glazer, DDS, deputy chief forensic dentist in the Office of Chief Medical Examiner, City of New York. Howard read the manuscript with an editor's eye to insure that Carly Mason did forensic dentistry proud.

Experts help turn ideas into realities for readers. Thanks to Paul Ginzberg, Professional Audio Laboratories, for explaining the world of tapes and surveillance. Waco, the World Trade Center bombing, your expertise is second to none.

My gratitude is extended to Mark Hart, managing director of the West Coast Zoological, Inc., for giving me a crash course on herpetology.

Pam Anderson, my publishing associate at iUniverse.com, deserves special recognition. Pam, your unwavering patience and professionalism was appreciated every anxious step of the way. You made a daunting task easy. Thank you.

I am also grateful to my family for their support and understanding that writers must follow their dreams. To my sons, Scott, Jordan, Ryan, Brett, and Dean: always reach for the stars. To Robert, Marshall, and Ariel, writers-in-arms. To Cheryl and Robin, the best sister and brother anyone could have. To my parents, Janice and Berny Winter, who taught me I could do anything I set my mind to do.

Five special patients must be publicly thanked: Lucy Gaston for forcing me to take up creative writing nearly twenty years ago; Laura Foreman, Sylvia Roberts, and Stan Friedman, who criticized, critiqued, and pushed me to be a better writer; and Richard Lingeman, ever the professional whenever help was needed. Your cares and concerns kept me going.

Finally, I must thank my muse and mentor, Susan Hall. Susan, you believed in me from the start, always knowing which buttons to push. Susan, you are the epitome of a friend.

I am lucky to have all of you.

I

"Aldous Fromm can't pull it off," Jeremy Steel said to Lute Aurum, "Fromm's a long shot at best. We can't count on him winning. Even if he does, who's to say he'll get *our* job done?"

The two moguls were standing in the basement of Lute's Institute of Humanetics, an inspirational empire jump-started by Jeremy Steel's millions.

"That's why I brought you here," Aurum said. "Watch. The show's about to begin; then you'll be convinced."

Lute Aurum felt that he could not have picked a better pigeon than Texas's Governor Fromm. Four words spoken by Fromm, "*I need your help,*" catalyzed Lute's long dormant scheme.

The men studied Aldous Fromm through a one-way mirror. For now, the governor twitched in his straight-backed wooden chair as his "monitor" prodded him across the plain Formica table. During the Korean War, this one-on-one exchange had been called brainwashing. But here, in the bowels of Aurum's Institute, it was the penultimate step to self-realization.

The monitor was a slight man who had clearly worked on bulking up to an MP's physique. His hair was cropped to a drill sergeant's buzz and matched his military dress: the Institute's unisex standard issue, a green Polo shirt and mustard-colored khakis.

Monitors were faceless drones. They did Lute's bidding like the flower vendors who stood on the city street corner for eighteen-hour stretches, selling wilted roses in the name of Reverend Moon. At the Institute for Humanetics, monitors were the teachers and administrators who kept Lute Aurum's juggernaut rolling.

Jeremy Steel didn't like the mental bashing process he was watching. He thought Humanetics—as a belief system—was a waste. In fact, Jeremy Steel didn't believe in anything. As far as he was concerned, "belief" weakened.

Power was a different story. He loved power as much as any man had ever loved anything. Over the five years he had known Aurum, Jeremy had observed that all his hocus-pocus was designed to deliver power.

So what if Humanetics drove a spike into its subjects' psyches? "Timetracks" and "enturbulated" were futuristic words Aurum made up purposefully to confuse those who sought his help. The weak-willed, the emotionally lost, and the aimless could never realize that Humanetics's twelve steps toward self-realization were nothing more than classic mind-fucking at its best.

Only when Jeremy found himself at a small dinner with John Travolta and Tom Cruise did he begin to take the magnetic quality of Aurum's work seriously. The actors had raved that they owed their successes to Aurum and Humanetics. Even their wives believed. These Hollywood stars straightened Jeremy out. Humanetics was not some cabal led by a glassy-eyed guru who hypnotized his followers. No, Lute Aurum was special; he was someone Jeremy Steel should get to know. Jeremy took their advice.

Jeremy was hooked the moment he met Lute Aurum. At the onset, Jeremy had thought Lute might be one of the few men in the world he could not lead. But in time, Steel's offer and delivery of cash to help build Humanetics's headquarters into a global force, altered that opinion. His manipulation of the IRS to grant

Lute's extraordinarily profitable enterprise the tax-free status of a church *bonded* the two men.

"Bonding" was Lute's word, not Jeremy's.

Anyone who did business with Lute Aurum had to be "audited" by the process Aldous Fromm was now undergoing. The timetracks of every enturbulated soul had to be erased. Not Jeremy Steel. His cash bought him a free pass to the world of Humanetics. Not that Jeremy would ever have tolerated Humanetics's pussy-whipping demands. Masters of the Universe didn't kowtow to anyone. There, standing shoulder to shoulder, Jeremy knew he was Lute's equal. Lute thought otherwise.

Now, the only thing that mattered was to determine how worthy a convert Aldous Fromm would become.

Lute turned away from the mirror and slipped his right hand into the pocket of a loose-fitting Nehru-styled jacket. He purred as he withdrew his pet tarantula, cupping it in his palm.

"Why do you always carry that thing around?" Jeremy asked, trying to mask his fear.

Lute stroked the back of the Antilles pinktoe with the tip of his index finger. In the world of tarantulas, the pinktoe was small, only an inch-and-a-half long. Lute raised the arachnid to eye level and mouthed a kiss at the spider.

Jeremy squirmed.

Aurum sliced his hand through the air; Jeremy jumped back into the cinder block wall with a bone-rattling thwack. His arms and legs flayed against the wall. He never took his eyes off the pinktoe. Jeremy hissed, "Get that thing away from me."

Lute made a shushing sound. "You should know when to pick your battles." He caressed the pinktoe's short hairs. "Save your childhood terrors for another day. This little fellow is as harmless as our governor."

It took all of Jeremy's willpower to stay in the room with Lute and his pinktoe, but he wasn't going to let Lute Aurum get the upper hand, no matter what. He cleared his throat, gulped, and then spoke, never taking his eyes off the little beast. "We've got too much riding on this to make a mistake."

"Are you forgetting Fromm came to me? After today, he's mine."

Lute stepped back.

Jeremy eased off the wall.

Lute cocked his head to the side, signaling ever-so-subtle twitches of his lips and brows that sent waves of anticipated pleasure to the pinktoe. The pinktoe moved a leg and Aurum hummed happily. Lute fished into his left pocket and brought his closed fist toward the spider.

Jeremy heard a chirp.

The tarantula?

Transfixed, Jeremy saw Lute tighten his fist in a practiced squeeze and drop a damaged, but still-breathing, cricket next to the hungry arachnid. The pinktoe's forelegs grabbed dinner.

While the tarantula was occupied with its meal, Jeremy was able to collect his thoughts. "Just because Fromm's got a pedigree second to none, doesn't mean he's got what it takes. He's raw and untested. The only reason the Longhorns voted for him was because he wrangled a deal for the Texas Rangers to stay in Arlington. That doesn't qualify him to run the country. Christ, I'm better suited for the job than he is."

"You want to be president?"

"I'm not the issue. Fromm is. Besides, you and I both know power is not in the hands of the person occupying the Oval Office. It rests with the puppeteers. Standing here, as far as I can tell, your Texas governor will never play in Peoria...and we need someone who will."

Jeremy Steel was used to having his way. When he talked, everyone listened. At six-three and a decade younger than Lute, he was a poster-boy for success wrapped in two thousand dollar suits. His slicked-back dirty-blond hair and billboard-smile were trademarks. The Post and the Times claimed he had more chutz-pah than Bill Clinton, which was more evident once Hillary forced Bill to endure Aurum's mind-bashing techniques after the Monica debacle. The mayor of New York consulted with Jeremy daily. Even Steel's ex-wives still talked to him. The only man Jeremy feared—and revered—in the entire world was Lute Aurum.

*   *   *

Lute was a man no one could forget, but he had not always had that effect on people. In fact, Lute was the forgotten face in high school. Rural Nebraska was never kind to mediocre students and poor athletes. Hard-pressed to make friends, he turned to Frank Herbert, Isaac Asimov, and Gene Roddenberry for company. He exhibited a flair for writing and then went on to major in English at the university. The Navy put his writing skills to use as an in-service reporter during a stint in Saigon. After his discharge, he crafted a successful career as a science fiction writer, and was best known for his Iotan Planet series.

In Aurum's invented world, aliens journeyed from the planet Iota to Earth. Unlike other evil inter-galactic creatures, Lute's were purveyors of good. His creatures invaded the human pod to create immortal souls. But eternal life came with a price: earthlings had to first rid themselves of every frailty that tied them down. In a manner of speaking, they had to wipe their slate clean. Invaded by an Iotan, the human vessel was a *pre-Clear* striving to morph into a *Clear*.

Only *Clears* were true Iotans.

Iotans lived forever.

In real life, Aurum believed *he* was an Iotan.

Lute's books became so successful and his following so great, that he refined the Iotan beliefs and published them as a guide for the living. He called his life-system Humanetics, declared it a religion, and anointed himself head priest. When the IRS gave Humanetics church status (thanks to Jeremy Steel's clout), every dollar Aurum collected from courses given at the Institute, from seminars held across the country and around the world, and from his vast publishing empire, was tax-free.

*   *   *

When the pinktoe finished its meal, Lute returned the spider to the depths of his pocket. "Can't you see the beauty of this? The symmetry? Fromm doesn't want to be president. He *has* to make a run for it."

"Who's forcing him?"

Jeremy's breathing turned more normal now that the tarantula was out of sight.

"Fromm, Sr., that's who. Junior's been groomed for the Oval Office from the get-go just like that kid in the movie 'Shine.' You remember, the one with the piano whose father stood over him like a Gestapo agent until he mastered the Rach 3. You remember what happened to him?"

"Expecting your kid will make it to the White House is a far cry from playing Rachmaninoff."

While Jeremy's voice raised a pitch, Lute remained ever calm. "Oppressive fathers create damaged children. That's what we have going for us."

"Then chalk it up to ego. Senior must want to go down in the history books as the second team of father and son presidents. After John Adams and little John Quincy."

"When is it not about ego?"

"Frankly, I'd tell my father to shove it. In fact, I *have* told my father to shove it. More than once."

"I'd expect no less from you. Fromm, on the other hand, is not you. He's incapable of countermanding the old geyser. That's why he's here. That's why we have him."

"Why do you think I'm so good at making deals? You're misjudging this guy. Fromm eats pressure for breakfast. He's not the patsy you think."

At that moment the lights flickered and then faded out. Jeremy, praying that the tarantula was under control, grabbed Lute's arm. "Does this happen often?"

"With all this heat, the public utilities can't meet the cooling demand. We get brown-outs all the time. How is it back east?"

"Con Ed has had their share, like all the others."

A generator kicked in and bulbs crackled back to life. A blast of air spewed from the vent. Jeremy wiped his brow.

"Bet you don't like scuba diving," Lute sneered.

"Tried it once." Jeremy wasn't going to tell Lute that he couldn't stand the sea grass moving back and forth, and schools of fish shimmering this way and that. Jeremy had used up his air in no time. When he had gotten to the water's surface, blood gushed from his nose.

"It takes discipline not to be afraid," Lute said.

"I've got the balls to do anything."

Lute was about to taunt him about dark rooms and tarantulas, but decided to let them pass. Better to file away Jeremy's weaknesses for another day. Instead, he said, "Let's listen."

Lute flicked on a wall switch so they could see and hear Fromm's auditing. The monitor had placed a lone rectangular instrument in front of Fromm. It was about the size of a shoe-box. The device was Lute's brainchild. It was called an H-meter, the "H" standing for Humanetics. Two wires stretched from the box and ended in metal plates that Fromm held in each hand...but not before the rubber-coated wires were wrapped around his arms like phylacteries.

What struck Jeremy as he watched the green-shirted monitor sharpen his verbal spears was that Aldous Fromm was a man uncomfortable in his own skin, a man who would rather have been a college professor than a budding political star. Fromm was in stark contrast to Lute Aurum. The two were about the same age and height, but that's where the similarities ended. Fromm was not certain that he wanted to rule the world; Lute already acted like he controlled it from the palm of his hand.

The governor's usually pale skin was now ashen and coated with a coppery sweat. He kept his eyes fixed straight forward. He appeared to be unfazed by the monitor in his face. Fromm opened and closed his fingers around the metal plates like a speed car racer eager to jump the gun.

"On your questionnaire, governor, you said you once beat the daylights out of your brother. Tell me why?"

The dial on the meter plunged to the far right as he answered. "He left my baseball mitt in the rain. It was my favorite thing in the whole world and he ruined it. My father got it from a famous collector in New Jersey. Livingston, I think. It belonged to Lou Gehrig."

"What did your father do when he found out?"

Fromm lowered is gaze. His voice became inaudible.

"I can't hear you."

"He caned me across the back. Out of love." Fromm looked up, his hazel eyes filled with tears. "I wasn't supposed to play with it."

"And I've got a bridge in Brooklyn to sell you. No one whips his kid with a wooden stick, not for any reason. Certainly not for love. I'd be pissed at him, too."

Fromm sagged. "I'm not mad at him. I deserved it."

The needle remained buried to the right.

"The H-meter says otherwise. The H-meter says you're so piss-eyed you can't see straight. It says that until you resolve these timetracks, you'll be enturbulated forever."

Fromm wriggled in the chair. His eyes darted around the room. His breathing grew labored. "It was my fault, not my father's. I'm the one who lost control. I never should have taken the glove outside."

The monitor threw up his hands and paced back-and-forth behind the governor. "You were right to belt your s.o.b. brother. You should've crippled him for what he did to you." He stepped toward the cinder block wall, and then wheeled about. "You're more fucked up than I thought."

Nose-to-nose, the monitor snarled; Fromm flinched. "If your father loved you, he would have praised you. You're all twisted."

A tear spilled down Fromm's cheek. Then another.

"Your father has been your enemy all your life. Can't you get that through your thick skull? He's the one holding you back from that *casa blanca* in Washington. You're here to prove to the Old Man that you've got what it takes. Don't deny the truth."

This time the gauge remained dead center neutral. The monitor had made a dent in Fromm's defenses. Fromm took a deep breath, and then threw his chest out. He had been plagued with these thoughts for forty years, but was too ashamed to admit them. Finally, someone gave him permission to air his hurts.

Fromm raised his head to the monitor. "Help me."

Lute flicked off the switch and turned to Jeremy.

"Is he Mr. Perfect or what?"

Jeremy stroked his chin. "From what I just heard, it will take a lifetime of auditing to get rid of his timetracks...and then he'll still be messed up. He'll never get through this program in time to be of use."

"He only got here yesterday, right before the others. I need time to polish the edges, and he's mine."

"Ours...and don't ever forget it. As for polishing the edges, Fromm's a major reclamation project. I can't believe you're wasting your time with him. There's got to be someone better suited."

A twisted smile crossed Lute's face. "I'm surprised at you. After all we've been through, all the years of planning. Where's your faith? Fromm is the one."

"Even if Fromm does become a player," Jeremy warned, "sitting in that Oval Office changes a man. He can never captain our team."

Lute rocked on his heels. "Trust me. We will form the greatest triumvirate the world has ever known."

Until one of us gets stabbed in the back, thought Jeremy.

Earth Sizzles to Record High Temperatures

by Elmore Gossage

The earth's average surface temperature reached its highest level since meteorologists first used a thermometer around the time of the Civil War. This year marks the twenty-sixth year in a row that the earth's annual temperature has exceeded the historic average. In fact, nine out of the ten hottest years have occurred during this last decade, with an ignominious streak occurring through this month: each of the last eighteen months have been the hottest single average months on record.

While some scientists maintain that the earth's temperatures fall within the normal cycles that have appeared every ten-to-twenty thousand years, some dissenters are adamant that the warming trend is a result of emissions of heat-trapping waste industrial gases like carbon dioxide, which are produced by burning oil, coal, natural gas, and even wood.

Besides tracking daily temperatures, changes in annual tree rings strengthen the theory that the earth is heating up. During the twentieth century, the earth had warmed up by 1.25 degrees. Though it may not sound like a lot, since the last Ice Age that ended about ten thousand years ago, the earth had only warmed 5-9 degrees. In this context, the twentieth-century increase was huge.

Scientists now estimate that the next century will see an acceleration of this trend, with the earth heating up an additional 2 to 6 degrees.

2

Carly Mason was a young dentist from New York who, at first glance, did not appear a likely candidate for Humanetics. A head-turner, Carly caused men to catch their wives' sharp elbows as they gawked at her lithe frame, cover girl skin, and aquamarine eyes. Carly was oblivious to men's stares and clueless as to how she affected them. To her way of thinking, she was another damaged soul seeking Aurum's help at the Institute.

Carly and Aldous Fromm had arrived at Aurum's Institute at the same time. Fromm expected star treatment; Carly was thrown in with the drones.

When Carly boarded the plane at JFK to go to the Humanetics makeover, she had three areas of critical concern. First was to grab a handful of life's riches, second to share them with a significant other, and third to start a family. Having long passed her thirtieth birthday, Carly's biological clock was ticking louder than ever. Each time her six-foot frame stretched for that brass ring, it seemed to slip further from her toned health-club arms. She could get her body into shape, but her goals were elusive.

Had she been more in touch with her childhood demons, she would have added a fourth concern to her list: coming to grips with a father who, over the last twenty-odd years, had not so much as called or dropped a postcard telling her where he was or that he still loved her. She didn't even know if he was alive. When her mother died years ago, Carly—for all practical purposes—was made an orphan.

There had been wonderful days when she was eight and nine. Although the family lived in an attached garden duplex in Queens—Fresh Meadows to be exact—Hack Mason loved to expose his daughter to Nature's wonders. They'd drive to Jones Beach together and collect multicolored shells. He taught her about starfish and sea horses and crabbing, and how lobsters were trapped in wooden cages. Further out on The Island, they went for hikes in the saw grass and skirted marshes to catch a glimpse of a blue heron or a nest of duck eggs. Her favorite drive was to northern Westchester. She would take off her white sneakers and socks, roll up her jeans, and stand in the cold spring water casting a thin fiberglass rod in the direction of a dark ripple that appeared to move. The glee when she caught a trout! Hack Mason taught her all those things and more...until he left home on her tenth birthday. That's when the lights went out for Carly. That's why she was vulnerable to Lute Aurum's teachings.

Hack Mason's sudden departure had turned Carly into a turnkey child at ten. Her mother worked the afternoon and early evening shift at the Five Corners Diner on Northern Boulevard. Day after day, Carly came home to an empty house searching for what she could say or do that would bring her father back.

The sulking didn't last long. One day, her fifth grade teacher asked her to stay after class. The spinster sat Carly down and told her not to be afraid of showing she was smarter than the boys, said that Carly should be proud that she had a quick mind and an aptitude for science and math. From that time on, Carly ignored the snickers every time she waved her hand with the right answer.

She went on to make the Honor Society at Francis Lewis High School and was named a National Merit semi-finalist. Everyone expected her to try out for cheerleading, but she chose volleyball and made first-team All-State. When it came time for the school's senior play, kids said she was too awkward to be an actress. Undaunted, she tried out for the lead...and got it. When it came to picking a career that would guarantee a steady income, she bypassed teaching and chose dentistry.

It was a good choice. Everyone knew that dentists made oodles of money and still could hit the links once or twice a week. If they weren't above-average golfers, they were more than passable tennis players or expert skiers. With only the rare emergency call, they had plenty of time for their families. Dentistry was the perfect career for Carly Mason...or so she thought.

Carly entered NYU's dental school primed to set the world on fire. She calculated she would have both success and a man in short order. Naturally, her one-point-eight children, her sprawling house with a white picket fence, and her golden Labrador retriever that barely fit into the rear of her silver-colored Range Rover, would all be courtesy of drilling and filling. The formula was a guarantee for happiness.

Except time doused her fire into a fizzle of broken dreams. Mr. Right was as elusive as Sasquatch. There was no baby—not even eight-tenths of one—to nurture. Talk about timing! Managed care was the iceberg piercing dentistry's hull, and Carly Mason's dental practice was being dragged to the depths of cold, still waters.

Years into being a dentist, her future should have been secure. Carly shouldered her worries—*money* worries, and *lack-of-a-significant-other* worries, and *is-the-city-going-to-cut-out-my-forensic job?* worries —as though she had not a care. Life was anything but good.

Then a brochure from the Institute of Humanetics crossed her desk. Something rang a bell. Wasn't Jonah Schoonover saying just the other day how Humanetics changed his life?

Jonah had been one of her four cadaver-mates freshman year at NYU. When it came to catching an angle on how to make a buck, Jonah knew all of them. While he was boasting about the geometric growth in his practice, hers was floundering. While he had an avalanche of patients, she hardly experienced a flurry. Most fortunate of all, Jonah had a beautiful wife and three-point-four beautiful children housed on his Old Westbury estate.

Jonah claimed he owed it all to Humanetics. So when the three-part missive came in the mail, Carly opened it instead of tossing it into the wastepaper basket.

*"Come to an introductory course and gain the
business skills needed for greater success."*

Carly scoffed at any system that claimed to not only have all the answers to stop life's hemorrhages, but to be able to initiate complete healing in one fell swoop. She read on, stopping at the phrase, *"...find success and gain happiness."* One hundred and ninety-five dollars would get her in the front door, refundable if she registered for the full four-day program. She shrugged, not wanting to think what the four days at Aurum's Institute for Humanetics would set her back. What the hell! It was good enough for Jonah.

Lute Aurum knew how to hook people into his belief system. If there were demons in your past, Aurum would shove the demons in your face until you cried, "Mercy." Humanetics was a magnet for the walking wounded. That's what made Carly Mason, Aldous Fromm, and all the others gravitate to the Institute. They were all damaged goods.

The introductory course was held at the downtown Marriott Hotel, on West Street next to the West Side Highway in New York

City. Though small by uptown standards, the Marriott was amply appointed. A black bulletin board atop a brass pedestal had an arrow pointing toward a marbled staircase: **The Lute Aurum Introductory Course to Humanetics** was on the second floor.

Carly registered at a long table. She clipped her plastic nametag to her pocketbook strap, and then entered the converted ball-room-to-lecture hall looking for a familiar face. The high-ceilinged room, rimmed by thick moldings worthy of Versailles, was drenched in gold-flocked moiré wallpaper and crowned with chandeliers dripping crystals. In truth she expected to find a room filled with well-dressed generation-Xers like herself, young people looking to get a business edge up. Instead, the registrants represented New York as the melting pot of the world. The hopefuls wore dashikis and polyester, turbans and baseball caps. Sprinkled between open-shirted Russians and French-speaking Senegalese were a smattering of Wall Street brokers and financial planners.

Lesson number one: there were no barriers to Humanetics's appeal.

"When something seems too good to be true, it usually is," Willie Robinson had advised her that morning. Carly adored Willie. As chief pathologist, Willie was her mentor, advisor, and boss at the Medical Examiner's office.

"I'm going anyway."

"For a hundred and ninety-five bucks, get it out of your system."

Waiting for the course to start, she was thinking how the one-ninety-five registration fee would have paid for a decent pair of shoes—more like half-a-pair—when she locked like a laser beam on a "face" animated in conversation. If *that* face had *anything* to do with Humanetics, then the program just hop/skipped two notches up her chart from a "wait and see" to a "probable buy." On second thought, she would buy "futures" in Humanetics if it meant getting to know the "face" better.

And that's how Humanetics wove its web. A pretty face, a bag of promises.

"Please find your seats," said the course director, fastening a lavaliere microphone to her smart gray suit Carly recognized as the Armani she could never afford. "We're about to begin."

The drone simmered. The director fingered magic markers lining the chalk runners of a white board. The word POSITIVITY, in black letters, punctuated an otherwise squeaky clean surface.

"Welcome to Lute Aurum's introductory course on *'Necessary Survival Skills for the 3rd Millennium.'* My name is Suzy Crenshaw and I will be your facilitator this evening. Around the room...," transfixed eyes followed her index finger from one side to the other, "...are staff monitors here to help you, in every way."

The first spoke on cue. "Howdy, folks! My name is Kirk Felter. I'm here to inspire you."

"My name is Cindy Adams. Looking at your smiling faces I know we are one big happy family."

"Owen Bucks here. Been with Lute six years, never met a finer man."

Then it was the "face's" turn to introduce himself. Carly soaked in his every detail. He was taller than the others. He wore a wide-lapel, blue Ungaro suit and handmade mesh loafers that cost more than Carly made in a week. A splashy tie of yellows, red, kiwi greens and a hint of hyacinth accented his subtle pinstriped shirt. The monitor had that wet look that invited the curious to suspect what was under his body-hugging threads. She memorized his chiseled face, his outstanding cheekbones, and the golden locks that covered his ears and curled onto his neck. Deep-set green eyes beckoned.

"I'm Conner Masterson. I look forward to working with each of you."

"And you can start with me," Carly Mason whispered under her breath.

          *   *   *

From across the room Conner caught Carly Mason's flicker of interest. Conner had balked when Suzy asked him to monitor this course. He had been working hard. Special jobs for Lute. Assignments that, when executed well, captured Lute's attention. This was fine with Conner because Lute responded to results. There was no doubt Lute had dubbed him a "comer," a "go to" man. No matter what was asked of him, Conner delivered. Monitors who received high marks moved up Lute's ladder of success. In no time, Conner would be the number one seed in Humanetics. Seeing Carly gave him pause.

She appeared tall to him, almost as tall as he was. It was hard to miss her. She brimmed with confidence, yet experience told him she probably had psychic rifts as deep as canyons.

For the next hour Carly glanced Conner's way enough to make her neck sore, with barely an ear to Suzy Crenshaw's spiel about Humanetics. She did hear scraps about "success" and "happiness." Gaining the "skills to go all the way" certainly appealed to her. When Suzy asked Conner to write the seven business skills everyone needed to succeed on the board—**Expert, Communicate, Financier, Marketer, Public Relations, Executive Administrator, Money Manager**—Carly bristled. Suzy was a woman with a fake smile plastered on her doll-like face. There wasn't a hair out of place, her makeup was perfect and on second thought, her Armani was probably a knockoff. Moreover, Conner not only jumped to do her bidding, but also *heated up* as he approached her.

"There you have it ladies and gentlemen, the ingredients for success. Take those seven blocks, roll them into a big ball, and...," she blew into her hand like a magician, "...what do you have?"

"Success," called someone seated in the front.

"What else?"

"Happiness."

They had absorbed the lesson.

"That's what this is all about folks, success and happiness." Suzy glanced at her watch. "Okay, it's break time. The food and restrooms are out the back. The monitors will circle about, answering any questions you have. Those of you ready to commit to the four-day course will receive a ten percent discount that's only good through tomorrow night."

The only bargain Carly could focus on was making contact with Conner Masterson. She stepped his way, plotting how to break the ice, only to feel her shoulder tapped. She turned to see Suzy's loaded smile.

"Carly? How do you like the course so far?"

The last thing she wanted to do was speak to little Miss Perfect at that moment. Carly glanced over her shoulder; Conner raised a brow.

"Carly?" Carly drew a bead on the course director, wishing she had worn sunglasses to deflect that blazing smile. "What do you think?"

"Uh, you've managed to highlight the shortcomings of my practice. It seems I was doomed to fail right from the beginning."

"I see you've been listening in spite of the distractions."

Carly's color changed two shades. *Was it that obvious?*

"Recognizing one's limitations is the first step to recovery. That's where *POSITIVITY* comes in: chasing out the bad ideas from the past and accepting better ones to improve ourselves. Lute made that word up. It says it all, doesn't it?"

"Seems to."

"Then I can sign you up for our full program?"

Suzy was in Carly's face now, her cheap perfume offending.

"How much is this four-day course?"

"With the ten percent discount, it's fifteen."

Carly seemed unfazed. Though she'd rather take a trip with the money, fifteen hundred for a four-day course was usual. In fact, it was cheaper than she thought it would be.

Suzy handed her a registration form, and then pointed to the bottom. "Just sign here and we'll be all set."

Carly was about to write her name when she saw the price. "I can't sign this. Is this a typo or something? Fifteen *thousand* dollars for the course? That's absurd."

"I agree. It is an absurd bargain for what you're getting. Besides, after tomorrow, it goes to sixteen-five. Next month, it'll even be more."

"Tuition cost that for my first year of dental school. You're talking about four days."

Carly had come to the Marriott courtesy of Jonah's good fortunes. Somewhere in the middle of the talk, she connected with the images Suzy Crenshaw painted. After all, how could one person be skilled enough to be an expert in her field while at the same time knowing how to market herself and manage her staff, everyday operations, and finances, too? She'd have to be another Bill Gates! Maybe an advanced course *would* get her practice to the next level. It was time for the moaning and complaining to stop. But fifteen thousand was a huge investment. Huge.

"Look at it this way," Suzy continued, "with what we'll teach you, your gross is guaranteed to double in six months. If it doesn't, we'll return every penny you've spent. Can we do better than that? The fact is, most people's incomes triple after taking the four-day course. In return for these new skills you'll be acquiring, all we're asking for is a small part of your new success. Think of it this way. We get the first three or four weeks of it, you get everything else for the rest of your life."

What did Carly's mother always say? *You've got to give to get!* Still fifteen big ones was a lot of giving, no matter how appealing Suzy made it. Carly licked her lips and looked away. A minor jolt, strong enough to register on the Richter scale, jiggled through her when she caught Conner looking right at her. Or was he looking at Suzy?

"I'm not ready to commit to this right now. I need some time."

"Let me blunt, Carly." Suzy did not blink. "The Lute Aurum course is extraordinary. Something worth doing. As a friend—I know we just met, but I am your friend—it's in your best interest to get the skills you're lacking. It's dog-eat-dog out there. We're talking survival. Food on the table. Paying the rent."

"What happened to happiness and success?"

"That, too."

"I've never spent so much money just for a course before."

Suzy looked Carly over from head to toe.

"It shows."

Carly bit her lower lip, not from anger, but because she hurt. She knew it was the truth. While most women her age didn't think twice about how much a dress or bag cost, Carly was always fingering price tags, hoping a zero would rub off so she could afford the dresses, too.

In deliberate fashion, Suzy brought her wrist up and scrutinized her Chopard watch. Carly knew the piece. It was the one with the diamonds floating under the crystal; it was in all the magazines. The watch costs almost as much as the four-day Humanetics course. Next Suzy opened her Prada bag and found her monogrammed compact case to do a quick inspection of her perfect face.

They couldn't all be knockoffs. Neither was the Armani.

Suzy snapped the bag shut. "While you're thinking about taking the plunge, remember how much money is slipping through your fingers. *Tempus fugit* and all that. Maybe a personal consult tomorrow night will convince you."

"I read something about that in the brochure. What does *that* cost?"

"It's gratis. We do it for the select few we sense want to take the course, but need a nudge. You're one of them."

"You're that sure of me? What makes you such a quick judge of character?"

"Gotta be in this business. There's too many fish out there for us to waste time trolling on the losers...and I know you're not a loser."

Suzy scanned her clipboard, and then her rubber smile stretched closer to her one-point-something-carat studded earrings.

"Do I come here again?"

"The consult is at your convenience. See how your day is going tomorrow. The monitor will call you at your office. He's pretty flexible."

"He?"

"Oh, didn't I mention it? You'll be meeting with Conner Masterson."

3

Carly left the Marriott feeling more giddy than prudent. For safety's sake, she splurged on a cab ride to her apartment. As the cab streamed up the West Side Highway past Gansevoort Street and the meatpacking district, past the all-night diner on Twelfth Avenue, past the USS Intrepid and the Jersey-bound ferry, Carly replayed her good fortune at drawing the handsome, sexy Conner for her consult. Carly was feeling so good she considered calling the Psychic Hotline to see what else was in store for her.

The cab pulled into Lincoln Towers off West End Avenue. The six towers were built decades earlier, a city-within-a-city. In contrast to the freshly planted gardens and tulip-lined paths, the complex had aged into a hulking composite of grimy brick and rusted casement windows. Clipped greens and unflagging maintenance could not offset beige buildings that had grown as tired and old as their inhabitants. On most days Carly's bouncy stride was in stark contrast to the legion of crinkled seniors trudging with walkers or limping on canes.

Miguel, the night doorman, glimpsed Carly coming in from the street. Carly always counted on Miguel who, along with the other doormen, took a special interest in protecting the few young single women living in the building.

Carly unlocked her metal cube. "Was Danny here today?" she asked Miguel, thumbing through her mail.

Danny was the everyday mailman.

"Danny went to the Yankee game. One of those inter-league jobs with the Mets. Sure hope the Mets tie one over on them Bombers. Why?"

Carly rifled through the letters a second, and then a third time. They had been stacked in an even pile, edge-to-edge, corner-to-corner. "They feel strange. Too neat. Like someone opened them."

"Nah, who would do that?"

Yeah, who would do that?

              *   *   *

Inside her apartment, Carly clicked on the lights. A dozen over-sized fringed pillows that she bought on sale at ABC Carpets rested on a long couch covered with a cream-colored moiré fabric. The distressed wood coffee table was cluttered with old magazines and a half-filled plastic bottle of Evian.

A built-in pine wood unit stretched across the opposite wall. It had come with the apartment. Its round-edged shelves were extra thick, and sagged in the middle from years of use. Sprinkled in front of books from college and dental school were a dozen silver-framed pictures, five-by-sevens and three-by-fives, of Carly with friends she rarely saw any more. There was a twenty-inch television on the center shelf that had a layer of dust on the screen; it had not been turned on in weeks.

Carly plucked organically grown carrots and fresh celery stalks from the refrigerator, blending them into a cocktail to drink with her vitamins. She munched on sesame flat breads while she thumbed through the latest New York Magazine. Here she was, living alone, drinking vegetable juice, and snacking on dry crackers. Whatever free time she had was spent at the Medical Examiner's. *How'd it happen?*

Carly replayed the day's messages while dabbing baby oil onto a cotton ball.

She heard a click, but no message.

She wiped off her eye make-up.

The next message was also a click and nothing.

The third message sparked a grin.

"Hi, Carly, it's Conner Masterson...from the Aurum seminar. Since you're my last appointment tomorrow night, could we turn it into a dinner? I'd sure like to have a normal evening, for a change. I'll call you at your office in the morning."

Pause.

"Sweet dreams."

*   *   *

Conner found Carly at the polished bar at Patria on Park Avenue South. Like most restaurants built in industrial areas, it had high ceilings that bounced conversations to the floor with a vengeance.

"Is it always so noisy?"

"Always." She lifted a white wine spritzer. "Want to catch up?"

Conner ordered a bottle of micro-brewed Long Shot Light Ale. The crowd pressed him against Carly's leg. He didn't pull back. Neither did she.

"How did the consults go?" she asked.

"Better than expected. We got six more to sign up."

"You *do* get a commission on each person who registers, don't you?"

She luxuriated in the way he focused on her. His eyes didn't wander to the half-dressed model-types around the bar, craning for *his* attention. (Who could blame them?)

"Let's save the business talk for later. How was your day?"

"You don't want to hear about my life. Dentists are boring."

"Not when they work for the Medical Examiner, they're not."

"I was in my dental office most of the day. Nothing glamorous there. In fact, that's why your program interests me. If I don't do something to bring in more patients, I'll be forced to work for other people. That's not why I became a dentist. Enough of that. Tell me about you."

"There's nothing to tell. I'm from a small New England town. My dad was a printer and wanted me to go into the business with him, but I had other ideas. We had the typical father-son knock-down battles over it."

"Who won?"

"I did, for a while." Conner leaned back and gulped down half the bottle.

Carly sipped her spritzer. "So I take it setting ens and ems wasn't for you."

"You're a Scrabble player?"

"Crossword puzzles."

He flashed his array of perfect enamel. "Printing's changed, like everything else. Most of it's computerized these days. The last thing I wanted was to be trapped in my father's shop."

"Were you one of the fortunate few who got to bum around Europe for a couple of years?"

"Hardly. I wanted to be an actor. I went to Emerson, it's in Boston."

"I know where it is."

"Most people don't. Anyway, I was an English major, took lots of acting classes. Made the lead in a lot of plays…"

"Funny, I was the lead in my high school play. That was ages ago. So what happened to you? You've got the looks. Speak well. I'd have thought you were a natural."

His gaze dropped, so did his voice. "Something happened."

The noise around them cranked up. She leaned closer to hear, inhaling his musk-scented cologne. Her pulse quickened.

"My father had a heart attack right on the shop floor. One of the men tried CPR but it was no good."

She touched his hand. "I'm so sorry."

He looked up. "There were so many things I never got to say to him." Struggling to gain control, he grabbed a cocktail napkin off the bar and blew his nose.

"Believe me, I know how you feel," she said.

Conner let out a long breath and continued. "At that point, I had no choice. So I left school to run the business."

"Couldn't your mother do it?"

"My father was the old-fashioned type. He would never let his wife work. She didn't even know that checkbooks were supposed to be balanced. My sister was still in school then. I had no choice. It was me or we go hungry."

"So you became the man of the family."

He finished his beer. "Something like that."

"When did you get involved with Aurum?"

Just then, an anorexic leggy blond with short hair and a sash that barely covered her vital parts announced that their table was ready.

"...after we're seated."

Once they trucked to the table, Conner started to read the menu. "What kind of food do they serve here?"

"Ever have Ecuadorian free-range chicken or Cuban polenta?"

"I can't even pronounce half these things!"

"Then let me order for you."

"We have a lot in common."

"How do you mean?"

Conner leaned forward on both his arms. "You know the way dentistry seems to be passing you by?"

"Not seems to be, is."

"Same thing happened to me in the printing business. My father did okay in the early days. He got to print all the handouts that go with living in a small town. You know, the annual July 4th parade, the 10K races, garage sales, charity auctions, and the stationery for half the local businesses. Throw in wedding and party invitations, and he eked out a living. Then, when the cheap copy places opened up and everyone had their own computers, half that went by the wayside. That's when he created this niche of printing church newsletters. You can't believe how many little churches there are in New England. Every one of them sends out a weekly letter. My father would get the merchants to advertise to help defray the costs. He was finally making money for the first time in his life. Then he died."

"The business was good?"

"For a time, it even got big. I expanded it until I had every church in five surrounding counties using me. Then some big outfit from Pennsylvania came in and cut the legs out from under me. Made a deal with all the churches to give them a higher percentage of the advertising dollars."

"Weren't there any contracts?"

"We're talking New England, here. Everything was a handshake. Besides, these churches weren't exactly flush with money. Along comes some fast-talking suit who promises to give them a revenue stream from something that used to cost them money, and they jump like bass at feeding time."

"You'd expect a church to be loyal."

"Wouldn't you? The kicker is these outsiders didn't give a hoot about the local merchants *or* the churches. All they cared about was their bottom line. They squeezed the stores.

Quadrupled the advertising rates. That's how the churches made out, and so did they."

"And you didn't."

"Which is why I took the Aurum course. The man inspired. Sure it was all the clichés—a new purpose, success and happiness—but he helped me regain my self-esteem. I realized he had more to offer than the printing business, so I sold whatever was left to those bastards for a song. At least it was enough to take care of my mom. I've been with Aurum ever since."

"All the traveling and sleeping in hotels has got to get to you after a while."

"It still has a glamour for me, and you can't beat the money. To answer your question before, yes, we do get a commission. We've got a good product. The best. I'm going to stick with this a while longer."

"Then what? Go back to acting?"

Conner didn't answer when the waitress interrupted to take their order. They made small talk until the food came. Each dish was more aromatic and delicious than the one before.

"You're easy to talk to," Carly said, between courses.

"Really? I do fine in front of a group. Get me alone with a woman and weights grow on my tongue. Half the time I never know what to say because I'm so worried about being p.c."

She yanked on her hair, making a screeching face. "I hate that everyone feels they have to be politically correct. They've made it so we all have to walk on eggshells. No one can be themselves anymore."

"Amen to that."

The dishes were cleared. Carly ordered a decaf cappuccino; Conner's gruel-thick espresso laced with Anisette, had three coffee beans floating in it. The waitress set a banana flambé between them. Rum-fueled blue flames hissed, shot upwards, and then dwindled and vanished.

"Go ahead, try it."

He scooped the caramelized banana onto a spoon. Carly waited for the syrupy desert to explode in his mouth.

He nodded, "There should be a law against this."

Carly was oblivious to the clamor of the restaurant as their spoons clanked in the gooey banana.

"You're different Carly Mason. I know you've got your guard up, but you've got a softness about you I'm not used to seeing."

"Thank you."

"Don't thank me for telling the truth. I've talked more tonight than I have in the last two months. It's getting late. I need to ask you...."

She studied his mouth.

"...I know it's kind of tacky now...," his brow and lip arched as one, "...if you want to sign up for the advanced course? There's a spot open. You'd have to leave Sunday. From what you've told me about your practice, you need this course."

Carly knew she'd be taking the advanced course somewhere between seeing Conner the night before and hearing that her gross would triple. It was her survival ticket...possibly in more ways than one.

"Will you be teaching it?"

"As much as I want to, I have another introductory course to give. Sometimes, I do teach an advanced course. Maybe we could work together then?"

Or sooner?

By the time the waitress slipped the bill onto the table at the "consult" dinner, Carly had agreed to leave for Phoenix that Sunday.

"I apologize for having to ask for this now," he said, copying her AMEX number onto the back of her business card, "but they won't let you go until this is processed."

She shrugged. "I can't get out of Bloomingdale's without paying either."

He insisted on seeing her home. When they entered her lobby, she winked at Miguel. Miguel nodded his approval and gave a thumb's up. As they stepped into the elevator, Carly's palms began to itch. By the time she reached her door, welts were forming.

It was dilemma time. She never knew what to do. Kiss at the door? Invite him inside? It was *almost* their second date. Not really. It was the second time they met; neither had been a date. Still, she wanted him to know she was interested without being too forward. When it came to men, no matter how hard she tried, Carly had two left feet. Now, all she could think about was giving him the right signals...and having a taste of Conner's magnetic lips.

Let him make the move.

As Carly unlocked the first dead bolt, she felt his stare caress her back. She took her time with the second lock. Fumbling for the third key bordered on ecstasy. The moment the last tumbler clicked, the stage was set.

The starters were in their blocks.

Carly turned.

Ready?

Conner placed his hands on her shoulders.

Get set.

Carly closed her eyes.

Go!

Conner inched closer.

Carly tilted her head, drawing in his sweet breath.

A second shot was fired.

Conner spoke.

False start!

"I'm glad we got to know each other better."

She straightened her head and opened her eyes to find him staring back. "I enjoyed myself, too. Thanks, again, for dinner."

What's he waiting for?

"They're expecting me in Philly, tomorrow. We've got an early session."

She licked her lips, and then brought her hands to his waist.

"I wish I didn't have to go," he said.

"They're expecting you. You know, commissions and all that."

He lowered his head, never taking his eyes off hers. "I'm entitled to a life," he said, more to convince himself than her.

Yes!

That's when he pulled her into him. She trembled at the touch of his chest and arms, the way his lips met hers, the way his tongue explored her mouth. He shifted his weight, and their bodies grooved together.

Oh, but to run a marathon with him!

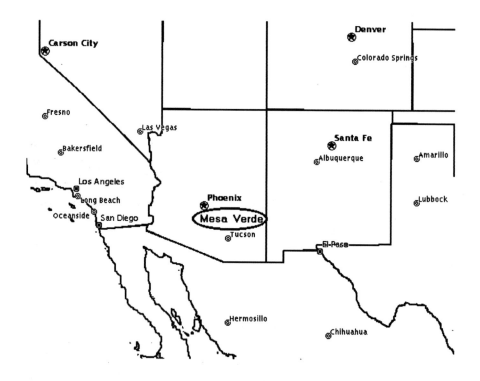

4

Except for the pilot's announcement that they needed to fly higher to avoid a huge tornado west of Harrisburg, Pennsylvania, the flight to Phoenix's Sky Harbor Airport was uneventful. The instructions in the Humanetics packet said a driver was to meet her at the gate and take her to Lute Aurum's ranch in Mesa Verde. When no one showed, Carly found the baggage claim area and waited at carousel seven for the conveyor to eject her black luggage.

An arm darted past hers.

"Let me help you. You must be the forensic dentist," said a pimply-faced youth dressed in a green shirt and mustard-colored pants. He set the piece on the floor.

She looked down. "How'd you know it was me?"

"Lucky guess. Actually, I read your file...and you're the last one. The others are in the van on the other side of the glass doors. I'm Jeff, by the way."

Even though she was long-legged, Carly had to trot to keep up with Jeff wheeling her luggage at a brisk clip. Jeff stowed the bag in a built-in compartment under the seats of the mauve-colored Chevy transport. The anxious buzz filling the van simmered as Carly squeezed passed the other course registrants. Ranged in age from thirty-to-sixty, most were men. Two women seated together were so engrossed in what they were discussing that they didn't even see Carly pass. She would connect with them later.

The only open seat was on the rear banquette next to a thickset man who was clearly too large to fit in the other seats. Carly wedged past him and nestled next to the tinted window. Even though the air-conditioner was on full blast, sweat poured down the man's face.

"Hot as a mother out there, isn't it?"

Carly took his meaty, clammy hand. "I don't know. How hot is a mother supposed to be?"

He had a gap-toothed smile. "Cute. You're the dentist."

"In the flesh."

Artie shrugged, only his shrug was more like Jell-O shimmying on a plate. "Want to know how I know? Saw Jeff's list. Only three women coming. Those two women are lawyers. It's elementary."

"Is your name Watson?"

"Like the detective? Very funny. I wish. Nothing that glamorous. Name's Artie Montefusco. From Cleveland. I sell magic tricks on the Internet. Mostly kids buy my stuff. I'm betting this course will get me to the next level. If everything falls right, I'm going public next spring. Not too many IPOs deal with magic, you know."

"I can imagine."

The van headed due east along Route 60 and Houdini of cyberspace fell silent, preferring to fan himself than to expend calories talking.

As Carly gazed out the window beyond the city limits and manicured gardens, she assumed she'd be driving through a vast desert filled with barrel cacti and low-lying scrub. The earth should have been parched and brown. It wasn't. Water trickled through gullies and culverts. Tall grasses swayed along the edges. Every few miles, they'd drive through a lush forest of willow cottonwoods and then pass acres of grasslands. A kaleidoscope of wild flowers spotted the tall grass.

Jeff's voice pierced the van. "Before all of you start asking about the desert, let me fill you in as to what's been happening here over the last few years. You've all heard of El Ninō. Lasted the entire decade of the nineties. Some places in the country grew warmer, some had more snow; we got rain. Our rainy season used to be a few weeks, now it goes on for months. We're passing what's known as riparian forests. A hydrologist over at the university did some soundings and discovered that the aquifer from the San Pedro River Basin was expanding northward. Creeks have come back to life, and the migratory birds have started funneling through here for the first time in history."

"I thought I saw a kingfisher out there."

"You did. We've got Song sparrows and Wilson's warblers, and Willow flycatchers, too. And dream-on about dry air. We've got humidity, pollen, mosquitoes, and more allergens than you can shake a stick at. Arizona isn't what it used to be."

A gurgling caught Carly's ear. She turned to Artie who broke into a guilty grin. He nodded at his gelatinous paunch. Climatic changes were not *his* concern at the moment.

"How about a bite to eat?" he called out across the van.

"Try to hold out. There's a barbecue at the ranch after you get settled in. That's when you'll meet the other registrants," Jeff snorted.

"Is the big boss gonna be there? For the money we're spending, Lute Aurum should be manning this course."

Jeff kept his eyes fixed on the winding road. He fielded the same questions with every group. "Not this go-round. You might catch a glimpse of him swimming laps in the pool or taking a walk with members of his inner circle. Those folks pay big bucks to spend time with him. Lute generally doesn't even speak to first-timers."

"Excuse me," said an accountant-type, "this is the most expensive course in the country. What do *you* call fifteen big smackers?"

"Chump change. You take Humanetics 101 so that you can get to the next level. Once you're rolling in dough, you can swim with the big fish, too."

Jeff's words perfumed the air with success. A dozen mental cash registers clicked away, creating imagined sums of great wealth.

"Where are we staying?"

"I'd stay in a hole if it meant making that kind of dough."

"You'll have your essentials. Lute doesn't believe in fancy," warned Jeff.

"Read something about the Institute on one of those in-flight magazines. What's Mesa Verde like?"

"Used to be a ghost town before Lute came here. He refurbished the hotel, moved his publishing company, and got the copper mines going again. His prize baby is the hospital. Has a neonatal unit, CAT scan, MRI, all kinds of stuff folks used to travel sixty miles for. The town's even got a soda shop that makes those New York style egg creams."

"When do we get to see the town?"

"Sorry. This course's all business. There's no time for sightseeing."

"There's got to be some fun stuff to do, isn't there?"

Jeff smirked. "Depends on the day."

"What's that supposed to mean?"

Jeff didn't answer.

Carly couldn't believe the others were carrying on so. She certainly didn't fly all this way to go sightseeing. Did breaking the chains that kept one from life's successes mean more to her than the others? One thing was certain: Humanetics was getting her full attention, unless one Conner Masterson showed his rakish face. Then she would go into a juggling act.

5

Before anyone asked about the black limo parked in front of Lute's white ranch house or whine that they'd like to take a dip in the Olympic-size pool or saddle-up one of the horses prancing in the coral, Jeff turned off the paved roadway. The van bumped along a graveled lane to a low-lying, ocher-colored building. It had a single hexagonal-shaped window above a red metal front door. The building was more fortress-like than guest lodging.

"*This* is the Institute. I suggest you like it 'cause you'll be staying here for the next few days." Jeff didn't beat around the bush.

"Where's my room with a view? Even Army barracks have windows."

Jeff unloaded the luggage without comment.

"Why are you making us stand out here? Can we go inside?"

"Find some shade or wait in the van. The chief monitor will be out in a second."

Artie Montefusco wouldn't wander from the van, but most recruits found refuge under a cluster of willows. Verdant grass lined the banks of an aged arroyo babbling with sparkling water. A breeze whipped up, sending sweet fragrances their way. Carly strayed from the group. She ran her index finger across the prickle of a barrel cactus.

Jeff looked up. "Be careful. They can cut you."

"Too late," she said, as she sucked a red droplet of blood.

Heads turned as the Institute's front door opened and another green-shirted, yellow-slacked man marched out. He gripped a clipboard in his left hand and a megaphone in his right. He was lean and muscular with brown hair trimmed military-short. He stood tall, surveying Humanetics's latest recruits...all raw to a one. It was his job to whip them into line, to bring them into the fold.

Legs spread apart, he barked through the megaphone. "My name is Bowden St. Clair, and you are my children for the next five days. Any problems during your stay, see me and I'll correct them. We run this course lean and hard. No frills. No filet mignon. No champagne."

"Any beer?"

"The Institute is alcohol free."

A few groans escaped.

"In a word, you'll find this experience 'memorable.' It's safe to say none of you have had a course like this...unless you've been in the Navy Seals or a participant on *The Survivor's Show*."

He scanned the group, reveling in their dismay.

"Sadist," someone muttered under his breath.

"We begin tomorrow morning. O-five hundred sharp. The course ends Thursday afternoon at sixteen hundred. Depending on flights, some leave Thursday, others Friday morning."

"Is it true we're not meeting with Mr. Aurum?"

"I'm certain Jeff explained that you'll meet him if you take an advanced course."

Artie Montefusco clutched his belly and brayed. "I know *I'm* coming back. I was made for this place."

Everyone smiled.

Bowden smirked. "This is not your everyday course. If I were you, I'd wait to make certain you finish before making promises you can't keep."

Artie glowed. "The only way I'm leaving early is in a pine box."

"Mr. Montefusco, is it? You'll find the Institute is first-class all the way. We only use mahogany."

Artie frowned, running a thick finger through his matted hair. "How'd you know my name? And that wasn't funny."

Bowden didn't miss a beat. "This is boot camp to your future. There are no bellhops to carry your luggage, no maids to make your beds. You're on your own. Room assignments are posted on the wall behind the door. Unpack, freshen up. We meet in forty-five minutes for barbecue."

*   *   *

Carly drew a ground level room. It had a single bed, a four-drawer chest, and an end table, all in early-American Shaker style. The wood was stained an amber honey that highlighted the knot-holes. A frosted glass hurricane lamp nested on the end table, providing the room's only light. There was no overhead fixture, no window, and no lock on the door. She would later discover that every room was exactly the same.

Carly draped her clothes on wooden hangers in the closet. She arranged her toiletries around the rim of the white porcelain sink, which was the only storage space available. As she showered, the water dribbled onto her skin, leaving her wanting. The dwarf-sized bath towel scarcely fit around her back. She remembered traveling cross-country between her first and second years of dental school, and staying in Day's Inns. The Day's Inns were half the price of the Holiday Inns. They also had half-sized beds, shrimp-sized towels, toilets with small seats, and no phones in the rooms. How she wished there was a second towel to wrap her hair now. She slipped into a DKNY hunter green tee shirt, light-blue jeans, and stepped out of her room, following the buzz of voices.

"This is disgusting," one of the registrants said.

One look told Carly why. The "barbecue" turned out to be rose-colored bug juice and soggy chocolate chip cookies.

Bowden appeared at the door and waved. "Everyone into the study chamber and take a seat. We'll go over tomorrow's schedule."

"What happened to the food?" Artie asked.

"You'll have to trust me on this one. It'll make you concentrate better. Scout's honor."

"You'll have to trust me on this one," Artie gave Bowden the finger. "Bullshit to you."

Bowden was halfway into the room and missed Artie's message.

There were twenty-four registrants in the class. They filed into what soon became known as the "learning center." Four rows of mud-brown folding chairs were clustered in the middle, forcing the class to sit knee-to-knee. Blond wood desks rimmed the outer walls, each topped with a computer including leather headsets. Posters of Lute Aurum lined the room. A wood lectern stood at attention behind Bowden.

There were no windows; the front wall was mirrored.

"Who feels funny sitting this way?"

Hands knifed up.

"The chairs are close for a reason. Why?"

"Makes us feel like a group."

"Sets us apart from the outside world."

"It forces us to lose our identity."

The recruits focused on Bowden as if their lives depended on him.

"Speaking of which, introduce yourselves. Tell us what you do."

Carly's compatriots ran the gamut: a stockbroker, a banker, a card-counting professional gambler, a used car dealer, two college teachers, a web page designer, a social worker, a shoe salesmen from Nordstrom's, a CEO, and an erotic bakery store owner.

Carly wondered how much she should reveal. She was a forensic dentist. A tooth sleuth. Sure she had the requisite training from Bethesda's Armed Forces Institute of Pathology and had volunteered lots of time at the Chief Medical Examiner's office, but that didn't pay the bills. So besides dealing with bite marks and postmortem x-rays, Carly rented a dental operatory off Park Avenue where she had a patient appointment book with more holes than aged Swiss cheese.

When it was her turn, she said, "I'm a general dentist hoping to gain the skills necessary to make my practice busier."

"Then you've come to the right place," answered Bowden. "Dentists love this course, especially the part about the quotas."

The man to Carly's right installed water sprinklers. Next came an accountant, a headhunter who specialized in HMO executives, a hairdresser, a tugboat skipper, an estate planner, a manager from Toys "R" Us, a priest, an optician, and a graphic designer. One woman was a medical malpractice lawyer, the other defended the First Amendment rights of porno web sites. And there was Artie Montefusco.

"Believe it or not, this is a typical mix for an introductory course. Lute's program is designed to help all of you. It's self-paced and exhausting. Get a good night's rest."

"It's only seven o'clock. My kids go to bed later than this."

Bowden stiffened. "This is your last free night. I suggest you take advantage of it."

Bumper Citrus Crop As A Result of Continued Tropical Weather

LAKELAND, FL., October 28 (AP) Florida's orange crop is turning out even bigger than expected, making it the twenty-second consecutive month that growers have seen record crops. The United States Agriculture Department raised its estimate of the state's orange crop to 360 million 90-pound boxes. This was a 2 per-cent increase from last month.

Growers expect record production to continue as long as Florida's three-year spell of tropical weather lasts. Experts from the U.S. Meteorological Department state that Florida's change in weather patterns may be permanent.

The larger orange crop continues to be good news for consumers as retailers are forced to keep the price of orange juice down. But this is not good for farmers, who have seen a steady decline in prices.

A side benefit to this increased orange production is a worldwide

decrease in scurvy, as more third
world countries are able to import
oranges as a cheap source of
Vitamin C.

6

Carly was in overdrive. The last thing she wanted to do was sleep, so she rummaged through her carry-on for the novel she'd been reading for the last nine months, *The English Patient.* Two pages later she tossed it down. She hopped up, absorbed the bleak interior, and started pacing.

She paced back and forth.

Would Conner surprise her and show up? Dream on, girl!

"You're doing it again," she said out loud.

How many times had Carly latched onto a pair of dark eyes, full lips, and white teeth only to have her heart torn into confetti? When it came to picking guys, punishment was her middle name. In high school, it was Rod Phillips, captain of the basketball team. Who else would ask her out? She was taller than all the other boys?

At first, she didn't believe Sami Jaspers, her best friend, when Sami told her that she had seen Rod playing tonsil hockey in the Great Neck High School parking lot one afternoon. She made the usual denials, showed the appropriate disbelief, but at the end of the day, she wasn't even surprised.

"What an appropriate place. Who was the creep with? And what were you doing there, anyway?" Carly asked.

Sami hesitated. She didn't want to answer. "I was picking up my brother from a jayvee tennis match to take him to the orthodontist. You should've seen them all twisted and tangled in his VW. The windows were steamy but I could see enough."

"Thanks for sharing. Now what am I going to do about the prom?"

"I'll take you. That will set them on their heels."

"You know I can't go with you Sami."

"It was just a thought." Sami popped two orange Tic Tacs. "Whatever you do, don't spill any tears for that one. Guys are nothing more than untrained puppies. They pee and shit at will, and follow anyone who'll scratch their bellies."

"So who was scratching his?"

"Some cheerleader with big tits and no brains. Heard she's a real blockhead."

Carly tapped her own chest.

"Hello! You're looking at the bimbo."

When Carly was at Duke, it was Ryan Jordan. Ryan played tight end on the Blue Devils football team. They didn't call him "Flyin' Ryan" for nothing. He broke every receiving record in the books. Soft hands, they said. Wandering hands was more like it…they wandered over everyone in the Sigma Phi Delta sorority house, including Carly's little sorority sister.

Carly stamped her foot. The jolt brought her back to Arizona, back to Conner Masterson.

"He's different from them," she said to the empty room. Did she need to hear the words out loud to believe them to be true? Not after the way they parted Thursday night.

By the time Carly convinced herself that Sami Jaspers was wrong, that not all men are the same, she had tagged the door for the tenth time. The walls were closing in. Conner on the brain was wiring her like a double espresso. She tossed a gray sweatshirt over her back, knotted the arms around her chest, and marched down the empty hall.

She pushed the latch on the red door leading to the graveled area in front of the Institute. It didn't budge.

She pushed again.

She looked up. There was a smoke detector all right, but it was as dark as a Vaudeville theater. Either the battery had gone dead ages ago or someone stole it for their Walkman. A last try convinced her the door was locked for real. "Why?" could wait until the morning, now she prayed no one fell asleep smoking in bed.

With nowhere to go, Carly ambled back to her room. The moment she touched her door, a scream sliced the still air. She couldn't tell where it came from.

The silence grew louder.

A pulse throbbed in her ears.

Thhh…thump. Thhh…thump.

Convinced that her exhausted mind was toying with her, Carly shifted her body weight and pushed into her room. Above the creaking door, she heard it a second time.

This time the pitch was higher, more piercing. More wail than howl.

She canted her head toward the outside door. Was it a coyote? Maybe a wolf. She knew two families of wolves were released in Yellowstone National Park in the mid-nineties. Had they migrated to Arizona?

Tired, she shrugged it off. She stepped inside and a split second before the door slammed shut, she heard the scream for the last time. Carly didn't know what to make of it, but decided to wedge a chair under her doorknob. With her clothes still on, she slipped between the sheets.

She tucked her knees to her chest and forced herself to think of anything that would get her mind off of what she just had heard. What she *thought* she heard. She forced herself to think about the Medical Examiner's office. What cases came in that day for her? A bite mark on a rape victim? Bones found in a brownstone renovation?

Thoughts drifted towards Willie Robinson and the rows of stainless steel autopsy tables. How many posts had Willie done since she left? Then it dawned on her. It was still Sunday and she had only left New York that morning.

Carly dozed, falling into her dream. She bolted upright. The dreams were getting more real by the day.

Her eyelids fluttered. When she heard the cry this time, she was certain of two things: it came from close by, and it was human.

7

The next morning, Carly saw Artie Montefusco enter the learning center.

"Is there any coffee?" she asked.

He turned around, sporting a cat-who-ate-the-canary grin. "It doesn't matter. I'm revved up without it. Last night was fantastic."

Before Carly could ask what he meant, Bowden St. Clair came catapulting through the door. "Please find your spot, Dr. Mason. We're about to begin."

Placards on the carrels indicated the seating was alphabetical. Artie sat behind her.

Bowden clapped his hands to get everyone's attention. "As I showed you last night, headsets are attached to your computers. This is a self-paced program. If you need help, push the button that looks like a doorbell. A facilitator will speak to you. Any questions?"

"When do we get a break?"

"Breaks are rewards for right answers. Coffee's a drug."

"No drugs at the Institute, right?"

"You're catching on. Now go for it."

It was five-fifteen in the morning.

*   *   *

Headsets in place, Lute's voice greeted them.

"You are about to embark on a journey of learning. My methods will teach you how to fulfill your dreams. Those who finish may become part of my inner circle. Your adventure is about to begin."

*   *   *

Carly touched the beige mouse and the monitor screen came alive. Each of the four program parts was headed by the day of the week. She clicked on "Monday" and read the instructions:

*   *   *

1. ANSWER ALL QUESTIONS IN THE ORDER THEY APPEAR.
2. DO **NOT** GO TO ANOTHER SECTION BEFORE FINISHING THIS ONE.
3. EACH SKILL IS BUILT UPON A SEQUENCE OF KNOWLEDGE.
4. YOU MAY BEGIN.

*   *   *

Carly plunged forward. She read a treatise attributed to Lute Aurum that described how conquering one's goals was like being an air traffic controller. One had to manage everything coming in and going out at the same time. We were time jugglers. To gain control of our lives we had to define and embrace goals. Once we had them, we could establish a purpose. Next we'd create a project to execute our programs so that we could deliver our product, no matter what it was. In order to be efficient, we had to create a flow chart to circumvent bottlenecks and communication breakdowns.

Carly discovered that "product outflow" was the Holy Grail. More outflow meant greater remuneration. What created outflow? Inflow. Inflow came from wanting product, whether it was a professional service or a haircut. As long as the individual's def-initions were correct, product—or outflow—would be created. A faulty definition ground outflow to a halt. Without product, there was no money. Without money, there was no happiness. This model only succeeded if he/she did not bring baggage from the past. Baggage interfered with success.

Outflow. Inflow. Product. Policy. Program. Goals. Plans. Projects. Everything was gibberish...yet it all made perfect sense.

Then it registered.

What kind of baggage?

The registrants were being spoon-fed the doctrines of Humanetics. It had taken Aurum years to understand that each person's intrinsic ability was layered with problems the way Italian frescoes were layered with centuries of grime masking the true colors beneath it. There were no exceptions. *Pre-Clears* were the walking dead. They sucked life through a mask, chok-ing on their own experiences, drowning in their collective past. By the time they uncovered these defects, only Humanetics could save them.

Some tried other methods. Therapy and pills. Chanting. Colonic enemas. Some discovered EST repackaged into a belief called The Forum. There were mystical lights and tenth insights, aromatic therapies, and celestial prophecies. Of late, Galun Gong, the spiritual movement banned in China, was gaining favor in the States. No matter. In the end, Lute knew nothing but Humanetics was guaranteed to make them happy.

The "how?" was simple enough. Aurum's sure-fire techniques stripped away life's cataracts. Only when his disciples cut the umbil-ical to their pasts known as timetracks, could Lute's believers "see" life as it should be. Rid of their timetracks, they were reborn. He called them *Pre-Clears*.

To be a *Clear* was to reach one's full potential and be eternally happy. For money, lots of it, Aurum could teach anyone how to achieve a *Clear* state. And from the looks of his Institute and the new wing awaiting the zoning board's approval, there was no shortage of people willing to fork over huge sums to throw off their psychic leg irons.

By dinnertime, the group was worthless. They had navigated more twists and hairpin turns than a Le Mans auto race required. Every so often, one of the registrants would be led from the room by a green-shirted monitor, only to return invigorated and alert. After Artie came back, Carly was sure she was next. They skipped her.

Bowden grabbed the microphone. "Who wants to offer a synopsis of the course so far?"

"It's repetitious."

"Confusing."

"Exhausting."

"Lute says the harder something is, the more beneficial the results. Isn't that what you're here for? To get results?"

No one answered.

"Dr. Mason, your test results were most impressive. What did you think of the course so far?"

"I thought most of it was...," she glanced around, "irrelevant."

"No problem. Stick with it and we'll change your mind."

Dinner consisted of assorted breads, lasagna, and ziti. For dessert they gorged on blocks of white powdered crumb cakes, chocolate glazed donuts, and jelly covered wedges. The red-purple fruit punch had the appeal of diluted Kool Aid. Monitors spoke to each registrant in a separate room during dinner.

It was Carly's turn. She knocked.

"It's open."

She hesitated. The voice was familiar. It wasn't Bowden's or anyone else's from the course. It had a memorable ring. She nudged the door open and leaned into the room.

She pounced on the green-shirt.

"What are you doing here? You said you had to be in Philadelphia."

Conner Masterson squeezed her as if they were separated lovers. At least it felt that way to Carly. So much for making him grovel.

"W.C. Fields got it right about Philadelphia. I'd rather be here."

"Philadelphia's loss is my gain."

"Why do you think I rushed back?"

They separated, but kept their fingers interlocked. He wagged their hands. "Look, I'm supposed to be grilling you about the course."

Before she could speak her mind, Conner drew her back into him. He tilted his head and kissed her, keeping his eyes open until Carly closed hers. She felt his hard body nestle into hers as his hands discovered the small of her back. She arched into him. He turned his head and kissed her again; a deep moan purred from a faraway place.

"Is the course more relevant now?"

"It needs more work."

Conner led her back to her room. She no sooner flicked on the light, than he flicked it off.

She turned it on again. "Aren't you assuming too much?"

His facial cast turned quizzical, like a cloud blocking the sun.

"The way you kissed me. I heard the noises you were making. I thought..."

"Who said anything about not wanting to make love to you?"

"Then what's holding you back?"

He reached for the light switch; she cut him off.

"Not this way. Not so soon. We just met last week."

"And I haven't stopped thinking about you since. Truth is I made three other people change their schedules so I could be with you."

"Don't think I'm not grateful."

He touched her shoulders; she stiffened. Conner dropped his hands and said, "Another day, another week, it won't matter. I can wait."

She leaned and kissed him.

"What was that for?" he asked.

"You're a nice guy."

"In that case..." Conner moved to wrap his arms around her.

Carly slid backwards until she thumped into the wall. She balled up her fists. "Where are you going with this? I'm sorry if I gave you the wrong message, but this isn't the time. I thought you were different."

He touched his cheek. "I thought...I mean..."

"You thought wrong." Her body tensed waiting to see what he would do.

Conner stared for a moment longer, and then dropped into the lone wood chair.

She opened her fingers.

Conner lowered his head. "I didn't mean to make you anxious. It's just that...that kiss...I mean I feel something for you."

"I'm glad you do, because that's what I want, too. But we hardly know each other. I don't want to make it easy for you. What would you think of me?"

He smiled. "Guess we'll have to turn it up a notch and get to know each other a lot better. Real soon, if you ask me."

Conner put his hand on the knob and had one foot out the door when he felt Carly spin him around. He felt her warm lips on his, and her tongue exploring his opened mouth. Now it was his turn to break away.

"Look, I don't know what game you're trying to play here, but I'm trying to be good. There were girls in high school...we called them CTs."

"I'm no cock teaser."

"You couldn't prove that by me."

He reached for the doorknob but Carly grabbed his hand. In the past, when it came to men, she knew when she was making a mistake, which was almost all the time. Carly chose to make them anyway, praying time would smooth out the wrinkles. It never panned out that way. Time was an ugly mirror that told the truth. This time? She exhaled. Conner was no mistake. Her one worry was what he would think of what she was about to do.

"If you go, I'll clobber you."

Conner closed the door. Humanetics 101 had just become relevant.

8

None of the registrants knew that the black limo they had seen the day before, belonged to Texas Governor Aldous Fromm. While Jeff was guiding the van up the graveled road to the Institute, Fromm was greeting Lute Aurum inside the white house.

"How did the meeting go in Tucson with the other governors?"

"They had some pretty compelling reasons why I should run for president."

"That's got to be flattering to a politician's ear."

Fromm loosened his tie and shrugged. "I still have my doubts."

"Nonsense. You'd make a superb candidate."

"It's nothing I ever wanted. Besides, who knows me outside the south?"

"Who's been selling you that crock? The Fromm name is synonymous with American politics. You're a shoe-in...if you want it."

"That's the trouble. I'm not sure I want the presidency. Besides, odds-long favorites rarely win the Kentucky Derby."

"That's bull. You want it so bad you can taste it in your sleep. The only thing holding you back is what your father will think if you don't win."

"You cut right to the chase, don't you?"

"It's a gift."

"You don't know my father."

"I know everyone's father."

In the months to come, Governor Fromm would describe how the days spent in the Institute of Humanetics were the turning point of his career. When asked about the auditing and mind-bashing tête-à-têtes exposed in Newsweek, the New York Times Magazine, and 20/20, he would stop to think.

"Those initial days following the mental assaults were unsettling. I had demons to bury, which I did."

"Like your father's legacy, sir?" asked a reporter.

Which legacy was the better question? It was public knowledge that Aldous Fromm, Sr. expected, to the point of demanding, that his son run for the presidency. Losing was unthinkable. The pressure forced Junior to seek Aurum's help. Then two weeks after Junior left the Institute, Aldous Fromm Senior, nearing eighty and ever-the-man-on-the-go, died in a Westport, Connecticut B&B. Confirmed reports said Senior died while in *flagrante delictus* servicing the ghostwriter of the last installment of his memoirs. The book was a tell-all exposé about the Iran-Contra affair, Ollie North, and how Jimmy Carter's personal notebook ended up in the hands of the columnist, George Will days before the Reagan-Carter debate. By the time the book was published, Jimmy Carter, now an evangelist, had forgiven all, Reagan was reduced to a vegetative state suffering from terminal stages of Alzheimer's Disease, and the writer would make a fortune from Pfizer in TV spots describing how both she and Fromm Senior used Viagra.

Junior wanted to set the record straight. "The only legacy I am running on is the strength I've gained from the one man in my life who has really mattered: Lute Aurum."

* * *

Tuesday. Day two at the Institute.

As Carly Mason lightly touched Conner's arm while he slept, Lute was greeting a bleary-eyed Aldous Fromm. "I take it the course is going well, Governor?"

Fromm's hair was rumpled. He was wearing an apricot Polo shirt and crisp blue jeans in need of a stone washing. Tired as he was, he grasped Lute by the shoulders. "I can't thank you enough. A lot of shi..., excuse me, stuff came out during the auditing sessions yesterday. Your monitor is one whiz of a genius. Would you believe he identified what's been holding me back? I'm sending my entire staff here first chance I get."

Lute basked as the governor praised the Institute and Humanetics. "Glad you found it so rewarding, governor."

"Rewarding? Wait until I tell my wife, Barbara. She should come here. You're a fucking national treasure. One day the world will build a monument to you. Point me to your torture cell. I'm raring to go."

*   *   *

Carly rolled over and thanked her lucky stars. Conner was not a mirage. Maybe coming to Arizona had, at last, broken the mold. She'd had her fill of pretty boys who offered little more than their good looks and charming ways.

She tapped Conner's shoulder. "You said something that bothered me last night."

"And a good morning to you."

"Was last night for real?"

"What do you mean?"

"Just that you said Aurum was a master at giving people what they wanted. I started thinking...I'm a single professional from New York. My age group got shafted six ways to Sunday. There are too few men for us. The good guys are married and the single guys are single for a reason. So who's left for someone like me? Losers in mid-life crises looking to score at health clubs, or post-pubescent studs who glory in servicing pathetic thirtysomethings who are more their mothers' age? You come along and I'm thinking serendipity is finally on my side. Then I realize this could all be a scam to get me to buy into Humanetics. Tell me I'm wrong."

Conner grabbed her shoulders.

Carly struggled to pull away, he held firm. They were both naked.

"You're right about Aurum. He'd do anything to give a client what they want, but that's not what's happening here. I care for you. Learn to be trusting."

She pulled strands of hair off her face. "What are you talking about? Trust is my middle name. See, it's even branded on my forehead…next to the word, 'schmuck.'"

The hurt on his face told her she had pushed too far. She finally meets a guy who's in touch with his feelings, who can reach deep down and expose a glimmer of his soul, and what does she do?

Conner stared off, taking in rapid breaths. "I should've expected this. Your profile said that you didn't trust men. I thought I'd be the one who could make a difference."

"Look at me! What profile are you talking about? Am I some sort of charity case?"

"Don't you remember the questionnaire they sent before the course began?"

"The one that asked everything from my favorite color to whether I prefer Rice Chex to Wheat Chex to Fiber One? Those questions were really stupid."

"Depends what you do with the answers. We have them professionally analyzed. Our people know if you like your toilet paper coming off the top or bottom of the roll. We know if your toothbrush is wet or dry before putting on your Crest MultiCare. No matter what your problems are, Humanetics can fix them."

"So which is it?" She wanted to know.

"What?"

"Top or bottom? How do I like my toilet paper?"

"You? You could care less as long as the roll isn't empty."

"Lucky guess."

"On the contrary, we know what we're doing…and so do I."

He knelt down and cupped her face. "Let me earn your trust. Let me make you a believer."

If his verbal plea didn't convince her, his Oscar-worthy performance that followed turned her into a true convert.

*   *   *

Carly entered the learning center a jumble of thoughts. Making love to Conner was like nothing she'd ever experienced. She could still see him hovering over her, feel his weight concentrated in one spot.

"You don't have to be so controlled," she said. She closed her eyes with his next thrust and turned her head to the side, biting the knuckles of her clenched fist.

"There's time for me," he whispered. "I want you to take yours, and then some, and I'll be right behind you."

She looked at him wide-eyed. "Are you for real?"

"As real as they come."

Conner shifted his weight to trigger a cascade of pleasure. It started deep in her thighs, then spread upward until she could see colors with her eyelids clamped shut. She bucked and moaned. Tears of joy spilled onto the sheets. Then, smoldering in the embers of delight, Conner took his.

Bowden's voice erupted over the microphone, scattering an image of Conner hovering over her.

"Take your seats, people. You've got a heap to do today."

Carly sighed as she adjusted the headset.

The second day was dedicated to acquiring those business skills needed to succeed, the same ones Conner had written on the white board back in New York. She learned that no matter how expert one was, other talents were necessary. One had to be able to communicate, market, micro-manage people, and macro-manage a business. Buzz-words filled a maze of verbal twists and turns. She became confused. What started as a march into the forest of financial expertise disintegrated into a muddle of verbal gullies.

Carly removed her headset as Artie Montefusco was escorted past her a second time. Where were they taking him?

"Is something the matter?" asked Bowden St. Clair.

She looked up at his green shirt and mustard-colored pants. "I've made a mistake," she said in a bold voice.

"Not from what we've observed. You're quick on concepts. Your reviews have been excellent. Stay with it a little longer. You won't be disappointed."

"I don't belong here. None of Aurum's techniques apply to my practice. It's too small."

Bowden cocked his head and Carly followed him out the door. They stood in the hallway. "Don't quit now. I know it can get boring."

"Boring, I can take. I've networked until I'm blue in the face and I've volunteered for more charities than I have dollars to give them. I teach at the university and belong to three study clubs. And what do I have to show for it all? Moths in my bank account and holes in my appointment book. Ain't life grand."

"You haven't had the special one-on-one sessions. It's part of the course. At least stay for that. Afterwards, if you still want to go, I'll arrange a ride to the airport. What do you say?"

"Is that when they sell the extra courses? I'm not interested."

"We're not just about making money. We want you to reach your potential. The one-on-ones try to uncover what might be keeping you from that success.

Carly wavered. While most of her friends were talking about retirement accounts and 401Ks, she was concerned about next month's rent. Something *must* be keeping her back. Even if she was destined to run a two-bit practice the rest of her life, she might learn something.

A door clicked open down the hallway. Artie came shuffling toward her.

"Was Artie learning how to succeed?" she asked.

"Ask him," Bowden answered.

Carly stepped toward the would-be wizard of the Web. When their eyes locked, he became energized. Revitalized. Artie pulled his shoulders back, stood taller, and jacked his thumb upwards. "Go for it."

She did...and what a mistake it turned out to be.

9

Jeremy Steel left the Institute ever the skeptic. Why waste time on the likes of Aldous Fromm? When Jeremy tried to name the last governor elected president, he stalled on old Rough and Ready. Governors had little national exposure and no hand at foreign affairs. They knew little about the ways of Congress or how insiders called the shots and made the rules. Imagine pitting Jesse "The Body" Ventura against Trent Lott and Jesse Helms, let alone Vladimir Putin or Tony Blair?

Then he remembered Jimmy Carter was a governor.

Where Lute Aurum was concerned, Jeremy should have known better. Auditing would remove the timetracks holding Fromm back. Getting Fromm elected was the easy part. Getting him on the team was what Lute had to guarantee if Jeremy was to stay involved.

They had stood in the small room an hour longer, observing the monitor peel away one timetrack at a time that anchored Aldous Fromm to his childhood fears. The monitor did so with the skill of an archaeologist sifting through layers of human detritus. At the moment no response caused the H-meter to waiver, Jeremy and Lute left.

A car was waiting to take Jeremy to his private jet. Lute went with him.

"Then you approve?" Lute asked. "I told you he was the one."

"Maybe."

"I need to have you convinced."

"There's too much at stake to commit to him right away. Let me think about it."

"Is it money? It costs a lot to run."

"That's not it. Fromm will have an overflowing war chest, so much so, that he'll forego matching federal funds. That way the sky's the limit. His campaign can be bought. It's not about money."

"What about the others? Forbes will make one last try."

"Even if the US Mint was behind him, Forbes couldn't get elected. And the rest? Pat Buchanan? Really. Kip Greeley's interesting. He's making noise about running. With all the problems we're having, Greenpeace is taking hold. Greeley knows the issues. I'd watch out for him."

"Don't forget Bradley. He's got people paying attention. Been at it for a long time, too."

"A six-five basketball player who could never dunk? Let him say whatever he wants. Besides, he's looking frail these days. Fromm's a lock over him."

"So if it's not the money, what is it?"

"I can see what you're doing *here* with him. What happens when he goes to Washington? Who's going to watch over him?"

Lute bubbled with glee. "Is that all you're worried about?"

"Can you blame me?"

Lute grazed Jeremy's arm with a friendly swipe of his hand. "After all we've been through, you don't trust me. You need to get back here and work on some timetracks of your own."

"I'm serious, Lute."

"So am I. Fromm will do as I say...no matter where he calls home. Texas, Washington, it's all the same."

"I had to hear you say that."

"So you approve?"

Jeremy smiled for the first time. "If I didn't?"

Lute brushed his hand against his pocket. "I'd have to feed you to my pets."

*   *   *

As they approached Manhattan, Jeremy picked up the in-flight phone on his Gulfstream VI.

"Take the scenic route, Travis."

Travis Billings had already plotted the course over Lady Liberty and up the Hudson before landing at Teterboro Airport. He knew Jeremy loved to soak up the Manhattan skyline. Why not? He had already left his imprint on more of it than anyone else in history.

Jeremy had started with rundown brownstones in Brooklyn. He would buy them for a song. His crew would patch the holes, slap on a few coats of Moore Paint, and then flip the row houses for a quick turn. Brownstones led to small office buildings and strip malls. In no time, greed stoked his appetite for more.

Jeremy didn't dip his big toe into Manhattan real estate, he dove in head first. When he realized that old and tired hotels were no different than an aging beauty's face, he bought the Commodore Hotel between Lexington and Park Avenues on Forty-Second Street. Bingo! Steel had his winning formula. Like a plastic surgeon, Jeremy nipped and tucked throughout the city to much acclaim. Banks liked winners, and the purse strings opened for the boy wonder.

Rejuvenating the old had its rewards, but starting from scratch proved intoxicating. Jeremy created Manhattan's first indoor vertical mall. He felt so proud of his achievement he named it after himself: Steel Towers. Detractors laughed and scoffed. This time the "bad" boy had gone too far.

Steel loved his critics; they were good for business. With white-gloved doormen greeting everyone and a concert pianist serenading shoppers with Chopin polonaises, Steel Towers became an instant landmark. A tourist must-see. Jeremy built Steel Plaza next. When New Jersey went head-to-head with Las Vegas, Steel conquered Atlantic City. A billionaire by the time he was forty, the NY Post and Daily News praised Steel the way they had venerated the erstwhile Robert Moses.

Being compared to the man who hammered modern-day New York into a Mecca was not enough for Jeremy Steel.

Jeremy once told a reporter, "I'm the embodiment of I.M. Pei, Frank Lloyd Wright, and Robert Moses all rolled into one. They were master builders, I'm the world builder."

*   *   *

"Was it worth flying down, Boss?"

Buddy LoBianco was Jeremy's right-hand man and CFO. They had been together since the early Brooklyn days. Not much on class or style, Buddy was loyal to the core.

"I should've known better than to doubt Lute Aurum. He's got everything under control."

"I'm glad you're in a good mood. Feast your eyes on this."

Buddy handed Jeremy a message written on a City of New York notepad.

"I see they didn't go for it," said Jeremy.

"The Mayor tried, but couldn't get it passed. What'll we do now?"

Television City was meant to be Jeremy's crowning New York achievement. He would strip away the varicose railroad tracks littering Manhattan's west side and build a series of skyscrapers to house the major television networks under one roof. The recipe would mix residential with commercial properties, renovate the West Side Highway, all beautified by an island-long park. The crown of this "city-within-a-city," would be topped with the tallest building in the world.

Jeremy knew the answer before he asked. "The environmentalists?"

"The planning commission couldn't get passed the fact that the shadows would fall half-way across Central Park."

"They nixed the project because the sun would be blocked out? Don't they realize business in the area would triple? We're talking about turning a major chunk of the city into a theme park."

"They said, 'One Times Square was enough.' There was also a stink about traffic."

"That's it? Finished? In the trash heap for good?"

"The mayor said to scale it down, and then he'll make certain it's approved."

Jeremy ripped the note to shreds. He stood in front of the tinted glass windows with an unfettered view of the gold-topped Crown Building across from Tiffany's. Down Fifth Avenue, he took in the spires of Rockefeller Center and the Empire State Building. In the distance, the Twin Towers loomed like smokestacks on the prow of one long ship.

"Why don't you build it somewhere else, Boss? That'll show them."

Jeremy tilted his head. His glare turned into a broad grin. "That's exactly what I'll do. I'll build it somewhere else. And I know just the spot."

10

Encouraged by Artie Montefusco, Carly stayed for the one-on-one consult. A verbal "assault" would better describe the experience. The room was nothing more than a cement slab surrounded by windowless cinder block walls. Decorating tastes ran simple: two metal chairs and a small wooden table that held a box resembling a polygraph. She soon learned about the H-meter.

"Have a seat," said a green-shirt she hadn't seen before.

The moment she nestled onto the chair, the room lights went out, and a lone spotlight blazed from above. "Do you have to shine that in my eyes?"

"It's for your own good."

Before she could tell him to take a flying fuck, the green-shirt body-slammed her with words that crushed.

"The reason you're such a loser, Carly Mason, is because you blame yourself for your parents break-up. You feel that if you had been a better child, your daddy would've stayed home. Instead he split for parts unknown."

Carly was stunned.

The bastard continued. "It's time to get a grip. Daddy's not coming home and mommy's dead. It's a cold world and you're on your own."

Her teeth separated, but her voice failed her. She tried harder and managed a squeak.

The monitor circled from behind.

She felt his hot breath on her neck, and smelled his tar-scented hair. She sensed his hostility, his disdain for her. Is this what they did to the others? Belittle them until they could barely remember their names? How did they return to the learning center with a spring in their step and a smile on their kisser?

The green-shirt paraded in front.

She clenched the rim of the chair seat. Her heart drummed against her chest. In a few words, he summed up twenty-five years of truths she was afraid to face.

How did they know?

"You're such a loser, you can't even defend yourself."

If there was a hole in the center of the floor, she would have sailed through the Looking Glass. Absent a hole, a tear formed, and then another, and then a torrent overwhelmed her until she couldn't breathe.

The green-shirt eased his behind onto the wooden table and kicked his foot like a metronome, waiting for her to gain control.

Carly wiped her nose with the back of her hand.

The monitor handed her a Kleenex.

She honked into it and reached for a fresh one. She felt hot and clammy. She tented her blouse to cool down. Her pulse raced. Sweat beads trickled from her forehead. There were no more tissues; she used her shirttail. When she forced herself back into a semblance of control, her fingers still trembled.

"What gives you the right to say those things? I've been on my own a long time. I've done the best I can."

"Your best is pathetic. Face it, Carly, you're dying for some S&M."

"I don't have to listen to this."

"I'm talking success and men. We can give you both."

Nothing like kicking her in the gut when she was already down for the count! If there was any doubt before, there was none now. Conner *was* part of their game; he was another one of her major screw-ups. Perfect eyes, perfect smile…she should have known.

She was about to leave when the monitor's words knocked her back down.

"Let's talk about your love life."

Carly took a staccato breath as a warm, gelatinous mass oozed into her panties. Conner went bareback, swearing six ways 'til Sunday that he had an insurance physical two weeks earlier—negative on the HIV—and hadn't been with a woman since.

"Shouldn't you be more discriminating in who you choose to fuck? That's part of why you're so enturbulated. You'll screw anyone, won't you?"

Then her hand clamped over her mouth. How could they possibly know?

Sami!

*   *   *

Carly and Sami Jaspers were strikers on the high school varsity volleyball team. Sami was a year older than Carly. Their team was favored to advance to the state sectionals. Francis Lewis High School had a shot to win it all…as long as no one became injured or got into an academic jam. Exams could not have come at a worse time. Sami was tanking senior math. If she passed a makeup test, they'd let her play. The coach asked Carly who was a junior but also taking senior math, to help.

Sami slammed the book shut. "Break time."

Carly reached for the book. "The test is in two days. If you don't pass, you'll miss the sectionals and we'll lose."

Sami grabbed Carly's hand and brought it to her cheek. "Have I told you how much I appreciate your help?"

"You would've done the same thing."

Carly tugged on her hand but Sami held firm.

"I've wanted to do this for a long time," said Sami.

Carly opened her mouth as Sami leaned into her. When their lips touched, she waited for lightning bolts to flash or James Earl Jones's voice to boom that they were committing a carnal sin. No such thing. Carly tasted Sami's sweet lips and let herself be pulled closer. A hand under her shirt stroked her back, and then inched until a finger skimmed her nipple.

Sami whipped off her own shirt then helped Carly remove hers.

Afterwards, Sami asked, "Why didn't you stop me?"

"I was curious."

For Carly, it was a fling of discovery. Dating boys had never been an issue. So when Rod Phillips showed a flicker of interest, Carly sparked back. Sami wasn't the least bit jealous. She had been down this road before, and knew that all high school courtships were short-lived. She'd give Carly all the slack she needed, even if it meant enduring her going to the prom with the school's number one jock. As luck would have it, tripping across Rod with the Great Neck cheerleader brought Carly back into Sami's fold...until Sami left for the University of Colorado.

Carly's experimenting left with Sami. Sami never returned to Queens. She graduated with a degree in marketing, got a great job and met the love of her life. Carly heard through the grapevine Sami was married and living outside Seattle, balancing her career with raising a son. She and her partner gained prominence when Barbara Walters interviewed them about the virtues of a child being raised by two mothers.

        *   *   *

Carly never got to answer; the room turned pitch black.

Blurry videotape lines scorched the wall, then it cleared to a sharp focus; it had nothing to do with Sami Jaspers.

"You bastards," she blurted, seeing herself and Conner naked. Every intimate detail had been recorded.

Legs spreading.

Conner mounting.

Penetrating.

Carly sunk lower in the chair. No one crashed through the door to save her. "What do you people want?"

"You're enturbulated and need help."

"Says who? So what if I can't pick the right man and I'm still affected by my parents' break-up. Neither has anything to do with me running my dental practice. As far as the tape goes, use it to whack off."

The green-shirt shoved an AMEX charge-slip in front of her.

"What's this for?"

"For your next course."

Carly gaped at the bottom line. "Eighteen thousand dollars? Are you crazy?"

"That's cheap to get rid of timetracks."

"I can do better than that."

"We don't make deals."

Carly stood. "Neither do I. It's been swell."

Carly marched out the door, not caring what happened next. She should have.

II

While Carly battled the green-shirt's hard sell, Aldous Fromm was in the adjacent room. This time the governor was clay for the experienced potter, Lute Aurum.

"So are there any other timetracks you feel we have to work on?" Lute asked.

"I have to keep remembering that everything my father did to me was out of love."

"No one ever taught a parent how to be a father or mother. We're all human, you know."

"Sometimes I wonder. Did you know that my father left a space on the wall next to his presidential portrait? It was to add mine after I got elected."

"He had high hopes for you."

"Unrealistic dreams, if you ask me." Fromm looked up with poodle eyes. "What if I don't make it? What if I lose the election?"

"With me by your side, you can't lose."

Aldous lunged and gave Lute a big bear hug. "My father never talked to me that way before."

"He should have."

The governor stepped back. "What's in it for you?"

"To know I've helped a fellow human attain his just rewards. When that happens, you'll be helping me find everlasting peace."

         *   *   *

He

He has lived for a quadrillion years...since before the beginning. *He* is all-knowing. An Iotan-being.

He can create or destroy Matter. Energy. Space. Time.

He is...and *He* is not.

He is more than the astral spirit that flits from carcass to carcass in the Lazarus connection. *He* is not a reincarnate, but different.

He resides at the base of the brain. *He* dances on synapses, hitchhikes on ganglia, swims in the pons, goes prospecting in the medulla oblongata, and picks pontine nuclei like daisies.

What intrigues him is the human's ability to start, stop, and change.

Control their change, and the future is His.

He will live for another quadrillion years.

12

Nothing happened when Carly left the mind-bashing cell. No one called her name; no one came after her. *Bullies were all the same.* They wanted to scare and intimidate, but in the end, they were ball-less wonders. Eunuchs.

Carly was packing to leave when she heard grunts and squeals from the next room. Chair legs screeched against the floor. There was a loud thump.

It was Artie Montesfuco's room.

She placed her ear against the common wall between the two rooms. It was dead silent now. Carly shrugged off her forensic-driven imagination, and swept up her toiletries as she heard a scream. It had the same shrill tone she had heard when she tried to take a walk the first night at the Institute.

               *   *   *

Artie loved the grill sessions. They had nothing to do with him wanting to create an Internet business or magic or gorging himself until he could bust. Once the monitors picked up that Artie loved his fantasies, they owned him. The more they played his games, the more he agreed to sign the AMEX charges. The bills mounted, and Artie couldn't have been happier.

At the same time Aldous Fromm was in his final audit and Carly was collecting her belongings, Artie was having his arms tied behind his back. Next the green-shirt moved the chair in place and slipped a black hood over Artie's head. All was ready.

Artie felt the monitor's cool hand touch his juicy thigh. "Step on the chair and spread your legs," said the monitor, guiding him.

Artie slobbered in ecstasy when the green-shirt threaded his ripe jingleberries through the brass ring, one hairy cojone at a time. Tiny goose bumps erupted on his thin skin as the cold metal slid until it touched the stalk of his aching blue-veiner.

Life is *grand.*

The green-shirt twisted the clamp until Artie screamed with pleasure.

The hood grew twenty degrees hotter.

"Tighter," Artie cried out.

Artie's nipples hardened.

A noose was slipped around his neck.

Artie giggled. His skin prickled. His stick ached.

"Artie, you are one perverse motherfucker."

Artie licked his purple lips. "Houdini never did *this.*"

Artie pictured his swollen branch quivering in the air, the head blue-red.

"You've got demons working inside you," said the monitor.

"I know."

"You need to cleanse yourself in order to become a *Clear.*"

"I know."

Artie shifted his weight from one foot to the other, like a kid needing to pee.

The monitor shifted the noose.

"Better, Artie?"

Artie sounded like Don Corleone. "Pull, you sonofabitch. Pull."

The volcanic blast would be perfect, the lava flow complete.

The green-shirt wrapped the cord end around his wrist. A last check for twists, and then the monitor squatted like the anchor in a tug-of-war. He yanked with all his might.

Behind the black hood, Artie's neck stretched. His face turned crimson. Sweat leaked from every pore. Blue lines criss-crossed his cheeks. His eyes bulged white.

"Tighter," he wheezed through clamped teeth. "I'm almost there."

The monitor gripped harder, then kicked the chair from under Artie.

Artie's body tightened into a coil; white cream spewed onto the floor. He felt the rhythmic pumping against the brass ring. He felt his reservoir empty, his body depleted.

Tears of joy dampened the black cloth. Had they asked, he would have paid ten times more for this experience.

The green-shirt held fast.

It's time to let go.

Artie's feet thrashed for the chair.

He cried out, but the booming scream echoed only in his mind. His vocal chords were crushed.

A brown stream poured down his leg.

Then Artie perked alive and the beat started again.

It was a fucking double! A two-time creamer.

*   *   *

The noises were too weird to disregard. She tiptoed in front of Artie's door and cracked it open. She saw the green-shirt bearing down on the rope. She saw Artie's feet thrashing. She saw globs of jism splattering to the floor. She didn't know if she should scream, help Artie, or mind her own business. In the end, her years of hanging around the Medical Examiner's had numbed her senses to what people did to each other...or even to themselves. She had seen victims impaled by broom handles in their rectums. Over the years, she had seen Willie remove every imaginable object from vaginal cavities, from Coke bottles to Lionel trains. They did it for sex, for torture, for pleasure. They did it to dominate or be dominated. If Artie got his rocks off swinging from a rope, who was she to stop him?

She finished packing with half an ear out to more noises erupting from Artie's room, as if the man had anything left in him to erupt.

Carly was zipping her luggage shut when Conner zoomed into the room holding a piece of cardboard in one hand, and a shirt and pants tucked under his other arm. He motioned for her not to talk until he taped the thick paper over the miniature camera lens hidden in the ceiling molding.

He never saw it coming. Carly swooped across the room and head-butted Conner in the solar plexus. Conner thumped into the wall, his arms flailing back. He slithered to the floor holding his belly, gulping for air.

Carly kicked his leg and he spun like a top. He rolled onto his shoulder when she grabbed a handful of hair and yanked his head until their faces were inches apart.

"Now you cover the camera? *Now* doesn't matter. My friend, Sami Jaspers, used to say all men were slime. You prove the point. How dare you come in here!"

She shoved his head into the floor, stepped over him, and grabbed her suitcase.

Conner made no effort to stand. He struggled for air. Finally, he squeezed out a sentence. "You've got to get out of here."

"No shit. The van's taking me to the airport."

Conner righted himself and tucked his knees to his chest. His face was flushed, his breathing shallow. He tried to stand but crumbled down. "You don't understand. I was monitoring the camera bank and saw you peek into Montefusco's room."

"Then you know what was going on in there?"

He nodded.

"Lots of people are into kinky sex. Big whoop," she said, "I see it all the time."

"What you don't know is that Artie was hired by one of the monitor's parents to expose Humanetics as a cult. They figured if the place was shut down, their kid had to come home."

"The Institute gives business courses. So what if there's a little side action between consenting adults. What's with the voodoo cult stuff? And what's wrong with this place? Is it as bad as you're making it out to be?"

"Worse, but there's no time to explain. They found a Nagra on Artie. He was taping them."

Carly shook her wrist. "That's a Swiss-made recorder. State-of-the-art. One of those costs half-as-much as this course. I thought Artie was a magician?"

"He was." Conner clapped his hands, then added, "Poof, he's gone."

"What are you trying to pull? I just saw him next door, kicking and coming waterfalls."

"Until he was lowered to the floor like a beached whale."

She started for the door; he blocked her. "We've got to help him," she said, pushing him aside.

"It's too late."

"Are you certain?"

He scrambled to hand her the shirt and pants. "No, but put these on. They'll be coming for you any minute."

She took them, looked at the blocked camera, and then sucker-punched him with a right hook. "If I had a knife I'd Lorraine

Bobbit you and grind your precious shlong into cat food. Then maybe you'd have time to think about how to treat women."

Carly swung again, this time he was ready.

He deflected the blow then grabbed both wrists. "I deserve that."

"No kidding." She struggled to free herself.

He held tight. "I apologize, but I was so excited to see you, I forgot about the camera. It was a big mistake."

"So was blowing up the World Trade Center."

She got her right hand free and tried to cuff him again. Conner wrapped his arms around her this time, but not before she clipped his ear. He held fast until she stopped struggling.

It was a Mexican standoff. His grip lessened. Just as she was about to break free, she felt Conner's hand slide to the back of her head. He kissed her. She tried to pull away but he wouldn't let her. They continued kissing until he eased his grip. Instead of letting go, she wrapped her arms around him.

When they broke apart, he cradled her head to his chest and spoke.

"I don't have time to explain but Aurum once did something to my family. I'm here to expose Aurum for what he is, except none of that matters at the moment. What's important is that you get out of here right now."

"Why do I think you're telling the truth?"

He cupped her face in his hands. "Because I am. This place is bad. Now let's get you out of here."

"They're sending the van for me."

"That was before Montefusco. I've made arrangements with the limo driver. He's bored to tears waiting for the governor to finish with Aurum. He can drive you to the airport and no one will ever know."

"Is that the car I saw parked in front of the ranch?"

"It's the only way you'll get through the front gate. They won't check his car."

"Conner, if they're as bad as you say, come with me."

"Believe me, I wish I could. I came here to do a job, and I can't leave until it's done."

"What if they find out you helped me?"

He shrugged. "Pray they don't."

13

The limousine driver was waiting in a culvert to the side of the Institute. Conner watched her hop in and wave. He stood there long enough to see the car kick up some gravel and pull away. He felt secure that the guard would let the car out the front gate...as long as no surprises cropped up.

Conner returned to the surveillance center reviewing what had just transpired. He knew there was little chance he would be spared Lute's wrath when they found that Carly had escaped.

What choice did he have?

Conner's assignment was Carly, so while she was going through the paces in the learning center and, afterwards, during the time she was being "audited," Conner hung around the surveillance room. The surveillance room had two components: audio and visual. Aurum's audio board made the Nixon tapes look like child's play. Not everyone became enamored with Humanetics, so Lute employed a corps of telephone installers to tap the phone lines of registrants who threatened to expose Humanetics to the authorities. When the *Pre-Clears* made what Lute considered an imprudent call, they were paid a visit. One talk was usually enough to straighten them out.

The Institute used visual surveillance. Roof cameras caught the comings and goings of anyone within a hundred yards of the front gates. Lenses were also aimed at Lute's ranch house, the pool, and the stable area. There was no point in covering the surrounding acres; wolves and mountain lions needed to eat.

He munched on a Power Bar, killing time.

"I'll take over for a while," he said to the green-shirt who had been staring at the screens for hours. "Not much going on."

The monitor pointed to the black and white screen. "Call me when Montefusco gets his. I wouldn't want to miss it."

Conner didn't call. He was transfixed when the black hood was placed over Artie's head. He couldn't believe it when the noose went around the fat neck. Scuttlebutt had it that the Cult Information Network planted Artie in an attempt to unmask Aurum. If that were true, Aurum would extract more than his pound of flesh. Then again, what would they do to him, Conner, if Aurum ever found out what *he* was planning?

At the same moment the monitor kicked the chair from under Artie, Conner noted Carly Mason opening her door on another black and white screen. A hall shot followed her traipsing in front of Artie's room. Conner saw the monitor holding the rope around Artie's neck and Artie kicking and stretching for something solid…before it was too late.

Then the green-shirt returned from his break; Conner stood to block the screen. He stalled long enough for Carly to return to her room. Relieved, but knowing Carly would soon be in trouble, Conner drew the green-shirt's attention to Artie's screen.

The monitor slid onto his seat and fiddled with a dial. The camera zoomed in for a close-up.

"Look at all that cum on the floor. Impressive."

Conner waited long enough to see Artie lowered to the floor. "Any chance of you making a copy?"

The monitor screwed his face. "You know that's against the rules."

Conner patted him on the shoulder. "You might want one for yourself."

"No way." Then he thought otherwise.

The moment the green-shirt left the console to get a fresh tape Conner flicked-off a bank of toggle switches that controlled cameras in the halls and the outside grounds. Then he bolted. On the way, he grabbed a uniform for Carly, praying he had bought enough time for her to escape...and for him not to get caught in the process.

Now, regardless of how much he had reassured Carly, as the limousine pulled away Conner knew there would be consequences from all sides. He was feeling more than a pang of guilt. Carly's instincts were dead-on. He *was* summoned to the Institute to seduce her. Aurum's thesis was "give them what they want and we own them." Except when it came to Carly, Conner wasn't acting. He was attracted to her the moment they met in New York. When he got the call to return from Philadelphia, he hopped the first available flight. His orders were to get to know Carly better. He jumped at the chance. Besides it gave him time to pursue his own agenda: snooping around the Institute for evidence that would incriminate Aurum and bring down Humanetics.

After Conner's father died and he returned to run the printing business, Conner became more father than brother to his younger sister. In a way (not the Oedipal way) he became a husband to his mother, too. She was an anachronism; a woman who thought a man's job was to protect her from worries and stress, to keep her on a pedestal every day of her life. Conner's father had done just that. When he died, Conner's mother was lost. Adrift. She was ill-equipped to venture out on her own.

One day, she called him at the shop. She needed cash.

"Go to an ATM and get what you need," he said to her.

"What's that? Where do I go?"

Conner's mother not only didn't have an ATM card, she had no idea what they were or how they were used.

His sister, Lizzie, was a couple of years younger but every bit the survivor. At the time of his death, Conner's father had found a niche in printing newsletters for churches. Conner was able to pick up the banner for a time, making enough money to pay for Lizzie's remaining college expenses. But the blush of success of business was short-lived. The competition smelled blood. Outsiders cut side deals with the churches that reduced Conner's base, and income, to less than half of what it was. Lucky for him, Lizzie graduated and soon got married, no longer needing his support.

Lizzie and her husband, Keith, opened a high-end shop near Boston's Quincy Market that catered to the discriminating souls who still believed writing was an art form. They carried gold Cross, Mont Blanc, and fountain pens, quills and fine bonded stationary, and inks of every color. They had a few loyal customers but the store could not sustain itself. Lizzie argued they needed more time; Keith wanted to ditch it and buy an Arthur Murray franchise. When they heard that the fabled Pineidar stationers was opening nearby, they took Aurum's course as one last stab at making a go of it. Then, if that didn't work, Lizzie would learn to cha-cha.

As soon as Lizzie and Keith started the self-paced program in Mesa Verde, Keith bolted. He told Lizzie the material was crap and that he was returning to Boston. She stayed on.

With Keith gone, they "mated" Lizzie with another lonely soul, a wannabe disc jockey. No one could prove it was murder, but exposing his sister to HIV was the same as pointing a gun at her head and squeezing the trigger. The DJ's virus remained dormant while Lizzie sero-converted to a full-blown case of AIDS. A few months later, she died in Conner's arms.

        *   *   *

Carly freaked when the limousine didn't head for the gate. Instead it swung in front of Aurum's ranch house.

Aldous Fromm lowered himself onto the back seat with her. "Who are you?"

Carly froze.

Fromm rested both hands on his knees and waited for her reply.

In the rearview mirror, Carly saw the driver's worried look. She glanced out the dark tinted window that hid her from the two green-shirts coming their way. She gripped the door handle, ready to tug it open.

"I've got to get home to see my sick mother. There are no buses out here, and the van's out picking up new people. Your driver said it was okay. He didn't think you'd be finished for some time. Please don't get him in trouble. It's not his fault."

Fromm patted her knee as he spoke into the intercom. "Looks like there's two of us heading for the airport."

To Carly's relief, they lurched forward. When they reached the electronic gate, the guard pressed a code into a keypad. She held her breath. In seconds, she would be...

A siren blasted behind them.

The guardhouse phone rang.

Carly saw the guard nod up and down, slam the headset in its cradle, and then stare at the waiting limousine. He was unarmed. He jabbed at the keypad to no avail; it had to complete its cycle before closing.

Carly prayed Fromm wasn't watching. When she turned a fretful eye toward him, she found him gazing out the other window.

The driver gunned the car and they roared past the guard the second he could clear the gate.

After a minute, she exhaled. She looked out the rear window: no cars were following Carly.

"I wonder what all the fuss us about?" Fromm asked.

"My name's Carly Mason," she extended her hand, "and I can't thank you enough."

Fromm gestured over his shoulder, toward the ranch. "Whatever it is, I'm sure they've got it under control. Aurum's quite a guy, isn't he?"

"To say the least. Someone said you were a governor. Is that true?"

"I'm Aldous Fromm."

"The president's son?"

"I'd rather think of myself as the governor of Texas."

"Why were *you* at the Institute?"

"I couldn't run for president without putting away some of my past."

"Me, too."

Carly knew she had to distract Fromm. "I barely remember my father. He left when I was ten. They were trying to blame me for my parents splitting up."

"You can't imagine. It was a nightmare living under the same roof with my father."

"At least you got to see him every day."

"I didn't. When I was a kid, he was in Washington. The few times he did come home, he'd snoop around my assignment books to check my homework. You'd think he'd want to spend some time and toss a ball around? No. Instead he bought expensive toys to substitute for parenting, and then he'd bully me if I didn't get a hundred on a test."

"I would've traded for your problems. I don't even know if my father's alive."

"If he is, I'm sure you'll see him again. Even bad fathers return, sort of like dirty pennies."

He pressed his hand on hers, the way a father would.

Carly didn't pull back. She tilted her head and took an immediate liking to him. For all the bad Conner claimed Humanetics did to people, it had worked for Governor Fromm.

Now they were both quiet. Fromm had faced his demons and stared them down. He was his own man now, making his own choices, answerable only to his wife, Barbara. Sweet Barbara. How he missed her. She was his first and only love. His one regret in life was that the Fates did not grace them with a child. No matter, they had each other. The thought of her as First Lady made him glow.

Carly replayed the last couple of hours. Conner said she was in danger. Was she? What had she seen? A rope around Artie's neck didn't add up to murder. When she peeked into the room, his legs were moving and jism was arcing to the floor. After all, the greenshirt was there to lower Artie after the last threads of white cum broke away. In New York, how many times had people come into the emergency room with rectal bleeding and torn tissues? For a New Yorker, Artie was normal fare. She'd extracted her share of Coke bottles, gerbils, and battery-operated dildos the size of overgrown zucchinis, so not much surprised her. Maybe Conner jumped the gun.

The limousine cruised along the twisting base of the Superstitious Mountains. On each turn, she gripped the hand rest so hard her knuckles turned white. She knocked on the glass screen separating the front from the back when the pinion tree-covered valley changed into a flat road lined with wild grasses. Here and there, a barrel cactus or thistle bush dotted a flourishing landscape. The driver caught her face in the mirror. She waved; he smiled. When she saw Fromm nodding off, she leaned back and enjoyed the rest of the ride.

The driver dropped her off first. With one foot out the door, Carly leaned and pecked Fromm on the cheek.

"I'm going to vote for you."

He lingered, holding her hand. "I hope your mother makes a speedy recovery."

"It won't be easy, but I appreciate your good thoughts."

"One last thing," he called after her.

Carly swung the door open and ducked her head inside.

"When you find your father tell him, for me, he has one fine daughter."

"I will, sir."

Again she started to close the door.

"You know, you never told me what you did in New York."

"I like to say I wear Siamese hats. I have a small dental practice, and I also work for the Medical Examiner as an odontologist. That's a forensic dentist."

Fromm mockingly made the sign of the cross with his fingers. "I hope I never need you for either."

"Good thing I have a thick skin when it comes to telling people what I do." She smiled. "Just the same, I always extend professional courtesy to governors and presidents."

"Isn't forensics about dead people?"

"Most often, but not always."

Forensics? Dead People? Presidents? In that instant, they both flashed on a November day in Dallas, when a lone sniper shattered JFK's skull.

Fromm broke the spell. "Forget the forensics part of what you do, Carly. If I ever need you, it'll be to fix my choppers."

They both laughed.

"Good luck to you, young lady."

"Good luck to you, sir."

14

"Ticket for Priscilla Jones to JFK," she panted, out of breath, at the America West counter in Terminal Four.

Conner explained it was safer to travel under an assumed name. Somehow he came up with a fake driver's license. It wasn't needed. When she came to reflect on the events leading to her swift departure, she realized Conner saving her was no spur-of-the-moment act. Booking the ticket and having the ID ready took planning.

Carly focused on the agent's gray roots while the woman scanned the computer list. Whenever someone approached, Carly flattened her body against the ticket counter as a reflex. Until the plane was in the air, she wasn't free of Lute Aurum. Of course there was no guarantee the green-shirts would leave her alone in New York, but it would be on her turf. She had miles to go and hours to sift through the day's events.

"Here we go, Ms. Jones. One-way to New York. Would you like your Aadvantage miles?"

Clutching the ticket as if she had won a twenty-state super lottery, Carly whisked past security. The gate was at the end of a tentacle erupting from the main building. She tucked hard into a corner. With her back against the thick glass overlooking the runway, Carly was hidden. For the next half hour she observed the waiting area in a stilted slow motion. She saw people tracking in and out of rest rooms, towing children and bags in all colors and shapes. She saw last minute ticket purchases sprinkled among the soldiers traipsing to the ticket counter, confirming seats and getting boarding passes. She saw passengers sleeping, eating, talking, or bopping to Country-western blasting through yellow and black Sony headphones. It was non-stop busy.

Carly craved a Snickers. Shoving her hand in her pants pocket, she felt a thickness she had missed earlier. What a surprise! A wad of dollars. Conner thought of everything! Now she could buy candy.

Carly tossed the wrapper in a gray litter can.

"Flight 1467 for JFK Airport in New York will begin general boarding in ten minutes. At this time, First Class passengers, people with small children or those needing assistance may begin taking their seats. Passengers in our Aadvantage Executive Platinum club may board at any time."

Carly ducked back into the kiosk to buy bottled water when she heard her name over the loudspeaker.

"Will Carly Mason go to the nearest phone and identify yourself to an airport operator. Carly Mason, please go to...."

Only Conner and Governor Fromm knew she was at the airport. No one else. Suddenly, two green-shirts barreled into the terminus. Carly peered over the rack of packaged nuts. The monitors fanned out in military fashion, and checked each person. She guessed that a third monitor was guarding the ramp leading back to the main building.

Boarding went swiftly; Carly stayed out of sight.

"This is the last call for Flight 1467 to New York's JFK International Airport. Final boarding call for Fli...."

Carly's throat swelled. The green-shirts weren't leaving. She never did buy the water and the Snickers made her thirsty. Her brain went into overdrive. She could race to the plane but they'd grab her. Or she could abandon this flight and catch another.

The agent changed flight signs at the gate. There would be no last call.

She had to figure something out...and fast.

The monitors flanked the terminus. She felt like a gazelle about to be turned into a meal.

At that moment two women strolled in front of the kiosk. The mother was close to fifty, the daughter half that. Carly made a long-legged dash. She slipped an arm through each startled women, kissed them on the cheeks, and then replayed her high school lead in *The Mad Woman of Chaillot*, dragging them to the gate.

"I was so worried you dears wouldn't see me off. It would have been terribly dreadful not having said, 'Ta, ta.' to each other."

"Why, uh...."

"I know, I know dears," breathed Carly, "it's been exhilarating for me, too. As they say, 'Ta, ta.'"

*   *   *

The monitors reconnoitered under the center dome.

"What're we gonna tell Lute?" said one coming out of the ladies room. "He'll string us to a cactus."

"We should be so lucky. You saw the plane's manifest: no Carly Mason. Either she used a different name or hopped another flight. Either way, we're buzzard bait."

One gate over, boarding began for a flight to Atlanta. When the flock of frenetic travelers settled into an orderly flow toward their door, three women approached the just-closed New York-bound gate.

"...*been exhilarating for me, too. As they say, 'Ta, ta.'*"

"That's her," said the third monitor pointing from his guard post at the main stem. "Over there. Wearing one of our shirts."

"She's taller than that. And she's got long hair."

"Under the baseball cap."

"I'm telling you it's...."

They watched the attendant unlock the door and Carly bolt down the expandable tunnel. In the moments it took for the first monitor to get to the door, the attendant sealed it shut a second time.

"Open that up. My sister just went through there, and I've got to give her something. It's a matter of life and death."

The attendant put on a doughy smile, but didn't budge.

The monitor glanced at the ticket receipt in her hand, and then softened. "Please? It won't take but a minute."

"I'm sorry, I can't do that. The captain's ready to take off."

"Look, her name is Priscilla Jones. Five seconds. I know how it works. If they haven't locked the inside door, what's the big deal?"

Another ticket agent approached. "There's a hold. Something about a governor needing to get on this plane."

"Now may I see my sister?"

With a look that could kill, the ticket agent located the key from the beaded chain around her neck. By the time she and the green-shirt got to the end of the ramp extensor, the pressurized door had swung open.

       *   *   *

Carly pressed her nose to the porthole-sized window. The terminal view was blocked by the walkway and the plane's wing. The longer the plane remained at the gate, the more she worried.

She surveyed the cabin: a smattering of empty seats remained. Most passengers talked or read. The flight attendants closed the overhead compartments. A woman scolded a shrieking toddler.

Carly heard the whoosh of air released from a hydraulic door and knew trouble was seconds away.

*   *   *

"Excuse me," the green-shirted monitor said to another flight attendant, "where did the last woman take a seat? A tall blond wearing a green shirt. Like this one."

"Middle left, by the wing."

The monitor traipsed down the aisle wondering if Carly would put up a fight. Lute wanted to know why she sneaked away instead of taking the van to the airport? Lute ordered everyone at the Institute to look for her. When they caught her, they would find out which stooge helped her escape.

*   *   *

Carly saw the monitor speak with an attendant, and then begin down the aisle toward her. She hadn't come this far to make it easy for them. She considered scrunching into an empty seat in the rear of the plane, and then tossing a navy blanket over her head. There was a hole in this stratagem: tall women are hard to hide, especially in planes. The lavatories were too obvious.

Her prospects were sinking fast when she spotted the blue curtain separating the flight attendants' galley from the main cabin. Lucky for her, the Boeing 737's galley was *behind* the last seat.

*   *   *

The monitor lifted blankets and peered over magazines. He disturbed anybody whose face he couldn't see. He growled like a caged lion poked by a trainer. He huffed and muttered and ranted for his missing sister.

*   *   *

Carly untied the drawstring and fanned the curtain across the rear. She pressed against the steel cabinets, not daring to breathe. If only she could rifle through the metal drawers for a knife. A fork would do.

The monitor was a step away.

She braced for the moment he drew back the curtain, ready to claw his eyes out.

"I'm sorry, sir." The flight attendant ducked under the monitor's outstretched arm. "No one is permitted beyond this point."

In a louder than necessary voice, he answered. "I need to find her. It's about her boyfriend, Conner."

He jostled to rip open the galley curtain.

The flight attendant stood her ground.

They both looked up when the overhead speakers crackled.

"That's the captain. Unless you want to fly to New York, you have to leave now."

"But the governor?"

"The governor must have made other plans. The tower wants us out of here. There's a plane waiting to unload at this gate."

The monitor stalled, waiting for Carly to show herself.

"Are you leaving or making the trip with us?"

He craned to see beyond the blue curtain.

"Or do I call security?"

He retreated a step, and then swiveled hoping to catch Carly peeking out. "Maybe I was mistaken." He turned again. "I thought it was her. I guess I'll catch up with her in New York."

The flight attendant winked over her shoulder as the green-shirt filed out the plane. "I'm sure she'll be happy to see you."

15

While Carly downed a Black Label on the flight back to New York, six monitors quaked on metal chairs in a basement cell. They sat in a semi-circle. For the moment, they were alone with each other. No one spoke. Conner was planted in the middle.

With each passing second, the air grew metallic with fear. Soon it would turn caustic and hurt when they breathed.

The door behind them opened

They faced forward, not daring to turn around. They knew it was Aurum.

Boots clicked on the hard floor, and then stopped. Tranquillity before the storm. Instead of thunder, they heard the soft padding of little feet. All were curious, but not enough to peek.

Aurum moved closer, followed by wisps of dainty feet. "I want you to meet my friends."

Aurum came into view stroking a snake wrapped around his neck, and holding a leash in his free hand. Conner followed the leash to where it encircled the waist of the biggest fucking spider he had ever seen. Aurum tugged on the leash.

"May I present Charlotte. Charlotte is a Goliath Birdeater. She has a leg span of twelve inches and stands six inches off the ground, certainly bigger than some dogs. She's nocturnal and doesn't like to be awake this time of day. Like your average teenager. I suggest none of you disturb Charlotte. She hasn't been fed in a day, and being hungry makes her—shall we say—a bit on the grumpy side.

Lute dropped the brown leather strap and the animal plodded toward the closest monitor. Its body was in two rounded parts, each segment larger than a black fuzzy tennis ball. Its furry legs—three to the left, three to the right, two in front—were colossal.

The snake poked its broad head toward the monitors.

Aurum used both hands to uncoil the snake, it was seven feet long. "This jealous beauty is a Rhinoceros Viper. She may seem tame to you, but I'd advise against getting it angry. Her fangs are two inches long. When she bites, she doesn't let go. Her venom, I may add, is about the deadliest on the planet."

Conner gawked at the snake's mixture of diamonds and strips set against its light buff-colored skin. Yellow bars lined its back, and its head was as big as Aurum's hand.

The tarantula crawled up the leg of the nearest monitor. The monitor shrieked.

Conner didn't know which beast was more frightening, the tarantula or the snake.

"Charlotte's being playful. Stay calm and let her explore you. It's rare that they bite...unless they sense fear."

Aurum stroked the viper.

The door opened and a green-shirt carried in a glass cage. He set the cage on an empty table, and then Aurum lowered in the snake. The monitor reached into his pocket and handed Aurum a white mouse, which he rubbed against his cheek and lips before tossing into the herpetterrarium.

Everyone except the man Charlotte was climbing over, watched in panicked rapture as the snake devoured the mouse. Charlotte climbed from the first lap to the next. The second monitor scrunched his face as if he mainlined sour lemons. His lips were welded shut. His eyes grew whiter as the spider climbed up his shirt.

The viper darted its head above the glass top.

Aurum's calm turned; his ranting ripped through the room like a grade four tornado trashing Candy Mountain. Now there was Charlotte, the viper, *and* Aurum to fear.

Aurum pounded his fist in his left palm. "I can accept someone leaving my course. However I will never tolerate anyone sneaking off this ranch and making a mockery of Humanetics. One of you helped Carly Mason escape. One of you is a traitor to everything we hold sacred and true. One of you is enturbulated beyond measure."

In a Jekyll/Hyde turnabout, his tone turned father-like. Accepting. "Maybe you were protecting her, worried that if we stripped her timetracks away, she would crack. We've seen it happen before, we know it happens." Then he thundered, growing seven-feet tall. "What I can't understand is why you didn't come and tell me what you were thinking. The betrayal of it!"

Lute turned grotesque.

The snake hissed. Charlotte moved onto Conner.

"What I can't understand is why the guilty one is still breathing."

16

Carly quit the jet way searching for a familiar face. She panicked when LeShana Thompkins was nowhere to be seen. They had talked on the GE Skylink phone. Carly met LeShana when they both worked on Carly's first case: the Happy Land Social Club fire. The tragedy, the largest mass murder in American history, was Carly's baptism in forensics. Eighty-seven young people who suffocated to death from the smoke had to be identified. It was LeShana's job to find the culprit, and she did. LeShana was the NYPD's peregrine falcon: a competent Afro-American female cop. The top brass had no choice but to give her a detective's badge.

LeShana said they would meet at the gate.

The terminus emptied out. It grew cold, like an empty hangar. With the last passengers waddling away, Carly trailed the fresh-as-ever flight attendants and the crisp pilots. When the entourage entered the main terminal, Carly did a three-sixty. She felt eyes on her back, sensed someone was following her...but no one was there.

She hustled after the flight crew and then heard a familiar voice. She didn't know where it was coming from, but it had the sweet effect of Julie Andrews singing, "The hills are alive...."

"I'm a-coming, child. Just hold on."

LeShana sprinted toward her.

Carly met her in mid-stride. "Whoa, if you don't let up, we're talking serious rib damage. C'mon, let's get out of here," said LeShana.

"When you weren't at the gate, I got confused. Either I gave you the wrong information or Aurum's people got hold of you.

"Always the paranoid New Yorker. Traffic was a mother coming out of Shea. The Mets beat Atlanta and a dozen cars were overheated on the parkway. Otherwise I'd have been here sooner. Forget all that, child. I ran Artie Montefusco's name through our computers. Nada. If he really died, no one's...."

"I saw him swinging with a rope around his neck. Conner—he's the guy who helped me get away—so much as said that Artie bought it. That it's happened before at the Institute."

"Appearances can be deceiving. We're hearing more and more about sex being coupled with near-asphyxiation. It's quite the rage these days."

"That's what I thought when I first saw him swinging there. In fact, I just shrugged and went about my business. Then Conner busts into my room and tells me I'm in danger, like I witnessed a murder or something."

"Aurum's a famous dude. He's not going to get his hands dirty like that. So much of what we have to deal with is people thinking they saw something when they really didn't."

"With hindsight, I know what I saw. Are you forgetting I'm a trained observer? Artie Montefusco was swinging from a rope, kicking his feet. Probably choking to death. If I'm wrong, why did Conner scoot me out of there?"

LeShana saw this was going nowhere. "Tell you what. Some folks in the Phoenix police force owe me a favor. I helped them catch a drug dealer once. I'll ask them to snoop around that

Institute, see if they hear anything. In the meantime, I'll keep my eyes peeled on the missing persons lists. Will that satisfy you?"

"Could they check to see if Conner's okay? If things have happened at the Institute before, there's no telling what they might do to him."

"Who is this Conner fellow? One of the other suckers taking your high-priced course?"

"He works for them."

LeShana put her hands on her hips. "You see? It's probably another one of their scams. They get you frightened to death, have you looking over your shoulder, and then blind-side you with another course in a week or two. You'll see, they'll be back."

"Can't you ever believe someone's telling the truth?"

"Not when I'm hearing a story. From what you're telling me, I'm hearing a story."

"Conner's not like that. He's there, I guess you could say 'undercover,' because he blames Aurum for his sister dying. She was taking a course at the Institute with her husband. The husband leaves and she's upset. They throw her together with some guy who happens to be HIV positive. You can figure the rest."

"Conner returns to the scene of the crime to seek retribution. Along the way, he sees a fair damsel in distress, and saves her pretty little ass. Now *that's* a story."

"Whether you believe me or not, when you call your friends, could you have them check to see if he's all right?"

LeShana bowed with a roll of her right hand. "Anything to humor you, milady. What's Sir Galahad's last name?"

Carly hugged LeShana tighter than before. "I knew you'd do it. Masterson. Conner Masterson."

"Sounds like a cowboy name."

Carly stifled a grin. "In some ways, he is."

Arm-in-arm, Carly and LeShana strolled out of the JFK terminal towards LeShana's unmarked car.

They were too relaxed to notice the man shadowing them.

*   *   *

Before taking her home, LeShana parked in front of a fire-plug and dragged Carly into Ben and Jerry's on Columbus Avenue. A treat was in order. They left the car and drifted toward Carly's West End Avenue apartment lapping the Coffee BuzzBuzzBuzz before it melted. Carly was describing Governor Fromm when they neared the corner of her apartment building. She stopped so suddenly LeShana broke the cone against her teeth.

"Oh my God," Carly said. She dropped the unfinished ice cream.

LeShana's eyes darted this way and that until she focused on a man donned in a green shirt coming toward them. LeShana tossed her cone, crouched, and whipped out her 9mm Glock in one fluid move. She was about to shout, "Halt! Police!" when she saw the "Jesus Saves" message written across his shirt.

Carly marched past the man without pausing or looking his way. By the time LeShana holstered her gun, Carly was running her fingers over the four-foot high ad in the glass bus shelter.

It was bold. Brazen. Chilling.

LeShana stole behind Carly, who was staring at a large poster of Lute Aurum smiling at them. "If that don't beat all."

Black letters howled the message:

Humanetics: A New Slant on Life

"How could the city let him do it? It's got to be against the law," Carly said.

"Child, no matter what we think about them, it's a free country. Can't go curtailing free speech, now, can you?"

"Don't you get it, LeShana? They're everywhere. Pretty soon, Lute Aurum's face will replace Michael Jordan's on the Wheaties Box. Aurum gains more momentum every day. Where's it going to stop?"

*   *   *

Carly plunged into the only thing she was sure would help: a hot shower. With the water stinging like needles, she closed her eyes and tried to see the real Conner Masterson. For starters, why did he seduce her? Was it part of his job or did he like her? They did connect that first night at the introductory course, so she put "like" in the plus column.

She turned the spigot further to the left; the water grew hotter.

Forgetting the camera?...that was bad. "Camera" went into the minus column.

The "escape" put Conner back on the plus side.

She toweled herself, combed out her hair, rubbed on body lotion, brushed her teeth, flossed, and dove into bed. She found a comfortable position, worked her head into the cool pillowcase, and then listened to herself breathe for the next hour. She tossed and turned, watching shadows dance on her ceiling. Light filtered across the river from an all-night golf driving range in Edgewater. Horns blared on the street below. A city bus rumbled by, and then she heard a motorboat sputter up the Hudson.

Carly's eyelids fluttered. She drifted off only to awaken to her phone ringing.

Please be Conner!

Silence greeted her on the other end. The seconds ticked.

"Hello."

No one responded. She wanted to ask if it was Conner checking to see that she made it home safely, but he would have identified himself.

"Is anyone there? If this is someone's idea of playing a joke, it's not funny."

"No one's laughing, bitch." The phone went dead.

The voice was unfamiliar. She hit *69, the number had been blocked. She shuddered. Was it her "brother," the green-shirt from the airport? Were they after her? Or, was her New York paranoia getting the best of her?

She tossed for hours, mulling over Conner. In one scenario, Conner remained undercover in Humanetics longer than he wanted. In another, Conner escaped undetected. That suited her, and she drifted off. Had she known Conner would be underground for years, she would have stayed awake figuring out how to free him.

17

Willie Robinson looked up with a scalpel in his hand. "You're two days early."

"Missed you too much to stay away longer, and stop gloating."

Willie pretended to rub away his glee. "*Moi?*"

She held her hands up in surrender. "Okay, I'll say it. 'Anything that sounds too good to be true, usually is too good to be true.' There, you satisfied? You warned me not to go. I should've listened."

While she helped Willie dissect the body of an eighteen-year-old victim of a drive-by gang shooting, she recounted everything that happened at the Institute except the intimate parts with Conner.

"You should've told that monitor to take a flying one when they started talking about your parents. You can bet I would've."

"I started to, and then I began thinking he was right. I remembered how I used to cry myself to sleep, night after night. I blamed myself for thinking something I did made my father leave. That's how ten-year olds think. I wracked my brain figuring what I could do to make him come back. Those kinds of wounds never heal, not really. Aurum's people knew what was festering in me, and jabbed away like I was a boxer with a glass chin."

"Excuse me, but when it comes to parental guilt, yours truly gets the blue ribbon. Try living with parents who made me feel guilty for getting polio. They claimed I ruined *their* lives! Can you imagine?"

Willie threw his hands up. "I grew up hearing them curse Jonas Salk and every other Jewish doctor for not discovering the polio vaccine sooner. My mother swore there was a conspiracy against her and my father. You see, they were more sorry for themselves than for me. I was a cripple sent to punish them. Now is that sick or what?"

Carly hugged him. "Willie, we're two of a kind, aren't we?"

He kissed the top of her head. "I think so, pumpkin."

"My father used to call me that," Carly said softly.

What might have proved awkward at that moment...wasn't. How many times had she longed to find her father and tell him she was sorry she forced him to leave? When Hack Mason bailed out on his family, he left Carly with an emptiness bigger than a celestial black hole. He had taught his daughter how to drain oil without getting dirty. Thanks to him, Carly could hit a curve ball better than any other Little Leaguer—boy or girl. Twenty-five years later, she was still grieving.

The other side of the story was that Hack Mason was guaranteed trouble. In and out of jail all his life, Mason rode bucking broncos in a small-time rodeo that toured the country. He met Carly's mother when the rodeo set up in a park off Kissena Boulevard. It was a sultry summer night. Carly's mom waitressed at the Five Corners Diner. She marched up to Hack on a dare. Sparks flew and Carly was conceived that very night.

Carly's mother tried traveling with the rodeo, but soon tired of the nomadic life. All of a sudden, waitressing and raising a baby in Queens was looking good. Hack had other ideas. He was a restless soul, with a quick mouth and fists to match. He tried to stay home, drifting from job to job. One day he came home with a wad of money. He wouldn't say how or where it came from, only that there was more to be made. Their good fortune lasted another year, and then he disappeared.

Willie punctured her reverie. "So you marched out of that Institute?"

"Not before a green-shirted goon tried to sell me extra courses."

"On top of the fifteen Gs?"

"Aurum's got some racket going. They try to convince you that timetracks from your childhood hinder your success. Someone said these hindrances pass through the placenta, that's why babies cry."

"If it comes from the mother, they may be on to something. That's why I still see my shrink after thirty years."

"Why don't you stop?"

"Can't. I knew I'd be going so I prepaid for the next twelve years. Got a great discount."

Carly rolled her eyes. "They talked about becoming a *Clear*. I never got a chance to find out what that meant because the chair got hot."

Willie gashed through the victim's kidney. "Run the chair thing by me again. Hot? As in temperature, hot?"

"We're talking, hot, as in scalding hot. The monitor controlled a wire going to the metal chair I was sitting on. At first I thought I was imagining things. When the chair started to burn, I stood up. I mean, wouldn't everyone? Anyway, this jerk orders me to sit back down."

Willie sliced the second kidney. "What'd you tell him?"

"I said, 'Not in this lifetime.' What could he do? Tie me to the chair? So I stood and left. That's when everything degenerated."

18

Carly was aching to call the Institute to speak with Conner when she spotted a child on the gurney. "Abuse?"

"The authorities want to take the parents' other children away," Willie said.

The boy was seven, eight tops. He had straight jet-black hair, a broad nose, and almond-colored skin. The day before, he was a Ninja warrior playing with his brothers and sisters. Now he lay in a serene calm, never to wake again.

"Got a cause?"

Willie pointed to well-defined bruises. "I'm glad you're here. Tell me about those wounds."

Carly studied the patterned marks that resembled a squared-off letter "U." The sides were dark and straight, with a deeper mark midway. The stained specks that connected the nearly parallel sides, held four faint dots. This same pattern was found on the boy's neck, right cheek, both arms, torso, and outer thighs. There was one on his groin, too, near his penis.

"Do they have a dog?"

"A rotweiler."

"That's the culprit. You knew that, didn't you?"

"Just wanted to be sure."

"Now, can you do me a favor?" she asked.

"Name it," Willie answered touching his legs, "as long as it doesn't require any sprinting."

Carly explained how she wanted to find out what happened to Conner, but was afraid to call the Institute. Willie agreed to help.

"Hi," Willie said to the receptionist answering the Institute's 1-800 number, "I'm Conner Masterson's uncle. I need to get a message to him."

"You can stop right there, Dr. Robinson."

Willie was never so startled; he held the receiver so Carly could hear.

The secretary continued. "If Carly Mason happens to be close by, tell her to stop trying to reach Conner. It's for his own good, as well as hers."

Carly was not about to be intimidated by Aurum's people. Besides, knowing LeShana was around gave her was an extra measure of security. Carly grabbed the phone and was about to demand they put Conner on the line when the call was disconnected. "Damn that caller ID."

That same day, LeShana's Arizona contacts drove to Lute Aurum's ranch. Without a search warrant, they were turned away at the gate. Had they managed to bust through, they would have learned Conner had been moved to a "safe" house in San Francisco where he had round-the-clock mind bashing to rid him of destructive timetracks.

*   *   *

For the first time in years, the Claypool Arizona Boy Scout Troop changed the group's task. In past forays into Lost Dutchman State Park, the boys collected picnic litter, beer bottles, and soda cans around the park's campsites. This year was different. It didn't matter that purists felt fires and disasters were part of Nature's life cycles. If there were any more ruinous fires, Arizona's tourism would be decimated. So in the spirit of helping local businesses and getting their merit badges, the scouts set out to reduce the local ground mass by carting away excess pine cones and dried needles.

Big Bill Slaughter wore two hats: he was the troop leader *and* Ray Gene Slaughter's dad. Big Bill was in charge of fifteen scouts on a scorcher of a day. He tried to get help, but no other father was willing to chaperone. All that heat, snippy kids and no cold beer…it was going to be a long day. The last thing he wanted was to be chasing down a straggling kid when it came time to leave.

Tyrone Piersal, all of twelve-and-a-half with a bad stutter, was a curious child. He also had ADD and hadn't taken his Ritalin because school was out. The second Big Bill turned his back, Tyrone wandered away. Tyrone hadn't been out of sight thirty seconds when he charged out of the brush quicker than a bobcat in heat.

The boy grabbed Big Bill's olive shirt and yanked so hard the two-hundred-and-ten pound man collapsed to his knee. Tyrone's eyes were wild, his face flushed.

"Calm down, boy. Take deep, slow breaths. Count to three."

Bill mouthed the numbers with Tyrone. He spotted his son. "Ray Gene, bring this scout some water."

Tyrone gulped for a canteen, slobbering onto his uniform.

"Now tell Big Bill what you saw. Take it nice and slow." Slaughter squeezed Tyrone's shoulder. "One word at a time, son. That-a-boy."

Wide-eyed, Tyrone got through it. "There's a big fat dead man up there, and his balls are in his mouth."

"Don't tell no stories, boy, you're scaring everybody."

"It ain't a story, Mr. Slaughter. Go see for yourself."

Big Bill stood and removed his olive-colored scouting hat. He scratched his red scalp. Fourteen scouts encircled him and Tyrone, waiting for his next move.

Jesus H. Christ! There's nothing in them scout manuals about handling fibbing boys with wild stories. Why couldn't Tyrone save it for a marshmallow roast?

"Everybody stand back and wait here." He turned to Tyrone. "Take me there, son. I got to make sure you saw what you saw."

Tyrone shook his head with enough force to put himself in traction for a week.

"I ain't going back there, Mr. Slaughter. It's right over yonder. You go yourself."

*   *   *

The police questioned the scouts. For nearly everyone, it was the most exciting day of their young lives. For Big Bill Slaughter, helping the authorities was what scouting was all about, and he was bursting to tell the guys back at Fogerty's Bar. For Tyrone Piersal, his stuttering became worse than ever. Tripping over a dead man triggered a basket full of trips to a child psychologist and a speech pathologist. It took years to get over the trauma.

The county medical examiner took scores of photos of Artie's body. Reports devoted ample space describing how the genitals— tied at the stalk with a brass cock ring—were found stuffed in the victim's mouth. What was considered of little import was the fact that Artie's tongue had been cut out and was nowhere to be found. Imagine what would have happened to Tyrone Piersal's stutter if the boy found Artie's tongue on the ground?

The police and the medical examiner should have made more out of the severed tongue. Instead, they were more impressed with Artie's big mouth wrapped around his bigger balls.

19

By the time the scouts discovered Artie Montefusco, Conner was long gone to San Francisco for intensive auditing sessions. He was confined in a Holiday Inn at the corner of Bay and Columbus. Conner had no clue he was being kept in one of the countless hotels across the country where Aurum Enterprises had "local" arrangements. Aurum paid a premium over posted rates…for special favors. It had worked this way for years.

The green-shirt in charge of purging Conner of his residual time-tracks interrupted Conner's "studies" one day. He handed him a piece of paper and a cell phone. "Read this to the bitch," ordered the monitor. Carly was the bitch. Carly had to be made to understand that she could never call the Institute again. Not ever.

*   *   *

The only thing to change for Carly in the days following her return from the Institute was that jogging around Central Park's reservoir became a thing of the past. The principle reason had to do with the environmental changes. In the back of her mind, however, Carly harbored a nagging thought that a green-shirt might spring out from behind a tree or bush at any time and harm her. Though the immediate threat that Aurum would retaliate for her escape from the Institute began to recede, Carly developed a keener awareness of her surroundings. These days, she took fewer risks. This meant avoiding dark and isolated places, or sucking in unfiltered air for long periods of time.

In New York, as well as in most major urban centers, outdoor exercise became a health hazard. While reducing exhaust fumes improved air quality, global warming accelerated at a deadly pace. Weather patterns were changing faster than Madison Avenue fashions. Oceans stayed warmer for longer periods of time, spawning freak storms, floods, red algae, and lots of blizzards. Droughts became commonplace.

Urban sprawl meant more streets and buildings using tar-based products. Asphalt, pitch, and creosote absorbed heat. Cities became heat cells. Higher temperatures meant increases in respiratory diseases along with extra thunderstorms. One suggestion was to put a thin layer of concrete over every street to lower the surrounding temperature and help reduce smog. Another was to plant millions of trees. These were desperate times, and too little was being done about it.

*   *   *

"There's a call for you," Willie said one morning after she had been home about a week.

Carly didn't bother to look up behind the yellow-tinted protective glasses. With an UV light, she scanned the skin of a five-year old for old bruises. "Take a message. I'll call back as soon as I'm finished."

"I think you'll want to take it now. He says his name is Conner Masterson."

Like the lead runner in a 4x100 relay, Carly tossed down the gun-shaped machine and bolted toward the phone. "Are you all right? Where are you? How come you didn't call?"

She tapped her foot waiting from him to reply. "Conner, why aren't you answering?" She heard labored breathing. "Conner, is that you?"

"Carly...."

It was Conner, but it wasn't. The voice was his, but the tone was mechanical, lifeless. He sounded drugged.

"...I wanted you to know that I'm okay. Don't try to call me anymore or send someone looking for me." Then the phone clicked and he was gone.

*　　　　*　　　　*

The monitor took the cell phone from Conner and tapped the dictionary-high stack of papers on the desk in front of him. "Finish this by tomorrow." Conner turned to the material without a challenge.

*　　　　*　　　　*

"To know knowledge is to know yourself. To know yourself,
is to have knowledge. There is the knowable and the unknowable,
and we have to know which goes with which. If knowing
does not solve the problem, then an aberration has occurred
and the human mind needs to be made clear. Neither the
human soul, mental telepathy, spiritualism, or the belief in
god will make you know more than you already know. To
know is to be, to be is to know."

*　　　　*　　　　*

After days of auditing, Conner no longer recognized that the convoluted material zigged and zagged only to return to the same starting point again and again. For reasons he could not plumb, courtesy of having his timetracks removed, Conner was convinced he was tapping into the secrets of life. His mentor and master teacher was Lute Aurum. Lute, the *Clear*. Lute, the Immortal.

                *   *   *

Carly swiped a tear away.

"Is he all right?" Willie asked.

"He didn't sound right. He told me to stay away and not to send anyone to look for him."

"You're not going to listen to him, are you? I'm sure there's something LeShana can do."

"What else can she do? Her people were turned away at the front gate. Aurum's green-shirts orchestrated Conner's call just now, I'm sure of it. It's their way of saying that if I stop trying to contact Conner, then we'll both be okay."

She plopped down on a chair.

"What's going to happen to Conner?" Willie edged back to the gurney where Carly had been working.

All Carly could think about were her last minutes at the Institute. Did Conner overreact when he rushed into the room and helped her escape? Maybe Artie Montefusco *was* having an erotic S&M experience when she opened his door. Carly wanted to believe that scenario with all her might. So why did she harbor nagging thoughts that what she had really witnessed was the end stages of Artie being murdered? If that was case, Conner was in deep trouble. She prayed Conner had the resources to survive because any further attempt on her part to try to save him could end in disaster...for both of them.

Carly stood and muttered out loud. "He's a big boy. He's going to have to help himself."

Willie caught what she said. "I hope he has better luck than this kid." He nodded toward the corpse on the gurney. "Did you find any long-standing bruises before the phone rang?"

Carly returned to the angelic face. "With the UV light, I could see more bruises under his skin than Dennis Rodman has tattoos. Crucify his parents."

Willie saw that Carly was still worried. He put both hands on her shoulders. "Carly, I know Conner touched you and, somehow, he'll get out of the mess he's in. If the two of you hook up later, that's great. If not him, I know there's someone out there for you. I can't help you find that guy but I'm in a position do something about your career. Are you game?"

Willie explained how the state of New York created a salary line to help educate every healthcare worker, policeman, social worker, etc., to recognize child abuse. "I've submitted your name. The money's good, great benefits, and you'll be doing a lot to help prevent *that* from happening again."

Carly studied the dead boy, and then hugged Willie. "I can't do it."

"You're the best one for the job. Someone's got to train other professionals how to detect abuses before more children end up like him."

"It's wonderful and all that."

"Then what's stopping you?"

"You."

"I'm the one who wants you to take it."

"Then I won't be able to work here anymore."

"Is that what's worrying you? It's not a full-time job. You'd still have to work. I just assumed you'd want to sell your practice and give me the extra time. What the child abuse program doesn't pay you, I can maybe make up with discretionary funds. What do you say?"

"I didn't go to school all those years to drop it like that."

"You'd still be using your degree. The truth of the matter is that you'll be doing a hellava lot more good than giving fluoride treatments and bonding laminates onto the pretty people. I thought forensics had become your first love?"

Willie couldn't have been more on target. The truth was that Carly found comfort in dealing with the dead. The dead never complained, but did they have lots to say! And the stories they told Carly were always the truth. Root canals, a silver filling, an impacted wisdom tooth, were all points for comparing teeth to x-rays, and x-rays to teeth. Teeth were used to identify or verify the missing, the dead...and the guilty. It was a dentist who declared that a skull found in Brazil belonged to the mad Mengele. It was a dentist who sifted through the Romanov bones only to find remnants of the "missing" Anastasia. And if not for dentists, the pathologists would still be toiling to identify shreds of flesh fished out of the Atlantic after the explosion of TWA Flight 800 or who each Russian sailor was when the Kurtz went down in the Barents Sea.

In a curious twist, death infused Carly with vigor and a sense of worth. That's where she found her comfort zone in life, and maybe—just maybe—it was part of the reason why she had trouble connecting with men. Who wanted to date a woman who was more comfortable slicing into bodies than slipping into lace panties?

Should she dare follow her heart?

"I could sell my practice to the guy who's renting me the operatory."

"Then you'll do it?"

"I'll try! I'm ready for a change."

Once the words escaped her mouth, she felt lighter; the every-day worries of running a dental practice weighed her down more than she cared to admit. Was being able to see the light a step closer to becoming a *Clear?* Perhaps Humanetics held more appeal for her than she imagined.

20

Two weeks later, Carly was about to give her first lecture on child abuse. Willie told her to take the morning off but she insisted she would rather come to work. Extra time would make her too nervous.

"In that case, we've got a rape/homicide with apparent bite marks," Willie said.

Carly opened the file. A twenty-nine year old woman was found nude in Central Park early that morning. She had blond hair and was tall like Carly.

"Where'd they find her?"

"By the tennis courts."

"I started jogging there, again, whenever they cancel the smog alerts."

Willie didn't respond. He didn't have to. They both knew Carly could have been the victim lying on the gurney.

Carly saw the bite marks circling the left nipple. They had a distinctive pattern. An accurate mold would go along way to match a suspect's teeth—once they had a suspect in custody—to the dead girl's wounds.

Carly shaped gray plasticine into a circle and pressed it around the woman's breast, careful to keep the edges away from the bite marks. She measured four scoops of pink alginate into a green mixing bowl and added the right amount of cold water. She began spatulating the mixture into a creamy blend when the carport doors swung open.

LeShana was pushing a gurney

"Since when does homicide wheel in corpses?" Willie asked.

"The mayor called me to make sure there was no monkey business in this one."

"Was there?"

LeShana hoisted the plastic garbage bag resting on the body. "Found the weapon, found the note. Classic suicide from where I'm standing."

Carly started ladling the mixed alginate, which had the consistency of crème brûlée, onto the ghost-white breast. "Why all the fuss?" She tapped the breast to jar air bubbles from forming in the bite mark area. If any voids occurred in the impression, she'd have to start over. She wasn't focusing on LeShana's answer, but she heard "dentist."

"Repeat that part about the dentist, again, LeShana."

LeShana patted the suicide victim. "I said that you probably know him. The *corpus delecti* is the mayor's dentist."

A dentist? The Mayor? Then it clicked.

"Oh my, God." The rubber bowl slipped to the floor and rolled in a circle until it stopped. "It's Jonah!"

*   *   *

Carly emerged from a cab in a daze. Her lecture started in twenty minutes, but all she could think about was the last two hours. She and Jonah were never ass-licking close. He wasn't her type. Jonah was a conniver but there was a glint in his eye that appealed to Carly. Maybe it was the mischievous way he played the system, making certain he got the best locker, the best lab desk, and the easiest instructors. Or maybe it was the larceny in his heart that she wished she had. No matter. If you showed any kindness to Carly, she would be a friend for life.

The entrance wound was a massive hole through the posterior wall of the back of the throat. Beyond the hole, there was not much to see. Half of Jonah's head was blown off.

The exam done, notes recorded, Willie began the autopsy. She knew the speech by heart.

Let the body tell its story.

"Cut along the scalp and peel down the forehead while I get the saw."

Carly hovered above Jonah's skull with a scalpel, telling herself the face wasn't Jonah's. The first slice was close to impossible. Her stare wavered for a split second, long enough to catch Jonah's ice-blue iris staring back at her. Her legs sagged.

"Need ammonia pellets?" He held an ampoule of smelling salts that he always kept in his lab coat pocket toward her.

"Give me a sec. I'm fine."

Carly's determined fingers peeled the forehead skin until it draped over Jonah's nose and onto his mouth. With the scalp stripped back, Willie flipped the switch on the electric rotary saw and sliced through Jonah's cranium like it was an aluminum can. He searched and poked the mixture of bone and brain parts.

Carly stared, but didn't see. How was this possible? Jonah Schoonover, ever the schemer and plotter, always had an angle for this deal or that bargain, but he was never out of control. Not Jonah. Sure he had suitcases under his eyes the last time they met, but suitcases aren't angst.

At their study club, Jonah's eyes had wandered when they were talking. He couldn't string two sentences together without glancing about the room that night. Carly thought him rude. She was about to lash out and tell him so when Jonah whispered that he knew how she could jump-start her stalling practice.

"Really?" she asked. "Do you promise it will make a difference?"

"Have I ever lied to you?" answered Jonah.

Humanetics was the answer. When the brochure crossed her desk a couple of days later, she ascribed it to fate. Having gone to the Humanetics mill, maybe it wasn't such a coincidence that the course description arrived after Jonah mentioned it? Jonah probably had it sent to her office...for a small commission.

Now that Jonah had been wheeled into the ME's and the initial shock had worn off, how surprised was she? After the Artie Montefusco fiasco and with Conner under their thumb, Lute Aurum's Institute of Humanetics seemed more threatening by the hour.

21

Carly swirled through the metal revolving door and scaled the tread-worn beige marble steps to the second floor. Inside, the bespectacled secretary greeted her. "You here for the child abuse seminar? Name please?"

"Carly Mason. I'm the speaker."

"That's nice. You've got thirty-two registered. Last room on the left. The slide projector is set up. The electric pointer and lavaliere mike are on the lectern. Need anything else?"

Carly nodded at the unfamiliar faces. Some glanced up at her, others continued to read the Wall Street Journal. Two or three labored over the New York Times crossword puzzle. Carly found the room and dropped the carousel onto the projector, tested the bulb, and focused the first slide.

The secretary ducked her head in the room.

"Sooner you start, the sooner you're out of here. It is Friday, you know."

*   *   *

"My name's Carly Mason and I am going to spend the next two hours discussing how to recognize and report physical abuse cases in children. The state of New York requires that all mandated

126

reporters take this course to maintain their licenses. By definition, every dentist in this state is a mandated reporter. So are physicians, osteopaths, nurses, hygienists, school officials, psychologists, police officers, and so on. Anyone whom the community looks to as an authority is a mandated reporter."

Carly detailed what evidence is needed and where to call when abuse was suspected. She talked at length about treatment at mental health facilities and family court procedures. The class could have made it rough for her. Few people were there by choice, attending one child abuse lecture was required for continued licensure. For an inaugural lecture, Carly drew a good group. Their interest dissipated any first time flutters she might have had, but it did nothing to make her wretched stomach condition go away.

"Let's take a five minute break."

Carly dashed out of the room before any questions waylaid her. She flung open the bathroom door, charged into the stall, and dropped to her knees. She retched chunks of bile-coated pretzels into the cool white porcelain bowl. Beads of sweat formed on the back of her scalp and rimmed her upper lip. Her eyeballs and throat hurt. She cringed at the globs of brown and green pooling in the toilet water. She groped for the lever. Just when she thought she had gained control, she heaved and heaved again, until the only discharge was a trickle of foul-tasting slime.

As the muddy swirl disappeared, she sat back on her haunches. She neither dared to stand nor was able to forget what happened that morning.

*   *   *

It was vintage Willie. After posting Jonah and verifying that the weapon LeShana discovered at the scene had killed him, Willie still had doubts.

Let the body tell its story.

"Ballistics confirmed this was the weapon. We have a note. Where's the mystery?" she asked the skeptical ME.

Willie ignored Carly. He grabbed a dusty skull above a glass case and tossed it onto an empty gurney. Next he placed a rubber block under the skull to prop it in a reclining pose. "Get two more blocks, and then stack these lab coats under the chin."

It could have been a Halloween staging. The reclining skull was angled toward the ceiling, with the white lab coat arms folded over each other.

"See," he said, showing her the photo taken in Jonah's operatory. "It's the way they found him."

Carly saw the resemblance. "Where are you going with this?"

Instead of answering, Willie removed the skull and coats. He left the rubber block. "Hop up there."

"Excuse me?"

"*Please*, hop up there. I've got to verify the gun position. I can't do it myself," he grinned with a 'what-choice-is-there?-it's-all-in-a-day's-work' sort of grin.

"In front of everyone?" Carly wriggled her backside onto the gurney. "Are you sure you want me to do this?" She hoisted one leg onto the table, and then the other, all the while glaring at Willie. "You're absolutely positive this is necessary? One hundred percent certain?"

His hand guided her shoulder down.

She cleared her throat three times before her head rested on the blocks. "Is that about right?" she asked with eyes clamped tight.

Willie shoved the shotgun into her hands. "Put it in your mouth."

Carly bolted upright, nearly smashing Willie with the gun stock. "Are you crazy? I'm not putting *that* in my mouth."

"It's clean. I washed it myself."

"Don't get cute on me. I'm not putting a gun in my mouth even if it's sterile and tested for HIV."

"Be a good girl. Do it for me, Carly."

"I'm not a child, Willie. Stop patronizing me. What're you trying to prove with this...this ridiculous display?"

She brandished the gun toward Willie.

He grabbed it. "If you'd stop blabbering and start helping, we'd have a better idea of what happened to Jonah. Now get in position."

She resented doing it, hesitated, and then dropped down. "Like this?" She jacked straight up again. "It's not loaded, is it?"

"It should be."

"I love you, too."

"Down."

"Yes, master."

Carly pointed the barrel toward her mouth. It quivered.

"*In* your mouth, not on your lips. Stretch your arms. As high as you can."

A light blazed, and a motor whirred. Willie had taken a Polaroid.

"Can I get down, now?"

"Not unless you like it up there."

"Was all this necessary?" she said, smoothing her lab coat.

Willie handed her the developing photo; she flapped it in the air to speed the chemical process.

"I'm ripping this up the minute you're through with it."

"What does it tell you?"

"That I looked pretty stupid."

Willie waited.

Carly studied the frame. She considered Jonah's remains on the gurney. "It tells me," Carly said with care, "that if Jonah held it the same way I did, there'd be a huge hole through the roof of his mouth into his brain, not through the pharynx and out the back of his skull."

"What do you make of it?"

Carly peered into Jonah's mouth. She took the barrel and held it as high as she could, like Benny Goodman really swinging. "My arms are too short to create that angle."

"Try Jonah's."

No matter how Carly tried to clamp Jonah's hands on the trigger, something was wrong: the barrel pointed past his skin-draped face, in front of his upturned nose!

"I don't get it."

Willie produced a corncob pipe stem from his lab coat. "Jonah's arms are shorter than yours, aren't they?"

"But his prints were found on the stock and muzzle."

"Jonah touched it. We don't know when."

Willie waited for her to digest what had become obvious to him. "Seems we have a departure from the expected, don't we?"

"Oh my God. Jonah didn't kill himself."

22

Carly splashed water on her face, reapplied her makeup and chewed five Velamints before returning to the lecture room. With the lights out, no one would see the red rings circling her eyes.

"Will someone turn on the slide projector, please?" One good thing about lecturing to dentists was that they were all familiar with how Kodak projectors worked.

The first slide jarred the group. It was a photo of a three-year old boy who appeared to be napping. The boy's eyes were closed, his pudgy fingers at rest. The next slide showed a close-up of the boy's chest. Black and purple marks were the landscape of his arms and shoulders.

"Both clavicles were broken. These are old wounds," she pointed to purple marks.

The door cracked open, and a spark of light flashed on a latecomer.

The next slide ratcheted closer.

"These dark reddish marks are cigarette burns. In cases of physical abuse, children are scalded and burned because the junkie parents can't bear hearing hungry kids ask for food. Innocent babies make the fatal mistake of needing diapers changed. The scenario we hear goes like this: the mother's boyfriend killed the child with one too many blows to the head, because the screaming kid got on his nerves."

Carly zoomed in on the fleshy thighs and inch-long penis.

"These are bite marks. Here," she pointed to the spots, "and here. Remember, bite marks are often associated with child abuse, so look for them. We convicted the boyfriend by taking an impression of his teeth, and then slipping his dental mold into these marks."

Her talk had the effect of Jeffrey Dahmer leading a Gray Line bus tour through life...as only Dahmer could know. Fifteen slides later, in a room silenced by the view of city life few ever saw, Carly Mason finished her lecture on child abuse.

"Will someone please turn on the lights?"

Carly began summarizing the key points when a form along the side wall drew her attention. For a moment no name went with the face. She stammered. Her mental retrieval system was misfiring. When it came together, her tongue ballooned in primal fear. Her legs turned rubbery. The pointer tumbled out of her grasp, clacking to the floor.

Lute Aurum gloated from the back of the class.

She stammered when she asked if there were any questions. When no hands broke the air, she kinked her head toward the door. "Have a great weekend," she told them.

*   *   *

Carly was left alone with Aurum. She surprised herself when she asked, "Learn anything? Then again, abuse is your forte, isn't it?"

Carly turned the carousel light off, but left the fan running to cool the projector. She replaced the slide tray in its carrying box, anything to avoid Aurum's drilling stare.

Aurum deflected her dig, but his answer chilled. "I particularly enjoyed the one where the rats ate the child's eyes."

Carly shifted toward Aurum, pressed with a singular thought. *Chianti and fava beans.*

"Why are you here?"

"I had a meeting with a dear colleague of mine this morning, Jeremy Steel. Maybe you know him? There's a spark in you that reminds me of him. You two would hit it off."

"The gossip columns have him pretty occupied these days. If anyone ever stands him up..."

"I'll be certain to pass the message. Speaking of which, I have one for you."

"From Conner?"

"No, from Jonah Schoonover, the poor soul. It's so unfortunate."

"How could *you* have found out? It happened this morning."

"Jonah was one of my prize pupils, you know. I got the call soon after his secretary discovered the body."

Carly believed coincidences were as rare as white tigers. "So what was his message?"

"I'll let you figure it out since I don't have time to explain. They're expecting me in Washington for an important announcement, and I can't keep them waiting."

Her immediate thought was that Conner was dead, too.

Aurum brushed passed her and whirled through the revolving door before Carly could ask what he meant. Ever since Conner's disturbing phone call, Carly was tormented by his hollow voice. It was distant. Drugged. Could auditing alone do that? She would have kept trying to contact him, but he made it so clear she should back off. Now, with Aurum's sudden appearance, how could she avoid thinking Jonah's death was somehow related to Humanetics?

She nearly caught up with Aurum at the corner of Madison Avenue. The light changed to green but Aurum's cabby was forced to wait for a mother wheeling a double-wide carriage with twins. Carly took advantage of the stall and sprinted between two cars. She reached the cab at the moment its path cleared.

Lute turned to see her at his window. He showed no surprise. Rather, if her eyes weren't deceiving her, he looked cocksure she would be there.

He flicked his wrist.

Her reflexes took over; she waved back.

He said something, but she couldn't make out the words. Her eyes followed the cab as it slalomed up Madison, swerving in and out of the lanes. Then it came to her. Aurum had said, "Ta, ta.."

*   *   *

No longer enturbulated and rid of timetracks, Conner had returned to the Institute from his auditing in San Francisco. Even so, green-shirts were assigned to watch him every minute of the day, until they were convinced they could leave him alone. Conner crapped, washed, and dressed in front of a monitor. Without a mirror, he couldn't see that his ribs poked through his shirt or how much weight he had lost. All he knew, but not on a conscious level, was that he had to cinch his belt an extra notch.

These days, Conner did what he was told. This meant he cleaned the latrines, he scrubbed pans, he hauled hay, and did any number of mindless tasks.

"Come with me," a green-shirt said one day.

Conner dutifully followed him into Lute's ranch house.

"Take off your clothes. All of them."

Conner complied. The green-shirt handed Conner a toothbrush and a bucket. "While Lute's away, clean the grout and bathroom tiles. When you finish here, there's another john upstairs. I'll be back in an hour or two."

Before leaving, the monitor put Conner through his mantra.

"How will you become a *Clear*?"

"By achieving inner peace through Humanetics. By climbing the steps of a *Pre-Clear*."

"Are you enturbulated?"

"Yes."

"Who can help you become a *Clear*?"

"Only myself."

"Who is the Commodore?"

"The grand master of us all."

"Do you believe in all *his* principles?"

"POSITIVITY."

"Are you worthy of *his* help?"

"Only after I rid myself of all my timetracks." And so it went, day after day.

Now alone, Conner poured a capful of Mr. Clean into the bucket and added scalding hot water. He placed the bucket on the floor, got on his knees and began to scrub. When he finished, he found the upstairs bathroom and a new toothbrush waiting for him. He was about to kneel down when he caught his image in the mirror and stopped. He touched his cheeks, his chin, his lips. He was a shadow of his former self. His gaunt looked reminded him of his sister wasting away to nothing during the terminal stages of her disease. Words flashed through his sleep-deprived haze. Audit. H-meter. Bashing. Numb. Fear. Survive. Pain. Hunger.

Add the word *loss*.

Loss tipped the scales.

He had lost his sister.

Conner found the phone on the night table and dialed Carly. On the fourth ring, Carly's message informed him she was unavailable to take his call, but if he...

"If you're there, Carly, pick up. Pick up, damn it. Please pick up. I'm at the Institute. You've got to…"

Conner never got to finish the message. He never heard the green-shirt return.

23

As Carly rode the stainless steel lift to her apartment, she considered canceling dinner. She had invited LeShana and Willie to celebrate her first "child abuse" lecture. She was in no mood to be charming after the shock of posting Jonah's corpse, retching her guts up in the middle of her talk, and finding Lute Aurum appear from nowhere. And she had new worries about Conner.

The elevator bell rang and the metal doors sprung open. In synch, she heard a door slam shut.

Carly stepped toward her apartment and froze. A man blocked her way.

"May I help you?" she asked.

Even though it was beastly hot outside, the man wore a tan raincoat and matching hat. The brim covered his eyes. What little she could see of his face was covered with a gray-flecked stubble. His cheeks were translucent. His lips barely moved when he spoke.

"I must be on the wrong floor," he answered. Then he spurted passed her, slid into the stairwell, and ran up the stairs two at a time.

She sneezed.

Add a strange man to the day's list.

All thoughts of canceling dinner plans were shelved when she inserted the key in the top lock. It didn't tumble. Medeco locks had a full spin to them. Carly went to unlock the second and third locks. They were open, too.

Her first thought was that in the excitement of the morning's lecture, she forgot to triple lock her door when she left. Her second was that she *never* forgot to set her locks. Her third was that it was *her* door that had slammed shut when the elevator opened...which led to her fourth thought: the strange man had been in *her* apartment.

She hesitated. It would be easy to return to the lobby and have the doorman accompany her in the apartment. It would be just as easy to call the police. "Easy" just wasn't her middle name.

Carly let the door swing open. She cocked her right hand, as her left groped for the light switch. She listened. No strange noises. She inched into the pint-sized entryway, grabbed her Public Television award umbrella, and bent for a fuller view. So far, all was in order.

She stepped tentatively into the living room. The refrigerator hummed to life. The battery-operated Seiko clock ticked. A housefly buzzed between the blinds and the dirty window. She leaned toward the kitchenette. The bedroom and bathroom were to the left. She counted to three, leaned hard on the bathroom door, barreled in and stabbed the shower curtain. Pity...it was a hard pattern to find.

She entered her bedroom intent on not destroying anything else. After a check under the bed and a look into the closet, she determined she was alone. That was the good news. The bad news was that she sneezed.

Carly checked her answering machine: no messages.

She sneezed again.

She retraced her steps, sniffing like a bloodhound.

Cologne.
Faint.
Lemony.
Same as the man's in the hall.

24

It took two glasses of Puilly Fuissé to settle her nerves. Nothing was missing, nothing out of place. She thought about calling the police, but the idea of spending the rest of the night answering questions held no appeal and she was sure it would accomplish little. Besides, her own personal cop would be along in a few...and she'd better start preparing or there would be nothing to eat.

First Carly sautéed leeks in a large skillet until they wilted, and then let them simmer in chicken stock. Next she poured the concoction into frozen pastry puffs nestled in a tart pan, sprinkling pepper and parsley sprigs on top. She would toss it in the oven when LeShana and Willie arrived. She didn't have to wait long.

The buzzer sounded from downstairs. Carly opened her door and waited in the hall, wishing the floor numbers highlighting the elevator's progress didn't move so slowly. She leapt when the bell rang and the doors opened.

"Anxious for company, are we?" Willie asked.

"You don't know," she answered, hugging them both.

LeShana sniffed toward the open door. "Smells good, child. Here." She shoved a box into Carly's hand, "This is for you. Better open it for desert. I intend to eat my share."

Carly shook the box. "Champagne truffles?"

"What else?"

Carly pointed to LeShana's left hand. "What's in the black bag?"

"I'll show you in a minute."

Once they were seated, Carly poured two glasses of white wine. "Here's to your first lecture," Willie said. "How did it go?"

"Which should we talk about first? The shock of the lifetime or the near disaster?" She eased her glass onto the coffee table and started by describing what happened when she got off the elevator. When she discovered her locks undone, she was convinced the man had broken into her apartment.

"Why'd you go inside?" Willie asked. "Nothing's worth it."

"If it was the guy in the hall, he was gone. Even so, I crept through the place expecting someone to clobber me. I never felt so vulnerable."

"Honey, it's the same as being raped. Your space was violated. Let me call the precinct. Willie and I didn't touch much. They can dust for fingerprints. Maybe we'll get lucky."

Carly shook her head. "He was wearing gloves."

"In the summer?"

"I didn't think quick enough. It was a dead giveaway and I missed it." She reached for the wine. "I think I'm going to pretend it never happened."

"Sort of like fiddle-dee-dee and Scarlet O'Hara? Like the Civil War was just a bad dream? Change your locks first thing in the morning," LeShana said.

"You're both taking this too lightly. I want you to call a locksmith, now," said Willie. "There's still tonight."

LeShana opened her bag, and pulled out her 9mm. Glock. "Ain't nothing to worry about with LeShana camping here tonight."

Carly blew her nose and refilled their glasses. She hugged LeShana. "You don't have to stay."

"I know, but I'm going to. Now tell us about the course. How did it go?"

"Given it was my first time and considering I threw up at the break, it went great…not to mention Lute Aurum paying me a visit."

Willie leaned forward. "What was Aurum doing there? He didn't take the course did he?"

"He was delivering a message."

The oven buzzer sounded and Carly sprung to her feet before she explained any more. "Appetizers are ready."

Willie blew on the steaming tart until it cooled. LeShana stuffed the whole tart in her mouth, and then slurped wine to cool her throat.

"That's good child. Gimme 'nother one of those. What you call them?"

Carly giggled for the first time that day. She watched LeShana devour the second one, lick each finger, and reach for a third.

"By the way," she said between bites, "did you know we were sitting with a celebrity?"

"Figures something great would happen after I left!"

Willie milked the moment. "There was a wee bit excitement at City Hall. One of the secretaries got angry when an assistant mayor sexually harassed her."

"Good for her. Did he get what he deserved?"

"A .38 caliber in the chest."

"There's a lady after my own heart," LeShana said.

"Trouble is, he shot back. Killed her in front of twenty coworkers. City Hall turned into a combat zone. Reporters were swarming over me worse than locusts during a plague. I'll be on the evening news in…," he checked his watch, "…thirty minutes."

Carly cleared the dishes and put the next course in the oven. When she returned, LeShana was fiddling with a white plastic box that was in her black case.

Willie spoke first.

"A clock radio! Does it have an alarm, too?"

"You've never seen one like this."

LeShana unscrewed the mouthpiece of the phone resting on a lacquered table.

"That's my favorite phone," Carly warned.

"Keep your feathers down. I'm about to demonstrate the wonders of drug-induced technology."

LeShana dropped a small object into the hollow, and then screwed the mouthpiece back. "Note bug in phone," she said in a clipped staccato voice, waving the receiver with the aplomb of David Copperfield. She replaced it in the cradle, and then plugged the clock/radio into the nearest electrical outlet. Its green luminescent numbers flashed. "There."

"I don't get it," said Carly, "all digital clocks flash when you plug them in."

Willie stifled a yawn as LeShana tapped the side of her head. "We're not thinking, children. What flashes when clock/radios are plugged in? Bong! Are we thinking twelve o'clock? This one's flashing the correct time."

"I'm duly impressed. What's the catch before dinner turns to ashes?"

"This is a reverse bug detector. It lets the drug dealers know when the cops have bugged their places. Kind of levels the playing field."

Willie was intrigued. "What's next? Crooks getting their own satellites?"

"The Cali cartel already has one."

LeShana retrieved the bug from the receiver and dropped it in the black bag. "This prize goes into my collection. I have a fountain pen that blinks and a Timex watch that vibrates when dope dealers stroll into bugged rooms."

Carly twinkled. "I need to borrow that watch."

"It's pretty tiny."

"I'll make it work."

25

Willie saw it first.

LeShana removed the phone bug and the clock/radio continued to flash.

"Your toy is broken," he said.

LeShana turned serious. She slapped a finger to her lips, demanding silence. She fished inside the black bag and plucked out a voltmeter that measured signal strength. LeShana aimed the dial toward the coffee table. It registered in the middle ranges. She stepped toward the window and the needle slipped to zero. Then she reversed her steps and angled toward the kitchen. The beam grew stronger. One step into the kitchen and the signal dropped again.

Willie and Carly eyed LeShana's every step.

LeShana angled toward the front door. With a lithe step, she knelt down and touched the two-gang ivory wall outlet with the voltmeter.

LeShana cast a knowing eye toward them, pointing to the outlet. She removed the cover plate with a blade from her Swiss Army knife, and then unscrewed the outlet, tugging it toward her. Limited by the wires set deep in the wall, the outlet could only move a few inches. LeShana loosed the white and black leads, plus the green ground wire to free the outlet. A fourth wire tethered it to the junction box. She disconnected that one and tossed it in the air.

"It's a bug connected to a dedicated wire."

"The clock stopped flashing."

Then Carly understood. "Someone heard *everything* we've been saying?"

LeShana nodded. "We have experts who can check the phone panel in the basement. They might be able to trace the source so we can find who did this."

"Can you tell if it's new? Maybe the man in the hall did it."

LeShana peeled back some of the rubber coating. "See how shiny the covered copper is? This was planted a while ago."

Then Carly remembered the mail a few weeks back, how she sensed someone had rifled through it. She had chalked it up to a vivid imagination and forgot about it...until now. Other things bothered her. Ever since she returned from Arizona, Carly had found herself spinning around...more than once. She had sensed eyes on her back, eyes following her on the subway, eyes shopping with her in the fish market, eyes behind her at the Lincoln Cinema. Now this!

The oven jet ignited, a horn blared from the street below.

Willie raised his glass. "May Humanetics and all the bullshit like it in the world be zapped to oblivion."

LeShana seconded it. "And may Aurum and his goons ride off on the Hale Bopp comet. L'Chaim."

They chugged the Puilly Fuissé like brew in a stein. Carly went for a second bottle.

LeShana snatched the remote control. "Let's watch for Willie. Then we can eat. I'm starved."

EYEWITNESS NEWS filled on the screen. The familiar blond-haired midwestern anchorman, with crow's feet fanning from his eyes, announced the headlines.

*   *   *

"Tragedy at City Hall today: Deputy Mayor McCarthy Brown was critically wounded during the noon lunch hour, and his secretary, Ina Fraddin, killed. EYEWITNESS NEWS was first on the scene and has exclusive footage of this tragedy, plus an interview with Dr. Wilbur Robinson, Chief Medical Examiner of the City of New York. But first, we switch to Washington, DC, for this late-breaking story."

*   *   *

The inset of a man's face appeared in the upper right part of the screen. As the anchor's face faded, the picture grew until it filled the screen.

"Willie, you're gonna have to wait for your fifteen seconds of fame. Hey, that's the Lincoln Memorial."

A dark profile came into focus. A rakish man leaned over stalks of microphones, his hair askew. His face was ravaged by fatigue, but the glint in his eye was unmistakable.

"Holy shit," said Carly, "that's Governor Fromm. He gave me a ride to the airport."

LeShana turned up the volume.

Throngs of men and women cheered.

Fromm held his hands up for quiet.

*   *   *

"Our country needs new leaders who will take bold steps to capture a future that is ours. We need to be more focused, to do

what is necessary to reverse the horrors of global warming and feed our hungry children.

"It is for these and many more reasons, my fellow Americans, that I declare my candidacy for President of the United States."

*   *   *

Salvos of approval exploded from the crowd. Fromm waited for the crowd to grow still. With a slight gesture, he turned toward the bronze hand of the sixteenth president. A man stepped from the shadows.

*   *   *

"I consider this man the foremost thinker in America today. He will run my presidential campaign, and be responsible for policy decisions. Most of you have never heard of him. By the end of the campaign, his name will be a household word, branded into our collective memories. It is an honor to introduce..."

*   *   *

Willie grabbed his scalp.
LeShana was wide-eyed.
Tears rolled down Carly's cheeks.
The three chorused in unison, "Lute Aurum."

Four Years Later

Pax Americana

by
Anonymous

I monitored the Merrimac and fought in Tripoli
A friend of Crispus Attucks, I rode with General Lee
I stalked the forests at Verdun, and battled for Alsace-Lorraine
And sailed my ship into Manila Bay, remembering the Maine
Oh I'm the universal soldier, here to fight again
In Operation Desert Storm against Saddam Hussein

I led the charge of Pickett's men, and heard "Four score and seven"
I held Old Glory high and proud, at Vicksburg and Antietam
I liberated Midway and fought at Iwo Jima
And piloted the Enola Gay over Hiroshima
I stood with Davey at the Alamo, and was at Appomattox
And plowed the dunes of Africa, chasing the elusive Desert Fox

From napalm bombs to preemptive strikes, rarely on the defensive
We lost so much in Viet Nam, starting with the Tet Offensive
For I am Pax Americana, the universal soldier
Who's spilled his blood in the sands of time, forever and forever
Let cannons blast and clarions call, trumpeting this one eternal certainty
It's never debated, always assumed, we conquer for Manifest Destiny.

Futures Markets: Wheat Prices Skyrocket; Crop Estimate Lowered Again

by Bloomberg News

Wheat prices set record highs on the Chicago Board of Trade yesterday, after the Agriculture Department not only lowered this season's expected wheat production, but also announced that for the first time in history, wheat had to be imported into the United States. In other markets, corn and bean prices fell.

The Agriculture Department cited that the empty storage silos across the country had prompted this crisis measure.

"Our continued bad weather is our trading partners' gains," said Walther Montross, an analyst with Salomon Smith Barney. "Russia, along with Canada, have become the world's major suppliers of wheat. America can no longer expect to feed her hungry citizens without outside help. This new order of things will continue into the foreseeable future."

26

Summer, autumn, winter, spring...the names were the same, but the weather patterns were not. Thanks to global warming, each had grown warmer, hotter, drier, and more parched. Summers blistered. Falls were too hot. Where snow used to fall, temperate winters found snowplows wrapped in spider webs. Spring rains became sun showers. On this particular November day, helicopter blades cut through the hazy Maryland skies. Heat shimmered in wiggly waves.

President Aldous Fromm had earned a rest. In ten glorious days, Fromm had silenced his critics with strokes of boldness. He accomplished what Presidents Bush and Clinton never dared: he blew the Iraqi military might to smithereens, while neutering their nuclear fission and biological warfare plants.

News writers, political analysts, and the public assumed Aldous Fromm was tired of hearing Saddam Hussein's invectives. Actually, the Iraqi leader amused the president. The reason Fromm killed Hussein was to show our Russian nemesis that this was a new America, an America with backbone. As long as Russia and its backers continued to support Saddam's right to keep UN inspectors at bay, Fromm had to teach *them* a lesson.

Them being both the Iraqis *and* the Ruskies.

Them being the Shiite fundamentalists and the Pakistani terrorists.

Them being anyone foolish enough to think America had slipped a notch in its resolve to secure world peace.

Kuwait showed we could attack, but we didn't have the killer instinct to get the job done. From there, it was downhill. Somalia. Kosovo. Karachi. Hot spots erupted around the world, and America grew tired of foreign involvements. Advisers, politicians and scientists proffered Fromm to take radical steps to stem the tide of a disintegrating economy. They urged him to take steps to quell the social unrest. They begged him to tackle the global warming that was deep-frying our breadbasket. Yet for all the advice, Fromm appeared distracted. Preoccupied. Unable to lead. Whatever his agenda, Fromm kept it to himself.

Lute Aurum, the president's personal advisor and long-time friend, changed all that the day he barged into the Oval Office.

"Russia's developed a genetically engineered form of Anthrax that is immune to all known vaccines. Guess who's making it for them?"

Fromm could throw the first punch without a care about the consequences, and then sleep baby-like the night after. He was the John Wayne of presidents.

Operation Annihilate was a monster success. Fromm roared out of the media's doghouse to, once again, become its darling. CNN's "Firing Line," Larry King *Live*, and a speech before the UN's General Assembly...they clamored for his appearance. Time voted him "Man of the Year" six weeks before year's end. Fromm accepted the accolades and gave the speeches until he was too exhausted.

In minutes, his holiday—and much deserved rest—would begin.

The helicopter hummed. All aboard basked in that day's latest poll: Fromm's job approval rating was higher than any other president's in recent history with the exception of FDR...and FDR's was retrospective, through the filter of treasured memories. Aldous Fromm was on top of the world. With Hussein out of the picture and Russia put on notice, Fromm could now unleash a frontal attack on domestic problems. Time was on his side. A second term was there for the taking.

Then without warning, the gurgling helicopter blades gagged on the thick air. The motor sputtered. Metal ground against metal. The whirlybird froze at its zenith. For the longest second, it hung there. The pilots tried every trick in the manual to jump-start the stalled chopper. Nothing worked. Velocity zero turned into a kamikaze plunge toward the forest below.

There was no midair explosion.

No phantom missiles shot from the ground.

No red-light warning signs.

No pilot error. The blades just stopped working.

Early reports were sketchy, but one fact was inescapable: a helicopter sporting the seal of the President of the United States nose-dived to earth that morning, like a speeding satellite reentering the atmosphere.

Only helicopters don't manage to land like crippled birds; they crash and burn.

The lucky are decapitated, the others deep-fry.

The unlucky survive.

27

Minutes after hearing that President Aldous Fromm's helicopter had corkscrewed from the sky, Coulter Bell, the president's press secretary, mopped sweat beads from his brow. First reports indicated that a miracle accompanied the tragedy: the president had been pulled from the wreckage with the weakest of pulses. Fromm was alive and being taken to a local facility for emergency surgery. There would be heaps of questions. Bell was a "yes" man, a detail man, a man who juggled the truth. Give him a few details, and he could keep a press corps busy—and happy—for hours.

But this? Presidential crashes fell out of the range of a press secretary's mien. This was critical business.

Coulter imagined the worst. The Man could bleed out on the table. Throw a clot. Have a seizure. Go into cardiac arrest. Walk…but not speak. Speak…but not walk. Or maybe, just pray it didn't happen, President Aldous Fromm would turn into a ripe squash.

Coulter had this sickening feeling that he'd have to dust off his résumé.

Coulter's rational side argued he could speculate until kingdom come. Aldous Fromm's fate was in the hands of hastily assembled surgeons in some remote Maryland clinic. For the time being, these doctors—plus the beneficence of the good Lord above— were all that mattered. As soon as Fromm was able, Coulter would have him transferred to the Walter Reade Medical Center.

The death of Lute Aurum and all the others on board had taken a distant second to the president's survival. At times, Coulter had been jealous of the way Aurum and Fromm interacted; each one knew what the other was thinking. Though Fromm held the most powerful job in the world, he still deferred to Aurum. Would the president suffer the pangs of losing his soul mate?

Then again, thought Coulter, how could Aurum be dead? *Clears* were supposed to live forever.

*   *   *

Vernon Barlow was the classic example of a busy man who had time for everyone and everything. He had time to run his home security business, time to help raise five children, time to volunteer for the Emmitsburg fire department, time to sing in the church choir, and time to visit his eighty-four year old mother in the nursing home every Wednesday. Except for needing a hearing aid, courtesy of the US Army radio corps, from being too close to an exploding shell in Saigon, Vernon was a fit man at age sixty. He liked to say that he was cousin to a shark, and that the day he stopped moving—and had nothing to do—was the day he died.

Vernon didn't like to keep his mother waiting, but he sure didn't like to hurry past the beautiful scenery either. He was coming from Waynesboro after calling on the widow Emma Richards. Emma Richards, like so many others in central Maryland, liked it better before city folks discovered their rural setting around Catoctin Mountain Park. Up until a few years back, the only local attraction in the area was the hundred-and-twenty-five acres FDR

carved out of the park so he could have a cool retreat away from
the hot, steamy Washington, DC summers. He dubbed it his
Shangri-la, and the name stuck until President Eisenhower
changed it to Camp David. Still, no one paid any mind to presidents when they needed to get away from the rigors of running the
country. They were entitled to peace and quiet, too.

The trouble was lots of other people wanted that same peace
and quiet. So of late, the area had experienced a building boom.
Maryland started competing with North Carolina as one of the
most desirable places for people to retire. Townhouses, assisted
living communities, and retirement villages were stamped out of
once profitable farms that could no longer support their owners.
The more the suburban sprawl stretched to the rural parts of the
state, the more people wanted Vernon to install burglar alarms in
their houses. Not that any were needed. The growth didn't change
the crime rate much. Just the same, folks liked to feel safe.

The nursing home was in Catoctin Furnace, a dot of a town
south of Thurmont on Highway 806. There was no quick way to
get there from Waynesboro, because the state park and Camp
David were in the direct path. Vernon either had to take the north
route through Flint and then south on 806, or pass through
Foxville and skirt around the southwestern fringe of Catoctin
Mountain Park. Vernon took the southern route.

Vernon always drove with his truck windows open; it helped
him hear what was going on around him. He was a few miles past
Foxville when the hum of his tires was eclipsed by a noise from
above. Vernon leaned over the steering wheel for a better look,
but couldn't see much with so many tall poplar trees lining the
road. There was a clearing around the next bend, and that's when
Vernon saw the glint from the humming whirlybird heading into
the park. Helicopters were always flying to Camp David, so
Vernon paid it no mind.

Vernon was about to turn on the radio and listen to his favorite country-and-western station when the noise above stopped. For someone always straining to hear, it got too quiet for Vernon, too fast. He craned his head out the window and caught a glimpse of the helicopter frozen in the one spot. It dangled there for a whole second, angled left, and then plummeted to the ground. Vernon went into action.

He scrambled out of his truck and tore-ass through the dense forest. In no time, he came upon the wreck. Flames were shooting from the smashed helicopter, which had hit the earth nose first, then keeled on its side. Glass and metal were strewn about. Vernon could see the pilot and co-pilot were dead. He tried to get closer, but a small explosion drove him back. There was no chance that anyone still onboard was alive.

Vernon circled the wreck. That's when he saw a man lying on his side. At first, he thought it was a log. The man had been thrown from the chopper and probably every bone was broken. Vernon put his index and middle finger on the man's neck; there was a faint pulse in the carotid artery. The man's skin was scorched and blistered and charred, but he was alive...for the moment. Vernon had an idea who it might be, muttered, "Thank God," and knew what he had to do.

The closest hospital was too far, but Dr. Labatelli's clinic wasn't. Enrico Labatelli was a plastic surgeon that fixed, mended, and altered anyone who had enough coin for his steep fees. The surgeon had built his posh digs in a serene setting that catered to the rich and famous; he was an operator in every sense of the word. Early in his training, Dr. Labatelli understood that managed care was ruining medicine. Undaunted, he picked plastic surgery because in the immortal words of the bank robber, Willie Sutton, that's where the money was. Dr. Labatelli was altruistic; he believed in helping the less fortunate. His exclusive plastic surgical center/spa permitted him to collect exorbitant fees for his excellent services. That's how he funded a clinic in India—totally at his own expense—to fix the disfigured faces of scores of lepers every summer. He took from the rich and gave to the poor, and had a ton left over for himself.

By noon, Dr. Labatelli had already put in a full day. His last surgery was a facelift that would extend the Oscar-winning actress's career another ten years. Then Vernon Barlow pulled into the open bay.

*   *   *

Coulter was moments away from informing the world about his boss's brush with death. Stock markets would plummet, currencies would falter. Cards and flowers would be sent by the truckload. The White House switchboard staff was doubled to receive the deluge of telephone traffic.

Calls had to be made to the vice-president, the Majority Whip, and the Secret Service.

The vice-president. The proverbial heartbeat away. It had happened before. Harrison. Taylor. Lincoln. McKinley. Roosevelt. Kennedy. Throw in Gerald Ford taking over for Tricky Dick.

Coulter clamped his eyes shut and prayed this VP wouldn't stay long enough to crease the White House sheets. During the primaries, Greeley was a worthy adversary. His died-in-the-wool environmental stances were in stark contrast to Fromm's nearly limitless oil industry support, support that expected energy from oil shale and tar sands...no matter what the environmental consequences. So when Horace "Kip" Greeley's name surfaced as a running mate for Fromm, everyone scoffed except Lute Aurum. Aurum reasoned that the best way to keep tabs on the one man who could damage *their* long-range plans—both his and Fromm's—was to put Greeley on the ticket. The closer Greeley was to the White House, the less power he could wield. Everyone knew vice-presidents were castrated politicos. Think Al Gore. Once Greeley got on board with Fromm, he became as effective as Jimmy Hoffa encased in concrete under the Jersey Meadowlands. Greeley could no longer take potshots at Fromm's jingoistic jargon to beef up the military, nor could he challenge Fromm for abandoning the domestic programs needed to slam the brakes on global meltdown. At least that was the game plan.

Fromm put an end to Iraq's plans for a nuclear winter. Fromm and Aurum's agenda was written in stone, and no vice-president was going to derail their plans with pansy-assed environmental concerns.

Until today. Until the crash.

Coulter Bell was in a tizzy. With Aurum dead in the helicopter crash and the president incapacitated—for who-knew-how-long?—Greeley could ruin everything.

What would Fromm want him to do?

Coulter studied the press release. The document was being telexed to every wire service in the world. At another time, in another crisis, Coulter might have run the country until Fromm recovered. Like Mrs. Wilson when Woodrow had a stroke.

      *   *   *

White House Press Release

PRESIDENT SURVIVES COPTER CRASH
VP GREELEY TAKES OVER WHITE HOUSE

WHITE HOUSE. President Aldous Fromm was the lone survivor of a fiery crash that killed all other passengers aboard the president's helicopter this afternoon. The president was on his way to Camp David to rest prior to Kyoto-II summit meeting on global thermal changes.

The pilot, Rear Admiral Mack Olson, and the co-pilot, Lt. General Winslow "Cap" Jennings, were both killed. Also killed were Abigail Kinsey Johnson, the president's personal secretary; Dr. Gerhard Stram, chief geothermal scientist at NASA; Lute Aurum, President Fromm's personal advisor, and two members of the Secret Service, Lane Contrell and Blair Bryant.

President Fromm's condition is listed as critical. Initial reports indicate that the President is expected to survive the massive internal and facial injuries he sustained from the crash, and is undergoing emergency surgery at this moment. Assuming the president survives his injuries, he will face numerous corrective surgical procedures and months of rehabilitation.

Vice-President William Horace Greeley was notified of the president's near-fatal accident while on a hiking trip in Colorado with the Sierra Club.

This is only the second time in our nation's history that a Vice-President has assumed the presidency after it was deemed the president could not "discharge the powers and duties of his office," as quoted from the 25th Amendment. The previous exigency occurred when George W. Bush assumed temporary control of the Oval Office while President Ronald Reagan underwent general anesthesia to remove a polyp in his colon. (Even when John Hinckley shot President Reagan, he remained conscious and in charge of his presidential duties.)

Members of the House and Senate have been informed of the president's condition, and will meet in a rare joint session when acting-president Greeley addresses the nation later this evening.

      *   *   *

Not since the beloved Camelot years of JFK and Jackie had the country been so smitten with its leader. It was a scant two-plus years ago, on January twentieth to be specific, when the legend began. On that day Aldous Fromm, Jr. was sworn in as president of the United States. An empty podium chair served to remind the world how Barbara Fromm had cajoled her metastatic body to last until she could watch a televised broadcast of the inauguration from her hospital bed. At the very moment Aldous Fromm promised to "uphold the laws of this nation," Barbara Fromm died.

Fromm ended his inaugural speech and an already sympathetic nation witnessed the new president's face crack as Vice-President Greeley whispered the news in his ear. A thousand camera shutters captured his tears for posterity. It was a picture second only to little John-John saluting JFK's horse-drawn casket. The country mourned for Barbara Fromm the way the world mourned for Lady Di, and later, for JFK, Jr. Fromm became the first bachelor in the White House since James Buchanan. Buchanan never married; Fromm would never marry again. His goals for the country and his relationship with Lute Aurum were all-consuming; they left no room for romance or time to enjoy the simple pleasures of life. The one joy he did permit himself was stolen days at Camp David, taking long walks through the pastoral acres. And that almost cost him his life.

*   *   *

An aide rapped on the hardwood door and entered.

Coulter turned.

"They're ready, sir."

"Another moment."

Coulter waited for the aide to leave. One chore remained before facing the lights and cameras. He plucked the phone receiver from its cradle on his polished desk, and stabbed the numbers from memory.

28

As Coulter Bell braced himself to inform the world of the president's helicopter tragedy and Dr. Enrico Labatelli went to work on his patient, a huge explosion tore apart the eighteenth floor of a Rockefeller Center building. Black plumes billowed through broken windows. Power was cut, emergency generators kicked in.

Preliminary reports indicated it was a bomb. The extent of the damage was unknown. City agencies feared the worst. The mayor declared a state of emergency. Anti-terrorist units were activated. The police commissioner canceled all leaves. City employees on vacation were ordered back to duty. The governor activated the National Guard. Yellow barriers were erected around the building. Police and SWAT teams flooded the area. Fire trucks and hoses were everywhere.

The Big Apple became an armed fortress, her bridges and tunnels sealed at both ends; there was neither entry nor exodus to the island. Seventeen million men, women, and children—residents, shoppers, theatergoers, and workers who were in the city that day—were trapped.

The throngs evacuated from Rockefeller Center were shepherded to the front of St. Patrick's Cathedral on Fifth Avenue and across from Radio City Music Hall on Avenue of the Americas. It was only then, after the bombed building had been emptied, that alphanumeric pagers delivered Coulter Bell's message to many of the bystanders.

"Did you hear about the president?"

"Were they Muslim terrorists?"

"Will the subways be safe to ride?"

"They gonna swear in Greeley?"

Put New Yorkers in a crisis and conjectures flow like champagne on New Year's Eve. One rumor linked the Brooklyn-based Russian Mafia as responsible for *both* the Rockefeller Center bombing and President Fromm's accident. The director, Oliver Stone, who was in New York to make a film about Puerto Rican freedom fighters, was quoted as saying, "When the smoke clears, the culprits responsible for these tragedies will be second-generation rogue CIA assassins trained by the same ones who killed JFK and Jack Ruby." Beat cops were overheard muttering that it was hotter than hell and shit happens.

Speculations aside, no lunatic fringe group claimed responsibility for the bombing.

*　　　　　　　*　　　　　　　*

Coulter Bell approached the thicket of microphones. The press corps had divided mitotically; the room was overflowing with double the number of reporters. He cleared his throat at the same time Willie Robinson's phone jangled.

*　　　　　　　*　　　　　　　*

"Isn't anybody going to answer that?"

Carly was in the middle of charting a victim's mouth. She made a detailed dental exam of every unidentified body that came through the Medical Examiner's post room, in case private records became available for comparison. When private dental records matched her exam, identities were established to a high degree of certainty. The latter left no room for error, no falsely named corpses.

In this particular case, a frozen carcass was discovered in the meat freezer of a century-old Brooklyn restaurant. The eatery was famous for sawdust-covered floors and aged steaks. Sassy waiters delivered the piping hot platters of sizzling beef, hash brown potatoes, and creamed spinach trimmed with Borscht Belt wit worthy of Jackie Mason. Patrons schlepped to the decaying neighborhood as much to clog their arteries as to be abused by the help.

Willie quipped that they hung the patron in the freezer for not paying his bill. Carly called it an "aged account."

By the fourth ring, Willie grabbed his crutches and brushed past Carly. If it wasn't his secretary's every-other-hour coffee break, it was a trip to the john. If it wasn't a trip to the john, it was jabbering in the hall with a lab tech. She spent half of the morning discussing what her sister was cooking for Thanksgiving dinner two weeks away. Willie rolled his eyes. Bless affirmative action.

Carly couldn't hear what was said, but Willie returned in high gear, his crutches closing the space between them in a hurry.

"Grab your camera. There's been an explosion at Rockefeller Center. I hope it's no one you know."

"Christ. Not the dental floor!"

That's where Jonah Schoonover used to practice.

Carly froze on Jonah's name. In her heart of hearts, she blamed Lute Aurum for her friend's death. No one could ever prove Lute or anyone else pulled the trigger that killed Jonah, but Carly believed his sudden death was somehow connected to Humanetics.

She had always thought that.

Every time Carly saw Lute Aurum's face on the news or his name in the papers, she cringed. Whatever Aldous Fromm's virtues were (and she didn't forget the kindness he extended when she escaped Aurum's ranch), it bothered Carly that the man turned a blind eye to his advisor's evil side. Could it be that Aurum had turned over a new leaf once he became part of the president's inner circle? Or was Fromm bamboozled?

Bowden St. Clair was running Humanetics these days. Without a dental practice, Carly was of no value to the green-shirts eager to milk huge sums from unsuspecting and weak-willed chumps. Even though flyers announcing new courses still crossed her desk, the goons from The Institute of Humanetics left her alone...and so did Conner Masterson.

Except for the wooden-sounding message, Carly never heard from Conner again. All things being equal, Conner should have been a faded picture in her memory bank. That's not how the equation worked out. Carly was never short on dates, except that no one came close to lighting her up the way Conner did. She never told a soul, neither Willie nor LeShana, that whenever she walked down a street, she hoped to see his pretty face. Though their fling was brief, it lingered. Thinking of Conner at that moment made her heart ache.

What price did he pay for saving her?

Willie maneuvered into the driver's seat of his city-owned Lincoln Town car equipped with hand-controls so that he could accelerate and brake. He and Carly sped up First Avenue and turned onto Thirty-fourth Street. Then it took twenty-five minutes to make it two blocks across Thirty-fourth Street to Third Avenue.

Willie pulled the key out of the ignition. "C'mon, we'll take the subway."

"You're going to leave the car in the middle of the street?"

"Christ, yeah. What do you expect me to do? Fly over everyone?"

Carly flashed her ID at the fare collector planted behind a bulletproof glass at Thirty-third Street and Park Avenue, and she and Willie bypassed the automatic turnstiles. They didn't have to wait long. Seated on the northbound Number Six train, Carly searched the car. Willie did the same thing.

"Are you thinking what I'm thinking?" she asked.

"Like why'd we do this?"

"Exactly."

"Tokyo?"

"You've got it. The Aum Shinrikyo cult."

"Sarin could take out a lot of people."

Carly clamped her legs together. She searched the faces of the other riders.

"Was this a mistake?"

"We'll find out."

29

Buddy LoBianco's craggy face jerked up from scrutinizing a ledger.

"Listen to all those sirens. It's like London when the Nazis dropped them bombs. I wonder what's happened?" Buddy stood and pointed. "Hey, look!"

Jeremy Steel ambled to the thick, green-tinted plate glass in the penthouse suite of Steel Towers that he used as his corporate center. He gazed southward at the smoke wafting from Rockefeller Center, and then flicked a speck of lint off his custom-made suit.

"It's unfortunate."

"Sounds like the whole friggin' city's on alert. You don't think it's those swami, tabouli-loving maniacs again, do you? I hate it when they blow themselves up before we get a chance to rip them wide open and give them their own hearts to hold in their hands. Remember when that nut job opened fire on the observatory deck of the Empire State Building a few years back? For no damn reason, this guy goes off his rocker. All those innocent people. What a shame."

Jeremy remained lost in thought.

"You know *this* building's got a pretty high profile, boss. We could be sittin' ducks if someone wanted to get to *us*. We oughta move, and pronto quick."

Buddy raised his voice when Jeremy didn't answer.

"So we gonna get out of here or what?"

Jeremy eased into the black leather chair behind his desk. He put his elbow on the lacquered desk and made steeples with his fingers.

"There's no need to be concerned."

"No place is fucking safe in the this city, anymore. That's why I'm glad we're building up in Canada now. They won't stand for any terrorist shit up there, not the way we do. Call your buddy, Lute Aurum? Ask him to speak to Fromm? Let them declare martial law in New York. Use this as an excuse to clean this place up, once and for all."

Jeremy reached for his solid gold nail clipper. A clipping flew through the air.

"Calling won't be necessary. All you need to know is that we're safe here." He replaced the clipper and leaned forward. "Now let's have a look at those reports."

Buddy scratched his head: Jeremy Steel had ice in his veins. Maybe he had reason to stay so calm, Buddy thought. He noticed that after his talk with the Canadian Prime Minister Honey Fitzpatrick that morning, Jeremy's mood had brightened. Or was it around the time the bomb went off and Jeremy had learned that the fucking terrorists must have blown themselves up? That's why Jeremy was so unruffled!

That wasn't it either.

When Buddy analyzed *all* the possibilities, he came to realize that the change in Jeremy's mood only occurred after Coulter Bell called moments ago. Jeremy uttered a lot of "Uh huhs," and

"That's good," and one, "Are you sure?" Jeremy was pleased about something because when he hung up on the president's press secretary, Jeremy lit up one mother of a Red Auerbach cigar.

Cave Yields "Iceman"

TETE JEUNE CACHE, CANADA. Scientists are calling the chilling discovery of a five hundred year old hunter one of the great anthropologic finds in recent years.

The hunter was discovered by veteran hikers, Bill Donohough and Terry Williams, who had never seen a cave in their many trips across the Thompson Ice Fields on their way to Mt. Sir Wilfrid Laurier in eastern British Columbia. This time, a curious hole was exposed in the ice. When they ventured inside, they stumbled over a bow and arrows, and an atlatl shaft. They also found an intact spear. Inching deeper into the cave, they discovered the hunter frozen in a block of ice.

Radiocarbon has dated Canada's "iceman," who is an Indian, to around 1450 AD. The tools found with him, however, were similar to those found in ancient caribou hunting grounds 7,000 years ago.

Global warming has caused the alpine ice to recede 20-100 feet during the last century, yielding a treasure trove of artifacts in its wake. One mystery surrounding this "iceman" centers on the small piece of iron found among his personal effects. The "iceman" died 300 years before Russian traders appeared in the area. Inuits who live 500 miles to the north, have long been known to work iron out of fallen meteorites. Or, perhaps it came from a Viking who landed on Canada's east coast around 1000 AD. However it made it across the continent, scientists agree that in the coming years, more artifacts will be found that will help answer many mysteries about North America's early inhabitants.

30

Jack Kinkade had worries of his own. The news of the day was lost to him as he sat on his tattered, pebble-skinned suitcase, hoping to hitch a ride.

An hour earlier he had been perched on the same oblong case, gazing at the clapboard church that he and his deceased wife, Mary, had attended all their lives. Jack noted the sun-bleached shutter that dangled like a broken wing. He studied the sway-backed steps that creaked even under a child's weight, the peeling paint that flaked off the walls dandruff-like and the barren garden that no longer bloomed in the abbreviated springs that had become commonplace. The building was old and dying, just like everything around it.

It was mid-week. The parson had called a special prayer meeting, thinking the extraordinary measure might help. It couldn't hurt. Pray for the weather to change, he exhorted. Pray for the winds to stop blowing. Pray for the dust to stop swirling. Most of all, urged the parson, pray for rain. Lots and lots of rain.

Might as well pray for the Messiah to swoop down and pay a visit.

The young and the old, the crippled and the sturdy, heeded the parson's call. Why not? There was little else to do. Even Rolfe

Lundgren, who was Jack's best friend since they were old enough to remember anything, hobbled to church, bum leg and all.

Sitting there, gazing at the nothingness of it all, Jack Kinkade knew praying was a waste of time. Rains were never going to come, not anytime soon enough to matter. In fact if the heavens did open her floodgates and let it rip big, the last shreds of soil would wash away sure as he was sitting there. Hadn't they raised money to send up that biplane and seed the clouds? And didn't he feel like a damn fool huddled around that huge bonfire for seven straight nights, watching them Injuns hoop and holler? Did even a drop of rain come down after their drunken, pot-eyed, naked dancing?

A lifeless prayer zigzagged out the church windows, and Jack couldn't help asking himself why were they wasting their time? Mary would've known it, and would've said so, too.

"Them is mighty defeated voices," she would've said. Then she would've added, "We got to help them, Jack. We got to do all we can."

But Mary was gone, and Jack knew there wasn't a thing anybody could do. Despair had replaced the last vestiges of hope in Kalvesta. Despair and doom.

It wasn't always this way. Their church, Jack's and Mary's church, had been built by farmers following the Cumberland Trail. They had trekked across the land in mud-caked wagons, seeking the rich and loamy earth of a promised land. When they found their acres, they stopped. The land was rich; life was good. Things grew then, and farmers were proud to be called farmers.

Then, like a flash flood, their world was destroyed. Turned upside down. Ozone layers. Fluorocarbons. Fossil fuel emissions. Slashing the rain forests. Why call it the "Greenhouse Effect?" Plants *grew* in a green house. Green was green, brown was shit.

Nothing grew on Jack's farm anymore. Nothing grew on *anyone's* farm anymore.

Jack couldn't wait any longer. He was about to leave without saying good-bye when Rolfe Lundgren grabbed the rusted railing with his left hand and wobbled down the wooden planks. Rolfe was three-legged now, the third being a pearl-handled cane courtesy of his John Deere tractor. Rolfe was working the fields one day, when he stopped aerating the soil to move a big rock. It was too heavy, he slipped, and his leg got chopped pretty bad, right down to the bone. Some foreign-trained doctor hardly speaking any English, was about to saw it off when Doc Smithers—half-sober—showed up.

"Say Jack? Why you sittin' by your lonesome? Why didn't you come inside? The parson done right good, today."

Crumbs of unfiltered cigarette butts, smoked until the nubs blistered the thick, patchy callous on his lips, were piled at Jack's feet.

"No point being inside. Only used to go 'cause of Mary."

"Jest the same you should've come in," Rolfe said. "Need all the help we can get. Gotta pray for the land, Jack. Gotta pray for rain."

Jack studied his friend. The lines on Rolfe's fractured face were ditched deep, his skin dust-gray. The smell of decaying mulch leached from Rolfe.

"Going somewhere?"

"Yup."

"Not much for words, today, are ya?"

"Nope."

Rolfe waited for Jack to explain why he was sitting on a suitcase and staring at the church. Jack remained silent.

"You always was a stubborn fool. Have it your way."

Rolfe wiped his veined nose with an embroidered handkerchief, and then turned to leave. He had taken two steps when Jack finally dredged up the words stuck deep in his craw.

"Come to say good-bye, Rolfe."

Rolfe cranked around and faced his childhood friend.

"Where'ya going, Jack?"

"Canada, I guess. Hear the farming's real good up there. Who knows? Possible I'll get a job in Steel City."

Jack stared at the parched earth the whole time he spoke to Rolfe. He couldn't bear to look him in the eye, not after what they had been through together.

"Kalvesta's in our blood. Been so for generations. No one ever leaves here."

"Ain't nothing left for me, no more."

Rolfe glared at his chum. He wanted to shout. *I'm here, Jack. Have some patience; it'll all turn around.* Instead, Rolfe remained mute.

Jack spoke. "When was the last time you saw something green come out of the ground? Tell me that?"

Rolfe shifted his weight.

"Been quite a while."

"You seen it yourself, those black twisters taking our topsoil so's we can't ever grow a thing. There's no dirt anymore. I'm tired waiting for rains that ain't never gonna come."

Jack grabbed the dark, red-brown powder at their feet. He rubbed it between his fingers. The silky dust hung between them.

Rolfe blew his nose again.

"Been getting at me, too. The damn dust's so fine it slips through the screen doors. I wake every morning and the only part of my pillow that's still white is where my head's been resting. Half the time my face looks like I been working in a coal mine."

Jack lit another cigarette.

Rolfe's hooked fingers dug into Jack's shoulders.

"Are you really going, Jack?"

"The wind blew away my reason for staying."

Rolfe dropped his cane and wrapped his arms around Jack. They hugged, squeezing the air out of their narrow chests, knowing they would never share barn raisings or hay rides or church dinners or Finney County fairs...ever again.

Then Jack did something he had never done before in his entire life. He peered so deep into Rolfe's soul that Rolfe fidgeted until Jack's face relaxed. Then he kissed Rolfe, full-lipped, right on his cheek. They looked at each other, and then Jack kissed him again.

Jack left Rolfe standing there. He didn't turn to see Rolfe touch the spot. He didn't see Rolfe pull out his handkerchief and pretend to wipe his nose so that he could really dab his eyes. And he didn't have to turn to know that his boots were raising a cloud of dust...on a lonely street...in the middle of a desert that map makers called Kansas.

*   *   *

Now Jack waited for a ride that would take him north.

North, to the *new* Promised Land.

North to Canada.

3 I

Coulter Bell fielded question after question from the wired White House press corps. "No, I don't know when the president can resume his duties."

"No, I don't know the extent of his damages."

"Yes, his mental faculties are intact."

"Yes, all government agencies will continue uninterrupted."

Coulter pulled himself out the side door, the reporters scrambling to deliver sidebars to this blockbuster story. The White House halls were hushed. Coulter paused in front of Lute Aurum's office, two doors down from the Oval Office. Then he pushed open the door. Aurum's death had left a vacuum.

He peered inside the glass cage Aurum always kept beside him. The viper was curled in a corner, under a branch.

Did snakes miss their masters?

Did the commissary serve live mice?

*   *   *

By the time Carly and Willie had reached the bomb-site, the streets were like an armed camp. It took another thirty-five minutes for them to clear the checkpoints manned by the police and National Guard. The building's generators threw off enough juice to operate the elevators and light the place, but not enough to cool it down.

They stepped off the elevator and sloshed through the tangle of men and hoses to find LeShana Thompkins questioning a fire official. Each floor in the Rockefeller Center building was configured like an old-fashioned square 8. Six elevator banks opened into the crossbar area that led to hallways lined with suites. Dentists occupied every office on the floor. Each intact door still had a large panel of glass with the doctor's name in black letters. Carly struggled past Jonah's old office, and caught LeShana's eye.

"Who have we here? The doctors of ghoul. Where'd you come from? Chicago?"

Willie growled. "Do you have any idea what's going on outside?"

"It's no hotter than here. This place is a fucking pizza oven."

"I was referring to the traffic. The city's closed down tighter than midnight lockup in a nunnery. We left our car in the middle of Thirty-Fourth Street, took the subway to Forty-Second, then hoofed it 'cause they closed the cross-town shuttle."

"No wonder it took so long."

Willie patted his leg. "Speed-walking's never been my event."

LeShana grinned. "Thanks for the flash."

He licked his dry lips. "Is there any water around here?"

A fireman pushed the brass nozzle of a hose toward Willie. Dribs trickled from the spout.

"It's clean."

Willie held it toward Carly.

"I'll pass. I like my water bottled."

"LeShana?"

"The pleasure's all yours."

Willie leaned on his crutches, tilted his head, and let beads of water drop into his parched mouth.

"See, still alive!"

"If you're finished sipping New York's finest champagne, I've got fifty people who would rather be somewhere else than dying of heat prostration. With the air off, the bodies in there are starting to get perfumed, if you know what I mean." LeShana took a step. "Shall we?"

Carly touched her arm. "Whose office is this?"

LeShana flipped through her note pad. "Here it is. San Martini. Dr. Rocco San Martini. "

When she heard the name, Carly's whistled.

"Dentist to the stars? His patient list reads like the index of People Magazine. Madonna. Jerry Seinfeld. Isaac Stern. Jagger. And it doesn't stop there."

"That could explain all those dark glasses hanging around the building. I was hoping one of them might have been waiting for whoever was inside." She pointed to Dr. San Martini's destroyed office. "The elevator starter said famous people come here all the time. Bodyguards and chauffeurs are always waiting in the lobby."

"It's not just San Martini," Carly added. "The entire floor is filled with dentists treating famous people. Kissinger's a patient in one of the offices. Steinbrenner's in another. On an average day, there are more dignitaries here than at the UN."

Willie shook his head.

"Are you two forgetting all the corporate headquarters? The large businesses? The record companies? NBC studios are here. The *Today Show*. At any given moment, high-profile people are marching in and out of these buildings, with and without their entourages. All I can say is that we're lucky this wasn't worse."

"Amen to that," LeShana said. "C'mon. We've talked enough."

They peered into an office with fourteen-foot high ceilings. It was shaped like the letter "T." The reception area was to the left, the business area to the right, and a center hall led to the treatment rooms. Amidst the ruin, two black and white photographs remained on the wall, arrow-straight. Others had fallen to the floor, their frames and glasses smashed, the pictures ruined. Dr. San Martini had wall-to-wall banquettes—purple in another life—that rested against the back and side walls. A marble coffee table had broken into pieces. Magazines and patient records were scattered about. A lamp was in pieces, its brass harp bent but the bulb still intact.

Midway down the short corridor, they could see scorched walls. Doors were blown off their hinges. Doorframes twisted into metal pretzels. Green and blue tanks—oxygen and nitrogen—were on their sides, deeply gashed.

"The fire marshal thinks it started near the tanks. We're working on the theory that there was a gas leak. The blast blew out the wall and everything on the other side of it, including Dr. San Martini and his patient."

"Tanks don't just explode," said Carly. "Nitrogen and oxygen support fires, they can't cause them. There's no way there was anything electrical in the closet to set the fire off. I know for a fact that Rockefeller Center is tougher than nails when it comes to following the building codes. Everything is by the book."

"But gas travels," Willie said. "The nozzle may have been open and something from the treatment room could have sparked the blast. Don't dentists still use Bunsen burners?"

"Sure, to melt wax. Old-timers used a flame to warm instruments when they condensed gutta-percha in a root canal."

"Everything you're saying is true...we know a spark started it. Let me show you the bodies first."

They stepped into the belly of the office, their feet squishing into the muddy slate-gray carpet. Acrid smells of fire stung their nostrils.

LeShana pointed to the secretary slumped over her keyboard.

As Carly stepped closer, water squirted under her weight.

"The door's only a few feet away. The blast didn't get her. How much smoke could there have been at the start? She should've escaped."

Willie peered over the buckled Formica countertop that separated the reception room from the business area. He saw melted plastic, cracked glass, ruined charts, water damage, and charred grime. Dr. San Martini's secretary was curled in her chair, her head face down.

"What are you thinking, Doc?"

"Let me see the others."

Willie absorbed details. He could process them in his computer of a brain better than the best.

Two victims lay prostrate in the forty-inch wide hallway, beyond the gas tanks, close to the treatment rooms. Willie hovered over them, and then raised a brow at LeShana.

"Who moved these bodies?"

"Are you crazy? We know better than to do that."

Carly caught Willie's drift.

"They're angled *toward* the explosion, not away from it."

Deeper into the guts of the office, they found what must have been the hygienist crumpled to the floor, a sharpening stone in one hand and a curette in the other. Next was a small lab. A dental assistant was slumped to one side, holding a plaster model in her hand. The model trimmer was still spinning and spraying water. Carly flipped the toggle switch. As the cutting wheel ground to a halt, the water died off.

At the entrance to the main operatory, the chairside assistant's stool was driven back three feet. The assistant lay arms outstretched, head pointed to the ceiling, legs spread apart. Dr. San Martini was curled forward. His legs were tucked under the chair, and his head faced down. Blood pooled at his feet.

The patient's skull was blown apart. Bone fragments were embedded in the ceiling tile. The left zygomatic arch, still covered with half a cheek, protruded from the wall-mounted glass view box. Brain tissue was splattered on the cabinets. The patient's lower jaw was missing. Afterwards, when the bodies would be examined in the Medical Examiner's office, Carly would discover the missing mandible commingled with Dr. San Martini's gut.

LeShana studied Willie's eyes and the way he stroked his chin. She followed his gaze around the room, attempting to squirm into his thoughts. Had she been able to, she would have learned that the puzzle parts here were not coming together.

"What gets me," Carly said, "is how the hygienist and the one dental assistant in the lab are still holding things. When anyone hears an explosion, at the very least, they drop what they're doing."

LeShana pointed to the hole in the wall where the tanks once stood.

"The blast came through there. The others could run, these folks never had a chance."

"But no one ran," Carly said. "It doesn't make sense."

Willie cleared his throat.

"Speculate all you want. You're both missing the obvious."

LeShana spread the fingers on her right hand.

"We've got what caused the explosion, when it happened, where it happened, and who some of these people are. Granted, there are three unidentifieds, but we are making progress here."

Willie shook his head. He opened his eyes and folded LeShana's spread fingers into a fist, and then nudged her arm downward.

"You're jumping ahead of yourself. The most obvious question to ask, is what was the motive? And what caused the spark to start it off?"

LeShana's head bobbed like a turtle.

"Who said anything about a motive? It was an accident." Then she pointed to the dental light mounted on a movable track fixed to the ceiling. "We figure the spark came from a short in the transformer."

Carly knew what Willie would say next.

"Maybe that's where the spark came from," he said, "and, then again, maybe it came from someplace else."

"Tell me what's troubling you," LeShana said.

"I need to run some tests, but what would you say if I told you these people were stone dead *before* the blast went off?"

32

Jack made his way to the highway without passing a soul. He wished he still had his '78 Ford pickup. That beauty hummed prettier than Tammy Wynette or even Patsy Cline, but the money he got for it kept the bank away...for a time.

Even before the sheriff came to his door a week back, Jack knew it was time to leave Kalvesta. One thing was certain: Jack wouldn't blow his brains out like Lloyd Erlich had. Lloyd lived down the road. He couldn't hold up to all the pressure of trying to grow things and pay the bills. Not that anybody blamed poor Lloyd, but killing himself wasn't Jack's idea of solving a weather problem. With the thump of the sheriff's retreating footsteps still echoing in his ears, Jack lit a match to the foreclosure papers and prepared to leave Kalvesta for good.

*   *   *

Jack set the case on its end and sat down. He was wearing a brown suit with wide lapels, the same suit his father used to wear. The suit used to be snug, now it hung on him. One lone car passed and then another, both filled to overflowing. Chairs and mattresses were lashed on the roofs. A zigzag of rope kept suitcases and boxes from spilling onto the road. Young and old, Jack could see they were all grim-faced. Sad what this country had come to. Unlike the Western expansion that brought his and Rolfe's families in Conestoga wagons to Kansas a century-and-a-half ago filled with hope and high spirits, these beat-up Chevys and open-backed trucks were cast in doom and despair.

Jack was patient. Most had no room for a dog, let alone a stranger.

An hour passed before an eighteen-wheeler blasted its horn. The monster truck lumbered to a stop, and Jack grabbed his case and sprinted to the cab.

"Where you going?" asked the blond driver, his ponytail wagging from under a bandana which, in turn, was covered by a Confederate cap.

"Canada, " then added, "but any place will do."

"Heading north, myself. Steel City, in fact."

Jack's face shed years.

"Got me a name of a man says they're hiring up there. Maybe he'd take you on, too, if that's what you want, mister."

Steel City was Canada's answer to Brasilia: a new city built from scratch. Except Brasilia was built in the Amazon jungle. Steel City was being erected as a cosmopolitan oasis by some fancy easterner named Jeremy Steel. From the little Jack knew, Steel aimed to build cities throughout Canada like McDonald hamburger franchises.

The driver cranked down the handle and Jack flung open the door. He yanked himself up, tossed his case behind the seat, and eased the door closed. He never looked back.

*   *   *

Hindsight makes everyone visionaries. The mayor and governor over-reacted to the blast. This was not, as they feared, a repeat of the World Trade Center bombing. True, eight people as opposed to six were killed, but this time the destruction was limited to one dental suite...not the Twin Towers. New Yorkers returned to work. Bagels were made, lipsticks sold, and panhandlers panhandled...all in the face of record high temperatures. The "wilt" index was getting to everyone.

*   *   *

Carly was snapping photos while Willie prepared for the bodies to be moved to the City Examiner's facilities. Willie tapped on the wall to get her attention. He had been in the hall comparing notes with one of the police forensic's team.

"Seems we missed a bit of news."

"What? Not another postal worker going ballistic?"

"Think catastrophic."

"Christ Willie, I'm almost finished. Afterwards, we can soak naked in a vat of ice cubes. It's too hot to play games."

"That won't be necessary. LeShana's news is going to chill you to the bone."

*   *   *

As they picked-up speed, the driver blew one bubble after another.

"Want a piece?" he offered Jack a blue-and-red wrapped piece of Bazooka gum.

Jack shook his head.

The rig got up to 80MPH. The driver kept his straw-colored eyes focused on the black tongue of asphalt that disappeared into the horizon. "What's your name?"

"Kinkade. Jack Kinkade. And don't think I'm not grateful for the ride, mister."

"Name's Lincoln Wilson. Friends call me Link."

Link grinned displaying yellowed teeth that made him look older than his thirty years.

"Lincoln Wilson?"

"You heard right. Mama read her history books. Got one brother named Cleveland, the other's McKinley."

"I'm afraid to ask. Any sisters?"

Link grinned.

"Eleanor and Mary Todd."

Jack twisted his neck more to the left, and raised his eyebrows at Link.

"Always wear a pony tail?"

Link's face lengthened.

"Don't you like it?"

"I just figured it was kind of hot hanging back there on your neck, like that."

The road hummed on and on, past farms that once had grown bumper crops of winter wheat, farms that could feed not only a nation but also many third world countries. Now the ground couldn't feed a kangaroo rat. On long stretches, clusters of empty houses cropped up with doors flapping in the wind and window-panes broken. Every so often they passed a family migrating with their movables piled onto a truck. Modern day pioneers.

Link cleared his throat. "Why not go to California? They say them vineyards are doing right well, especially since the French stuff ain't nothing but vinegar these days. Heard they're hiring plenty up Napa way."

"Those Chinks are tough to work for, 'specially when you're not one of them. If I'm gonna work day and night, might as well work where I'll be appreciated. How come you're not going west, Link? Heard they pay top dollar. Better than those Maple Leafs you'll be getting."

"Money don't mean much to me. Principles make a man. The way I see it, a man ain't a man if he don't keep his self-respect and do what he thinks is right."

"A job's a job. What do you care what you're hauling?"

Link snarled at Jack. "You think I'd put just anything in *Ol' Betsy?* I'll be damned if foreigners are going to put their greasy hands on my baby. That's why I'm heading for Steel City."

Jack didn't have to ask who *Ol' Betsy* was. Her name was painted in gold letters above the polished grill.

"Them Canucks are foreigners."

Link tapped his chest.

"But they're our kind of people."

*   *   *

No amount of cajoling by Carly could get Willie to roll over and tell her what happened. She ducked under the yellow ribbon and caught LeShana wringing information out of Rockefeller Center's director of operations. Despite the sweltering air, the man's gray pinstriped suit was neatly pressed and his white starched shirt looked early-morning fresh.

Before Carly could ask what happened, LeShana filled her in on what she had learned. "Mr. Boyle manages the whole shebang. He said because so many heavy hitters come to Rock Center, everyone knows to stay cool and not make a scene."

Mr. Boyle dabbed his narrow eyes with a maroon-monogrammed handkerchief. "We never clear out the lobby for anybody. Didn't do it for Lady Di when she was here once with her children. If it's someone important with special needs, we insist they come after hours, like Saudi sheiks and princesses."

LeShana resumed her questioning. "What if it was someone from, let's say, the Witness Protection Program? Like when Sammy the Bull was in it. What then?"

"The only time we cordoned off this and the other buildings around the plaza was when the Pope wanted to go ice-skating."

LeShana clapped her hands. "Child, I would have liked to have seen that."

"Actually, he was quite good."

Carly crossed her arms. "Willie said something happened today."

"You mean you haven't heard?" Mr. Boyle asked.

LeShana touched his arm.

"That about finishes us, anyway. Let me tell her."

"You know where to reach me. Please let me know the minute you find out anything."

"I will, Mr. Boyle. I'll be in touch."

Carly watched the director hike up his pants and leave through the puddles. "So what the hell did I miss? Everybody seems to know but me."

LeShana blurted it out. "The president's helicopter crashed."

"Survivors?"

"Only Aldous Fromm."

Carly clenched her fist. Ever since she had attended the Institute, she felt a warm spot for Fromm. Lute Aurum aside, she volunteered to help Fromm's campaign when he won the party's nomination. Whenever she had extra time, she helped register new voters, mainly senior citizens on the upper west side. As the election neared, she took time off to hand out "Fromm" leaflets during the morning and evening rush hours at the entrance to the Seventy-second Street subway station. She was a fan.

The corners of LeShana's almond-shaped eyes crinkled.

"Know who else was with him? Lute Aurum."

"Excuse me?"

"You heard right. Lute Aurum is dead."

Carly raised her head toward the smoke-covered ceiling in a silent prayer of thanks. How many times had she felt the tug of someone's eyes tracing her every step, measuring her every purchase at Zabar's or Fresh Fields or Citarella's? How many times when a stranger had brushed her on the street was Carly's first thought that an Aurum goon trying to get her?

"Aren't you going to say something?"

"There is a God."

Vice-President Takes Over as President Has Surgery

WASHINGTON, DC. Vice-President William Horace Greeley reassured a worried nation and a watchful world that he will steer a steady course until the injured Aldous Fromm can resume his duties as President of the United States. As acting-president, Mr. Greeley has already contacted each leader of the industrialized eleven, the Secretary General of the United Nations, Premier Lin Chou Fong of China, and Russia's newly restored figurehead monarch, King Nicholai Romanov-Castillo. Mr. Greeley told these and other world leaders not to expect any changes in the policies of the United States.

When asked if he felt comfortable assuming the presidency, Mr. Greeley stated, "The vice-presidency is an internship for the Oval Office. I've been trained to lead our nation, and I will."

Reporters tried to pin down the exact date President Fromm would resume his duties. The Vice-President was vague when he answered. "Plain and simple, it's a miracle President Fromm survived the accident. We've had crises in the past, when the president was so compromised it was not clear who was running the country.

This happened when Woodrow Wilson had a stroke toward the end of his term of office, and when Dwight Eisenhower had a heart attack. At present, President Fromm is heavily sedated and incapacitated. There is no indication as to when he will be able to resume his mantel of leadership. Rest assured, when the moment comes, we will all welcome him back with open arms."

Though reports concerning the president's medical status were to have been kept secret, reporters learned the president's spleen was removed and that he received nine pints of blood during surgery. His doctors stated that all broken bones have been stabilized with surgical pins or casts.

A Senate aide wishing to remain anonymous, reported that Senate majority leader Hugh Covington was heard to say after hearing of the many bones the president broke, that he "hoped President Fromm would permit his largest campaign donors to sign his casts the way President Clinton had done when he hurt his leg."

White House sources stated that the president will require many surgical procedures before he can resume the duties of his office. He asked that the nation be patient during the President's protracted recovery.

33

Jack and Link barreled through Nebraska. The road was an inferno. Fingers of heat caressed the cab. The men's lips were as parched as the land they passed. When Jack pointed to the road sign: **Gas, Food,** Link's foot was already on the brake. They took turns in the truck stop's stench-filled bathroom. Jack was back in *Ol' Betsy* when Link returned carrying two six-packs.

"Place makes me gag," Link said.

Jack took a can for himself and held one for Link, while Link stashed the other ten cans in a tiny refrigerator behind the main seat.

"Smells like any other place animals shit and piss."

Link turned the key. *Ol' Betsy* picked up steam. Link downed long swigs of the ice-chilled brew; Jack sipped from time to time. They drove in silence, eager to make South Dakota by nightfall, and Canada the following morning.

Jack studied his hands, first the right then his left. He goosed each knuckle, and then squeezed the flesh. He made a fist and rotated one way and then the other, studying it the way Mary used to stare at sculptures.

"You live long enough, things start to happen. This heat makes my knuckles swell. I'm getting old man's hands."

"Shit, you're not so old."

Jack turned to Link.

"I could be your father."

"I got me a father, and he don't look anything near as good as you. His idea of exercise is opening the mail. I bet you could lift a calf."

Jack raised his arm.

"With one hand."

They laughed, and then Link turned serious.

"What's going to happen?"

"To what?"

Link waved his left hand.

"The land's baking into a crust of sand. You seen all them people on the road, people like you losing their farms. Where's it all gonna end?"

"It's a cycle. We been through it before. The pendulum always swings back the other way."

The road hummed on.

"I don't see it. Every year it's getting hotter. Every year there's less water. Every year there's more cars and fumes. Where's it gonna stop?"

Jack fiddled in his shirt pocket for a cigarette. He held it out to Link.

"Want one?"

Link checked the side mirror.

"I'll pull over. Gotta keep *Ol' Betsy* pure. 'Sides, the beer went right through me."

Link relieved himself and then wandered through dry brushwood, kicking up swirls of dust. He returned to see Jack light a second Camel with the embers of the first.

Jack closed his eyes and luxuriated in the sharp burn as the smoke hit the back of this throat. He felt the nicotine jolt through his body. He looked at Link. "Got it figured out."

"I was getting worried this brain trust of yours wasn't going to solve all the world's problems today."

Jack took a long drag. "All the troubles started when they discovered oil. 'Black gold,' they called it. If you asked me, I'd say it's 'fool's gold.' We're kidding ourselves. A few more years of this, and we'll be gone. The dinosaurs will have the last laugh."

"I thought you said pendulums always swing back."

"Sometimes they get stuck 'cause they ain't been oiled right. That's when you got to keep your eyes and ears open, your mouth shut, and try to dodge what's coming at you."

"Sort of like survival of the fittest."

Jack licked his thumb and middle finger, then squeezed the lit ember until it hissed out. He put the half-smoked cigarette pack in the pack for later. "Sort of."

34

The next morning LeShana barged into the autopsy room in the basement of the Medical Examiner's Office.

"Got them sorted out yet?"

Willie pointed to the first five gurneys. "The secretary, both assistants, and the hygienist. They were easy. So was the good doctor."

Willie held up a chest X-ray.

"Look at this."

LeShana broke out into an ear-to-ear.

"Teeth in the stomach. Heck of a way to chew your food."

For a split second he considered explaining how a unique tumor—a teratoma—can form in a woman's ovary. The teratoma is caused by pleuripotential cells which can grow into teeth and jaws. More than once, he'd extracted teeth from a woman's reproductive organs.

"Makes sense given ground zero for the blast. It's the patient's lower jaw."

Carly paused from charting the teeth of one of the two victims found in the hallway.

"If Dr. San Martini sat with the patient's head at lap level, the chin would be sticking up in the air, the way it leads for a boxer. The blast ripped it from the skull and turned it into a missile. Half the cranium was embedded in the seat cushion; a piece of the occipital bone got lodged in the ceiling tile like a picture hook. Any missing persons reported?"

"Not a word, child. After the *Post* ran its cover story on 'Dental Doom,' we should've gotten calls. I mean there were three of them. By now, we always have a list of names to weed through. It's been goose eggs all the way."

Carly clipped a black plastic holder filled with dental X-rays onto the wall-mounted fluorescent view box. She beckoned LeShana to come closer.

"This is the jaw in Dr. San Martini's belly."

"Cute little buggers, sort of shaped like Halloween candy corn. I love that orange and yellow stuff."

"This guy did, too. Every tooth was getting a crown. You don't see that very often. I could live half-a-year off of what this guy must have been paying San Martini."

LeShana studied the X-rays. She scratched her cheek.

"All this done in one visit?"

"It's grueling work. First you have to drill the teeth down. After making the impressions, temporary crowns are fitted and worn while the bridge is being made in the lab. Then the bite has to be right. San Martini's famous for tackling cases like these."

LeShana snapped her fingers.

"What if someone came from out of town? That could explain why no one's called just yet. They probably haven't heard about the blast."

At that moment, the door rattled and a messenger rolled a metal cart into the morgue. Willie looked up.

"That's my preliminary toxicology report."

Willie grabbed the paper and scanned the results. Then he lifted his head. A patented "I-told-you-so" smirk spread across is kisser. He extended his hand toward LeShana.

LeShana grimaced, and then fished through the leather pouch attached to her belt.

"You're really going to take this?"

Willie took the crisp Andrew Jackson and brought it to his nose.

"I love the sweet smell of victory."

"Stop gloating. Are you going to tell us what killed them?

"Carbon monoxide."

"Like in a bad muffler?"

"Explains why we found everyone at their respective work stations."

Carly jerked her thumb at one of the unnamed victims.

"That doesn't explain why we found these two in the hall, headed toward the back."

Willie thought about that one.

"They were furthest from the source. Maybe they heard the secretary's head hit the keyboard, or something fall in a room."

Carly grinned. "Maybe they had to go to the john."

LeShana wagged her index finger.

"Two at a time? It's New York, but I don't think so. Something tells me they were hustling to check on San Martini's patient. Maybe they were there to protect him. What I want to know is, where did the carbon monoxide come from?"

Willie looked at LeShana.

"Can you get a team to search every crevice of the office? Check the ceiling tiles and air vents. Have them look for a hole big enough to slip through a rubber tube."

LeShana saluted Willie.

"I'm also going to start checking missing persons from all over the country."

"Doesn't only have to be from the US," Carly said. "Dr. San Martini had patients fly in from Europe and South America, too."

"I like cases that have narrow limits."

Just then, a security guard stuck his head through the doorway. Willie turned.

"What is it, Julio?"

"There's a man here to see you, Dr. Mason. Suit. Sort of harmless looking. Says he has some papers for you to sign."

LeShana stopped. "Watch out, child. Sounds like a lawyer to me."

"Can't be a malpractice suit. My patients are already dead."

35

As Carly Mason tramped down the fluorescent-lit hall to discover what the stranger wanted, Jeremy Steel attacked his blinking speakerphone button.

"Honey Fitzpatrick on line three," announced Jeremy's longtime secretary.

The mountain comes to Mohammed.

"Tell the prime minister, I'm flying up this afternoon. I'll be there by three."

"He says it's urgent."

Jeremy put the prime minister on.

"What's so important that couldn't wait until I get there?"

Jeremy reached for a Cuban.

"Pick up the receiver, Jeremy. I hate talking to an entire room. Are you alone?"

He struck a match, and sniffed the phosphorous vapors. He puffed until the end was evenly lit.

"Are you there?"

Jeremy picked up the black handset. It had taken a little convincing to get his first audience with the Canadian prime minister, but Lute Aurum smoothed the path by getting Aldous Fromm's father to intercede. Senior and Fitzpatrick had worked on many projects together in the past; so access was easily arranged. Jeremy got what he wanted, and Senior banked a consulting fee far larger than his yearly presidential pension.

"Can't you let a man enjoy a good cigar?" Jeremy poked his finger through a smoke ring as he listened.

Honey Fitzpatrick didn't sound like the way he looked. At six-foot eight, he impressed. He had a handsome angelic face, but when he spoke, his voice betrayed him. Instead of resonating, it squeaked, ratcheting up in scale when be became excited. At the moment, it approached a squeal.

"You might not be in a such a good mood when you get here. That's why I'm calling you. Parliament is getting antsy about this latest venture. They're beginning to make a stink about foreign investments here."

"You tell your mamsy-pansy ass-wipes that without me, your fucking country would still be back in the Stone Ages. You people had a hundred years..."

"One hundred and thirty-five."

"Whatever. It was certainly enough time to tap the world's greatest natural resources. You've got minerals, all the land you could hope for, and what do you do? Export Molson Light. My cities are going to let you grow into the next superpower. So you tell those ungrateful twits not to mess up a good thing. Is that clear?"

Jeremy slammed down the receiver. He was in no mood to take any crap from anyone, especially the prime minister of Canada...especially after Coulter Bell's second call in two days.

He started to puff on the Cuban, but ground it out; it had turned bitter.

"Is Greeley causing damage already?" Jeremy had asked Coulter earlier.

"He's not the problem."

When Coulter finished explaining their latest setback, all the blood drained from Jeremy's ruddy face.

"Shit, this cannot be good."

*   *   *

Carly followed Julio to the waiting area that fronted the First Avenue entrance to the Medical Examiner's Office. Gray cloth chairs with stainless steel frames formed the letter "U" around a glass coffee table. A maroon area rug, with a paisley print, covered a large part of the speckled granite floor.

Julio returned to his raised chair behind a mahogany wood security desk.

Carly squinted as light streamed through the huge floor-to-ceiling windows. She could make out a man in front of the plate glass wearing a dark suit. His back was toward her; he was gazing at the Kips Bay apartments across the street. He turned when he heard the door click open.

"I remember when those were some of the most exclusive digs in New York. It must've been before you were born."

"Lots of things were. I'm Carly Mason, I understand you wanted to see me."

The man was in his fifties. A rim of thinning gray hair encircled his bald area above deep worry lines. Carly noted his polished shoes. Trim and sallow-faced, even the tailored suit could not hide the fact that he would never be a poster boy for physical fitness.

He handed her a white business card embossed in black lettering.

"My name's Alexander Prescott, Carly. You can call me Lex."

She fingered the card.

"What kind of attorney are you? Is some patient complaining about a bridge I made years back?"

"This has nothing to do with your profession."

The heavy glass door opened from the street. A sobbing woman supported by a brittle, dry-eyed man, asked for the morgue. Julio pointed the way.

Lex Prescott cleared his throat.

"Is there someplace we could talk? In private?"

She waved for him to sit in the corner next to an over-watered ficus tree, its yellowed leaves scattered about the floor.

"This is as private as it gets. They don't give me my own office. Now what's this all about?"

He trawled inside his battered leather case and came up with a bulging document. He handed it to her. Flowery writing was scrawled across the cream-colored sleeve. She had seen something long and thick like that once before.

"Is this a will?"

Prescott didn't answer. He blinked for her to pull at the papers in the sleeve.

The paper was stiff and thick. It felt important.

"My mother died years ago. She didn't have anything."

"I'm sorry, but it's not from her. Why don't you read it?"

Carly scanned the first page. She reread the top paragraph twice, and then dropped the document to her lap.

"It must be some other Hack Mason. I haven't seen my father in twenty-five years."

"I've been reassured he's the right one. Can you give me your social security number so I can verify this *does* belong to you."

Carly grew suspect. Handing her a piece of paper with all the markings of a loaded gun was one thing, asking for her SSN was something else. How dumb did he think she was? This certainly was a variation on an everyday scam.

"Try something else," she said.

"He said you wouldn't believe me. He was right."

"You spoke with him?"

"By phone. Last week."

Her hopes bubbled up. She closed her eyes and smelled her father. It was too long ago to remember if it was his after-shave or the way grime clung to his clothes. Maybe it was the Irish Spring soap he used to use. Whatever the smell, it belonged to him and she could smell it now. Then she remembered her mother's bruises, the crying jags, and not hearing from him when a simple postcard would have been more than enough.

Carly got to her feet.

"I'm sorry, Mr. Prescott."

"Lex."

"You've gone out of your way for nothing. I'm not the person you're trying to find. My father has to be dead. Even if he were alive, he wouldn't know where to find me."

"There's a birthmark on your right inner thigh. Midway above your knee. It's shaped like a butterfly, with one bent wing. He said you'd remember how he taught you to hit a curve ball and change the oil in a car faster than they did at Jiffy Lube. He said you'd remember all that."

Carly sank into the cushion. She studied the man's eyes to see a break in his gaze, to prove he was making it all up.

"Did he tell you where he was all these years?"

Carly struggled to remember her father's face. She'd ripped up every last picture of him the day she buried her mother.

"He didn't say."

"Didn't...or you don't want to tell me."

He studied the blue dial on his Breitling watch.

"Could you sign this so I could get going."

Carly drew her lower lip over her teeth. How many information bits could she inhale about her lost father?

"Where's he now?"

"Look, I didn't quiz him about every detail. I'm a two-bit lawyer he contacted to draw up a very unimaginative trust. There it is," he said, touching the document. "How about signing it so we can both be on our way."

Carly looked down at the paper.

"What's this, again?"

"A trust."

"He's the one creating it, isn't he? Why do I have to sign?"

Lex Prescott nodded approval. "I told him the same thing. He said he wanted you to know it existed...now."

"So I know he's alive?"

"It's the only reason I can think of. Maybe it's his way of reaching out after all these years. Saying he's sorry."

"Oh, like he ever cared."

"Just the same, sign it and I'll be going."

She penned her name next to a yellow marker that had "Sign here" printed in red ink. Then she noticed her father's signature. She choked as she ran her fingertips over the ink.

"Is he well?"

"Seems to be."

He folded the first document and had her sign a second copy.

"This one's for you."

"What am I supposed to do with it?"

"For now, nothing. When the time comes, I'll get back to you."

"Why didn't he call himself?"

"He's not ready, Carly."

Carly had a sinking feeling in her gut. She wasn't ready to be rejected all over again.

Now they both stood. "Will you tell him...tell him, 'Hello,' for me?"

"If I get a chance. Good luck."

Prescott was almost out the door, when Carly called to him. "Mr. Prescott, how'd you ever find me?"

"Some guy named Conner Masterson put me in touch with you."

36

After standing for fourteen hours straight and then sitting by his patient's side for another six hours, Dr. Enrico Labatelli's head bobbed in a cotton-filled dream. It was always the same dream. He was inching down a long, narrow stairway. There may have been walls on either side, but he couldn't see or touch them. One step at a time into the coal-black abyss, and then he would trip. He always tripped. The plunge hurtled him down an endless mine shaft. His arms flailed to grab onto something—anything—to break his descent. He always jerked awake to find the sheet damp from his clammy skin.

This time he awoke to a piercing blare. President Aldous Fromm was in full cardiac arrest.

While the code-blue sounded, Dr. Labatelli instituted CPR.

He crossed his hands and put the heel of his right hand below the sternum.

He pushed, mindful of the recent surgery.

One...two...three...

Labatelli's right index finger and thumb pinched the president's nostrils.

He covered the blue lips with his.

Nothing.

He returned to the chest, this time harder, less concerned with causing damage.

One...two...three...

Out of the corner of his eye, Labatelli caught the crash cart being wheeled in.

He gripped the paddles. They sparked.

"Stand clear."

The president's body heaved off the bed.

The monitor's beep droned on.

Labatelli could not accept losing the president under his watch.

One more time and open-heart massage.

"Again."

This time, a blip appeared.

Enrico Labatelli sagged; the President was still with them.

When he was certain the president was stable, he went into his office and called Coulter Bell.

Coulter Bell, in turn, called Jeremy Steel.

That's when Jeremy Steel's mood changed.

37

Everyone in Emmitsburg knew everyone else's business, so it was easy to find Vernon Barlow most evenings; he'd be at the firehouse playing pinochle. Vernon and his buddies played cards at a table set on the black asphalt in front of an open bay. There was enough light spilling from inside the station to see their cards, not to mention being outside meant they could catch an occasional breeze and see who was driving by. That's where Kip Greeley found Vernon, the day after he saved the president's life.

"What'd he say?" asked one of the volunteer firemen when Vernon returned from taking the call. The man smacked a mosquito against his skin.

"The usual. The nation thanks me. Wants to meet me personally. That kind of stuff."

"Did he invite you to the White House?"

Vernon sat down on the vinyl-covered metal chair. "I told him I wasn't much for photo opportunities. Said I would've done the same thing for a cat stuck in a tree."

At that moment, four men in dark suits drove up in two royal blue Buicks.

"Vernon Barlow?" asked the man who appeared to be the leader.

Vernon breasted his playing cards. "If you fellas got a pen, I'll be happy to give you my autograph." The other card players grinned from pride at sitting so close to their local celebrity.

The leader nodded toward the parking area. "That your truck over there?"

"Already told a feller it ain't for sale."

The man reached into his breast pocket and handed Vernon a court order and a set of keys. "We're borrowing your truck for a day or two. After we're finished with it, you can have it back. In the meantime, we're leaving you one of our cars. Sorry for any inconvenience."

"Taking a man's truck isn't looked upon as right kindly around these parts, mister."

The leader shrugged. "We understand that, sir, but we've got our orders." When he saw that Vernon made no effort to take them, the leader put the keys on the table.

From his days in the Army and then his dealings with the Veteran's Administration, Vernon knew not to butt heads with the government. "Answer me one thing," he said to the leader.

The man didn't flinch. "If it's not classified, I'll be happy to."

"You know the man I saved? The one they're saying was the president?"

"What about him?"

"He wasn't really the president, was he?"

The man glanced at his cohorts then adjusted his dark glasses. "Why are you asking?"

"Well, I got to thinking. That helicopter was sure different than any I'd ever seen. The way it maneuvered up there, dodging one way than the other. I was thinking maybe this was like one of those Roswell episodes. You know, like when these aliens came to earth and the government does everything in its power to hide the truth from the people."

"You know," chimed one of Vernon's friends, "X-Files sort of shit."

"Is that what's going on here?" Vernon asked.

The leader turned to the other suits. "I told you these hillbillies were smart."

*   *   *

Jack and Link stopped in a motel soon after crossing the Canadian border.

"Don't heat and perspiration have a smell all their own?"

A snore was the only answer he got. Jack smiled and headed for the shower. He let the needles of spray pelt his back while he marveled at how much the scenery had changed since the first light. The contrast was the harbinger of hope.

Early on, low-lying shrubs began to dot the landscape. These graduated into stunted trees. Here and there, a patch of green offered promise. The further north they drove, the more scattered saplings punctuated their view. By noon, plowed fields with furrowed rows of greens were commonplace. As the air cooled, their spirits picked up.

Navigating to the south of Moose Jaw, Saskatchewan, Link broke a long silence.

"Been awfully quiet."

"Thinking," answered Jack.

"Ain't healthy to think so much. Might become a habit."

The highway curved north when they hit Alberta Province. They passed through Medicine Hat and Drumsheller. The rose-colored sky gave way to purples and grays. By Red Deer, Link's eyes were on their way to shutting.

"Hey, Reb. Sign says there's a motel at Rocky Mountain House. How 'bout it?"

Twenty-minutes later, Link's head touched the pillow and he was out for the count.

His hair still wet from the shower, Jack ambled out into the graveled parking lot, leaving the door part way open. The yellow light from the room cast a pie wedge on the gravel. Jack cut a Camel from the crinkled soft-pack. He took a long drag. The coal-black sky was aglitter with stars. A shooting star streaked by, and then another. Without back lighting, they seemed so close. He wanted to reach up and grab one and tie it around his neck.

He looked back to see Link's boots pointed straight up. How long had it been since he was close to anyone? No one after Mary passed. Not even Rolfe, and Rolfe was his best friend. Now, far from Kalvesta, under a foreign sky, fate threw him into bed, so-to-speak, with a southern Reb. Truth be told, Link wasn't half-bad.

Jack flicked the butt to the ground. Two days had elapsed since he hugged Rolfe good-bye. Hooking up with Link had been his first break in a long time. Though he hadn't done so in close to forty years, he had actually enjoyed sleeping under the stars the night before. Tonight, the motel was one more step closer to a new life.

Jack closed his eyes. He was grateful for a new beginning; grateful to smell the color green again. And grateful he wasn't in Kansas anymore.

*   *   *

"President Greeley...."

"Coulter, save the title for Aldous."

It was William "Kip" Horace Greeley's second day standing in for Aldous Fromm. On the first, he had trembled when he eased behind the huge polished desk in the Oval Office. It took a minute of slow, deep breathing for the location to register. He caressed the leather chair. He looked about, absorbing each object in timid wonder.

A day later, Coulter Bell was no longer addressing him as an interloper. "Who knows, it may be yours. I mean his heart has already arrested once," said Coulter in a matter-of-fact tone.

"Day two and switching loyalties? That's not your style."

"On the contrary, I call it like it is, Kip." Coulter brought his hand up and scrutinized his manicured fingers, breathed on them, then burnished them with the jacket of his blue pinstriped suit. "Call me a pragmatist."

"Two-faced is more like it."

Coulter feigned hurt feelings. Kip knew Coulter was a chameleon, shifting whichever way the wind blew. It was something Coulter would even admit to himself.

"I might as well earn the taxpayers' money. What do you have for me?"

Loyalties notwithstanding, Coulter Bell was a die-hard pro. "A bill will be introduced in the Senate today limiting immigration into the United States."

"That's ridiculous."

"Not when the Public Assistance programs are bankrupt. The economy is in the toilet. No one wants more illegals here when our own people have empty bellies. And if they stay long enough, we risk countless numbers of them becoming legal. Then what do we do?"

"Who's behind this?"

"The Majority Whip. Says he has the votes."

"Tell him to shove it. If that bill touches my desk, it will sit there until the very parchment it's written on crumbles to dust."

Coulter continued as if nothing had been said. "We can no longer afford to be so generous, sir. There was a time when putting everyone on the public dole was a good idea. It didn't matter where they came from or how long they were here. Times have changed."

"There will be no changes while I'm president. Anyone who qualifies will always be welcomed in this country."

"How? We don't have the resources."

"We'll tighten our belts if we have to. Who knows? We could be turning away the next Mozart or Rembrandt."

Coulter's eyes drew a narrower beam on Greeley. "Need I remind you that President Fromm has already given his support for this bill?"

Kip Greeley rose to his full measure, which was half a head taller than the press secretary. "Need I remind *you* that at the moment, *I* am the president? This bill is dead in the water."

Coulter Bell stood soldier-straight, furious.

Greeley continued to bellow. "If I were you, I'd be praying that Aldous Fromm has had the last of his setbacks and makes a speedy recovery."

*   *   *

"Take a deep breath." Enrico Labatelli warmed the stethoscope in the palm of his hand before touching the president's back. "How do you feel?"

"Like a Mack truck ran me over...backwards and forwards. They tell me you saved my life."

"You're lucky twice over."

Dr. Labatelli watched the president lick his parched lips, and then nod off. The surgeon glanced at the half-empty intravenous drip, checked his watch, and then increased the flow. He would change the orders to hydrate his patient.

The surgeon was exhausted and took the opportunity to ease into a green vinyl chair next to the bed. He watched Fromm's chest rise and fall. He found the drone of the suction tube (draining the post-operative edema) and the steady beeping from the cardiac monitor peaceful. Here he was, Enrico Labatelli, born in the Pelham section of the Bronx, baby-sitting the president of the United States. He even had the power to keep Secret Servicemen outside the room. As a first year surgical resident at Georgetown Hospital, Enrico had scrubbed on cases involving Congressmen and even a governor or two. By the time he made chief resident, he had put hip replacements in a handful of bigwigs, including a Supreme Court justice. Now *he*—little Ricky Labatelli—was charged with putting Humpty Dumpty back together again.

Satisfied the president was dozing in comfort, Dr. Labatelli rose to leave.

"Will I be the same?"

Enrico froze in his tracks. He felt Fromm's eyes peering through his back. He turned. "Bones mend."

"Will I ever get to...?"

"...look like yourself?"

"My *old* self."

How could he tell the president he had months of skin grafts ahead of him, that he'd end up addicted to oxycodone to kill the pain? Right now, with a Demerol drip and a Valium push every four hours, Fromm was somewhere east of the Twilight Zone and west of La-la land. Dr. Labatelli was about to remind the president how lucky they were to have the bronze bust to serve as the template for the healing-mask, but he was cut short by a deep nasal rattle.

Dr. Labatelli touched Aldous Fromm's shoulder. There would be time to tell him not to worry. After the last surgeries healed and the physical therapists finished torturing the president back to full capacity, and long after the healing-mask did its job preventing scars, the new Aldous Fromm would be indistinguishable from the old one.

Inside was a different matter. Near-death experiences had a way of changing people, and Dr. Labatelli knew some of those wounds never close.

38

After Lex Prescott grabbed the signed papers and left, Carly had every intention of returning to the bodies. Instead, she went outside into the blast-oven heat blanketing the metropolitan area. Skipping down the granite steps, she turned left on First Avenue, making a left again at the corner. She followed Thirtieth Street to the East River. At the water's edge, she watched a tug nudge a barge loaded with steel drums downstream. A police patrol boat cruised toward the Harlem River. A chopper landed at the nearby heliport. Smelling the saltwater spray, seeing the small white caps churned by the small craft, hearing the cars whiz by on the FDR Drive, helped her forget to feel sorry for herself.

*　　　　　*　　　　　*

"Sorry I bolted out like that, but something came up."

Willie was about to level one of his patented snide remarks, like, *I'm elbow-deep in the Rock Center victims, and you go out for tea and crumpets,* but he didn't. Instead, he came up sober. "Nothing serious, I hope."

Carly wanted to just shout out that her father was alive, but she couldn't bring herself to say anything. It was not that she didn't want to share the news with Willie; he had become her surrogate father. She cherished him for his warm and caring ways, and that he was always looking out for her best interest. She would tell him after she sifted through her emotions, and could comprehend what it all meant.

"Nothing you need to worry about now." She looked at the body on the gurney. "So whatchya got?"

Willie wiped his sleeve against his forehead. "We're going to need one fantastic break to identify these bodies from Rock Center."

"Whoa! Is this the ever-optimistic Willie Robinson I know and love? We're only hours into the case and you're throwing in the towel? What's with you?"

"Pros did this."

"So?"

"They removed anything that would help identify these bodies: wallets, rings, watches. Everything. They knew the blast and the fire would destroy whatever they didn't take with them. Clothing tags, for instance. They were slick. Pros, I tell you."

Carly cleared her throat. "They still have their teeth."

"I know teeth bail us out time and time again, but a little birdie's whispering in my ear that we're barking up the wrong tree with these three."

Carly was determined to prove him wrong. She had been up against odds worse than these. "Remember when the Air Force sent me a single tooth a kid found playing by that crash site four years ago?"

"It made all the front pages. You were able to identify which of the crew, from a B-29 bomber that had plowed into an Okinawa mountainside during World Word Two, it belonged to. I can still see the look on his mother's face when they handed her the box containing the tooth."

"If I can do that with one premolar fifty-five years later, I can do it with three bodies with full sets of teeth. I'll figure out who they are."

"Twenty bucks says that the N.C.I.C. will have zip on these guys. That's why whoever killed them, left the teeth in the jaws. They knew we couldn't identify them."

N.C.I.C. was the computerized national repository for missing persons. With over one hundred thousand people on file, not even four percent had dental records charted and available for possible matches. While the FBI promised to improve the record keeping, N.C.I.C. was still of little help when it came to helping find the lost and missing.

"Are you forgetting it takes time to extract a mouth full of teeth? They couldn't very well yank them knowing a bomb was about to explode."

Carly was about to accept Willie's bet when LeShana marched into the autopsy room with open palms.

"Sorry folks," LeShana said, "no persons reported missing, nothing at N.C.I.C."

Willie beamed. "I told you."

"Stop gloating...and you can't collect because we didn't bet." She turned to LeShana. "What about the Witness Protection Program?"

"Sammy the Bull is accounted for. So's everyone else in their program, child."

Carly pointed to a folder on which the familiar FBI logo was prominently printed. "That looks like trouble."

LeShana broke into her patented ear-to-ear grin. "For you, it is. Thank your friends at the Bureau. They've been looking for three fugitive bank robbers. Want you to make certain they aren't those three." She pointed to the unidentified Rock Center victims.

"What would three bank robbers be doing in a dental office? Getting their teeth laminated for their next mug shots?" Willie said with a wry smile.

"Don't laugh. Anything's possible," LeShana said. "One time we were called to Umberto's II, you know, down in Little Italy. There was an argument in front of the restaurant; one guy bought it. Know where we found the perp? Getting his hair cut around the corner."

Carly was Hamlet holding up a skull. In her hand, she rotated the lower jaw that had been extracted from Dr. San Martini's abdomen. "This is a tough one. Every tooth has been ground down to make caps. All twenty-eight. The drilling removed every bit of enamel and destroyed any fillings or crowns we could've used for points of comparison."

"Still, there might be something if you had the person's chart," LeShana said.

Willie grabbed the jaw. "But all the records were destroyed in the fire."

Carly snapped her fingers. "Did anyone bother to look for the appointment book?"

LeShana put her hands on her hips and said in her best, do-you-think-I'm-an-idiot? voice, "It's missing."

39

Assured by Dr. Labatelli that the president was stable and out of danger for the moment, Jeremy continued to Teterboro Airport where he kept his private plane. He was looking forward to his meeting with Honey Fitzpatrick.

Thirty minutes later, he emerged from the shower on board his Gulfstream VI with Aldous Fromm's recovery still very much on his mind. It had taken years of planning. The final stages were critical if the master project was to succeed. Jeremy hated to depend on anyone but himself. His concerns were never more evident now that the president's helicopter had crashed.

An antique clock fixed to the wall chimed. Thanks to Travis Billings, his pilot, they had made up for a late start and would get to Ottawa on time.

Steel glanced at the semi-clad woman sleeping on the circular bed. She was a stunner. She should be for the money she cost. Ringlets of wavy blond hair fell onto the pillow in wild disarray. The raunchy smells of jazzing her to the end tingled his nostrils. He glowed. She hadn't disappointed.

The beauty clutched the peach-colored satin sheets in her fastidiously manicured hands. The glossy fabric rose and fell with each slumbering breath, reminding Jeremy of all that lay beneath the coverlet. He considered ravaging her again. When he checked his gold Piaget, he sighed. His one worthy adversary—time—had beaten him again.

Jeremy picked up the antique-white phone next to the French armoire.

"Yes, Mr. Steel?" said Travis, in his clipped Liverpool accent.

"How much longer?"

"Six-and-a-half and down."

Jeremy's gaze lingered on the blond. "Be a good chap and occupy our friend while I'm with the Prime Minister. She'll have more than one type of craving when she wakes."

Travis flipped a shock of straight sandy hair off his forehead and grinned. He had tasted Jeremy's women before, but never on the same day. This was one job perk he enjoyed. He gathered today had a special meaning.

*   *   *

Honey Fitzpatrick stood in the middle of the high-ceilinged office in the Langevin Building that had housed the Canadian prime minister since 1976. Before then, his predecessors had governed from second floor chambers across the way in the East Block, one of three architectural gems that made up the complex known as Parliament Hill.

The Langevin Building was a four-story structure standing on Wellington Street, between Elgin and Metcalfe. Erected in 1891, it has been described as Romanesque with a Gothic influence: a ten-foot wide corridor with semi-circular arches on either side the length of the building. Its main feature was a grand central staircase supported by granite columns and garnished with detailed risers and banisters made of heavy wrought ironwork.

"Quaint," was how Jeremy once described the Langevin Building. It was no White House. Further into the project, he would suggest changes to improve the PM's office.

Jeremy studied Honey Fitzpatrick. The Canadian PM had a powerful grip. At six-foot eight, he had played small forward for the University of Minnesota's basketball team....without distinction. Mediocre by American standards, Honey Fitzpatrick was good enough to start on the Canadian Olympic team in the ill-fated '72 Olympics in Munich. Rosy-cheeked, the prime minister still had the cherubic looks of the choirboy he had once been in a small log church in Prince Albert.

"Did you have a good flight, Jeremy?"

"It had its distractions, Mr. Prime Minister." Steel thought about what Travis Billings was doing at that very moment.

"There's so little time on those short flights. Glad you got something accomplished."

Jeremy grunted that the flight back should be just as rewarding.

"Bully for you. Why not come this way? I took the liberty of having tea ready for us."

They ambled to the round alabaster table tucked in an alcove. Here seats faced outward to take advantage of the East Block's splendor. As he sipped the green tea, Jeremy's builder's-eye roamed through the arched window. He absorbed the details of the copper-topped roof that covered the Gothic Revival building, noting the pointed arches, the repulsive gargoyles, and the high leaded-glass windows, all shouldered by flying buttresses. If anything, the building reeked more of beauty than power.

Jeremy caught the prime minister studying him. "Mr. Prime Minister...."

"Call me, Honey. Everyone else does."

Jeremy hesitated. "I'm sure I should know your real name."

Honey Fitzpatrick didn't miss a beat. "Aloyicious. Can you imagine being saddled with that? I was large for my age, with a baby face. It was a living hell. By the time I coughed up the courage to ask my mother to change my name, I was covered in hives so bad they thought I had chicken pox."

"What did she change it to?"

He hiked up his pant legs and leaned forward. "Get this. My mother says to me, 'It's okay, honey'. I thought 'Honey' was my new name. It's been Honey ever since. Pretty stupid, eh?"

"Not at all...Honey."

They both laughed.

"Enough of me, Jeremy. I've got to tell you the Canadian people will be forever grateful for what you've done here. You've changed the quality of so many lives."

"No need to thank me. I'm not some altruistic saint. I did it for money."

"But you've helped so many."

"Then I consider myself lucky you see the benefits and not my profits."

"It's typical of us. Money's never been the issue. Canada's always been long on resources and short on vision, especially when it comes to our future."

"Which is why I flew up today. Steel City's functioning pretty well, and Steel Metropolis is off to a good start. It's time for my next project to jump from the planning boards to mortar and wood."

Jeremy spun his web.

"I have a vision...a vision of happiness and harmony...of families living together in peace and tranquility. I want to build a series of villages—Steel Villages—about the perimeters of Ottawa, Toronto, Montreal, Calgary, Edmonton, and your other cities. They will be futuristic communities with controlled environments that will enable their inhabitants to be creative and prosperous. By the time I'm finished, ten million of *your* people will live in my cities and villages. Plans have already been forwarded to the Minister of the Interior for approval. You understand, of course, that an undertaking this size will require deep pockets."

"Very deep." Honey Fitzpatrick hesitated. "Would you finance this yourself?"

"I've got the necessary people lined up. It's a monster of a project. Guaranteed, it's the largest one ever undertaken in this hemisphere."

The prime minister sidled up to a wall-sized map of Canada. He ran his thick index finger across barren lands Jeremy Steel had already transformed into burgeoning cities. A string of Steel Villages would only enhance his own public opinion polls and guarantee he would remain in office. Under his breath, he thanked the day Aldous Fromm, Sr. called and arranged that first meeting with Jeremy Steel and Lute Aurum. Too bad about Junior's accident.

"This is an opportunity for you to change the face of your country," Senior had said at the time, "without costing your citizens a penny." Honey Fitzpatrick was newly elected. The former president was offering a chance for Canada to leap into the twenty-first century with both legs churning. She had more untapped minerals and oil deposits than any other country on the planet. With the right blend of know-how and financing, Jeremy Steel would stir history's drink. Honey Fitzpatrick would be remembered as the mover and shaker who unleashed his country's pent-up power.

"After all this time, I still don't get why you're doing this here? Why not back home?"

"My so-called beloved country throws roadblocks every place I turn. Take my building opposite the United Nations. I sat through all the hearings, got all the approvals, and then, only after the building was half-up, the neighbors decide they don't want it there. Where were they when they had a chance to say their piece? Walter Cronkite was one of them. Wherever I turn, laws are passed to nix my projects. They made it tough for me because my successes kill them."

"Look what you've accomplished!"

"New York and Atlantic City are the bush leagues compared to this." Jeremy swept his hand across the Canadian map. "This is the Majors."

"I hope the honeymoon continues for a long time, Mr. Steel." He offered his huge paw to Jeremy. "Build your Steel Villages." When Jeremy didn't react, Honey added, " Is something wrong?"

Jeremy turned pious. "I hesitate to ask."

"Fire away. You're on a roll."

Jeremy clasped his hands together, praying. "You know I own a shuttle service that flies between Boston, New York, and Washington. My fleet needs more routes. I'd like to fly into Canada. After all, when the new airports we're building are finished, someone's got to fly into them. Can you give Steel Airlines a shot?"

"You should have those routes."

Jeremy raised his fist in victory.

"But you know I can't do that," Honey said softly. "There are procedures to follow. This isn't my little fiefdom, you know."

Jeremy rallied. "This is something that will benefit everyone."

"Of course it will, but I have to be careful. I can't let the naysayers have their day with either of us. You understand."

Jeremy looked away.

"Don't take it so hard. I'll see what I can do."

"How long will it take?"

"You're a bit eager on this one, Jeremy. Are you certain there's not more to it than plane routes?"

"Why Mr. Prime Minister, whatever could you mean? I see profit here."

40

Dr. Labatelli wouldn't leave the president's side until he was confident the president's condition had stabilized. The doctor was dozing in a chair next to the bed when the phone rang. A reflex developed from years of on-call, he answered on the first ring, before he had time to clear his head.

"Yes?" He sat up, nodding to the unseen caller. "I understand. He'll be ready six months from today." Then, as quickly as his smile appeared, the good doctor turned ashen. "No one can heal that fast, not even the President of the United States."

He tapped his fingers on the portable top that held the serving trays.

He scowled and bit his lip.

He started to protest, but was told to shut-up and listen.

At the end, he slammed the phone down. With degrees from Johns Hopkins and Columbia, and residencies and fellowships performed at Georgetown Hospital, even he, Enrico Labatelli, couldn't perform miracles.

41

Link and Jack gobbled a breakfast of fried eggs draped over thick slabs of round bacon and hot-coal biscuits drowned in thick amber honey. After a last smoke and java refills, the traveling troubadours took their show on the road. On their way to the rig, Linked stopped and squatted to read a super bold headline plastered in the window of a coin-operated newspaper dispenser.

"Get a load of this," Link said, "they say the President's going to be all right."

"Big whoop. While he was bombing them Arabs, he could've been feeding millions of starving babies. As far as I'm concerned, this country's had its priorities screwed up for too long. Been paying too much attention to the rest of the world while neglecting us everyday folks, especially us farmers."

To seal his words in stone, Jack marshaled the biggest wad of yellow-green phlegm he could, and spat it right on Fromm's picture. He drew his sleeve across his mouth, dabbing white spittles that lingered at the corners of his lips as the mucus dripped down the faceplate.

"What'd you do that for?"

"Hate all politicians, 'specially that one."

"But he's the President."

"Far as I can tell, he puts one leg at a time through his boxers, same as us. What the hell's politics all about anyway? Big boys having big toys? They've got more money to spend than God can print. They toss it around like it don't mean nothing. There they go shootin' people and droppin' bombs 'stead of feeding babies. The way I see it, being President means you can get away with murdering anybody you want."

Link rose from his haunches. It didn't take much to size Jack up: rebutting him when he was this headstrong was about as safe as strolling into a lion's den. Link shrugged and climbed aboard *Ol' Betsy*. With Jack inside, he eased his special lady out of the parking lot. As soon as the land turned prettier, Jack would sing a different tune.

Before long the arrow-straight two-lane highway gave way to a twisting roadway. The black asphalt snaked between creeks and lakes and gorges that were meant for four-legged transportation, not steel rigs whose strength was measured in horsepower. By late morning, they reached Brazeau Reservoir.

Link pointed to a sign.

STEEL CITY-30 Km.

"Look at that that!" Jack said, like a gleeful child pressed against a department store window, all wide-eyed at the fake snow falling on the Lionel trains threading through a maze of shiny red and green wrapped Christmas presents.

"Have you gone loco."

"Hell no. I never thought I'd see the likes of it again. It's so beautiful."

Jack jumped from the cab and ran to the edge of a wheat field. He collapsed to his knees, clutching handfuls of dark rich soil. He closed his eyes and sucked in the fecund aroma. The fertile smells bombarded his senses. He felt dizzy.

Link edged up behind him. "Hey Cochise, you look like an Indian."

Jack's face was smudged like a grease monkey's. "Can't you smell it, Link? It's the sweetest damn smell in the whole world?"

"If you say, so. I always thought a girl dressed in laced panties, her body all sprayed up with those designer perfumes, was as good as it got. Never did think dirt in the middle of nowhere would be so sweet it'd make me bend over and put my nose to it."

"No wonder you lost the Civil War."

Jack, who had propped himself by now, eased onto one foot then the other. He held out two handfuls of dirt.

"Rich soil like this? It's better than sex itself. It's better than all the money in the whole world. Goddamn it, Link, I'm holding life in my hands."

"Right, Jack."

Jack remained undaunted. "Make all the fun you want. This dirt is our fucking future."

"I know it is, Jack. Now put it down like a good boy. You can play with it after we get to Steel City. We gotta be on our way."

Jack didn't budge. "I know you think I'm crazy, but feeling this here dirt, smelling like it does…shoot, now I know we're going to be saved."

For the rest of his life, Link would never forget the way Jack's face looked that day, all smudged in dirt. For a second there, he thought the fool was going to eat the friggin' dirt. Right then and there, Link knew he was bonded to Jack for life.

"Clean your hands and let's get going."

Jack chucked the dirt down, and stepped toward the wheat field while Link headed toward *Ol' Betsy*. Filled with good thoughts about what they would find in Steel City, Link almost missed it. He wouldn't remember what made him turn his head, but he turned. Out of the corner of his eye he caught a pair of legs poking out from the base of a gray-flecked boulder.

Goosebumps covered his arms. So the Garden of Eden was no Shangri-La.

42

Jeremy Steel slammed down the receiver. "How many does this make, five? Six? When's it going to stop?" Another American worker, the one Link and Jack found, one of *his* American workers, had been found dead in the outskirts of Steel City. "What are the blasted Canucks doing about it?"

He didn't expect his secretary to answer.

Rosemarie Crimshaw had held the building magnate's life together for more years than she cared to count. There was a time when she dreamed that the debonair boss would at least bed her. The fantasy was never fulfilled. The only thing that did change through the years was her bank account. Jeremy Steel's ascendancy as New York's building tycoon made Rosemarie rich—at least by her standards. The man was generous, but retirement would have to wait until this next wave of building was finished…because Jeremy needed her. Canada was Jeremy's greatest career risk. It was way bigger than Atlantic City or rejuvenating the West Side railroad yards, and it dwarfed constructing the tallest residential building in the world. Stick it out a little longer and she would hit "three cherries" soon enough.

"This makes eight."

She slipped the signed contracts that would get Steel Villages rolling into a manila folder. Jeremy was standing by the window, his back toward her. His shoulders hung low. Who else but Jeremy Steel would pick up the expenses for every victim's family? He was a one-of-a-kind wonder.

"What are they thinking?" Jeremy said.

"They?"

He whipped around to face her, and then smiled. "I'm sorry. I thought you had left."

"I'm still here."

"The only reason we've got Americans working in Canada is because *they* don't have enough skilled workers. And someone's knocking them off. Why? With every other place turning to shit, it's become the best place to live. A real Utopia. The way I see it, they could even be in a position to take us over one day. So these murders make no sense."

Rosemarie inched closer. She smelled his lemon-lime fragrance. "Men have killed since the beginning of time. Jealousy, envy, greed, who knows why? Human frailties exist everywhere, even in your precious Canada."

Jeremy squeezed her hand. "They're killing *my* workers."

Rosemarie broke away and smoothed her French-designed skirt, then waved the manila folder with the just-signed contracts. "Then put Steel Villages on hold. Finish the projects you've started, and wait 'til they catch whoever's doing this."

"Not on your life. Canada is my future. Our future. Steel Villages will be built. Nothing will stop us."

"Not even more men being killed?"

"Did sacrificing a few workers cancel-out building the Empire State Building? Shit happens."

"Why the flip-flop? A second ago, you were pining away for your men being killed. Now you're ready to lose a few more for the sake of finishing your projects. I don't get it?"

He plopped down in his high-backed chair. He grabbed his temples and looked down to see his reflection in the polished mahogany. "Forgive me. I don't know what I'm saying. Of course I don't want any more men killed."

He looked up. "Did this one...was he...did they say anything about...?"

"If you mean his tongue, they're still looking for it."

43

Carly and Willie were stymied. Not only were there no local reports of missing persons matching the three unknowns from Dr. San Martini's office, but also there were none nation-wide. It didn't make sense. A single unclaimed body happened all the time. A trio rang all the bells.

The last dental film taken of the jaw found in Dr. San Martini's gut dropped out of the automatic X-ray developer. Carly held it to the light.

Willie waved his scalpel in the air. "Any markers?"

"Only this three-rooted lower right molar. The endodontist did a good job getting all four canals."

"Are four canals common?"

"They happen. What's unusual is the three-rooted molar. I've only seen it once before."

Willie returned to his neck dissection. The victim had been found dead by her husband. Suspecting their stepfather might have tinkered with Nature, the socialite's daughters demanded an autopsy. Willie found the cricoid cartilage.

"Can you make a positive ID with that film?"

"If I had something to compare it to, it'd be a cinch," answered Carly.

"Something will turn up."

Carly mounted the X-rays, one-by-one, in a black Adamount. The plastic holder had clear edges so no part of a film was obscured. "If nothing turns up or we strike out at N.C.I.C., I'll show this film at the upcoming Forensic Academy meeting. It's soon. There's a special section for case reports. Maybe the oddball molar will strike a chord with someone."

Willie grunted without having a word she said register. He was too engrossed in what he was doing to listen.

She watched him dip his hand into the neck area and fish around. "What are you doing?"

Willie's head bobbed up, with a smile plastered across his whiskered face. "They were right."

"Who was?"

"The daughters. Instead of making a dorsal scissors incision through the cricoid cartilage, I did a complete resection of the thyroid cartilage first, and then a horizontal incision through the cricoid before opening the larynx dorsally. I could see a lot more this way and wouldn't you know it, there was a hidden fracture. This lady was strangled to death."

"Bravo for you."

Willie tossed the scalpel onto the corpse. It embedded in the muscle and quivered like a javelin. "Now about these Rock Center bodies. I've never had a case where we didn't have an inkling as to who we were dealing with soon after an accident like this."

"It's the third day. People call home no matter where they are. I say LeShana should start canvassing the midtown hotels. Housekeeping will know who hasn't messed their sheets for two days, especially if their rooms were side-by-side."

"This case is starting to stink big time. What if they *are* from New York? Then checking the hotels is a waste. I say it was a

Mafia hit, the three lived nearby, and no one's about to call the cops and report them missing."

Carly disagreed. "Doesn't our local Cosa Nostra send a message with every hit? It's their calling card to tell everyone else not to mess around...or they'll be next."

"Oh, so now you're a Mob expert? Better stick to teeth."

"I saw it in *The Godfather*."

Willie winked as Linus Rawling, the aide who kept track of all the corpses, rolled a gurney through the swinging doors. Linus was long beyond retirement age. Everyone knew he had been collecting Social Security for years, and he couldn't do that—and work full-time—until after he turned seventy-two. Rumor had it Linus had formaldehyde running through his veins.

"Got you a live one, doc. The Bloods and the Crypts at it again. Bled to death before they could get him to Bellevue."

The Bloods and the Crypts were LA gangs who invaded New York in the mid-nineties. Neophytes gained entry to their ranks by slashing innocents in the subways. This time, the blade went too deep and severed the carotid artery.

"They should teach the bastards where to cut," Willie said.

"Why don't you give the gangs a quickie anatomy lesson." Carly placed the last X-rays in the plastic mount.

"You're making a joke...I think it's a good idea."

"I'm dead serious. It would be a great community relations thing."

"I'm going to give it some thought."

"You do that."

She filed the completed X-ray series in a chart.

"By the way, do you have any plans for tonight?" he asked, pulling a thick cream-colored envelope from his coat pocket.

She scrunched her face and turned the pages in an imaginary day planner. "Am I in luck or what? Tonight was going to be Lean Cuisine and an episode of *Spin City*."

"Richard Kind can wait. Tape the show and go to this affair. You need to get out more."

"What affair are you talking about?" she asked, taking what appeared to be an invitation with her name written in black calligraphy.

"It's a black tie job at the Waldorf. A command performance by the Mayor."

As a city employee, Carly knew that Willie received last minute invites all the time. So being handed one, hours before the affair, was not unusual.

"What time do we have to be there?" she asked, scanning the invitation.

"*You* have to be there by seven."

"What about you? Weren't you invited, too?"

Willie shook his head. "Seems they wanted a pretty face on the dais."

"Shoot!"

Willie reached out for her. "It's good for you to get out. Meet some new people. But if you're that upset, I'll dust off my penguin suit and tag along."

"It has nothing to do with that. I'm a big girl. Lord knows I can handle any function this city throws."

"Then what's the problem?"

"I have nothing to wear."

44

"Rig 'round back. I'll get someone to take you to your bunk," the foreman barked. "Report here in the morning to get your load and papers."

"Yessir," Link said with a crisp salute. He back-pedaled as he left the wood-planked office.

Jack was leaning against a fence.

"You gonna ask for a job, too," Link asked.

"Thought I was when we hooked up in Kansas. The land's so rich here, got me thinking about farming again. Don't know if I want to ride a rig all day...nothing personal."

Link poked him in the ribs. "Give it a chance. *Ol' Betsy* needs two when she's loaded up. I kinda got used to your company, even if you are a Yank."

Jack shifted to his other foot and looked away. He dabbed at the corner of his eye with his sleeve. "I guess farming could wait a little longer. I wouldn't want to be trouble."

"The only trouble there'd be is if you said 'No.' I already signed you up." Link slapped his knee and did a jig.

"You're not so stupid for a Reb."

Link stopped prancing and slapped his right hand over his heart, hoisting his left arm high into the air. "Don't ever underestimate the cunning of a Southern gentleman. I am here to tell you, suh, that the South will rise again."

Jack pursed his lips in mock disbelief, glanced in either direction, and then put both hands on his hips. "I don't see no gentleman 'round here, do you? And for shittin' sure the South ain't never going to rise again."

"Ain't that the truth!"

Then Jack and Link touched closed fists together and broke into hysterics. Another worker, Slim Armstrong, interrupted their jocularity. "Foreman caught me walking past his office. Says you'll be staying in my bunk. Name's Slim Armstrong. From Omaha. C'mon, I'll show you the way."

Introductions made, they headed toward a row of wooden bungalows that resembled army barracks.

"What do they have you doing up here?" Link asked.

Slim, who was a shade taller than either Link or Jack and a lot more toned, scanned the area. He leaned into them. "You fellas sure you want to be here?"

"Hell, yes. I just got me my first job in months. Looks like there's plenty of work up here for me and *Ol' Betsy*...she's my rig."

"Oh, there's jobs all right, but this place ain't good for your health."

Jack nodded to Link, and then said, "We come across a body on the way up. People get killed everywhere. Besides, what's there back home for us?"

"All I'm saying is that if you know what's good for you, keep an eye behind you and stop your tongues from wagging too much."

RCMP Seeks Help from Henri Plumme

ALBERTA. After two Americans traveling into Canada from the U.S. discovered an eighth victim in what is being dubbed as the Pembina River killings, Loren Chesterfield, head of the RCMP is reported to have met with detective, Henri Plumme. Though one can only speculate as to what occurred at their meeting, readers will remember that it was Plumme who caught the assassin who killed former Prime Minister Witt Enslow after the PM signed NAFTA II, eliminating all restrictions on American companies wishing to do business in Canada.

Soon after, the new PM, Honey Fitzpatrick, bestowed the Royal Order of the Maple Leaf, Canada's highest honor on Inspector Plumme. Plumme then retired to pursue his lifelong interests in history and archaeology, often traveling to South America to work in jungle ruins in the Amazon and on the plains of Nasca.

When Chief Chesterfield was asked, he said the idea of bringing Plumme back to help track the Pembina serial killer was PM Fitzpatrick's idea. "In fact," Chief Chesterfield said, "enlisting Plumme was a *stroke of genius.*"

45

"Are you sure it's not going to hurt?"

Dr. Labatelli was set to remove the last of the bandages wrapped around Aldous Fromm's face. With a halogen light beaming atop his head and with magnifying loops perched on his nose, the doctor teased off the medicated gauze.

"I started to tell you yesterday—but you fell asleep—that we were able to take an accurate mold from your bronze bust in front of your college library. It was tons better than making the mask from scratch."

"And what is this mask going to do for me?"

"The mask helps guide the healing by pressing on the scars. This limits the blood flow and the scars can't grow. It's based on some recent studies. You'll look good as new."

"I expected nothing less, but is this necessary?"

"Consider it an insurance policy. Try it on for size."

The president's pale legs hung over the side of the examining table.

Dr. Labatelli held the see-through mask up to Fromm's face, checking to see if it would fit over the healing tissues. "Here goes."

Fromm clamped his eyes shut, girding himself for a stab of pain. He felt the cool acrylic slip over his raw face. It was painful,

246

in an exquisite sort of way. Each twinge reminded him how lucky he was to be alive, how lucky he was to have this second chance. The more it hurt, the more aroused he got.

With the mask fully seated, Dr. Labatelli stood back and admired the handiwork. Time had just been reversed, the clock turned back. He was staring at the Aldous Fromm of old. The features were perfect right down to the ruddy complexion. In a few weeks, the skin would heal without telltale scars or marks.

The doctor reached for an oversized chrome-handled mirror.

Fromm drew-up the mirror, not certain he wanted to look. What if he was horrified? What if he looked so bad Labatelli had to repeat all those surgeries? The prospect of more surgery made him queasy.

"When's the next audition for the lead in 'Phantom?'"

"Sorry, but you're too handsome."

With the mirror teetering in front of him, Aldous Fromm searched the doctor's eyes for a flicker of weakness. He saw none. Convinced the doctor was pleased, Fromm forced his eyes to look at the silver-backed glass.

Full head.

Lips.

Eyes.

He touched his cheeks.

He was stunned at how good he looked. "Ouch. It hurts when I smile."

"That will stop in a few days."

Like a savvy sports announcer who knows not to talk when the final out of the World Series has been made, the doctor made no comments. For Fromm, the shock of seeing himself after all those surgeries and bandages and salves and intravenous drips was overwhelming.

He lowered the mirror with a look of wonder. "Never in a million years did I think this was possible. I thank you from the bottom of my heart."

"It was a team effort, sir."

"The good ones all say that. Take credit for patching this old geezer back together, son. When do you think I'll be out of here?"

"You still need time to heal, to gain back your strength. It'll be over faster than you think."

"My first act when I return to Washington is to get Congress to award you the nation's highest honor for achievement. You, the Wright Brothers, Thomas Edison, DeBakey, you're America's gifts to the world."

46

Carly raced from the Medical Examiner's Office in a panic. Why hadn't Willie given her more time? She was expected at the Waldorf Astoria in three hours and her only black dress was four years old and out of style. It would have to do. Then she remembered Chantel's, the women's boutique on Lexington a few blocks north of Hunter College.

Standing in front of the three-paneled mirror while the seamstress pinned the hem, Carly frowned. "This isn't me."

The blond-streaked shop owner stood admiringly to the side. In her strong French accent, she tried to assuage Carly's fears by cupping her hands under her own breasts.

"Darling," said Chantel DuPaix, "I paid plenty for these. I flaunt them every chance I get. *N'est pas?* Yours are exquisite. I hate you because they are real. Don't be afraid to show them to the world. I do."

"But I'm a doctor."

"You look *fantastique.*"

Chantel patted herself under her chin as she spoke, Carly had seen other women do the same to keep their jowls from sinking.

"Darling, you must be daring. With that dress and your body, you promenade into that ballroom like a princess. Men love beautiful women who are strong-willed and talented, and the fact that you cut-up bodies for a living is a plus."

Carly scrutinized Chantel's flawless skin, red lips, and dazzling eyes. No matter what was real on her body and what wasn't, Chantel was one voluptuous package that any man would love to unwrap.

"You always know how to look, Chantel."

"It's my business to look good, but I'm a fake from top to bottom. Even my teeth. You are the real thing. When Chantel tells you that you're beautiful, you are beautiful. Tonight belongs to you, Dr. Carly Mason. I feel it in my bones."

*   *   *

With her new dress dangling in a garment bag from her index finger, Carly tackled the Medeco locks on her apartment door. What followed was Carly's version of "Supermarket Sweepstakes." In a flurry of arms and legs and makeup and shoes and switching handbags, Carly got ready for the fancy shindig.

She was out the door and waiting for the elevator when she heard the muted ringing of her phone. She was not about to unlock the door and answer it. By the time she hit the lobby, a brief message had been recorded.

"We need to talk."

When Carly heard this message later that evening, she would tremble.

*   *   *

Carly emerged from the yellow cab amidst a throng of perfect faces and perfect bodies traipsing into the Waldorf. Inside, she paused at the entrance to the gold gilded ballroom. In all the rush, she didn't stop to consider if she'd know anyone. She hated attending affairs unescorted. Despite Chantel's assurances, Carly was at ease meeting strangers on the autopsy table, not at gala events.

Carly drifted toward a tuxedoed maître d' standing in front of Louis XIV marble-topped table. An ocean of place cards was spread across it. She was about to give her name when a man, two inches shorter than she was, seized her arm.

"Dr. Mason? We've never met before."

"And you are?"

"Here to escort you to your seat."

The man wore a thick gold bracelet around his wrist, had a smoker's voice, and greased-back hair.

"I'll be able to find my own seat, thank you."

"My boss is expecting you. Cut me some slack and make it easy, okay?"

"Who's your boss?"

"That's the surprise. Shall we?"

He looped his arm through hers. What was she to do? With a thousand people in the room, her safety was not at stake. Why not play the game? They threaded their way through tables set for ten to get to the front of the room.

"I'm not going up there. Willie told me about a dais. I thought he meant a first-row table, not something in front of a thousand people."

"I don't know any Willie, but that's where you're sitting."

He pulled out the gold-gilded seat for Carly before excusing himself.

From the raised seat, Carly absorbed the room. Glittering crystal, shiny brass sconces, and an army of servers poised to cater to men and women decked to the nines. Carly glanced to her right and nodded to the head of the Health and Hospitals Corporation, the head of the Police Department, and the rotund Superintendent of Education. Other notables were to her left. The chair next to hers remained empty.

The mayor tapped the microphone then raised his hand for silence. When the room erupted into a rolling applause, he turned into Rocky Balboa doing a victory lap around the ring with his hands clasped over his head. Right before he introduced the guest of honor, the mayor winked at Carly. She had met him the night she paid a condolence call to Jonah Schoonover's wife. That night, the mayor had been there, telling everyone what a great dentist and friend Jonah had been.

Carly barely heard the mayor say, "...a man who has left an indelible mark on this great city, and who has gone on to conquer even greater vistas. By all accounts, he will be known as the greatest builder who ever lived. It is a privilege and honor to introduce our man of the night, Mr. Jeremy Steel."

The rest of the evening became a blur.

47

Jack was staring out the window of their new quarters. Like everyone else working at Steel City, Jack and Link had been assigned beds in an open bunk that slept a dozen men. As high-tech and modern as Steel City was, the workers' parts were little more than crude shantytowns. No one complained because they were warm when they were supposed to be warm, cool when they were supposed to be cool, and dry during the rainy season which was longer each year. With indoor plumbing and company stores, they had what they needed. What they didn't have, they didn't need.

"How long you been up?" Link asked in a hush, fearful of waking the others.

Jack took a last drag on a cigarette. "Mama always said I got rooster blood in me," he said without turning. Smoke escaped his nostrils in two steady streams. "Slim left already. Whatever they got him doing starts mighty early."

After spending a couple of days together, Jack knew Link was a slow starter. That was all right, it gave him more time to think. At quiet moments like these, Jack thought about his Mary. Good Lord, he hoped she was at peace now. The end had been terrible. The big C had spread from her colon into her liver and pancreas.

When it got to her bones, she begged to be treated with the dignity given to any farm animal. But Jack couldn't shoot her; he was no Kervorkian. He watched her suffer 'til her last breath.

Jack lit another butt. When Link appeared at his side, they headed for the dispatch office.

"Here are your papers and directions to Steel Metropolis. Your rig's already loaded."

The man returned to his paperwork.

"What're we carrying?" Link asked.

The foreman gave a dirty look. "Does it really matter, cowboy? Be grateful you got this job. Here's the last advice I'm gonna give you: if you make it on time and behave yourself when you get there, we'll load you up again tomorrow. Got that?"

"Loud and clear."

Outside Jack grabbed Link's arm. "He was only doing his job."

"I've met dispatchers like that one before. They're all condescending bastards who think they're doing you a favor giving out work. I don't cotton to attitude from no one."

"Be grateful he's giving us work."

Link drew in a long breath. This was a side of him, Jack had never seen.

"Seems we got a job to do," Jack said. "Now you going to Steel Metropolis or do I have to drive *Ol' Betsy* myself?"

*   *   *

That morning, Carly floated into Willie's office. "I got a great idea about the San Martini case last night," Carly said.

"What's on your face?"

She ran her fingers across her mouth. "I had a dry bagel. No creamed cheese. Is it off?"

"Nope, it's still on," Willie said, in a singsong voice.

She grabbed a compact case from her purse. "There's nothing there, Willie. What are you talking about?"

"It's not *what*, it's *who*? You've got Jeremy Steel all *over* your face."

Crimson would not do justice to Carly's color. "How'd you know?"

Willie thrust the NY Post in her hands. She read the headline:

NYC Doc Bewitches
Steel Magnate

The phone rang.

Willie nodded to the paper spread between her hands. "I've got connections at the paper. Want a dozen glossies?"

"Get real." Her eye lingered over the picture of her and Jeremy. Willie crooned. "It's lover boy."

"Enough of the games. Who is it, really?"

Willie feigned hurt feelings. Then, in his best Stan Laurel voice, said, "The gentleman didn't say."

Carly tried not to run to Willie's office. If Jeremy Steel could learn to wait for her, she might have a chance. By her own estimate, she should have made him wait longer, but she *was* eager. She turned her back away from Willie. Before she could say, "Hello," a strange voice spoke in a whisper. "Did you get my message last night?"

It wasn't Jeremy Steel.

"I did get a message last night, but I wasn't sure who it was."

"Think...as in past tense."

More than anything, Carly wanted the future to unfurl. She didn't want the past to come crashing down on her. "Let's keep the past buried. I've moved on."

"So have I, but now we can't."

"Is this about lawyer who came to me? Lex Prescott?"

"He's not one of them."

"Are you certain?"

Conner didn't answer right away. "Yes. His kid got into a jam. I helped him out. That's all. If you're thinking I'm still with them, you're wrong. A lot has happened since I left."

"For me, too."

"Do you think about them anymore? You know, the green-shirts? The Institute?"

"Some. But I stopped after Aurum was killed in the president's helicopter crash."

"I bet you still look over your shoulder, from time to time, don't you?"

"How did you know?"

"That's why I've got to meet with you. Name the place."

48

Jack and Link were each lost in their thoughts as they passed vineyards brimming with ripened wine grapes. Ever since the hole in the ozone layer had widened, the rich Maple Leaf soil had turned even richer than at any other time in the last five billion years. Wheat fields blossomed with bumper crops. Canola and barley plants were colossal. Once barren plains were now transected into rows of orange and grapefruit trees, and orchards filled with mangoes and persimmons and guava. Canada had become the world's garden.

Bounty had its price. Once pristine roadsides were now blemished with the campfires of migrants hoping to find work. These itinerants offered their backs and their souls to be part of the agricultural empire blossoming all around them. They would do anything for work. Anything for food. Anything so long as they didn't have to return to their arid homesteads in America.

"I heard so many are coming in, they're settin' up refugee camps," Link said, covering the brake in case an unseen child darted into the road.

"It's still better than what we got home, that's for sure."

"Get no argument there. Say, wonder where Slim went so early?"

*　　　　　*　　　　　*

Slim struggled through a second set of fifty pushups. His sweat mixed with soot kicked up from the ground to form an itchy crust. It itched so bad he wanted to rip his skin off, but he couldn't stop pumping up and down. If he did, the consequences would be more extreme than what was ailing him at the moment.

Each man counted for himself. When they hit the fiftieth, most collapsed. Their arms seared from the lactic acid build-up, their shoulders ached. They were miserable.

The leader, who they had come to dread, stood on a wooden box, legs astride and hands clasped behind him. The more the men grunted and groaned, the more he reveled in their pain. Their pain was irrelevant. His job was to make certain they were ready. And they would be.

"Two miles in full gear, and then down to the shooting range for an hour."

The leader scanned the so-called recruits. When he appeared distracted, Slim seized an opportunity. "Who does that bastard think he is? He can't even speak American proper-like," he murmured quietly to his neighbor who could do the push-ups in half the time it took Slim.

His compatriot commiserated. "I agree. I'm ready to shoot the sonofabitch. Why are they making us do this?"

Slim didn't get a chance to answer. He hadn't seen the feared leader rotate their way and point at them.

"You two take an extra mile, now."

Slim and his sidekick bolted knowing what happened to those who didn't jump quickly enough when the leader said, "Jump."

Once out of earshot Slim muttered, "See what I mean? The fucker thinks he's some kind of general in the fucking Army. He treats us like soldiers, not farmers." He wheezed; his body ached.

"We *are* in some kind of army. They just don't call it that," said the other man.

While Slim and his friend covered the trails in full gear, the leader assessed what had been accomplished over the last few weeks. He would never say so in so many words, but he was pleased with the headway these rubes were making. They would shine when the time came. His video/wristwatch beeped.

"Gadol, here," answered the former Israeli Army commandant into the small screen on his arm. A veteran of the '67 War and the Yom Kippur War, Zvi Gadol was one of the world's best instructors of troops. Gadol and his band of rebels catered to exotic tastes. They made lethal weapons out of the drug cartel's foot soldiers in the Colombian jungles; they gave refresher courses to Fidel Castro's bodyguards. *Both* sides of the never-ending Ethiopian civil war paid Gadol to train their troops. It was one of Gadol's best that went on to head the winning insurgent army fighting to free Liberia. Bosnia. Chechnya. Albania. Kosovo. Kashmir. East Timor. His résumé echoed past hot spots.

"How much longer?"

"Tell your boss that Gadol *always* delivers. He does not have to check up on me...ever again."

Gadol disconnected the call before another idiotic question could be asked. When the time came, the world would know how Zvi Gadol transformed these bumpkin farmers into a skilled fighting machine. He would become a media darling, a superstar, with a price tag to match.

49

Willie was reading Cindy Adams's gossip column when Carly returned from her phone call with Conner Masterson. "How come you never told me about old blue eyes?"

"They're hazel, and I never met him before last night," she answered, trying to puzzle out why Conner Masterson had called her after all this time.

"So?"

"What?"

"Must've been some night. I can understand if you don't want to talk about it. Say the word and I'll button up."

"There's nothing to tell. We spoke non-stop for two hours, and then he whisked me home to my castle in his chauffeured limousine. Sure beats the subway."

"And then?"

"You gloating pervert. Nothing happened. He walked me to the door, shook my hand, and left. End of story."

"No wet-lipped kiss? No body hug? No promises of riches and homes on the Riviera?"

She tapped his forehead. "Earth to Willie. We're talking Jeremy Steel here. You know, the Jeremy Steel who could have any woman in the Western hemisphere. He's not interested in me. He was just being a gentleman."

"So it was no big deal, right?"

"Nothing at all. Now leave me alone."

"I will," a sly smile crept across his whiskered face, "after you tell me when the next date is."

"Tonight. Are you satisfied now?" she asked.

"Couldn't be better," he answered.

"Now I have a question for you. How did the invitation come to you in the first place? After all, it was addressed to me."

"Would you have gone knowing it was some sort of mayoral function?"

"I would've tossed it."

"That's why it came to me. Obviously, the guest of honor was interested in meeting you."

"He could've called."

"That's not how the rich and famous work."

"I wouldn't know."

"Now you do," Willie said, and added, "you know you never told me what your great idea was about."

"Are we finished talking about Jeremy Steel?" she asked.

Willie genuflected. "Cross my heart and hope to...," he looked around the morgue and gulped, "die. Now what was it, again?"

"The obvious. It was right in front of our eyes and we missed it."

"You mean at San Martini's office? LeShana fingerprinted everything but the water bugs."

"Think harder, Willie. What did we miss?"

Willie scratched his head.

"Try his appointment book?" she said.

"LeShana did look for it. There wasn't any. It must have been destroyed in the fire."

Carly strolled to Willie's desk, and slid her elbow on top of the 17" monitor. She stood there without speaking.

"What?" Willie asked, trying to get onboard her train of thought.

"What do you see?"

"Your elbow on my computer monitor."

Carly was all smiles now. "Now we're getting somewhere."

Willie was all disbelief. "You mean...?"

"Exactly. It was right in front of your nose the whole time."

"The broken monitor! He made all his appointments on the computer." Then he frowned. "But the computers were destroyed, too."

She tapped her forehead. "Think backup tapes."

"What's the chance of him keeping them at home?"

"If I know my man, I'd say they were pretty good."

Willie turned when the door swung open. "What's she doing here?"

LeShana waltzed in waving a paper.

"Is that the court order?" Carly asked.

"Do peaches get ripe? If there's a backup tape at Rocco San Martini's house, we'll find it."

50

O*l' Betsy* made Steel Metropolis by midday. At the entrance to
the receiving dock, they waited for the guards to pull back
the metal hurricane gates. That didn't happen. Instead the guard
sauntered over to them, lifted his reflective sunglasses, and jerked
his thumb in the air.

"What gives?"

Jack understood. "He wants us out of the cab."

While Jack hopped out, Link glared at the guard. The man
stepped closer, resting his hand on his holstered gun. The guard
jerked his thumb again.

This time, Link eased open *Ol' Betsy*'s door and slid down the
steps. He was brushed back by the guard.

"Hey, where you going?" Link asked.

The guard got behind the controls. "You did your job, now it's
my turn, cowboy."

Link trotted after *Ol' Betsy* until a second guard stopped him at
the gate. He saw his lady disappear behind a long metal-sided
building, and he cringed hearing her brake to a screeching halt.
"Why couldn't I take her around? That guy doesn't know how to
treat her."

"It's procedure. The smart ones leave their rigs at the gate and don't ask any questions. You're new. You'll get the hang of it."

"You're talking about driving 'round the corner! What's the big deal?"

The second guard shrugged. "I've worked here two years and I've never been there myself. This is farthest I've ever gotten."

Jack piped in for the first time. "That's crazy."

"No argument from me, but that's the way it is. So why don't you let me do my job and you can do yours? We'll unload her and fill her up for the return trip."

"And what are we supposed to be doing in the meantime?"

"Visit *Pinky's Place*. That's were everybody goes."

*   *   *

Chrissy San Martini opened the door wearing a Nike sweat suit with a black ribbon pinned to the collar. She had met both Carly and LeShana during the preliminary investigation into her husband's death.

"Did they find out who did it?" she asked, the door half-open.

"We're still working on it," answered LeShana, "that's why we're here. May we come inside? There's something we need to ask you."

Seated in the living room, Carly explained. "We know that your husband used computers in his business."

"He was one of the first."

LeShana leaned forward. "What we're getting at, Mrs. San Martini, is that we need to know if your husband kept copies of his office records here? When we first searched the den and his desk, we were looking for clues about his death, nothing about how he ran his practice."

"You're treating me like I'm some sort of a porcelain doll. I can assure you I'm a strong woman. Now what is it, exactly, that you want?"

Carly answered. "Did your husband keep any diskettes from his office here? We're looking for his appointment book and financial records. If not, they may have been destroyed in the fire."

"I know for a fact there were no diskettes from the office here."

LeShana grimaced. "So much for him being fastidious about his computers."

"It doesn't make sense."

Chrissy ambled to the fireplace mantel. She picked up a silver-framed picture of her husband standing in the middle of a fast-running river. He was wearing hip-waders, a green canvas flak jacket with a dozen pockets for a dozen gadgets, and a white base-ball-style hat with Painters Lodge printed on it. Fly lures hung from the hat. In one hand he held a fishing pole, in the other, an eleven-pound Coho salmon.

She seemed lost in her memories. Then she turned to Carly and LeShana. "You mean the tapes?"

Carly's heart skipped a beat. "Did he bring one home every night? Where did he keep them?"

"Rocco was a nut about those tapes. He had a safe lowered into the cement when they were pouring the foundation. We keep a rug over it. It's fireproof and all that. Besides the daily tapes, Rocco had monthly and quarterly ones, too, just in case he needed them for some reason."

Seconds later, Chrissy returned holding eight micro cassettes.

Carly cradled them to her chest.

"What are you looking for?"

"Anything that can help figure out who the mystery patients were. The appointment schedule, financial records, patient names, any clue that will get us one step closer to solving your husband's murder."

5 1

Pinky's Place was like any modern frontier saloon in the movies. A computerized upright played current CDs while a rotating strobe cast hues of red, green, amber, and blue on topless dancing girls clad only in garter belts and fishnet stockings. The dancers slithered snake-like around poles planted at the edge of a wooden stage, close to the customers. There was a wall of odd-shaped bottles filled with a rainbow variety of liqueurs and clear high-priced vodkas. A black-lettered sign hung on a brass-linked chain: "There's No Place Like Home, Toto."

Jack and Link sashayed up to the mahogany bar and rested their boots on the brass foot railing. They waved for two beers. They leaned their backs to the bar to watch a large-breasted woman grind across the stage, stopping each time a patron waved a dollar bill at her. She had smeared a sticky substance on her skin and the money stuck to her like Velcro patches on a wall.

Pinky Struthers, who was the sole owner of the saloon, and also its bartender, raconteur, local historian, and amateur psychologist, slapped down two beers. "Where you fellas hail from?"

"I'm from Tuscaloosa. Jack, here, he's from Kansas."

"Well, well, a pair of home boys. My name's Pinky Struthers, I'm from Council Bluffs."

Pinky sported a large walrus mustache and an ample midriff under a soiled apron. He wiped his hands on his apron before grasping theirs.

Jack drew a long one from the chilled mug, wiped his mouth with the back of his hand, and then asked, "Been here long?"

"Since the beginning."

Pinky's tone had the ring of an intergalactic barkeep serving Neptunium mixers to soldiers from the Dark Side.

"The beginning of what?" Link asked.

"Steel Metropolis and Steel City. No reason to be up in these parts 'fore them."

Jack took another long swallow. "And now everything is peachy keen. Right?".

"Damn straight it is. Jeremy Steel, you heard of him, well he took himself a big chance building here. Now he's cashing in…big time. He goes and builds cities smack in the middle of Nowheresville, and goddamnit, if the whole country doesn't get fired up and take to them."

"I'm no economist," Jack accentuated the "e" in economist, dragging the sound out like it had a life of its own, "but Canada's been guns o' blasting ever since the damn weather turned. Your Jeremy Steel had nothing to do with that. Shit, any place that could grow corn nine feet high and have three crops of wheat a year can't help but being major successful. It just don't seem right that we Americans have to buy food from this here country and ship it back to the States. Ain't right at all."

"Maybe so, but you looked around? This place sure beats home."

Pinky refilled their mugs.

Jack wasn't convinced. "Soil's richer than anything I ever seen. The good Lord did that too, not Jeremy Steel."

"Don't pay to have sour grapes. Steel's the one who had the vision and did something about it. Give him credit for seeing the future."

"Even so these yokels don't have a clue about farming. They still need our American know-how to do it right."

"I'd watch what you say around here. These people are mighty proud now that they can go head-to-head with them Japs and the European Common Market. Shit....Canada's a world player, now. A powerhouse when it comes to big boys. Right or wrong, to a man, they believe it never would've happened without Jeremy Steel."

Jack drained his mug, and waved off a third refill. "What's with the secret stuff? We delivered our load like we were told and them guards...."

Before Jack could finish, two uniformed men walked through the swinging doors and sat down within earshot. The color drained from Pinky's face. He leaned closer and spoke in whispered tones.

"Hush up with them here. Don't ask me any more questions. We'll all stay healthy that way. Got it?"

Pinky straightened up, and in a contrived voice, addressed Link and Jack. "Can I get you fellas another round?"

Link, who had been staring at the gyrating girls, grunted.

Jack threw a twenty-dollar bill on the counter. "Nice meetin' ya," he said, and nudged Link toward the door.

Pinky pushed the bill back. "They're on me, friend. We don't take that kind of money anymore. Ain't worth the paper it's printed on. Ask your foreman for Steel Company script or Canadian money. They're the only legal tender we accept since the American dollar went into the toilet."

Everyone within earshot broke out into raucous laughter. What could they expect from tinhorns?

Aldous Fromm on Road to Recovery

WHITE HOUSE. (Washington Post). Still wrapped in shrouds of seclusion, physicians for Aldous Fromm indicate that the president, who has been on a medical leave in order to repair the severe damage from his near-fatal helicopter accident, is making excellent progress.

Doctors will not speculate as to how much longer it will take for the president to mend well enough to return to office.

Coulter Bell, acting-president Greeley's press secretary, has indicated that President Fromm will not return anytime soon. When asked how Kip Greeley was holding up, Mr. Bell grinned and said, "Carrying out the duties of the most demanding job in the world, would tax the most seasoned of politicians. Given the tragic circumstances of how he assumed the office, the American people can be proud of how Mr. Greeley has risen to the occasion."

52

Coulter Bell rapped on the door and waited. He thought he heard a faint acknowledgment from the other side, so he squeezed open the door. Kip Greeley was peering over a mountain of papers.

"Excuse me, Mr. President," Coulter said, "we've got some problems that can't wait for Aldous's return."

It was apparent from the moment he received that fateful call that Kip Greeley needed Coulter Bell. Coulter Bell was a Washington insider. He knew the ropes. He knew when to press hard and when to lay back. He knew whom to corner in order to squeeze an extra line or two into a new piece of legislation. In short, Coulter Bell became Kip Greeley's eyes, his ears, and his right hand. He became to Kip Greeley what Lute Aurum had been to Fromm.

The acting president tossed his pen down, leaned back and cupped his hands behind his head. "With you around, I could get used to this."

"You may not want to after you hear about the Ways and Means report. It seems like every actuary in the world blew their predictions as to when the Social Security fund would dry up."

Kip Greeley uncupped his hands and hunched over the desk. "Between using the tax surplus and raising the retirement age to sixty-eight, I thought we bought fifty years, if not more. Are you telling me otherwise?"

"It's the baby boomers, again. Seems they took great advantage of all the plans put into effect through the years. There's too many retiring all at once, something like ten to fifteen thousand each day. They're breaking the system."

"We're fucked."

"Exactly, sir."

"Could we lower monthly benefits?"

"Political suicide. We'd never get the votes from Capitol Hill."

"Then we'll raise the retirement age again. Make them work longer. Not everyone can afford to retire early...can they?"

"No, sir, but you'll make your mark in history along with George Washington."

"We can't be mentioned in the same breath."

"You can, if you are the only two presidents involved in a revolution. In his case, it created the country."

"And in my case, we'll be doomed."

"You're a quick study, Mr. President."

Kip Greeley trudged to the window and peered out at two gardeners struggling to salvage the rose bushes withering from the oppressive heat. He swayed back and forth, the death knell of the Social Security system ringing in his ears. Fromm's accident couldn't have come at a worse time. "How much time have we got?"

"Two months before the well goes dry."

"How could we have made such a gross miscalculation?"

"We have worse problems than that, sir."

Greeley's masseter muscles flexed. "Do you get pleasure dishing out bad news in dribs and drabs. Like it or not, you're stuck with me for a few more weeks. Stop dancing around and tell me everything. What else is wrong?"

"The government's running out of money. We can't cover Friday's payroll checks."

"Use the surplus funds."

Coulter expected that answer, and was prepared with his response. "No can do! The Burns-Trazewski Amendment forbids borrowing money to pay for social programs. We're bankrupt, sir."

Greeley sat stunned. He expected a frontal assault, but not an avalanche of problems that would smother the country. Why didn't he listen to his mother and become a doctor? "Is there any good news?"

Coulter shook his head. "There are reports of unrest in the migrant camps."

Greeley bit his lip, tasting the blood. "Aren't they getting enough relief?"

"The farm subsidies have run out."

If their minds were meat grinders, they were churning out vexing answers by the pound.

"What if....?" Kip Greeley caught himself and swallowed a bad idea. "I guess not."

Coulter Bell had been standing the entire time, he slipped into a chair. "May I be frank, sir?"

"Haven't you been up until now?"

"Yes, but what I'm about to say may upset you."

"Let me ask you this, what would Aldous Fromm do?"

"That's what I was going to suggest, sir."

"Out with it, man, what would a real president do?"

"Start a war."

Silo Gas Buildup
May Cause Explosions

ALBANY. (The Union). Perpetual dry weather is posing a new danger to farmers this fall: "silo gas."

The constant drought does not permit crops to achieve full size. Nitrates that plants usually convert to proteins for grain formation have been found to accumulate in plant stems. This causes the corn and hay stored in silos to ferment at a quicker rate, producing more nitrogen dioxide.

When inhaled, nitrogen dioxide, or "silo gas," can dissolve the moisture in the lungs and form nitric acid. The acid burns the lungs, causing them to fill with fluid. When this happens, death can occur in minutes.

Farmers are warned to watch for bleach-like odors and yellowish-brown fumes, both signs of "silo gas." Scientists at Cornell University urge farmers to enter a silo during fermentation only after venting the silo for thirty minutes with a powerful air blower.

53

D r. Labatelli assessed Aldous Fromm's progress. Each day since the Code Blue, the president gained strength. His vital signs were strong, his appetite increasing. He had moments of humor, and flashed a rare display or two of anger. His mental scars were receding, and he grew more alert as he needed less medication. As far as Labatelli was concerned, his baby-sitting days were winding down. In a day or so, he'd risk leaving the clinic for a few hours.

"Are you getting used to the mask?" he asked the president.

"Until it itches and then it drives me mad."

Labatelli studied the healing wounds through the clear plastic.

"It's doing what we want. There's no sign of scarring or necrosis."

"I'd expect no less. When will my voice return? It sounds scratchy."

"There was damage to your vocal chords. I'm afraid this is the best it's going to get."

"Actually, I rather like it. The nurses say I sound sexy."

          *   *   *

Carly and LeShana met at Paul Trevino's office. Paul ran Professional Audio Studio. He was the expert the police used for everything from James Bond surveillance equipment to filtering

274

out background noises on tape-recorded messages. Paul's credentials read like a Who's Who in spy work. He had played a role in nailing John Gotti, Jr.; he was instrumental in getting the scamming radio announcer, Sonny Block, arrested. Without Paul, the World Trade bombers would have gone free. He determined that the FBI did not fire the first shot at the Branch Davidians in Waco. In short, he knew his work.

"Any luck?" Carly asked.

LeShana sat alongside Paul, who was working in front of a twenty-inch monitor. "Grab a chair. We need your help."

Carly first met Paul when Willie Robinson discovered that Jonah Schoonover's death was anything but a suicide. Jonah's killer left no telltale clues. They hoped to match his/her voiceprints on Jonah's digitized answering service. That's where Paul came in. He was the forensic audio specialist for the NYPD.

At first, Conner Masterson was the prime suspect. Carly prayed they were wrong. In the end, the closest voice match belonged to Lute Aurum, but not enough spikes lined up to prove it was him beyond a doubt. Nothing could be done without proof. Carly could never get over the coincidence: Jonah died the day Aurum showed up at her first "abuse" lecture. This was also the day Aldous Fromm declared for the presidency. Carly did not believe in coincidences...or serendipity.

That was four years ago.

Now Aurum was dead.

         *   *   *

"Once Softdent™ sent me their read-only software, it was easy to download everything off of Dr. San Martini's tape so we could see it."

"So who was the patient in the chair?" Carly looked at them, rather than at the monitor.

"That's why you're here," LeShana said, "we don't understand the dental jargon."

"Scoot over."

After a few keystrokes, Carly opened up the daily scheduler and brought up November 19, the day of the bomb blast. They gawked at the screen.

Carly turned to Paul. "Can we print this?" Seconds later, the HP laser printer spit out the day sheet. "Here it is, plain as day: Mr. X, sixteen time slots."

"Translation, please," said LeShana.

"Each time slot is fifteen minutes. Mr. X had a four-hour appointment. And look at this," Carly waved the paper in front of them, "see the hygienist's column?"

"Why is it blocked out?"

"Because Dr. San Martini closed his office to all other patients, except Mr. X."

"Then who were the other two?" LeShana asked.

Carly stood and paced. "Bodyguards? You know how crooked Prince Charles's teeth are? Maybe it's him?"

"And no one in the royal family is searching for the good prince? Try again, child."

"Move over, Paul."

"What are you doing?" LeShana asked.

Carly tapped some keys and another screen came up. She reached for the phone. "May I?"

"Who you calling, child?"

Carly pointed to the screen. "It's common to confirm appointments. They called Mr. X to make certain he would be there."

"Damn, mine doesn't. Do all dentists do that?"

"Only the obsessive compulsive ones...,which means most call. If yours doesn't, it's time to get a more anally-fixated dentist. Anal compulsives are the crème de la crème of dentistry."

"If you ask me, you're all nut jobs."

Carly smiled. "That, too."

54

Aldous Fromm's eyes fluttered open. He heard the comforting background gurgles and bleeps and the whirs of machines kicking on and off. These umbilical cords monitored his every breath, his blood pressure, his temperature, his cardiac rhythms; they measured every drop of urine he peed. The habitual sounds made him feel safe and secure.

For a moment, Aldous Fromm was at peace. Then a sixth sense jolted him to the awareness that he wasn't alone. He tried to turn his head to see if anyone was there, but a pain lanced through his neck like a hot knife. He touched a pulsating point on his temple to will the ache away, forgetting he was wearing the healing-mask. His fingernail made a dull sound on the acrylic.

"They said I could stay for a few minutes."

Hearing the familiar voice, Fromm relaxed his head back into the pillow. He shifted until he found a comfortable spot.

Aldous reached for his press secretary's hand and asked, "How's he doing?"

Coulter leaned closer. "Who? Greeley? He's behaving."

"Bet the sonofabitch is loving every minute of this. In his wildest dreams, he could never see himself in the Oval Office."

"You better come back. He's getting too used to the place."

"Let him have his day. Pretty soon it's going to be over, and then where will he be? Turning pig shit into fuel?"

Coulter hesitated. He licked his lips as the president's eyelids pulsated, and then closed. The drugs were having their effect. He turned to leave.

"Not yet. You're the only one who's come to see me."

"They wouldn't let me before."

Fromm spoke with his eyes closed. "So Greeley likes the big chair, does he? What's he doing about the camp riots?"

"He's out of his league with things like that. He told the governor to handle it."

"The schmuck's like Dr. Doolittle. He's better off talking to the animals."

"Sir?"

"Spit it out, Coulter."

"Honey Fitzpatrick's got a call in to him. Should I say anything?"

"What could the big Canuck say that could ruin anything? Let it all play out."

"Should I call Jeremy, just to be on the safe side?"

"You'd think he would have called," he said, with more than a tinge of hurt. Then his voice grew stronger. "We don't want him to get too comfortable doing things on his own while I'm here convalescing. The man has to know he's never gonna run the show."

"That's a tall order when it comes to Jeremy Steel. If I may be candid, sir, I've never trusted him from the beginning."

"Neither have I, but that doesn't mean a thing. At the end of the day, Jeremy Steel will do our bidding."

"But a smart pawn can still get a king in checkmate," Coulter said.

Coulter made out a smile through the acrylic mask. "But a smarter king will always keep his pawns in place," Fromm said. "Steel's not half the trouble he appears to be, son."

Coulter knew better than to argue. What was the point? Always a role player, he was now a behind-the-scenes guy. Fromm relied on him, Greeley depended on him, and Steel confided in him, too. Who could doubt Coulter's star was rising?

Fromm's eyes fluttered shut.

Coulter turned to leave; there was more to his step than when he had come.

Fromm whispered. "What ever happened to that viper of Lute's?"

"I've been keeping it alive…for old time's sake. I think Lute would have liked that."

"You're a good man, Coulter Bell. A good man." Then Fromm dozed off.

55

By late afternoon, LeShana had exhausted every resource for finding out where Mr. X's phone number was located. "The only thing I discovered is that it was disconnected the day before the blast."

"Makes sense," Carly said, "they did it after the appointment was confirmed."

Paul added his two cents. "Can't a judge force the phone company to open its records."

"We did. The phone number belongs to a corporation registered in the Cayman Islands. Everything about it is off limits."

Carly shot back. "At least we know Mr. X was not in the Witness Protection Program or connected to any other government agency. He was probably some hotshot business man."

"Arab sheik is more like it," said Paul.

"So where does that leaves us?"

Carly and Paul looked at LeShana, and then said in the same breath, "Up shit's creek."

* * *

"Oh my god," Carly said when she turned into the oval courtyard thinking she had minutes to spare. Quick strides brought her to the driver's side of a block-long limousine. She rapped on the window to get the chauffeur's attention, then followed his index finger as he pointed to lobby. Carly dashed through the revolving door.

"I see him, Miguel," she said on the fly to the uniformed doorman.

Jeremy Steel was pacing the gray-flecked granite floor like an expectant father. He tapped his diamond-studded watch without a trace of being annoyed. "I was hoping to catch you so we could have drinks at the Terrace. The sunset is spectacular from there this time of year."

"If it's clear, you can see the Tappan Zee Bridge."

"You've been there? I was hoping you hadn't."

"Sorry. A date once had the romantic notion that if he took me there, he'd end up lucky."

"Did he?"

"You'll have to do him one better to find out for yourself. What's wrong?"

"You're feistier than I thought. I didn't expect that kind of talk from you."

"Just because my patients are dead, doesn't mean I am."

Carly headed toward the elevator. "By the way, where *are* you taking me? I need to know what to wear."

Jeremy grabbed her shoulder and spun her around. "How fast can you throw some clothes together?"

"Ten minutes, and where are we going?"

"Make it eight. The minutes count."

Jeremy made the necessary calls while Carly tossed whatever she thought she might need into a traveling bag. Every attempt to extract their destination failed. He was still mum when they crossed the George Washington Bridge into Jersey. By the time they rolled onto the less-than-picturesque Route 46, a highway dotted with auto body shops of all types, grease pits for quick lube jobs, stores for new tires, and the golden Midas Muffler sign next to the golden hamburger arches, she vacillated between piqued and pissed.

This part of Route 46 had as much appeal as a toxic waste dump.

"Nice place to take a date."

"I can't very well take you where past dates have tried to put the make on you, now can I? It's your fault. You challenged me to think of something different."

"Hoboken would have been better. What's in Lodi?" she asked, reading the green sign.

He patted her knee, and when she didn't move it away, left it there. "What's that saying? 'Essence of patience, tincture of time?'"

Patience was one thing; passing scenery with the appeal of searching through a rack of used dresses from Bangladesh was something quite different. Carly lowered the window and caught a glimpse of the autumn sun evaporating into a pallid ooze of gray and purple. Any hope of catching an early star was lost in the twinkling highway lights. So far, it was a shitty ride.

The plot thickened when they turned into Teterboro Airport.

"Is it correct to assume you have your own jet?"

"Jets…as in plural. It's the only way to travel when you have as many business ventures as I have. Time is money and waiting at commercial airports is a waste of both."

They coasted next to a sleek Gulfstream VI. "We don't have much time."

"For what?"

"Jeremy Steel's version of going to Oz."

"But where's my Toto?"

"I can't think of everything. You'll have to use your imagination for that one."

Carly closed her eyes, clicked her heels…and went for the ride of her life.

*   *   *

Their second run was identical to their first. Link and Jack planted themselves at *Pinky's Place* and were enjoying their drinks when guards appeared at the door. Hushed whispers turned to blank stares. No one liked the guards.

Jack and Link signaled that they were leaving, but Pinky avoided their nods.

"Did you get a load of how Pinky clammed up?" Link said outside the bar. "Wonder what they got over him?"

"It don't matter. Bullies are bullies no matter where they are."

Ol' Betsy was outside the fenced-in compound, pointed for the return run, loaded to the gills. A guard handed Link a manifest for Steel City.

"Who's got the keys for them mother locks you fellas clamped on my gal's rear end?"

"Guard at the other end. You asked the same friggin' question last time, Reb. I don't have to do this, but I'm gonna give you a bit of friendly advice."

Link yawned.

"I call them the *don'ts*. Don't ask any questions. Don't try to see what you're carrying. Don't do anything but what you're told to do. And don't be stupid. Have I made myself clear?"

Jack reached into his shirt pocket and popped a Camel into his mouth. "Got a *don't* for this, mister?"

"I got one more, but I'm not wasting it on smokes. Kill yourself if you want. There's plenty more waiting to take your place."

"I know we're new, but we're the best you got, mister. No need to lecture us about how to do our jobs," Link said.

The guard peered over the gold rim of his dark glasses. "Here's what I see: a middle-aged wannabe farmer who get can't a job anywhere else and a grease-slurping Rebel who's too stupid to know that being a smart-ass can shorten his life expectancy."

He tipped the bill of his cap with his revolver. "So here's the last *don't*, for your health's sake...and your partner's, too. Don't be a goddamned know-it-all smart ass. You'll be pushing up petunias faster than you can spell *fertilizer.*"

Link and Jack put twenty kilometers between themselves and Steel Metropolis before they spoke.

Link wrinkled his nose. "It's beginning to stink up here, and I don't mean no manure-smell, either."

"He was just doing his job."

"So was Hitler."

"I'd listen to him."

Link grunted, but didn't answer.

Jack's left arm shot across Link's chest.

"Watch it."

Jack braced his right hand against the dashboard as Link swerved to miss a red fox zipping across the road. *Ol' Betsy* teetered on her outside wheels, before settling back on the asphalt track.

"That was close," Link said. "Don't take much to tip over."

"Kinda puts the guard business into perspective, don't you say?"

Link became all business. Mandarin rays drenched lush vineyards in a golden bath. Twilight cast long shadows across the winding road making it difficult to see an oncoming steep grade. Link shifted into low gear.

Pinky's words started to play with his mind. Though he seemed not to listen, Link heard every word the guard had said.

All of a sudden, his stomach turned queasy and a sickening taste filled his mouth.

His heart froze when he jammed on the brakes.

They worked this time.

56

The glistening steel door was clamped tight and the jet taxied to takeoff. Carly sank into the plush seat covered in Moroccan leather and buckled her seat belt. "*Now* will you tell me where we're going?"

"For starters, Travis will take us to fifty-one thousand feet, above commercial flight paths. Then we'll cruise until I can make good on my promise…at least what I had hoped to share with you tonight."

"Secluded private dinners are one thing, but aren't you taking this a bit too far? There are other restaurants in New York besides The Terrace."

"Food is part of the agenda…but afterwards."

She scanned the cabin for a clue as the plane sped down the runway. She eyed a closed door. *Do airplanes have bedrooms?* "After what?"

With the plane leveling, Jeremy unbuckled his seat belt, eased his way to the polished cherry wood bar, and popped a vintage bottle of iced Dom Perignon.

Carly pressed her nose against the portal-shaped window. Nine miles above the earth, the brittle cold air was speckled with a spangle of lights. Some were bright, others faint. Some pulsed strong, most flickered.

Soon Carly watched the lip of the horizon turn a purplish red. She took the slender flute from Jeremy, clinked it against his, and then tipped the crystal. The amber liquid was cold and bubbly. She licked her lips. "You're going to pull this off, aren't you?"

"I'm glad you figured it out."

Careful not to tip her champagne, she angled her face against the window, looking westward. The wing grew more visible. The sky grew brighter. They were catching the sun.

"I thought it would take something special to get your attention."

"Are you that arrogant or just sure of yourself?"

As she spoke, she absorbed the cabin filled with antique furniture and Persian rugs.

"Only way to get things done," he answered.

Jeremy drained his glass.

With her face back against the window, Carly saw that the deep purple night had melted into the pastel blue of a sunny day.

Carly spun around. She tipped her glass toward him, finished her champagne, and said, "I don't care how many others you've pulled this stunt on, it's unbelievable. Thank you."

"I know you won't believe this, but you're the first."

"You're right," she said, throwing her head back, "I don't...but it sounds awfully good."

She loped back to her seat, "Why me?" She crossed her legs and leaned into him, "I don't get it."

"Straight?"

"I'm a big girl, I can take it."

He raised his right arm. "Here's the gospel. Rarely do I come across a woman as intelligent and beautiful as you. I've had my share of trophies glued to my arm. At best, any pleasure derived from those relationships was fleeting. They were more like

Christmas ornaments put on display once a year, only to be tucked in a box until the next season."

"Tucked in a box until a new one comes along. Good thing you're not a chauvinist."

He didn't miss a beat. "You're different."

"That's what they all say."

"You don't believe me?"

"Forgive me. It sounds great, has a nice ring to the ear…but it's a bit hard to believe."

"If you think it's easy for me to be this candid, you're wrong."

Normally Carly would have challenged his claim about being candid, but instead she asked, "One thing's been bothering me since the Waldorf. You made certain I'd be there by having Willie give me the invitation. Why?"

"I've followed your career ever since you started at the Medical Examiner's. I first saw your picture in the papers when you were working on the Happy Land Social Club fire."

"I had help."

He squeezed her hands. "You're selling yourself short. You're the type of woman who has no clue how beautiful she really is. From afar, I always thought you were a gem. Now that I'm getting to know you, you're even better than I imagined."

"You're glamorizing me for no reason. I'm like a million other young professionals trying to make ends meet. If I do get some press, it's because people are dying every day, and I help find out who they are. That doesn't make me very special."

"Listen to me, Carly Mason, I know from whence I speak. My first wife was an Olympic downhill skier before I met her. She loved the limelight until it went to her head. My second wife was a so-so model who forced me to buy her a part in a Broadway musical. You're different. You're a blue-chipper who doesn't have a clue."

She closed her eyes.

Why do they always sound so good...in the beginning?

Carly had never been a good judge of men. She had had her assortment of lovers and boyfriends through the years. The fact that they came in all shapes and sizes didn't matter to her. They started out nice. Pleasant. If she'd learned anything from the New York dating scene it was that "nice" and "pleasant" masked the kiss of the Death.

Carly found she could be "in like" with most of them, but never had been "in love" with any. Recently, two had touched her...only to clobber her in the end. One miscreant actually stole her ATM and PIN number, and cleaned all the cash out of her accounts. LeShana urged her to prosecute; testifying against him eased the pain. The second left her bed one Sunday morning only to jump into someone else's for a mid-afternoon romp and the crossword puzzle. It's not that she was a sore loser. She believed in being fair. Fair in this case was praying he'd have a perpetual chancre on the tip of his penis, kind of a keepsake of her eternal "like" for him.

Then there was Conner Masterson. "Oh my god."

"Are you all right? Can I get you something?"

She opened her eyes to measure Jeremy's concern. "I didn't mean to startle you, it's just that I remembered I was supposed to meet someone before you picked me up tonight. I forgot all about it."

"Thanks for the compliment!"

*   *   *

Conner was just about to call out Carly's name when he saw her tap a limousine window. He fell in step behind a Jamaican nurse wheeling a baby carriage. They strolled past the glass entrance to Carly's apartment building just long enough for

Conner to see her embrace Jeremy Steel. Conner fled and didn't stop until he reached Amsterdam Avenue.

"Are you okay, Mister?" Conner looked up to see a destitute man holding two black plastic bags filled to overflowing with soda cans. "You look like you've seen a ghost, mister."

Conner took the paper towel the man held up and wiped his face. "Worse."

The homeless man pointed to the center kiosk where Broadway and Amsterdam crossed at Seventy-second Street. "There's a cop over there."

Conner slipped into a breathing technique he had learned from an exit-counselor when he broke from the Institute. Ten...nine...eight...by the time he would get to "one" he would regain his composure. Conner knew that the deprogramming had saved his life. He didn't like to think what would have happened to him if the Cult Information Services had not shuttled him to Toronto for detoxification from Humanetics.

In the months that followed his treatment, Conner managed to avoid contact with anything and everything about Humanetics. Seeing Jeremy Steel brought back a panic that deep breathing didn't make go away.

                    *   *   *

Carly willed Conner from her mind as Jeremy refilled her champagne flute.

"Are you thinking about that missed appointment?" he asked.

"Long forgotten. I'm trying to figure out why we're still heading due west. You're not intending to catch six or seven sunrises along the way, are you?"

"Wouldn't that be a nice trick, but we'd run out of fuel by the next sunrise."

She tried to figure out where that would be, but couldn't. Then she grabbed his arm. "We're headed for Steel City, aren't we?"

"I'd like to show it to you. Do you mind?" Seeing her glow fade, he added, "I've already called Willie Robinson. He sends his regards and hopes you're having a good time."

"He said that?"

"If you don't know by now, let me explain one thing. I always get what I want."

Carly glanced at what she thought was the bedroom door, considered all that it meant, and wondered if Jeremy Steel would be able to make that statement in the morning?

57

Willie tossed LeShana a thick folder.

"What's this?" she asked.

"The final results on our mystery men. Maybe you can catch something we missed when we did the posts."

"This is one of those cases that needs a break out of left field, like a bank robber getting a parking ticket while he's in the bank. It'll be something stupid like that because three bodies parked in a midtown dental office are not going to go unclaimed forever. Something will pop up."

Expecting a break in the case was one thing, having a number of men—six blue-suited versions of granite blocks—barge into Willie's office was quite another. One approached Willie, nodded toward LeShana, and then flashed his credentials the way a pervert exposes himself...long enough for someone to zero in without really revealing anything. For all Willie knew, the metal shield might have been store bought or purchased over the Internet. He didn't know if he should laugh or cower.

LeShana knew the men were for real...and dangerous.

"Whatever it is you want, I'm sure you're in the wrong place," Willie said.

Grim-faced, one man passed Willie a set of papers.

"What are these?"

"A court order authorizing a release."

Willie brought the papers into focus. LeShana sidled next to him. When they finished, Willie looked from LeShana to the men. "I don't recognize the signature at the bottom."

"Judge Waldo McCoy, Chief Justice of the Southern District. He's authorized you to release the Rock Center bodies to us. Look at it this way, you were just relieved of three headaches."

*   *   *

Leaving the homeless man behind, Conner crossed to the west side of Broadway, repeating out loud, "Ten...nine...eight...." Sawyer Glenn, his exit-counselor, had predicted the day would come when something, or someone, would trigger a relapse in Conner. Seeing Carly with Jeremy Steel was just such a setback.

By the time Conner reached the curb, his clothes were drenched in sweat, his teeth were chattering from the chill, and fear wracked his body. Each number was meant to calm; he gasped for air.

Conner staggered against a wall. His body went from frost cold to boiling. He ripped his shirt off. He needed water. Conner ran into the corner Korean grocery store and poured a bottle of Poland Spring water over his head. He opened a second bottle and emptied it.

Then he blacked out.

Conner might have been out ten seconds. Twenty tops. The Korean grocer was jabbering away, ordering his wife to call 911, hacking at a block of ice with a pick. A chunk of ice was soothing to Conner.

Conner came to and waved off the protesting Samaritan. Sliding into an Oriental mode, Conner bowed and thanked him, bowed and thanked him, bowed a third time and was out the door.

He stopped to buy a shirt on Amsterdam Avenue, and then made his way to his room at the Wyndham Hotel. There, he filled an overnight bag and grabbed his passport.

"LaGuardia Airport," he told the cab driver.

*   *   *

"We could have done this over the phone," Sawyer Glenn said. "There was no reason to fly to Toronto."

"Maybe I missed the Four Seasons Hotel. It was my home for nearly a month, remember?"

"When people come here for exit-counseling, this is the last place they ever want to see again."

"Unless they freak out...like I did today."

It had been two years since Conner sought Sawyer Glenn's help. Then, Humanetics had stripped away every human defense from Conner. All he had left was a heartbeat and a functioning digestive system. Any independent thought brought more mental torture. That's why no participants in the Humanetics program challenged Aurum or any other messianic-led cult. Moonies, Branch Davidians, and members of the Universal Church of the Triumphant knew what was in store for them if they did.

Conner had paid the price for trying to call Carly. After his latest so-called timetracks were purged from his so-called defective system, he did menial work around Aurum's ranch. Most of the time, he cleaned toilets and collected horse manure. One time, after Bowden decided the Olympic-sized pool needed sprucing up, Conner scrubbed every square tile by hand for three weeks. Buck-naked.

"Shackle the brain, and the body will follow," was one of Aurum's mottos.

After a year of model behavior, Conner was allowed to enter the Institute as a janitor. At first, he went about his business cleaning the small rooms as new registrants rotated through Humanetics 101. In time, he graduated to cleaning the learning center, then the basement cells where the auditing took place. Even then, little of his past registered. He couldn't—wouldn't—remember what went on in those cells. The mind-bashing. The H-meter. None of it.

One day when he was swabbing out the kitchen garbage cans, a new Aurum green-shirt—a cook—sidled up next to him and whispered, "I can get you out of here."

Conner knew—only on a subconscious level—that such treasonous talk was a technique to catch an itinerant mind. It was a test he couldn't afford to fail. So without so much as a blink of the eye, he answered robotically, "I am not enturbulated. I am here to serve Humanetics."

Then the heavyset woman leaned closer. She cast furtive glances around to make certain no one was watching. "I'm Artie Montefusco's sister. Tell me what happened."

Hearing Artie's name was all Conner needed to break out of his deep trance. Artie's sister helped Conner escape the ranch by hiding him in a weekly food delivery truck that was secretly owned and operated by the Cult Information Network. Once Conner was away from the compound, the group arranged for him to be deprogrammed by Sawyer in Toronto. That was two years ago. Afterwards, Conner returned to Boston and got a Master's degree in psychology. Though he often thought about her and wanted to, he never called Carly...until now.

Four years after first meeting Carly, Conner described to Sawyer how his throat caught when he had glimpsed her hugging

Jeremy Steel. It brought back all the nightmares of the two years he spent being audited of his timetracks, the two years he had swabbed floors and washed toilets. The fact that the last two years were spent in Boston in relative calm had all but been erased when he blacked out on the Korean grocer's floor.

"You're sure it wasn't jealousy. I recall how special you thought she was."

"It was like I was back at the Institute the day Carly escaped. I could feel his snake around my neck and that hairy tarantula climbing up my leg at the same time. I couldn't breathe."

"Has it ever happened before? Since you left me two years ago?"

"That's why I ran up here. It was like an asthma attack with an epileptic chaser. I never want that to happen again."

"I'm surprised it hasn't happened sooner."

"Bowden St. Clair tried to contact me soon after I left, but I was stronger then. Everything you taught me was fresh in my mind. I was able to tell him where to go. Today? I wasn't expecting Steel. My guard was down."

"He didn't see or do anything to you, did he? For all you know, he was calling on Carly for personal reasons."

"Do you remember how I told you they had these one-way mirrors at the Institute? Steel visited—no, surveyed was more like it—the Institute for one day. Aurum wanted Steel to observe then-Governor Fromm being audited. Afterwards, Steel spent time checking out the registrants taking the routine course. Carly was there. I'm certain Steel saw her. Why now, after four years, does he show up on her doorstep?"

"For a date."

"She's not his type, and besides, he's certainly not hers."

"Like you are?"

"I didn't say that."

"You didn't have to, but enough of this, let's get to work. First of all, why didn't you say to yourself that you're not in the Institute and no one can hurt you?"

"It worked for a second, but seeing Steel with Carly, made no sense. Besides, I had to talk to her. With Steel there, I couldn't."

"Why did you want to see her?"

"To tell her she was in danger."

"From whom? Steel?"

"I dunno. Someone else, I think."

"Who told you Carly was in trouble?"

"I was contacted by one of the other green-shirts two days ago."

"To recruit you back into Humanetics?"

"No, to tell me Carly was in trouble."

"And you believed him? That's how clever they are. They'll use any trick to get you back. I'm surprised at you."

Conner grew agitated, his arms and legs moved about. "He didn't ask me to come back to Arizona. He told me to go to her, to tell her to be careful."

"And did you?"

"That's what I was trying to do when I saw Steel. That's when I freaked."

"Conner. Think about this rationally. You've had no contact with Humanetics for two years. Then out of the blue, someone calls to warn you about Carly. They know she's your Achilles heel."

"Then what was she doing with Steel?"

"You've blown this way out of proportion. Carly is safe, she's not in danger. It seems you're the one needing help."

Conner edged toward the door. He had been shredding a napkin in his lap and when he stood, the bits fell to the floor.

"You don't understand. They're out to get her. I have to warn her."

*   *   *

Later that same evening, about the time Carly and Jeremy Steel were headed for dinner after a grand tour of Steel City, Henri Plumme's phone rang.

"Meet me at the Melange Cafe. Midnight. It's about them murders," said the unidentified man's voice.

Click.

Henri Plumme considered the call. He had been summoned out of retirement to help solve the string of serial murders gripping Alberta Province. Getting a break after being on the case one day was beyond luck. But if that's what it took to get him back to his beloved fishing, he was all for it.

*   *   *

Though Steel City boasted the greatest technology in urban living, it was maintained and serviced by men and women living in quarters reminiscent of 19th century London. The Melange Cafe was their chipped-plate dining spot. Inspector Plumme rounded the corner and was confronted by blue and red flashing lights that cast tall shadows on unlit buildings. Police cars blocked the avenue and a flock of onlookers congregated in front of the blinking orange neon sign that read:

THE MELANGE CAFE

Plumme made his way through the swarm and showed his ID to a policeman barely old enough to shave. He angled toward a stretcher that two paramedics were navigating into the waiting ambulance. Plumme lifted the black tarp. To his trained eye, the victim was thirty or thirty-five. He had matted blond hair. Blood dripped from his mouth, the eyes still open.

"Plumme," was all he said to the man in charge, as if the world knew him by a single appellation, the way they knew Pelé or Madonna.

"It's another one of those murders," answered the man in charge.

"Are you certain?"

Without another word, the detective reached into his coat pocket and unfolded the neat corners of a stained handkerchief. With a delicacy reserved for removing a lady's undergarments, the detective peeled back the four corners.

Plumme knew this was another Pembina River killing the moment he saw the lifeless triangular mass of flesh that once moved easily in the victim's mouth.

58

They were seated in Jeremy's private booth in the city's most expensive restaurant. The room was hung with crystals and tapestries. Gold leaf shimmered wherever Carly turned.

"Do you own all this?" She meant the city, not the restaurant atop the forty-eight-story building.

Jeremy tossed his head back and laughed, revealing the whitest teeth she had ever seen on a man. The laminates were damn good. "Steel City is the center of my operations up here, but for the most part, the government owns what you see. I'm just a poor builder."

"I should be so poor."

"It comes with a lot of headaches."

"Why do it? It can't be to make more money?"

"It's a game to me now. To see how much I can accomplish."

"But to what end?"

Jeremy held her hand. "Behind it all, maybe I need to know I make a difference. That I touch people's lives. When I'm long gone, people will be living better because of buildings and cities I created. You don't believe me?"

"I think you do it for the power," she answered.

"Power doesn't interest me."

"Then ego. Why else would you name everything after yourself?"

"Here's a lesson I learned in business a long time ago: don't be so quick to blame. Did you ever stop and think that I'm a lonely man? That after two wives and no children, my family name can only survive in the building's and cities that carry it?"

Through all the pomp and glitz, Jeremy finally showed her his soft side. The man was vulnerable. Carly squeezed Jeremy's hands. "There's still time to have those children."

*   *   *

After a magical evening, Carly awoke the next morning on overload.

Fact: she was in the swankiest bedroom suite she had ever seen.

Fact: when Carly invited Jeremy to stay the night after dinner, he declined. He claimed he wanted to get to know her better before they bedded.

Fact: the kiss at the door was memorable.

Fact: Carly couldn't wait for Jeremy to return from his business meeting toward noon.

Fact: Carly's tapeworm needed to be fed.

After she showered and dressed, she had room service deliver the lumberjack special: three eggs over easy, a slab of Canadian bacon, a pitcher of freshly squeezed OJ, and a stack of wheat cakes smothered in homegrown maple syrup, along with the morning paper. The headline was a grabber:

Ninth American Dead:
"Copycat Killer" according
to Inspector Henri Plumme

Anytime Carly caught the words "serial murders" or "copycat killer," her professional curiosity was tweaked. She wondered what evidence they had and if they had a psychological profile on the killer, when an item on an inside page caught her attention.

"Shit!" Her call was picked up on the second ring. "Willie, what the hell's going on? I turn my back a few hours. How could you let them do it?"

"If it isn't the prima donna."

She sneaked in a forkful of wheat cakes. "Cut the shit, Willie, what happened."

For the next five minutes, Willie told her everything about the blue suits, starting with their court order to confiscate the three stiffs from the San Martini blast.

"Who were they?"

"Feds, but we don't know why."

They tossed around a few more ideas, and then Carly changed gears. "I read in the paper that there's a serial killer on the loose. Cute signature. Cuts off part of the tongue. It says that they've called in a retired special investigator. A Columbo type."

"Henri Plumme. He's the best they've got. Give him a call. I'm sure he'd welcome any help we could give him."

"Do you know him?"

"He came to New York one year. Took a course I was giving to police investigators about crime scene evidence. He'll remember me."

With their good-byes said, Carly let the receiver dangle. Was there time to meet with Plumme before Jeremy returned from his meeting? Jeremy was expected back at noon. Shouldn't she be there, in the room, waiting for him? Then again, maybe she had misread his advances. Her signals were clear: she was interested. Maybe under all that bluster and bravado, Jeremy Steel was gay?

That would be her luck! Whatever lack of talent Carly had for picking mates, most men had been more than willing to jump in the sack with her whenever she showed an interest in them.

Jeremy was the odd one. Maybe it was just because he made so much money and she came from....

If it wasn't for sex, why was Jeremy interested in her? Could it be he needed a new dentist? Great! She hadn't practiced dentistry in four years, and now there's a chance to land her first A-list patient. With Jeremy in her stable, scores would follow. Maybe this was the time to cash in and give up forensics? It wasn't too late.

No matter what was going on in Carly's personal life, being in "the hunt"—not for men, but for clues—was what turned Carly on. Maybe she was a bit distorted, but she did work with dead bodies for a living.

She picked up the phone and called Plumme.

*   *   *

Carly found Plumme's office housed in a sleek showcase. Score *One* for Jeremy!

Henri Plumme rose from behind a cluttered desk and spoke like he and Carly were old friends. "Imagine my surprise when I learned you were here in Steel City," he said.

"I didn't think you'd mind a call. Colleagues do it all the time when they're in New York. Sometimes, it's an interruption. But in general, I like to meet them."

"I hope this is more than a social visit, I could use your help."

He nodded to the strips of newspaper articles detailing the nine murders pinned to a corkboard. To the right, red Xs marked the location on a map of Alberta where each body was found. Plumme gestured for her to take a seat in the chair in front of his desk. He returned to his open-backed chair, which squeaked as he sank back down.

"I'm not even sure I can help."

"Willie said you were modest."

"You called him?"

"To make certain you were the famous Dr. Carly Mason, *non?*"

"I think you have me confused with someone else, inspector."

"Not at all. I've been an admirer of yours for some time, ever since you solved the murder of that horse trainer. Willie discussed the case with us when I took his course. You were very good in that one."

*   *   *

The case had sent shock waves up and down Central Park. Brynn Coughlin, a much-loved horse-riding instructor at the Claremont stables, had been found stabbed to death inside her sub-street level West Side apartment. There was a handyman who always lingered under the first floor steps as he packaged discarded newspapers for recycling. That was his usual time to spy through Brynn's gated window. Instead of catching Brynn's undulating hips wriggling out of her riding breeches, he saw a pool of blood congealing on the hardwood floor.

Moments after Willie Robinson arrived at the scene, he called Carly. There was evidence of a struggle. A struggle meant there might be bite marks. And to Willie Robinson, the possibility of bite marks required Carly's expertise.

Carly was just returning from two loops around Central Park Reservoir's cinder path when she got Willie's message. Now she leaned over the body, oblivious to the lingering eyes of assorted police specialists who gather at grizzly events. Carly hadn't bothered to change. Her sweat-drenched tee shirt left little to the imagination.

She inspected the victim's bruised wrists. "These are defensive wounds."

"I needed to hear you say it."

Wrist wounds meant a struggle, and a struggle meant the off-hand chance that the victim had bitten the assailant. If a captured suspect sported telltale bite marks, the victim's dental molds would go a long way to nailing the criminal. That's how the cops nailed Jesse Timmendequas, the twice-convicted pedophile, who killed Megan Kanka after luring her into his home with the promise of seeing a puppy. Timmendequas was convicted when his wrist wound matched casts of Megan's teeth. That horrific murder spawned Megan's Law.

In this case, a local delivery boy had brought a package of groceries to the murdered victim. While the boy took forever to return, other delivery orders backed up. Ben and Jerry's melted. But when he charged into the bodega dripping with blood, the store owner's anger evaporated. The gashes were deep so he sent the boy to Roosevelt Hospital's emergency room.

The next day's screaming headlines made the boss think twice about the boy's explanation, that he'd tripped and cut his arm on a broken beer bottle. When he questioned the boy further, the youth turned skittish. There was something in the way he answered that made the bodega owner call the local precinct. Let them figure out if the boy was telling the truth.

Police always pray for this sort of break. Without breaks, many crimes go unsolved. It turned out that Brynn Coughlin *had* bitten the delivery boy. The victim's dental molds fit into the suspect's wound the way a missing jigsaw part completes a puzzle. Seeing the evidence against him, the delivery boy confessed.

*   *   *

Carly turned crimson. "Anyone in my place would have done the same thing."

"But you're the one who did it."

Carly didn't want to appear rude, but it was close to eleven and Jeremy would be looking for her in the hotel sometime after noon. "I wish I could share more stories with you, but I'm meeting a friend for lunch."

"Silly of me to think you had all the time in the world."

Plumme was in his early sixties. Jowls. Bloodhound, droopy eyes. Creased face. Thinning salt and pepper hair. Forty pounds overweight. White shirt two sizes too big. Mud brown pants. He wore a curious ceramic fish around his neck that bobbed on a worn leather strip. Squiggly lines ran through the fish's body.

He held the piece toward her. "Know what it is?"

"There's great trout and salmon fishing up here."

He caressed the object.

"It's from Peru. The Incas. It represents an offering of thanks to their god."

Carly leaned to examine the fish. She felt his scrutiny, and then raised her head and looked him square in the eyes in triumph. "It's the Lines of Nasca."

Watching the Discovery channel on lonely nights reaped strange rewards.

Plumme clapped his thick hands together. "You're the only one who ever knew that. Bravo!"

"I'll take the compliment, inspector, but I wish I hadn't known the answer." Carly was not about to explain about her social life. Besides, her prospects were taking a turn for the better.

Plumme explained. "Somewhere, back in my family tree, a relative came from Peru. I like to think of myself as part Inca, that's why I wear it. They were a great society."

Carly remembered Lex Prescott and the papers she signed. So much for *her* relatives. The map with the red Xs was more interesting. Carly studied their pattern. "What do you know about the killer?"

For forty minutes Henri Plumme reviewed each Pembina River killing. When Carly interrupted about a detail, he answered with patience. It was clear that he respected her. When he was done, he pushed back, cupped his hands and waited for Carly to sift through the grizzly details. Nine men, all Americans, were murdered at close range. So close, in fact, that logic dictated each victim knew his killer. Only friends and co-workers got that close.

"So you think there's more than one? A copycat?"

Plumme hesitated before answering. "Partners, perhaps."

"Serial killers don't usually work in pairs."

"That's the trouble, but these are the facts."

The chance that two killers were working in concert was rare, indeed. Serial killers were loners. Social outcasts. They trusted no one, not even their mothers. When two hooked up, psychological profiling went out the window. If it were true that a pair was involved in the Pembina River murders, then Tarot card readers had a better chance of predicting the killers' future behavior than the police.

"Were the murders similar?"

Plumme handed her a sheet describing the murder weapons. The differences were startling. Two were stabbed to death, one asphyxiated, and one strangled. Five were shot with different guns. Shells or bullets were retrieved from a Ruger Bearcat .22, a Walther PPK, a Sauer P38, a 9mm Beretta, and a 357 Magnum.

She looked up. "It's like he, or they, were flaunting how easy it was to kill their victims. They varied each murder for the sake of change. Is it a game to them?"

"I wish I knew," answered Plumme. "What do you make out of this?"

Plumme described three similarities that linked each victim. Each was a young male. Each was an American. Each had the anterior portion of their tongues removed. It was sometimes left as a memorial, posed on a chin or a forehead. Other times it was in a shirt pocket or in the back of the victim's throat. Once it was in an eye socket. A couple of times it was missing altogether.

"Cutting the tongue is one signature that's new to me," began Carly.

"*Moi aussi.* Crosses. Swastikas. Missing eyeballs. Garter belts around the neck. Props and poses, but never the tongue. What is the meaning?"

"Hear no evil, see no evil."

Then he added the obvious, "Speak no evil"

"Have you studied the striations? What kinds of knives were used?" she asked.

"We did every test possible, and found nothing."

"Where are the slides?"

"I was hoping you had the time to look."

She looked at her watch and shook her head, knowing any chance of being on time for Jeremy was evaporating. But maybe she could help. "Lead the way."

Carly studied the slide preparations under the microscope. No two patterns of knife serrations were alike.

She looked up from the ocular. "He's toying with you, challenging you to catch him. They're all different."

"Maybe he does it to show how clever it is. He wants his genius recognized. *Non?*"

"Personally, I think it's meant to confuse. Before you indicated you thought it was two killers, why not three, even four or five? A conspiracy. That would explain the differences in every killing."

"That's what the killer would like us to think," Plumme said, "but it's a one man show, plus an assistant." Then he rubbed his arms with his gnarled fingers. "Besides, I feel it in my bones."

"How can you be so sure?"

Plumme broke his gaze with Carly and leaned forward. He fingered his medallion of the Lines of Nasca, dwelling over its detail before he spoke again. "I just know."

"Just knowing" wouldn't fly in New York. Not with Willie. There was little time for impressions or feelings when it came to Willie's cases. "The cold hard facts, nothing but the facts," were Willie's motto. It was Carly's, too.

She shrugged. *It's Canada, what did she expect?*

59

Carly returned to her hotel room spinning from the faint leads and blind alleys of the Pembina River killings. They were frightening and intriguing, and she wanted to tell Willie what she learned before Jeremy—who was now late—showed up.

"If it isn't Nanook of the North. How'd it go with Plumme?"

"For one thing they have a serial killer, possibly two working in tandem."

"Are you sure? Serial killers only like the playmates they kill."

"I know that. But two of the murders fitting the profile, right down to the cute little signature of cutting off the tongue, happened within minutes of each other."

"So the killer had another urge. That happens."

"Not three hundred kilometers apart, it doesn't. Not even Superman gets around that fast."

"Unless you're Jeremy Steel in his jazzed-up jet."

"Do I detect a note of jealously?"

"Not at all. I'm glad to know a high flyer. It gives me a chance to see how the other half lives."

Carly knew Willie had a soft spot for her. She needed to talk about the murders. "So what about the tongues? Sometimes the piece is left at the scene, sometimes it's missing."

"Depends if he brought the rye and Dijon."

She gulped. "Pleasant thought."

"Could you tell anything from the histology?"

"The serrations were unique. Each came from a different knife. Know what I think? The main killer is playing with them. He knows what the behavior of a serial killer is supposed to be, and deliberately doesn't follow the profile. He's a smart one."

"That becomes a clue in itself."

"But what does it mean?"

"Time will tell, it always does."

Carly then asked whether there'd been any news on the three Rock Center bodies?

"I was up all night searching the Internet for any word about three missing persons. Couldn't find a thing. I rechecked with NCIC, but you know how they are. Then, first thing this morning, I got through to someone in Intelligence at the Hoover Building...he swore six ways to Sunday, it wasn't their doing."

"Do you believe him?" Carly asked.

"For now."

"This is getting to sound like one for *Unsolved Mysteries*. Or maybe like what happened at Roswell."

"Get serious. You saw the posts. They weren't aliens." Willie's tone was not convincing.

"Are you sure?"

"Not any more. By the way, I almost forgot."

"Don't tell me there's been a sighting of Lute Aurum with Elvis? He always said he was immortal?"

"Elvis?"

"No, Lute," Carly answered.

"On that one you can relax. Dead is dead. But a voice did resurrect itself from the past, asking for you. Conner Masterson."

Carly was annoyed at herself for catching her breath, when she heard Conner's name. There had been a time when he was always on her mind, but fortunately memories fade.

"I was supposed to meet him at my apartment the other day. That's when Jeremy surprised me with the trip up here. What did Conner want?"

"Said it was important. Some bit of melodrama about life or death. Hope you don't get pissed, but I told him where you were staying. I figured a phone call couldn't hurt. He sounded so insistent."

"He better call soon. Jeremy is already late."

Carly needed to freshen up fast. She found it hard not to think of Conner as she applied her lipstick.

*   *   *

LuAnne Sternweiss was relentless.

"One more time, Mr. President."

She was charged with getting Aldous Fromm literally on his feet. A veteran physical therapist, she whipped Fromm into pushing a stainless steel walker down the hallway lined with Secret Servicemen.

"The more I walk, the more this mask itches," he paused to claw the plastic veneer pressed against his face.

"We've been through this before, Mr. President. The mask keeps those nasty scars from forming. You must wear it all the time, even during therapy."

"Cut me some slack. I never expected I would need to go through all this. Doesn't being the president give me any leeway?"

"All that matters to me is that you make it to the end of the corridor and back, two more times. When you do, I'll ask Dr. Labatelli for some Benadryl. That will make the itching go away."

"LuAnne, you're a saint."

"You won't be saying that tomorrow. Now move it...please."

*   *   *

Carly glanced at the wind-up traveling clock she always took on trips. It was one of the few things she had that belonged to her mother. Carly remembered her mother's voice made raspy from smoking too many cigarettes during her breaks at the diner. She could still smell the heavy, old lady-type perfume her mother doused herself that some salesman with an ill-fitting toupee gave her each time he stopped by. Carly could feel the light touch of her fingers even though bouts of arthritis made her knuckles painful and swollen. And there were the times her mother braided her hair—before her fingers got too bad—into pigtails so tight it hurt, but Carly never complained. As time went on, Carly found it harder and harder to picture what her mother looked like. Oh, she still could recall her face, but not in the crisp detail she swore she'd never forget.

"No time for nostalgia, now, Carly Mason. Jeremy'll be here any minute."

Then she smiled. Her mother always called herself by her full name. Out loud, too.

"Shirlaine Mason," she would say, "why'd you go off and do such-and-such a thing?" Then she'd add, "There you go again, jabbering to yourself."

Carly touched her face. She was looking more and more like her mother every day.

Carly wriggled into a black skirt. As she slipped a pink cashmere sweater over her head, her thoughts flipped to her phone call with Willie, and then to Conner who was looking for her. In a perverse way, she might not mind seeing him again, if nothing else to reconfirm that the spark she felt between them was gone...or had never existed in the first place. Maybe, after all this time, thinking there ever could have been anything between her and Conner was a figment of her fertile imagination. Regardless of her true feelings, she was relieved that no harm had come to him after he helped her escape from the Institute.

She slid one foot into a sandal, then the other. Straps tied, Carly searched for a full-length mirror; there was none in the room. She stepped into the bathroom, primped her hair, and checked her makeup. Then she climbed onto the toilet seat to see as much as she could see from the waist down.

"Yes!" She punched the air in victory. Carly was pleased with how she looked and pleased that for the first time in her life things were falling her way. "Let Conner Masterson find me. See if I care."

There was a click and the door opened.

She stepped off the toilet seat. Thoughts of chewing Jeremy out for being late vanished when she spotted a bellhop struggling to get through the door with the largest bouquet of red roses she had ever seen. She stretched to hug Jeremy; whims about Conner vanished.

"Who were you talking to?"

Carly felt trapped. "No one."

"I know I heard you say something when I walked in. Please don't tell me you're one of those women who babble to themselves and think no one can see or hear them? It's because you've got no one to talk to at work!"

"On the contrary, I've got plenty of people to talk to at work. My problem is they don't answer back."

"What would they say if they could answer you?"

"They'd say that they couldn't wait until this." Carly pressed against him, her head on his shoulder, taking in his lime-scented cologne, his crisp sapphire blue shirt, his Italian patterned tie, his Valentino suit. She felt his arms slip down an inch or two, and his biceps flex, molding her body deeper into his. It felt good.

"Will that be all, sir?"

Jeremy slipped him a crisp bill. "For now, Claude."

She waited for Claude to place the flowers on a round, glass-topped table, then she guided Jeremy to the sofa. Seated leg-to-leg, she basked in his hungry cat-green eyes. There was no mistaking the effect he had on her. In fact, there was no mistaking the effect Jeremy had on everyone. When Jeremy Steel entered a room, the airwaves danced and nerve endings tingled...the way hers were doing at that moment.

She shifted under his gaze.

Definitely not gay!

"I didn't except this to happen, Carly, not in the way it did."

"Nothing happened, it was only a hug."

"And I hugged back. You looked so radiant when I walked in. The strangest thing of all was that I missed you. It makes no sense. We hardly know each other."

Hearing his words stirred a beat deep inside her that pulsed against her black-lace panties. She removed a strand of hair dangling over her eyes and felt she was the luckiest girl in the world. She was sitting in a hotel room, being wooed by one of the world's greatest catches. The tabloids would have a field day with this little development:

Jeremy Steel Loses Head Over DDS.

Was she assuming too much, again? That's how she always got hurt.

"I can't say that I expected *that* sort of greeting either, but it was nice."

And you can continue holding my hands, thank you very much.

Unable to read her mind, he let go.

"So what'll it be? Lunch? Take a walk? What's your pleasure?"

She rose, feeling his stare strip her naked, which was exactly what would pleasure her at that moment. She dimmed the lights. "We'll eat later."

National Guard Quells
Camp Riots in Midwest

DES MOINES PRESS. Governors of
four states were forced to call out
their National Guard units, today,
after rioting broke out in the newly
formed migrant camps. Relief camps
in Nebraska, Iowa, Kansas, and S.
Dakota, were designed to offer shelter and food to the masses of homeless wandering the countryside. The
vast majority of displaced persons
interred in these camps are farmers who have lost their lands as a
result of the global climactic
changes that turned their farm-
lands into acres of dust.

While some resisted being placed
in these newly built government
compounds, most welcomed the
chance to get food, take showers,
get de-liced, and have a roof over
their heads. But the honeymoon
was short-lived. As the days wore
on and promises of work failed to
materialize, agitators rallied the dis-
enfranchised into burning several of
the housing units to the ground. At

last report, six have died and scores have been injured.

In light of the blunders made to Japanese-American citizens during World War II, acting President William "Kip" Greeley has asked the Attorney General to investigate these events to determine if the civil rights of these migrant farmers have been violated by detaining them in camps.

60

Link left *Ol' Betsy* at the designated point, signed some papers, and caught up to Jack. "I could eat a bear."

"I swear I don't know where you hide it all. You eat enough for three men."

Link aped Charles Atlas. "I'm still growing." Another time, he might have hammed it up more, but Link's spirit was elsewhere.

They were about to step into the cantina when Jack said, "Something's wrong with you."

Link slapped his sides. "I hate the way they take *Ol' Betsy* every time. No one's ever driven her before 'cept me."

"This ain't 'before,' no more. They got their routines and they aren't about to change a lick to please you or me. Way I see it, we oughta be thankful we have work given what's going on back home."

"Well right about now, home's looking pretty good to me. Maybe with all them farm subsidies throughout the years, you got used to working with Big Brother. Not me. That's why I'm a trucker, so I can go and come as I please, and call my own shots. I'm beginning to feel this place ain't for me."

Jack spun Link around. The canteen door swung open and two workers sidestepped them. "You telling me you'd leave all this?"

Jack saw Link survey the clean grounds and new buildings, and glance at the Steel City skyline in the distance. He watched him take off his cap and run his hands through his matted blond hair, tugging until his scalp danced back.

"I'm telling you I don't like it here," Link answered.

"I don't see anybody hungry."

"Yeah, well I ain't seen too many smiles, either."

"You would leave me after all we've been through?"

"It's not like we're married, Jack. You ain't my type."

That's when Jack knew Link wasn't about to give up, not on him and not on Canada. As it turned out, Link should have followed his instincts.

*　　　*　　　*

Carly had expected to have lunch in the hotel room, but Jeremy had other plans. "Why here?" They were seated in a small bistro in the outskirts of town. The table was covered with a red-checked cloth.

"Despite what People Weekly magazine and The Post say, I shun the limelight. I'd rather go where they don't know me."

"Try Timbuktu. Your picture is in the paper every day. Your face is plastered on half the billboards in the world. Get real. You're the Michael Jordan of building."

Carly caught the glint in his eye; she had struck a major chord.

"It's nice to get away from it once in a while."

A lank gum-snapping waitress wearing enough material to cover her vitals, sauntered up to them. She tossed a menu at Carly, and then put her elbow on the table and leaned into Jeremy's face like they were the only two humans left on the planet. "Want to hear the specials, Mr. Steel?"

Jeremy made a 'what-can-you-do' face.

Carly cleared her voice. "Excuse me, I'd like to hear them, too."

"Just a minute, honey, you'll get your turn."

Carly grasped a fork and pretended to stab the retreating waitress's back. "I thought no one would know you here?"

He shrugged.

"Here" meant a smoke-filled, wood-paneled room that had a small bar in the corner. A knot of men wearing jeans and overalls downed pints in animated talk. Aside from them, Carly and Jeremy were the only other patrons.

Jeremy grabbed her hand. "We need to talk."

"We could have done that in the room."

"I thought this would be more romantic."

"Romantic is nibbling food off each other's body. Why *did* you bring me here?"

His lower lip trembled. "For starters, tell me what you did this morning."

The skinny waitress was back. "Are you ready to order, Mr. Steel? We have sausages and beans."

Her flippancy no longer amused Jeremy. "I was thinking something lighter, less phallic."

She snatched the menu from him, champing on her wad of gum. "How about melon balls?"

"Cute. Garnish it with some other fruit, that is, if it's not too much trouble."

Carly ordered Caesar salad with grilled buffalo meat. "Where did *you* go this morning?"

He tapped his steepled fingertips in a slow rhythm, considering his answer. "I met with Honey Fitzpatrick."

"Here? In Steel City? He flew to meet you? I'm impressed."

"If I had flown to Ottawa, we wouldn't have experienced the last couple of hours. It was wonderful."

Carly reddened. She was about to tell him how she liked being with him when the waitress tramped to their table with plates in hand. She plunked down Carly's order and bits of Romaine toppled onto the table. She gently eased the fruit salad in front of Jeremy. The waitress's every gesture sent a singular message. Carly hoped *she* wasn't as easy to read.

The woman swooned. "Will there be anything else, Mr. Steel?"

"Yes. Stop pandering to me and don't be rude to my friend. Otherwise, you'll be traipsing the streets looking for a new job. Have I made myself clear?"

Her gum crackled. "I hear the chef calling me. Please excuse me."

When she disappeared behind swinging doors, Jeremy said, "That's what you get with full employment. Anyone *not* worth their salt, can get a good job here."

"I resent that." Carly spoke up. "I waitressed every weekend I could when I was in college. Even though I had a scholarship, I needed the spending money."

"That's different. Here the low-lifes do it. If she had anything on the ball, she wouldn't be here. It's that simple."

"Did you ever stop to think she likes being a waitress?"

"The thought never entered my mind."

Carly poked at an herb-flavored crouton. "Why doesn't that surprise me?" She rested the fork on her plate, and then folded her hands. "Since you asked, I met Henri Plumme this morning."

"Canada's Hercules Poirôt? He's a living legend. He's solved more murders than you can shake a stick at. Was this professional or social?"

"A bit of both." Carly described how she decided to contact Plumme after speaking with Willie. "You must have heard about the Pembina River killings?"

"Don't tell me there's a tenth!"

"For the moment, they're holding at nine."

"I hope you catch whoever's doing them. It's a waste of good men."

"You know about them?"

"I should. Every one of them worked for me."

Her mouth dropped faster than her fork. "Plumme didn't tell me that."

"How would he know? I have companies here that wouldn't be connected to me."

"You mean, they're not all named 'Steel?'"

"What you must think of me." Jeremy sat back. "For what it's worth, tell Plumme every victim was on my payroll. Is he sure these murders are connected? They could have to do with local crime."

Carly shook her head. "Canadians have one of the lowest murder rates in the world. They don't go around killing people. Everything points to a serial murderer."

"The paper said something about a copycat killer?"

"Newspaper talk. There's no copycat, it's two working in tandem." Carly looked around. She lowered her voice. "Copycats only know what the papers feed them. They get fixated on the murders and for a reason no one will ever understand, copy the act right down to the last part. If they can, the police hold back a detail only the real killer would know about. Usually it's their personal signature, their way of distinguishing their killings from anyone else's. In this instance, two of the Pembina River murders happened minutes apart, but separated by hundreds of kilometers. The signature was the same on both. Ergo, no copycat."

"You're talking about the tongues, aren't you?"

Carly bolted upright. "Plumme said no one knew about it."

"I also know that the Feds whisked three unknowns out of your Willie Robinson's clutches after we left, yesterday."

She reached for the crystal clear water, not knowing what to say. She swallowed.

"Do you happen to know who they were? It would save us a lot of time and trouble."

"What if I did?"

She gripped the edges of the table so hard her chair squawked. "How could you?"

"I'm joking." His face relaxed. He reached for her hand; she gave it to him. "I wanted to see what you would say. I have no clue who they are."

She pulled her hand back. "Now I don't believe you."

"That's good."

"Don't you want me to trust you?"

"Trust is a rare commodity these days. It has to be earned and I've done nothing to earn yours."

"I just gave myself to you. What do you call that?"

Jeremy didn't answer fast enough to suit Carly.

She looked away, dabbing the corner of her eye with the white napkin. "Are you telling me I made a mistake? Because if I did, the fun's over and it's time for me to go home."

Jeremy scooted around the table, and with one knee on the floor, guided her chin until she looked at him. "If I said anything that would make you think you're not special to me, then I'm sorry. I want you to trust me. You have to understand my high profile makes me a target for every money-grubbing schemer around."

She stiffened and pulled her head away. "Maybe that's the kind of women you're attracted to, the glitzy high-maintenance trophy-dolls that take, take, take. Well, if you haven't noticed, that's not me. Remember, I didn't go after you."

"You can tell me the truth. Don't you enjoy the power and the pleasures that surround me?"

"Jeremy, I'm not sure you would know the truth if it fell from the sky and clunked you on the head. I'm a simple girl who never dreamed she'd get to know a guy like you. I mean I'm not Cinderella or anyone else like that. Don't lump me together with the rest of the world. Where I come from, power is meaningless. How you treat a woman is all that matters."

He stood. "Then let me treat you the way you deserve to be treated."

She softened. "And how is that?"

He put his lips to her hand. "We had an appetizer before coming here."

"And now you want dessert?"

"Don't you?"

She stood and studied his face for a crack of insincerity. Finding none, she put her arm through his. "Lunch wasn't very filling."

61

It had gotten dark and Jack was napping after two beers at the cantina. Through a fuzzy haze, he heard someone say, "I gotta talk to you."

Jack opened his eyes to find Slim Armstrong with one knee on the floor. "What's so damned important that a fella can't sleep in peace?"

"This friend of mine, he's disappeared."

Jack swung his feet onto the floor. "Maybe he took a walk."

"No way, not with what's going on."

Since the last Pembina River murder victim, most men had taken to walking in pairs.

"What's his name?" asked Jack.

"Billy Squires. He's from Sioux Falls. I know you seen him hanging around. Bit younger than most. Looks like a doe with lights shining in his eyes."

"He have a lisp?"

"Not that bad."

"Where do you think he went?"

Slim hitched his belt. "Dunno. He never went anywhere without telling me. We became like brothers. He didn't have no family and we took to each other. Tough as nails. A curious sort. Always

327

wanted to understand this or have that explained to him. I tell you, it's got me real worried."

Slim looked around. "Any of the other fellas in the bunk?"

"Go check. I was sleeping."

When he returned from peeking into the shower stalls and toilets, Slim continued in a whisper. "Billy was on the crew building that grain holder 'bout six clicks out in the fields. You know, the silo detail. He worked there for weeks and never did see the inside of that sucker. Tried to once, but a guard stopped him."

"Same thing happened to me and Link on our first run. They took the rig from us, unloaded it, and then brought her back filled up. Might say it was a division of labor."

Slim's face grew longer by the minute. "It's fuckin' strange, if you ask me. Everything's ass backwards up here."

Jack scratched his head. "A feller could get in trouble thinking so much."

"That's what I'm trying to tell you."

"About what?"

"Billy seen something he wasn't supposed to have. He started telling me when we was eating yesterday but clammed up when he caught some dandy staring right at him. The greenhorn was reading Billy's lips. Like he was some sort of spy."

"Ever see the guy before?"

Slim shrugged. "Must be new. Don't know who he was. But that don't matter now. Billy's all I care about. Will you help me find him?"

*   *   *

The search didn't take long. It was Jack's idea to head for the small church at the edge of the compound. The church's outer shell was sheathed in white metal siding. There were no shutters because there were no windows in the building. The roof was peaked as a reminder of the steeples dotting the American landscape. A slatted picket fence set the building apart.

Slim swung through the front gate. "Billy loved to come here."

Inside, they waited for their eyes to adjust to the dim light. Four rows of empty wooden benches served as seats. A crude lectern stood alone. Next to it, the Canadian Maple Leaf hung limp on an oak flagpole. A plain wooden cross creased the wall. There were no pictures of Jesus.

Slim was the first to see it, breaking into a trot down the center aisle. "There!"

When Jack caught up, Slim was kneeling in a congealed pool of blood. The dead man's ash-brown hair was matted into clumps, his face pressed against the hewn lumber.

Jack moved a bench out of the way.

Slim lifted Billy's head.

The boy's eyes were fixed in the terror he had faced in his last moments.

Slim eased the eyelids closed. "I think I'm gonna be sick."

Slim dropped Billy's head and cupped his hand to his face. He started to retch.

Jack guided Slim outside; tears were streaming down his cheeks. "Why are they doing this to us, Jack? What did we ever do to them?"

Jack didn't answer. He couldn't. What could he say that would make the hurt go away? How could he explain why young American workers were being killed for no apparent reason, then further violated by having their tongues cut out?

62

Dr. Labatelli lifted the acrylic mask off Aldous Fromm. He checked the chief executive's pupillary response, peered into his ears, then used a wooden tongue depressor to check his throat. He tapped various points along both arms and legs with a rubber mallet. Finished, he helped the president ease onto the paper-covered table.

"What are you looking for?"

"An infection. Your white blood cells are up."

Fromm felt nothing out of the ordinary as the doctor pressed into the sides of his neck, and poked his armpit. The exam was sailing along. If it continued without a hitch, Kip Greeley could count the days left in the Oval Office with the fingers on both hands.

"That hurts!"

"It's not your appendix or your spleen, they're both out."

Fromm remained silent. He was tired of convalescing. He didn't know if he could bear one more setback.

Dr. Labatelli lowered the president's gown. He wrote an entry in the chart without comment, slipped the treatment record into the manila folder, and then slid the chart into the wall-mounted lucite holder. The doctor studied his patient the way an art collector would absorb a Van Gogh or a Matisse. He touched Fromm's forehead, and then his cheeks, nose, and lips. "You're almost ready."

Fromm grabbed the doctor's wrist. "Fuck the white blood cells. Give me some pills to fix them. I'm ready now."

Labatelli pried Fromm's fingers off, one-by-one. "I'll prescribe an antibiotic, but you're nowhere near ready. Not with the amount of pain meds you're taking."

Fromm's glare set the doctor back a step. When the president started peeling back the surgical tape holding the IV needle in place, Labatelli lurched to stop him.

"I don't care who you are, it stays. You need fluids and meds."

"Then unhook the pain dispenser. I'll stop cold-turkey."

Labatelli permitted himself a rare smirk. "I don't think so. Wean yourself some each day. That's the best way to do it."

"I'm a lot stronger than you think. I don't need the stuff."

"Junkies would rather die than go through withdrawal. The lucky ones shiver and shake, then barf their guts out. With the amount of medicine you've been gobbling up, you'll start convulsing quicker than you can say Herzegovina."

Fromm fell back into the bed. "You see the papers? The country's in shambles. I've got to get back to Washington."

"The fact that you're complaining is a good sign. Soon."

Fromm lifted his arms then let them drop to the sheets.

"One last thing," Dr. Labatelli said.

Fromm moaned. "Not another X-ray or blood test."

"It's your teeth."

"What's wrong with my teeth?"

The doctor handed him a mirror. "A few chipped along the way. Besides, they were never your strong suit. Get them capped."

"Truth is Coulter Bell told me the same thing years ago. I was about to do it before the election when Barbara took sick. With her getting chemo and all, teeth were the last thing on my mind.

After she died, I didn't care anymore. Last year Lute Aurum tried to bring them up again, but I wouldn't hear of it. Damn, I miss that man."

"Then do it for him. Get them fixed."

Labatelli waited for Fromm to dab his eye with the gown sleeve. Then the president asked, "Could you arrange for my dentist to come here? He'll do a crackerjack job."

"I've already discussed it with Coulter. There's no need to bring any Washington people here before you're ready to return to office. That'll bring the press and media back, and I don't think the locals could take any more of that. Use my guy. He's ex-Army and a terrific dentist."

"Can he be trusted?"

"If not, I'll kill him. He's my brother-in-law."

63

Earlier that day, a special phone rang in the Oval Office.

"What do you mean, there is troop movement all over Canada?" Kip Greeley queried Rear Admiral Buster Jorgenson, the nation's security adviser.

"We're not certain, Mr. President, but folks down at Langley are concerned. It may be nothing, but I'd like to show you the aerial photos anyway."

Greeley heard the alarm in the voice of the former linebacker from Annapolis.

"Now's as good a time as any, Admiral. Get your ass over here."

"Be there in a flash, Sir."

Minutes later, Kip Greeley poured over blowups spread across his desk. Rear Admiral Jorgenson was by his side, instructing the acting president how to interpret the images.

"See these specks over here, Mr. President? Those are men. And the white color indicates heat…like around those square things. They're military vehicles."

Greeley waved a magnifying glass. "How do you know this isn't a bunch of farmers and well-used farm equipment?"

"The Canadians want us to believe that, but there are simply too many. That's no farm and *those* are not farmers. Otherwise, these photos make no sense, Mr. President."

Aldous Fromm was expected to return to his office any day. As far as Kip Greeley was concerned, this would have been a good time.

"Why would the Canadians hold maneuvers in the middle of farm fields? Didn't you stop to think this wasn't a military base?"

"Truth is, we didn't know what to make of it, sir."

"Then there is no immediate threat?"

"Not at the moment, sir."

"Correct me if I'm wrong. We could afford to watch what they're doing a little longer. Isn't that right?"

"In theory."

"Then we wait."

"Begging your pardon, sir, I wouldn't advise that."

Greeley looked across the White House lawn. Beyond the gates and barricades, people strolled without a care in the world. Children held multicolored balloons and vendors hawked steaming hot dogs and miniature White Houses. Although it was January, it was warm enough for lightweight jackets and short sleeves.

Greeley whipped around. "What would *you* advise, Admiral? Attack our neighbors?"

"Go to Defcon One."

"You're fucking serious, aren't you? I'm not putting anybody on alert," Greeley snapped back. "The way I see it, a bunch of farmers got together for a weenie roast in the middle of some Canuck pasture. Bomb them and we'll be the world's laughingstock."

"Begging your pardon, sir, if President Fromm had seen these maneuvers, he would've had planes in the air by now."

Greeley glowered. "Then maybe it's a good thing he's not here. Tell your men to back off, Admiral. And a word of advice..."

"Yessir."

"Don't be so quick to look for conspiracies under every rock. Nixon did that. Most of the time, all you find is dirt."

"If I may remind the president, snakes hide under rocks, too."

64

The day after Billy died, Gadol ordered the men to take extra laps. He almost had a mutiny on his hands. The last thing the men wanted to do was run in full gear. In the end, they obeyed because it helped get Billy off their minds. Gadol barked that training was almost over and furloughs were around the corner. Given the prospect of time off, the men's enthusiasm was aroused.

At day's end, sweaty and grimy from the long run, Slim went straight to the bathroom and took a "from-the-sink" shower. Then he tramped to his bunk to take a nap. Boots off, he dropped into the sack fully clothed. He rolled onto his side. That's when he caught a glimpse of the white rectangle hidden under the pillow. He sat up. This was the first letter he had received since leaving Omaha. It had to be from his sister.

He held it to the light, but couldn't see anything special. He shook it. Nothing rattled. The handwriting appeared scribbled, like it was done in a hurry. Slim turned it over. After some moments, Slim tore open the flap. His mouth dropped. It was from Billy, postmarked the day he died.

*　　　　　　　*　　　　　　　*

Dear Slim,

I sure hope you get this letter and those sonsabitches don't. I'm writing you just in case something happens to me, 'cause of what I seen the other day.

Don't show this letter to nobody.

Remember how we both thought it was strange that I never got to work the inside of that big silo job? It made no sense, right? Well, the other day, I left my best hammer outside the sucker. It's the only thing I have that belonged to my daddy, and I wasn't about to lose it. It was dark by the time I found it. Just as I was picking it up, I heard a rumbling on the other side of the silo...I was over on the backside. Since I'm a curious so-and-so, I climbed up a ladder that was sitting there, and crawled into the hayloft.

All of a sudden, the main doors to the silo grind open. Did I tell you they were motorized? Then this flatbed backs inside it. I'm leaning for a better look and you won't believe what I saw. The fucking floors start opening up!

Promise me, if you're reading this and I'm not next to you that you'll come and see for yourself.

Billy

P.S. Watch out for your own ass, Slim.

    *   ***   ***

"Holy shit."

Slim started to shake. He shook so hard he rattled. He held the letter by its edge; it was high-grade plutonium. There was little choice as to what he should do; he had to destroy the letter. Slim swung his feet onto the floor and padded to the crapper. With the stall door open, he tore the letter in half. He was about to tear it in quarters when he stopped. Without the letter, it was his word against a corpse's.

Where could he hide it?

He searched the bunk, but no place seemed right. The communal bathroom was no better. Slim cranked his head toward the ceiling to relieve the lancing pain in his neck. He noticed that the corrugated ceiling had thin tiles. Slim maneuvered onto the sink, pushed a stained tile aside, then placed the letter behind a jumble of pipes. He managed to get the tile back in place when he heard his name called. He hopped off the sink and faced the wall.

A co-worker ambled toward him.

Slim prayed the man would pick the end urinal. Slim fiddled to make it look like he was zipping his jeans. Slim snorted, making a gurgling noise. "Sure does smell in here, don't you think?" Slim's voice was muted by a case of jitters, but the man didn't notice.

Slim doused water on his hands, feigned an inspection of the seedy room, and then stretched his already stiff neck and sneaked a glance at the letter's hiding place. Any two-bit actor would've given a better performance. Given the audience, Slim's passed muster.

Slim shuffled to his bed. Who would have dreamed that working in Steel City meant putting your life on the line? It was safer to pull up stakes and return to the States, but with Kip Greeley pretending to run the country, Old Glory was a fading star.

Then there was Billy Squires. Billy got a peek at something he shouldn't have. He got a glimpse of the future, Jeremy Steel's future, and he got killed for seeing it

65

Carly Mason was seated in a dark room on the sixth floor in the Marriott Marquis Hotel in Times Square. With all her obligations, the pressures of the Rockefeller Center bombing, and the newness of Jeremy Steel, she almost begged off the program of her favorite part of the American Academy of Forensic Science's meeting: the Last Word Society. For two hours, the obscure and arcane were discussed in this forensic equivalent to television's "Unsolved Mysteries." Some mysteries were current. Some happened ages ago, some were measured in centuries. Carly felt she owed herself this treat, especially if there was a chance one of her colleagues had a clue how to help her identify any of the three blast victims.

The first report chronicled the disinterment of English skeletons uncovered by workmen in 1674. It was thought their bones belonged to Edward V and his younger brother Richard, the Duke of York. The princes disappeared in the Tower in 1483. Their murders were the subject of many investigations, none more famous than Shakespeare's Richard III. The bones were studied by forensic experts in 1933, and left unchallenged until the evening's lecturer reopened the case. Maybe Richard didn't kill them?

One speaker analyzed the mysterious fire that destroyed Jack London's house in the Valley of the Moon in Glen Ellen, California in 1913. Another discussed the disarticulated remains uncovered on the site of the University of Michigan Medical School when new construction began. Forensic anthropologists determined that the skulls were of Native American Indians who had been buried there in the mid-nineteenth century.

Carly endured a talk about the saffron scourge—yellow fever—that decimated Memphis, Tennessee in 1878. She imagined how CNN's late breaking coverage would report six thousand dead and another thirty thousand fleeing for their lives. The speaker tonight chronicled valiant acts by those who tried to stem the plague.

Next, Dr. Ken Rosenberg ambled to the lectern. His topic: the exhumation of President Zachary Taylor. Zachary Taylor had intrigued Carly ever since she took U.S. history at Duke her freshman year.

"As most of you know Zachary Taylor was known as old Rough and Ready. He defended our country against General Santa Anna, of Alamo fame. Following a stunning victory at Buena Vista, Taylor helped win the war. He went on to be elected our twelfth president. Highlights of his administration include battles in the Senate over admitting California and New Mexico as free states, and passage of the Clayton-Bulwer Treaty guaranteeing the neutrality of any Atlantic-Pacific canal built through Nicaragua. The Industrial Revolution was gearing up. We were a nation of unlimited energy and raw materials, in need of markets to sell our goods. Gold had been discovered in California, Texas was ours, and nothing would stop our expansion from the Atlantic to the Pacific. Manifest Destiny was in full swing.

"Zachary Taylor had only been president for sixteen months when he died after a brief illness. It was reported that he became sick from eating too many cherries and drinking cold milk at a

July Fourth celebration. A recent historian theorized that Zachary Taylor, not Lincoln, was our first president to have been assassinated. She suspected arsenic poisoning. It was widely known in 1850 that, if a civil war broke out over slavery, President Taylor would have sided with the North. Southerners may have been...."

Carly moved to the end of the row.

She waited for the polite applause to simmer down.

She felt a flutter in the pit of her stomach.

As soon as Dr. Rosenberg was finished, she was up at bat.

66

They made the run from Steel City to Steel Metropolis with Billy Squires on their minds. Jack rolled the window down, cleared his throat, and hucked out a yellow-green wad. He wiped his lips on his sleeve, and then reached for a cigarette.

"You're killing yourself," Link said.

Jack struck a match and smiled in a haze of smoke. "Hate to quit with the killer loose. Could be I'm his next victim. Look at all the pleasure I would've missed!"

"Don't talk like that, and nothing's going to happen to you. Billy went where he shouldn't have."

"No one deserves to get killed, not for any reason." Jack drew in until the tobacco embers crackled and the paper flamed.

Link took his eyes off the road. "Then why are you so worried?"

Jack snickered. "I ain't crapping out on you so fast, Reb. All I meant to say is that it don't appear likely they're going to catch whoever's doing this to those boys."

*　　　　　*　　　　　*

On the return trip, Link almost ripped the door closed when they drove off. Then he slammed his hand on the steering wheel

343

twice, nearly bent the gear shift, gave the finger to two kids waving, and blasted the air horn at an elderly couple driving too slow.

"Was it what Pinky said?" Jack asked.

"Naw, and nothing about the guard they posted at the bar all the time, neither."

"Then what's eating you?"

"I'm sick of the whole thing. Sick of the way they take *Ol' Betsy*, sick of the way Billy was killed, and real sick that we're nothing but two cents up here."

"*Canadian* cents."

"Thanks for reminding me. The whole place stinks. How come you're so calm about it all?"

"I mind my business, they pay us. If that's how it is, I'm accepting of it."

"Well, I'm not."

Earlier, Jack and Link had been perched on a rock outside the gray hurricane fence, waiting for *Ol' Betsy* to be loaded. From their vantage point, they saw heavy machines drilling deep into the bedrock. They saw an armada of trucks with rotating drums waiting to dump wet cement into vast pits. They saw earthmovers and cranes, and an army of yellow-hatted workers scurrying about. Horns blared, whistles screamed, dynamite blasted, the pace was dizzying. Then, when they went into *Pinky's Place*, the mood was darker than night. It was too much after Billy's death. They left.

Link braked for *Ol' Betsy* to stop, and hopped down.

"What are you doing?" Jack asked.

"It's my rig. Stay inside if you don't want to see."

"If you're about to do what I think you're about to do, you'll be getting us both killed."

By the time Jack rounded the back of *Ol' Betsy*, Link held the big lock in his hand. "Christ, how'd you do that?"

Link jangled a makeshift key. "I've got some talents I ain't shared with you."

He explained how, days earlier, he lubricated the tumbler with silicone. He squirted hot wax into it and then inserted a notched wire. When the wax cooled, he withdrew the replica. Afterwards, a key blank was whittled into a perfect copy.

Jack grew more concerned by the minute. "Now what?"

"Now we're gonna see what's inside *Ol' Betsy*."

The door creaked open; Jack slammed it shut. "It may be your rig, but it's their merchandise. I'm not putting my ass on the line for whatever's in those boxes. Don't you either, Link. It won't be healthy for either of us."

Link pushed him away. "You can't stop me, Jack, and I'm not stupid, either. I'm not gonna break anything or mark a box. They'll never know."

*   *   *

Carly cleared her throat. "On November 19th of last year, America panicked...."

Carly had rehearsed the opening with Willie. He thought it dramatic; she felt it struck a chord. "...The helicopter carrying President Aldous Fromm crashed on its way to Camp David. Everyone on board perished except the president. Reports indicate he will make a full recovery and is expected to resume his duties in a matter of days."

She waited for an outburst of huzzahs, whistles, and foot-stomping to simmer.

"Lost in the chaos that day was another tragedy, that went straight to the hearts of every New Yorker. Most of you know that I am referring to the Rockefeller Center bombing that killed eight individuals. One was my colleague and acquaintance, Dr. Rocco

San Martini, plus his four staff members. Three bodies recovered at the scene remain unidentified."

Carly described the known facts about the bombing. She showed pictures of the blast, and the positions of each body. There was a simulated computer video that recreated the position of Dr. San Martini in relation to his patient moments before the bomb exploded. The simulation showed, in slow motion, how the blast blew through the wall and ripped the patient apart. It showed how the patient's jaw was impaled in Dr. San Martini's abdomen, and how parts of his skull splattered against the walls and ceiling.

Carly concluded with the dental findings on each of the three unidentified victims. She asked if anyone in the audience recognized anything about the victim's teeth that might help identify any one of them. No one raised a hand. When she signed off, there was polite applause. Carly accepted the moderator's thanks, but did little to hide her disappointment that no one raised a question.

She drifted to the back of the room to retrieve her slide carousel. Slipping the plastic tray into a black and yellow Kodak box, Carly sensed someone standing behind her. She turned to find a sun-wrinkled man, decked in traditional Navy whites. He had short-cropped silver hair, and a twinkle in his gray-blue eyes. His military name tag read, "Montgomery."

Carly cradled the slide box against her chest.

The man spoke without preamble. "I've seen a molar just like the one you showed in that last case. It's someone in my practice. I can't picture who, but I doubt he needed all his teeth capped like the man you showed."

Carly's heart skipped a beat. Dr. Montgomery was referring to the patient who died in Dr. San Martini's dental chair, the one whose jaw was embedded into the dentist's stomach. "Are you at Bethesda?"

"Head of the restorative department. I get to treat a lot of the top brass in DC."

"I know the chances are slim, but can you check your records when you get back?"

"Do you have any idea how many thousands of people we've treated through the years? Military? Civvies? We've got tens of thousands of files. Even if I find the chart, I doubt it's your man. We don't do many cosmetic rehabs at the hospital. Not right with the public's money."

"Could be why he came to New York."

"My first thought was that your victim might have been a drug dealer getting a makeover? Make it harder for the cops to ID him."

This was the first lead—if it could be called that—since the blast, and she was not going to let it pass. Carly accepted LeShana's theory that the two other victims were there to protect Dr. San Martini's patient, that's why they were headed down the hall instead of out the door. Everything focused on the patient in the chair. A connection to Washington would explain a lot.

"What made you say something, Dr. Montgomery?"

"Can't tell you why, but it seems familiar."

"How 'bout if I send you a copy. If you come across the one you're thinking about, do a quick comparison and tell me if they match. Would that work?"

She had broken through. The Navy man rocked back on his heels, pleased with himself. "I'll do you one better. I don't need your copy."

"Then how will you know?"

"I'll check every damn chart in the place. I'm certain there's only one patient with a three-rooted mandibular right first molar. When I find it, I'll send you a copy."

"You're making me feel guilty. That's a lot of work. How about if you just check the X-rays of the patients who come through the clinic for their routine care. You might come across it that way."

"Nonsense. When I say I'm going to help somebody, that's what I'm going to do."

"But that's a Herculean project."

"Dr. Mason, I can tell you've never been in the service. Grunt work is why God created privates in the Army and ensigns in the Navy. Don't worry, your X-ray is as good as found."

67

Jack jumped out of the way as the heavy door opened. Link stepped on a metal rung and hopped up; Jack was right behind. *Ol' Betsy* was filled with stacks of boxes. They closed the doors behind them and flicked on flashlights. The narrow beams darted this way and that, settling on black markings.

"Whaddya figure," Link asked, "Korean? Japanese?"

Jack checked boxes at the bottom of another stack. These had Arabic, Russian, and Greek writing.

"What're you doing?" Link screamed.

Jack had his thumbnail pressed into a box seam, ready to zip it open. "How else we gonna know what's inside?"

"Christ, Jack. I only meant to take a peek, not open anything. Now *you're the one* gonna get us both killed."

"We can't stop now."

Link stamped his foot. He was having second thoughts. "Damn you. This ain't right."

"Hey, you're the one who opened the lock, not me. Now stand back or leave. I'm finding out what's in here."

Link wrenched Jack around. "If you're going to be stupid, wait here."

Seconds later Link returned, brandishing a roll of tape.

Jack scoffed. "How clever is that? They're going to know the box was taped again."

Link rolled his eyes and nudged Jack aside. "You don't know everything."

Link flipped the box upside down and cut through the factory-taped seam with his Swiss Army knife blade to free the box flaps.

"This way, it will still look untouched from the top. With luck, they'll never check the bottom."

They withdrew a Styrofoam insert and gawked at the contents of the first box. Without a word they opened a second, then a third, each time amazed at what they found. After they sifted through a dozen, grime covered their faces.

"Who's gonna believe this?" Link asked.

"We better find someone," Jack answered.

68

Willie was doing paperwork when Carly returned from the Marriott. "How'd the lecture go?"

"They were more interested in learning that the legend about Zachary Taylor's death was actually true. The historian who dreamed up the idea was really disappointed. She thought Taylor had been assassinated."

"I'm glad. I never thought it was arsenic. Anyone have an idea about our cases?"

"There was a Navy guy who came up to me afterwards about the three-rooted lower molar. I don't think he had anything."

"Has he seen one like it?"

"He said he has."

"Then what's the problem?"

"Half the time he was talking, he was looking at my breasts."

"Let him look if it's going to help solve a case. Will he send you a copy of his X-ray?"

"He's got thousands of charts to sift through. I'll doubt he'll find it."

"Seems Plumme has put you on his Xmas list. You're in the loop, now."

"How's that?"

"Called while you were at the meeting. There's been another one. Thought you would want to know."

A voice came from behind her. "That makes ten."

Carly twirled around to see who it was. She gave a dirty look to Willie. "Why didn't you tell me he was here?"

"He wanted to surprise you."

"Some surprise," she said, turning back to Conner. "I thought you were going to call me when I was in Canada." She looked at his hand. "Break your dialing finger? Then again, why should I be surprised? The last time I heard from you, you sounded like a robot. What was wrong with you, anyway?"

"After four years, cut me some slack. Remember the Institute? After you left, they grabbed six of us. Put us in one of those basement cells and bashed us trying to find out who helped you escape."

Carly knew what they were capable of. She whispered, "Did they hurt you?"

"Not in the physical sense. But I was a mess for two years."

"Just because you helped me get out?"

"That first call *was* made on automatic pilot. I was a mess then. A couple of weeks later, I came out of it. I would've escaped but they caught me trying to leave a message on your machine. Didn't you get it? It was the same day Fromm announced he was running for president."

"That was the day Jonah Schoonover was killed."

"Coincidence Aurum was in the city that day, wasn't it?"

Carly groped for a stool and sat down.

Conner stepped closer. "What are you thinking?"

"That same day, someone burglarized my apartment. I found a man outside my apartment when I got off the elevator."

"Did he take anything?"

"Only an extra passport photo I had laying around. I realized it was missing months later. I needed it for the bulletin describing a lecture I was giving. At first I thought I lost it. Then I realized the man in the hall might have taken it."

"Was he thin, about your height, pale complexion? I've heard about that one," Conner said.

"Could be. The lighting was pretty fierce."

"Maybe he listened to your messages, too," Willie said.

"Which would explain why you never got mine," Conner added.

Carly pressed. "How bad was it?"

For the next hour Conner described, in detail, everything that happened to him once Carly left the Institute. He recounted how six monitors were tormented by the gigantic tarantula, how he felt during the days and nights of food deprivation and auditing, and finally, how they sent him to San Francisco once Willie tried to contact him.

"Now you're making *me* feel guilty," Willie said.

"You shouldn't. I don't know what I was thinking the first time I went there. Aurum's a pro. I was out of my league. I'm just lucky I got out of there alive. In the end, I never did get the goods to incriminate him."

"What does that matter? At least you got out."

"You wouldn't believe how!"

Once his timetracks were stripped away, Conner was subjugated to the duties of a neophyte. He cleaned the barn stalls and anything else they could find until he graduated to the kitchen. "That's when I came across Artie Montefusco's sister, Sophie. You remember him? Sophie's the one who saved me."

"Poor Artie. I hope she's all right," Carly said.

"Sophie's a tough lady. She works with the Cult Information Services, same as he did. Once she helped me escape, CIS shuttled me straight to Toronto. I spent a month there with Sawyer Glenn; he's an exit-counselor. After he deprogrammed me and I got acclimated to the real world again, I returned to Boston and got my BA from Emerson. Now I'm in the doctorate program at BU. Psychology. After I get my PhD, I'm going to be a deprogrammer, too. You can't believe how many lost souls wind up in these cults."

"That still doesn't explain why it took so long for you to call me. You've been out of there for two years."

"And fucked-up the whole time. I always thought about you. Wondered what you were doing. How you were. Whether or not they left you alone. Then your name came up in a teaching session. It was a tape of a green-shirt, from Washington, getting exit-counseling. When he mentioned your name, I knew I had to reach you. So here I am."

"What about my name? And what about the other day? You were supposed to meet me at my apartment."

"I was there."

"I didn't see you."

"That's because I had a panic attack when I saw you hugging Jeremy Steel."

He looked wounded; she took his hand. "I like that you were jealous."

"You don't understand," said Conner, "Jeremy Steel is Lute Aurum's friend. They're in cahoots. When I saw him with you, I lost control. Christ, I passed out in some Korean grocery store. The moment I recovered, I made a beeline to see Sawyer."

"Then you were in Canada the same time I was."

He nodded. "But I was in no shape to speak to you."

"I'm glad you're back to your old self now."

"Only in appearances. They have a way of messing up your brain. I don't know if I'll ever be the same. Enough about what happened to me. You need to know they're sending someone to get you."

"Who is?"

"Lute Aurum. Jeremy Steel. Maybe it was the man who broke into your apartment. All I know is that you better watch out."

"Aurum's dead, and Jeremy Steel has become my friend. I think you inherited a case of paranoia along the way."

"I'm not delusional. There's a bounty on your head, and more than one hunter would like to collect it."

*　　　　　*　　　　　*

Jack and Link drove up to the gate at Steel City with their hearts jackhammering. Link handed the manifest to the guard and then relinquished the rig so *Ol' Betsy* could be unloaded. Now Jack and Link knew the contents of their cargo. The second they were out of the guard's earshot, Link whispered to Jack. "Think *he* knows what's in there?"

Jack kicked a rock. "Seems no one knows much about anything here."

"So what're we gonna do?"

"About what?"

Link jerked his thumb over his shoulder.

Jack grabbed Link's shoulder and spun him around. "I thought we had this settled on the ride back. We're not telling a soul about this, not a soul. Do you hear me?"

"I know, but it don't seem right not telling anybody. Someone's gotta know."

"Get this through your thick, cracker skull: there's no one we could tell that's gonna give two shits about what we saw. You gotta mind your own beeswax."

"We could tell Slim. He'd have an idea what to do."

Jack made a face. "Slim's an old lady. He couldn't keep his mouth shut if his life depended on it. Look how he told us all that stuff about Billy. Besides, what could he do for us 'cepting get us in deep shit."

Gravel crunched and Jack turned to see a guard coming their way. Link blanched and tripped over his words. Jack picked up the tempo and jabbered about how the days were getting hotter. His stream of words didn't stop until the guard strolled into the main office.

"I froze, I'm sorry," said Link. "We never should've opened those boxes."

Jack punched his arm. "Don't be so hard on yourself. I've been wanting to open them ever since the first day."

Link shoved Jack back a step, and none too playfully, at that. "You bastard. You made me feel guilty as sin."

"Still don't make it right what we did."

"It would have made it easier knowing you was behind me."

"So what? I'm sorry we did it. C'mon, it's time for a tall one."

∗   ∗   ∗

An hour and two brews later, Jack and Link meandered toward their bunk. As they neared, they found Slim standing in the doorway.

Slim snapped his index finger to his lips. "Get in here."

"What's all the fuss?" Jack asked. "Nothing can be that important."

Inside, Link strutted passed Slim. "Gotta pump the bilge. The beer went right through me."

"I hope I'm doing the right thing telling you guys," Slim said.

Jack glanced at Link's disappearing back. "Telling us what?"

Instead of answering, Slim grabbed a wooden chair and charged after Link. For a split second, Jack tensed. Then he started after them. At the bathroom door, Jack's worries eased. He saw Slim mount a chair and push aside a water-stained acoustic tile. Link watched, aiming his fire hose at the porcelain urinal.

The three returned to the main bunk area.

"What's that?" Jack asked.

Slim handed Jack Billy's torn letter. "Read it."

Jack pieced the two halves together.

Slim followed Jack's darting eyes across the handwritten scrawl.

Link read over Jack's shoulder and let out a low whistle. Jack glared at him, afraid he would blurt something about *Ol' Betsy's* cargo. Reading Billy's letter made sense out of the cargo they were carrying. So did not mentioning a word of it to Slim.

"When'd you get this?" Jack asked.

"Day after Billy was killed. Think we should tell the bosses?"

"I'll go with you," Link said. "Let them figure out what to do."

"The two of you are crazy. Seems every time someone pokes their nose where it don't belong, they stop smelling things…permanent-like."

Slim pulled out a red engineer's handkerchief and honked his bugle into it. It took two more swipes to remove the hangers-on. "Maybe Billy didn't mean much to you, but he was like my kid brother. I gotta go out there."

Link started to answer, when Jack cut him off. "It ain't our fight, Slim. If you was smart, it wouldn't be yours either."

69

Night was falling. Without Jack or Link's help, Slim was having second thoughts. He could go to the silo alone and try to learn what Billy saw, but common sense told him that was a bad idea. That's when he remembered Johnny Ray Mabe. Billy made a habit of befriending recent arrivals that were assigned to his detail. When Johnny arrived a week or two back, Billy adopted the man, even though he was a lot older. Slim found Johnny Ray in the center of a knot of men chugging their draughts.

Slim shunned the barkeep with the back of his hand. He wanted to spurt out, "*What can you tell me about Billy's death?*" but couldn't right away. Homeboys had a time-honored ritual in the way they greeted each other. There had to be mention of the weather and how one was feeling. They needed to ask about the wives and children and if any animals were sick. Talk filtered down to details about the crops and prices the combine was paying.

"How you feeling today, Johnny Ray?"

Johnny Ray slapped Slim on the back. "Find me a fiddle and I'd show you how good I feel."

Johnny Ray winked, and the group broke out into a round of surface chuckles that meant nothing but polite tittering. It was homeboy bullshit laughing. They all knew it meant nothing.

"That's good, Johnny Ray, real good." Slim shot a furtive glance at the others, making them understand a private talk was about to take place.

Johnny Ray's smile evaporated. "What's on your mind, Slim?"

Slim shot a last look toward the others, and whispered, "When you and Billy was out by the silo, did you see or hear anything kind of strange?"

"Nothing that got me thinking about anything special. Why'ya asking?"

Johnny Ray reached into his pocket and extracted a pouch of Red Smokey. He placed a pinch of tobacco between his cheek and gums, and then offered the tinfoil sack to Slim.

"Thanks," Slim said, but didn't take any. He edged closer to Johnny Ray. "'cause Billy mighta seen something out there when he went back 'to get his hammer."

"His daddy's? That one?"

"Only reason he'd go back fer it. Anyways...," Slim said, "...he saw something mighty peculiar."

"Did he say what it was?"

"Never really said. But whatever it was, it sure got him killed."

Slim figured he had struck a dead end. He didn't know much about Johnny Ray, only that the man did his job, kept his mouth shut, and blended in with the other workers. If he had seen something, it didn't impress him the way it did Billy. "Sorry to take your time. I just thought, with you being on Billy's crew, you might o' seen something.

Johnny Ray banged his mug on a nearby table and motioned Slim outside. "I thought something fishy was going on, too. Just didn't want to say anything because, like—you know—who's gonna believe any of *us*?"

Slim's ears buzzed. Was he hearing right? "That's my point, too. We're plain trash to them."

"Exactly."

"What can we do?"

It was Johnny Ray's turn to make certain they were out of earshot of everyone else. "Time we put an end to all this worrying. Let's go out to the silo together, see if we find what Billy saw. What do you say to that?"

Slim wet his lips. "It's dark now. No one would be the wiser."

Johnny Ray slapped him on the back. "I like the way you think."

*   *   *

Slim and Johnny Ray used moonbeams to light the way to the silo. The night noises changed with each step away from the compound. The nimble notes of a homesick harmonica gave way to the plaintive cries of coyotes and wolves. For a while, a gurgling river kept them company, its white waters rushing over rounded stones, its murmurs suggesting that little changes in the world.

With the silo up ahead, Slim and Johnny Ray grew cautious. They neared the building silhouetted against the coal black sky, then froze...a squealing rig had rounded the bend from the far side and was now rolling toward the silo doors.

Slim saw it first. He grabbed Johnny Ray's arm and pointed.

Johnny Ray saw it, too.

The silo doors opened. The rig slithered inside to disgorge its cargo.

"Billy was right," whispered Slim, "this is a fucking...."

Slim never got to finish his sentence.

When the silo doors whirred closed, the nighttime noises could be heard again.

Crickets chirped and bullfrogs called from a nearby pond. A pike broke the water's surface. Yellow beams escaped the silo window, washing the road below in a warm hue.

An owl hooted at the sight of a lone man sauntering back to the main compound. Hearing the man whistle a happy tune, the owl hooted in harmony, then dove from his perch and snatched a field mouse in his beak.

70

When Carly opened the letter postmarked Bethesda, Maryland, a manila coin envelope fell to the floor. "Duplicate" was hand-written in pencil on the outside. She unfolded the accompanying note. It was from Dr. Montgomery. The Navy drones had located the X-ray of the three-rooted mandibular molar. Here was a duplicate of his patient's film.

Carly let out a whoop. She held the film's edges in her fingertips so as not to smear the image or leave a fingerprint. She held it high toward the overhead light. It was definitely a three-rooted mandibular molar. What were the chances of it matching the X-ray taken from the blast victim's jaw?

Shit!

All she could think about was that the victim's original X-ray was still in the Kodak carousel from her forensic academy talk. Comparing the two would have to wait until she went home.

          *   *   *

"Got what you came for?" the doorman, clad in a mocha uniform, asked the retreating doctor.

Later, when the police interviewed the doorman who was substituting for Miguel, all he could remember was that the man was

clean-cut and wore green surgical scrubs, and that he had a stethoscope draped around his neck. Try as he may, the doorman could-
n't put any distinguishing features to the face. The one thing he
did recall was how the man tucked the yellow and black Kodak
carousel under his arm.

"It was right where she said it would be," the doctor had
answered the doorman upon leaving the building.

*   *   *

Carly dashed into her building and considered sprinting up the
twenty flights to her apartment. She was that sure the X-rays
would match. If they did, she was to call Dr. Montgomery and he
would reveal the victim's identity.

Carly bolted past the opening elevator doors, her key already
out. One, two, three locks, Carly almost ripped the metal door off
its hinges. She didn't bother to flick on the closet light; the
carousel was on the shelf above the coat rack.

When Carly couldn't find the Kodak box, her first thought
was that she left it at the hotel after the forensic lecture. Her
second thought was that she put it elsewhere and forgot what
she did with it. She ran into the kitchen, checked the cabinets,
and even looked under her bed. It was nowhere to be found.
She grew worried. Did she have "sometimers" disease, a precur-
sor of "all-zheimers?"

After she checked the last place in her apartment—her locked
luggage—three facts hit her. The first: there were no scratches on
the door locks. The second: someone stole her slides. These led to
a third: she was scared shitless.

The next day she learned that someone had slashed all four of
Miguel's tires so he *had* to miss work. Miguel, being the responsible sort that he was, called the building's superintendent in plenty

of time to get a temporary doorman. The employment agency the building always used to supply temps insisted they never received a call for any substitute doorman for Carly's building. The superintendent knew otherwise. He had placed the call for a replacement for Miguel.

Undaunted, LeShana had the superintendent's phone calls traced. The phone company discovered that superintendent's line had been connected to a rogue relay that rerouted the call to a disposable cellular phone bought from a vending machine. The call never got as far as the employment agency; it was intercepted by whoever wanted to steal the X-ray from Carly's apartment.

Whoever they were, they were that good.

71

The uniformed tour guide repeated her mantra for the last time that day: "This concludes today's tour of Canada's largest corporation. Feel free to spend as much time as you want looking at the energy display. Thank you for visiting us, and have a nice day, ladies and gentlemen."

*   *   *

Interactive computers filled the room's center. Screens explained how rainwater collected in dams and was used to power colossal generators. These generators not only converted the raw power to electrify Canada, but also goosed enough excess juice to supply the Northeast Corridor as far south as Washington, DC. A wall map identified every facility Hydro-Quebec owned and operated across the country. Pictures of dams, power plants, and research facilities were described in bold, black print. Colorful pamphlets provided a treasure trove of detail about Canada's main utility company.

Three *tourists* milled around in the middle of the room. In the course of three days they would inspect more hydroelectric plants.

"We need to concentrate on the EHV power transmission centers. They control all the high-voltage power to the States," said the swarthy man wearing a khaki shirt with matching pants; he was the apparent leader of the three. With a camera around his neck and a tote bag strapped on his waist, he lifted a plastic bottle of water to his lips.

"How will we infiltrate the installations?" whispered one companion.

The leader revealed a missing front tooth. "With all the construction taking place these days, no one will suspect some harmless vehicles transporting workers to a job site. It's been arranged."

"When?" asked the shortest man, whose purple scar was earned fighting in Angola, or maybe it was in Mozambique. Or, It might have been during the cartel skirmishes in the Colombian jungle. He'd fought in so many places through the years he forgot where and when it happened.

The leader with the camera spoke. "Nothing can stop us now." He clasped the forearm of the smaller man and bid him farewell. "Shalom."

"Shalom aleicham," replied the shorter man.

"Aleicham shalom," whispered the third compatriot.

72

The bar on Phillips Street in south Boston was one of the oldest in New England. For over a century, Reynolds was a sanctuary where men could be men and women were not allowed. At Reynolds, men kicked off their shoes and basked in the exquisite comfort that wives and girlfriends were off limits. They puffed on thick stogies and laughed at gross jokes without giving a hoot if anyone heard them. The tap house was legendary for dark port and honey-colored ale. Their only fare was a block of tangy cheddar cheese served on crisp Saltines. The "sandwich" was topped with raw onions so hot that breathing after eating a few of these crackers would etch glass. There was a dartboard nailed to the sidewall, with more errant holes in the wood paneling than the moon had craters.

In time, Reynolds was forced by the courts to serve female corporate types dressed in tailored suits, designer ties, and gold cufflinks, women who felt they had a right to lift a brewski or two with their male counterparts. So be it. The law was the law. They could enter the establishment, have their drinks, leave their coin, and expect no special treatment from Reynolds regulars.

Women were last on Len Dobbens's mind when he needed to use Reynolds's *pissoir*. Len planted himself in front of the tall white porcelain urinal that had craze-lines running top to bottom.

Five feet high, they jutted out like wrap-around cockpit wings, giving the princely gunner command of his private ship.

Len aimed high, low, and to the sides. No matter where his clear yellow-tinged stream splashed, the slick porcelain sucked the liquid downward. He looked down at the pyramid of ice cubes covering the pitted brass drains, which were meant to cover up the stink of urea and uric acid. He wondered if anyone had ever added the urine-coated ice to his drink! The image made him laugh.

As he squeezed out the remaining whizz, the toilet behind him flushed. A woman in her early twenties exited the stall adjusting her skirt.

"For crying out loud," Len said seeing her bare legs and flowered panties. In his stupor, he had forgotten Reynolds had only one bathroom. Len's gaze followed her to the sink when he heard a wet thudding sound. It was the noise a stream of water makes when it drenches fabric. Only this wasn't water or any old fabric. Len was pissing on his pants. She smiled; he shrugged.

Len returned to his friends knowing there was no escape.

"Is that a huge *come* stain, or what?" one asked as the group convulsed in spasms.

Like they never pissed in their *pants!*

When the laughter died down, Len tried to change the subject. "So what do you think?"

"Don't take the gunnery position. Your aim is awful," said Eddie O'Hara. Hearing that, a new round of laughter broke out.

"I mean about what they've got us doing at the hangers."

"We're paid to work and keep our mouths shut. That's what I'm doing."

Len wouldn't let them off the hook that easily. "I need the money bad as the next, but cutting Bombay doors into shuttle planes is more than strange. What good are they?"

"Mail drops," answered Eddie. Then he looked square at Len, "You think too much."

Eddie was right. Len Dobbens should have minded his own business.

*   *   *

Jeremy Steel strutted along the wooden plank leading to the edge of the cavernous hole in the ground. The site would house the electronic hub controlling his next Canadian project: STEEL CENTRE.

"Has the concrete crew arrived from New York?" Steel asked the foreman wearing the yellow hard hat.

"Yesterday."

"And the installation people from Galveston?"

"Winding down at Steel Metropolis as we speak. Be here tomorrow."

"And the blueprints?"

"Separate set for each group...," answered the foreman, "...like always."

Like always...as in Steel City.

Like always...as in Steel Metropolis

Like always...as in Steel Villages.

Like always...as in Steel Airlines.

Like always.

Even the foreman, an eight-year Steel veteran, did not know the final plans for the underground bunkers. It was his job to get each crew and have them complete their jobs before the next team arrived on their heels. Only in rare instances, did crews overlap.

Steel could build his cities anyway he wanted. Steel paid the bills; Steel called the shots. The foreman insured that each project ran with military exactitude. When the rare hitch did surface, he saw to it that it was eliminated. In return, he and his family would be taken care of for the rest of their lives.

*   *   *

"What do you have, sergeant," asked one of the few high-ranking Afro-Americans on the Boston police force.

The cop pointed to a rubbish-filled back street. "Some homeless guy found him in the alley over there, lieutenant."

"Any ID?"

"Stripped clean. Name even ripped off the front of his shirt. But look at this," said the officer who carried thirty extra pounds. He marched up to the body and lifted the back of the victim's shirt.

"At least we know where he worked," the lieutenant said.

The insignia read: **Steel Airlines.**

73

Henri Plumme found Luc Reardon editing an article he was about to submit to a psychiatric journal. The paper was entitled, "The erotic love-hate conflict serial killers have with their victims."

"It's a classic example of the serial killer leaving his signature," answered the noted shrink after the inspector finished describing the Pembina River murders.

The rumpled detective jotted a few words down, and then flipped through his notes. "Let me ask you this, Dr. Reardon, would it make a difference to know that every victim was American?"

"That wouldn't change my thinking."

"I'm not finished."

Plumme had little use for the academic-types who passed themselves off in the forensic specialties without getting their lilywhite hands dirty in actual field studies. On that score Luc Reardon was unsullied. Still, the man had his strengths. If Reardon could supply him with a loose set of characteristics that might help catch a killer, then the trip—not to mention swallowing his pride—was worth his personal suffering. The pressure was on. The newspapers added to the maelstrom claiming that a psycho-driven killer was on his own Son-of-Sam warpath, and no one was safe in any of the provinces.

"Here's the rest of the profile: American...."

"You said that."

Plumme lifted his head. "I believe I did. Maybe it was worth repeating."

"Perhaps, and then again, perhaps not."

Plumme counted to ten until the "red" disappeared, then continued. "They were all rugged and strong. Worked outdoors. Had callused hands. Muscles. You know the type. The police found no motives or clues as to why any were killed. Each time a body was discovered, their friends were shocked."

Reardon tapped an expensive pen on a notepad, making random dots. "You're making it more complex than it is, inspector. You have to understand the killer's mind. Every murder he commits is done to satisfy an inner need for love. He ritualizes the final act, savoring every moment. He memorializes it. For all we know, he's taking videos of each killing so he can watch them over and over again."

"Since all were men, are you saying there's a homosexual component to these murders? Is this another Andrew Gannon killing Gianni Versace? Gannon left a trail of murdered gay men across America before they caught up to him in that houseboat."

Reardon looked away for a moment. There was a fire in his eyes. "Why is this so hard to accept? Every serial killer is reaching out. They're begging society to help them purge the demons from their souls. When you study the deviant behavior of these killers, sex is percolating under the surface of every one of them. Men kill for love."

Plumme met Reardon's stare. "Then how do you explain that two murders occurred within minutes of each other, hundreds of kilometers apart?"

Reardon broke into a controlled smile. His eyes sparkled. "I'm surprised, inspector. Your killer is a latent homosexual who can't deal with the realities of his orientation. At the same time, he's enlisted—shall we say—a special friend to commit murder for him. It's the friend's proof that he loves our killer, that he would do anything for him. They're a team."

Reardon folded his hands exuding superiority and triumph.

"That's what I thought, too," Plumme said in tones meant to contradict. "Where do the tongues fit in? What's he trying to say with them?"

"He's challenging the police. He thinks they can't catch him because he's too clever. When he cuts the tongues out, he's being brazen. Bragging, if you will. He's shouting to the world that his victims won't reveal secrets about him."

"He's so certain he won't leave any clues?"

"Oh, but he *does* leave clues, inspector. It's just that you and the others have missed them. Keep looking."

Plumme closed his notebook. "For what? Any ideas?"

"Not at the moment, Inspector." Reardon sat taller. Reardon pitched his parting shot. "You know, of course, there will be more murders? You knew that before you walked in here."

"I was hoping you would prove me wrong."

PRESIDENT RETURNS TO OFFICE

VP GREELEY STEPS DOWN

WHITE HOUSE. In a changeover taking no longer than a blink of an eye, Aldous Fromm resumed his duties as President of the United States. At noon Eastern Standard Time, acting-president William "Kip" Greeley, vacated the Oval Office and returned to his role as vice-president. Mr. Greeley told reporters that the experience had altered the way he would tackle his job, and that he was relieved to have President Fromm back.

Though the usual contingent of White House reporters was present to chronicle President Fromm's return, no photographers were permitted to attend. Speculation raced through the corps of veteran reporters that while the President looked the same as before the fiery crash that killed seven others, he was self-conscious about the acrylic mask he continues to wear to control scar formation.

The consensus among press corps reporters was that the President looked as good as new, but moved with a deliberate gimp in his left leg. More than one observed that the president appeared an inch shorter than before, which is a direct result of his helicopter accident.

74

Jeremy Steel stood in a side corridor—out of sight—until the reporters left. He waited where Monica had hidden more than once, measuring time until foreign dignitaries or staff members took their leave so she could have her way with Bill. Now it was Jeremy Steel's turn. Except the only fornicating he and the president would be doing was at someone else's expense. Jeremy looked forward to bringing his old friend up to speed. At last, they were alone.

"Is it a go?" asked the President without a preamble.

Some people never change, thought Jeremy. No, *Take a seat and tell me how you are.* Not even, *Who are you fucking these days?*

What was Jeremy thinking? Fromm learned a while back not to dilly-dally. After all the years of coaching by Lute Aurum, Aldous Fromm went for the jugular. Sure the press would cut him some slack while he got back into the presidential swing of things, but coasting on sympathy was not Fromm's style. There was a job to do, and Fromm would take bold strokes to do it.

"Fitzpatrick has agreed to everything," Jeremy answered.

"Even oil exploration in the St. Lawrence?"

"We foot the bills from the rigs to drill bits, while he sits back and collects. I had to guarantee him there'd be no repeat of Exxon Valdiz."

"Still a fifty-fifty split?"

"Like you said."

"And the Frenchies in Quebec? Are they going to be any trouble?"

"If Fitzpatrick can't keep them in line, he'll be out on his ass in a week. How'd you like it if Congress could call an election anytime it pleased them? How long would Clinton have lasted? Their form of government sucks."

"If Quebec gets wind of this deal before it goes into effect, they'll declare independence and go it alone. Canada will be cut in two. As for our plan, I've been rethinking it."

The plan. It had been months since the two men had been together, and a lot had been accomplished. This was no time to rethink any of it. The wheels were in motion. Yet, Fromm was still the president.

Jeremy squirmed. The room suddenly grew hot. He opened his collar. "We agreed before. If we have to, we go to Phase Two. You're not getting cold feet on me now, are you?"

"That's what I want to tell you," Fromm said, "I don't ever want to visit that place."

"That's why I've been busting my ass meeting that big goon so many times. Everything has to go without a hitch. It hasn't been easy. We're almost there."

Fromm tapped his acrylic mask with the head of a pen. "You talk about easy? The surgeries and dental remake were a piece of cake compared to wearing this fucking mask. I feel like red ants are crawling across my face all day. You try wearing it."

"I'll pass, but it is intriguing. Imagine them making a second mask for me? There'd be two Aldous Fromms. Think the world could handle that?"

"I know they could."

Fromm sipped tepid sparkling water through a straw. Dr. Labatelli's brother-in-law dentist, Dr. Urquetti, said the sensitivity to cold would lessen in time. Soon, was not quick enough. His lips stretched through the mask. "We'd be quite the dynamic duo, don't you think?"

"We are already."

Fromm took another sip of water and winced. His right hand shot to his ear.

"What's wrong?" Jeremy asked.

Fromm massaged his jaw angle. "I felt a sharp pain, but it's gone. The dentist told me this could happen after the marathon sessions I went through. I'm fine, now. What do you think of the job he did?"

Fromm bared two rows of porcelain teeth through the mouth opening in the mask.

"Very Hollywood."

"A bit too perfect? I agree, but what the Hell. It goes with the territory." Then Fromm clapped his hands, the sound echoing off the walls. "What's left to do?"

"Get Fitzpatrick to open the airports to us. He told me it had to go through channels. After that, it's a go."

Fromm reached for a painkiller. He had tried to wean himself off them, but couldn't. He placed the pill as far back on his tongue as he could reach, then sipped water through a straw. The water caused another stab of pain. "Everything I do, hurts." Fromm shook another pill out of an amber plastic bottle.

"I thought Labatelli took that stuff away?"

"He had no choice."

Steel waited for Fromm to swallow the pill.

Fromm continued. "I spoke with Fitzpatrick this morning. He's pushing for your fleet to get the landing rights."

"What's holding them back? Don't they realize the tourist dollars it'll bring?"

"Money's the last thing those Canucks need these days. They're worried about Americans staying and taking jobs away from their people."

"So promise them it won't happen. What's the big deal?"

"There is no 'big deal,' Jeremy. I did what I had to do," Fromm said with a twinkle.

Jeremy tasted victory. "When?"

"I fly there tomorrow to sign the agreement."

"Flying could be pretty rough when a tooth acts up. Better see a dentist."

Fromm rubbed his jaw. "I'll take care of it as soon as I'm back."

Steel stopped as the door swung open. He saw Coulter Bell coming through with his arms full, and moved to give him a wide berth.

"Where do you want it?" Coulter asked.

"Jeremy, would you be good enough to put the bust of Teddy Roosevelt on the floor. We'll have to find another place for it."

"Why keep that thing?" Jeremy asked. "Lute's not here, anymore."

Fromm ignored the question. He focused on the diamond-marked viper in the cage. "Did you have any trouble feeding it while...?" Then he caught himself, unable to finish the sentence.

Coulter put his hand inside the glass herpetterrarium. "It's really gentle. They're easy to like."

Seeing Jeremy back-pedal, Fromm added, "Once you get over your fears."

Jeremy grabbed the doorknob. Then Fromm called to him. "If you recall, there was one last fly in the ointment?"

"Which is being removed as we speak, Mr. President."

Man Killed in River Explosion was Pres. Fromm's Doc

SILVER SPRINGS, MD. Police discovered the body of noted surgeon Dr. Enrico Labatelli, a mile downstream from the charred remnants of his 55-foot twin-engine cabin cruiser. Authorities speculate that the explosion that destroyed the doctor's boat occurred when a spark ignited excess fumes leaking from his gas tank. A receipt found in the victim's wallet confirmed that he had filled the tank at the Chesapeake Marina only minutes before the blast.

Dr. Labatelli is best remembered as the surgeon who treated President Fromm after his near fatal helicopter accident months ago. Dr. Labatelli leaves a wife, and two small children.

Dentist Reported Missing

SILVER SPRINGS, MD. In what may be related to the tragic boating accident that claimed the life of Dr. Enrico Labatelli, his brother-in-law, Dr. Santo Urquetti, has been reported missing. Dr. Urquetti's wife, sister to Dr. Labatelli, explained that her husband often joined her brother for a late afternoon fishing jaunt. Though there is no reason to expect foul play, Dr. Urquetti's wife, Rachel, was concerned for her husband's safety. Police are dredging the river in case Dr. Urquetti was on his brother-in-law's boat when it exploded.

75

Aldous Fromm's stay in Ottawa didn't last an hour. Aboard AIR FORCE ONE for the return flight, he extracted a fine Cuban from the handmade humidor given him by the present head of the Christian Coalition. Who was going to tell him that it was bad for his health? Besides, the victory was enormous. He secured enough wheat from America's resource-rich northern neighbor to stave off civil unrest for years to come. The price was peanuts compared to what he got. His end of the bargain was to limit the mass exodus of Americans into Canada. Landing rights and flight routes for Steel Airlines were a throw-in. Fromm would abide by the deal...for now.

Fromm was about to strike a match when a wrinkle of pain turned excruciating. Since yesterday, radiating flashes were tripping up his jaw, stabbing his ear, and then vanishing as quickly as they appeared. At first, cold drinks set it off. Then having tea with Fitzpatrick leapfrogged "heat" to the list-topping cause for pain. This time it lingered. Describing it as "acute" would not do it service. Percocet took the edge off the pain as the president's entourage left the Langevin Block for the airport.

On the return flight, Jeremy's warning proved true: the plane's cabin pressure triggered a snare drum rat-a-tatting in Fromm's head that became louder by the second. In moments, the drum-beat grew into a tympanic crescendo. Fromm waited for it to abate. He sipped brandy to take the edge off. Instead of helping, the electric heat turned white, taking refuge behind his right eye. Pain was one thing; this hot poker was off the Richter charts.

Fromm yelled.

Coulter Bell heard the screech and ran to the president. The press secretary was no stranger to armrest clutching dental experiences. When he saw Fromm rip off his acrylic mask and press a fistful of ice cubes to his cheek, he knew a tooth was the culprit. Coulter returned from the bathroom with two more Percocet.. Fromm downed the tablets with the last of the brandy.

"I'll make the necessary arrangements, Mr. President. You'll be out of pain in no time."

*   *   *

The red phone pierced the air a second time. Was it a mistake?

Dr. Lucian Whitmore remained transfixed. He was in the middle of deciding how best to treat a fistulous tract that pierced a forty-five year old man's chest wall. The head of NYU's surgical radiology department had seen infections like this travel right to the heart and kill the patient before antibiotics had time to kick in. The conservative choice? Cut before it was too late.

With the treatment decided, Whitmore intercepted the third ring. As he brought it to his ear—rearranged courtesy of college boxing—two tons of reality smacked him in the kisser: this was not a test. President Fromm had a medical emergency. Whitmore flashed on all the boring hours spent in Bethesda, listening to one speaker after another. He was one of sixty doctors across the country on call at a moment's notice for a presidential medical crisis. The helicopter accident aside, Whitmore would have bet that a meteorite would have landed on his own head before that red phone would ever ring.

"It's a red alert, Whitmore. The real McCoy," Coulter Bell said, in a chopped staccato voice. "Touchdown in fifteen minutes."

"We're ready, Mr. Bell. What are his symptoms?" asked Dr. Whitmore.

*   *   *

Carly's beeper vibrated against her belly. With her gloved hands in the mouth of a partially decomposed corpse, she waited until the shaking stopped. She was perplexed. Her beeper never went off during the day. Anyone who wanted to reach her knew to call the ME's office.

Must be a mistake.

No sooner had Carly refocused on the victim's teeth than the pager went off a second time. Carly ripped her gloves off. Who was bugging her? "Oh, Christ."

This is not supposed to happen.

When Lucian Whitmore asked if he could pen her name to the roster of doctors NYU could call on a moment's notice whenever the president visited New York, Carly reluctantly agreed. Since NYU didn't have a general dental residency in the hospital, she was the lone, full-time staff dentist. The fact that she was in dental forensics didn't seem to matter.

"Get someone else," she said when Whitmore asked. "You know, I'm no longer one of those wet-fingered dentists who work in the trenches everyday. My patients are so compliant these days, they don't need Novocain."

"Relax. What's the worst that could happen? He'll have a toothache and you'll plug the cavity? Write an Rx, and he's on his way. Christ, when I was in the Navy, we trained monkeys to fill teeth, so what are you worried about? Besides," Whitmore said, "you'll never be called in a million years."

Carly was used to the potshots and jibes about dentistry. After all, when it came to being liked and appreciated, dentists rarely received bouquets. In the end, Carly agreed to be part of the dental unit headed by Dr. Murphy O'Harrigan, who was a DDS/MD and chief of maxillofacial surgery at Bellevue Hospital. O'Harrigan's team would handle any facial swellings or head and neck trauma; Carly would take care of the teeth.

The beeper went off again. She caught the pager before it crashed to the floor and stole a last look, praying for a different message. It was the same.

Code Red! Stat!!

76

For the first time in her life, an elevator felt small. Cramped. Carly struggled to breathe. She pressed against the cold steel wall as if that would make her anxiety over President Fromm disappear. At least he wasn't a stranger to her. When they were leaving the Institute in his limousine four years earlier, he was easy to talk to. Had time and the accident changed him? She would soon find out.

The elevator doors parted. A pack of dark-suited military types accosted her. A female agent flashed an ID without saying a word, and then whisked Carly into a chart-filled records room.

"Is this necessary?" Carly asked.

"What do you think?" the agent answered, patting her down.

The Secret Service agent had her hair drawn in a tight bun. She wore dark-tinted glasses, a tailored suit, and matching pumps that had never been stylish.

"He's waiting," the agent pointed to the clinic.

Carly nodded to the agents on either side of the doorjambs, and slipped into the only suite in the hospital, built for in-patient dental emergencies. The president's head was down, focused on a clutch of papers. When he heard her enter he dropped the papers to the floor.

"I'm glad it's you, Carly."

"How are you, Mr. President?"

The president had a plastic, toothy smile. He was stiff with pain, his skin white and pasty. When he stood to greet her, he was slightly smaller than she remembered.

He touched his cheek. "I must look like the ghost of Christmas past. I've been wearing this acrylic mask for a while now. It's meant to limit scarring after all those surgeries. When the pain hit, I ripped it off. I hope I didn't ruin anything. Can you tell?"

Carly stood inches away. She inspected his face; his skin had become as translucent as Chinese paper. It had the same chalky texture and feeling the skin of corpses did.

"As far as I can see, no harm done."

Out of habit, she stared at his mouth as he spoke. "From a distance, I'm told I do look the same. What do you think?" asked Fromm.

"Approximately. Once the new skin weathers and you get some color, you'll look more like yourself close-up, too." She stepped back. "I think it's time to look at that tooth."

Fromm reached for the armrests.

"Do you need any help?" she asked.

"That's kind of you, Carly, but my therapist—LuAnne—preaches that pain is good for me. Let me do it."

Carly clipped a daisy chain onto the patient bib and fixed it in place, then leaned against the gray Formica cabinet. She slipped her hands into her lab coat's pockets, still focusing on his lips. The corners of his mouth crept upwards.

"What are your symptoms?"

Fromm tugged at his right ear. "It started yesterday. When I think about it, I felt some slight twinges last week, too. With all the pain pills I'm taking, it didn't bother me enough to complain."

"Do either hot or cold bother you?"

"At first, it was only cold. Now both hot and cold send me through the roof."

"How long does the pain last?"

"Seems like minutes. It's probably only a few seconds, I guess."

"Do you feel it now?"

He gave a plastic chuckle. "Does it ever hurt when you see the doctor? An hour ago, I was ready to jump out of Air Force One. Now? Nothing."

She picked up a mouth mirror and a #23 explorer. She examined the gums. Nothing appeared swollen or inflamed. She touched the crown margins, all fit well. She put the instruments down and palpated the outside and insides of the jawbone. "That's tender," he said, when she placed her finger close to the apex of the mandibular right first molar.

Carly made no comment. She picked up the mirror and used the flat end of the handle to tap each tooth in the sextant.

Fromm's eyes widened, his head nudged away from her. "That's the one."

Carly placed the instruments back on the bracket table, and folded her arms.

"You've got a pulpitis. It can come from decay getting into the nerve or, sometimes, it just happens. Especially when a tooth has been crowned."

Fromm tapped his teeth. "These are brand new since the accident. How could there be a problem with them already?"

"The drilling. It stresses the pulp. The water spray is supposed to cool everything down, but sometimes, high-speed drills fry the pulp. Then there's always the chance that your dentist nicked a pulp horn while he was preparing the teeth. That kills the nerve, too."

"Sounds like the more dental work a patient has, the more annuities will be coming the dentist's way."

"In a manner of speaking, dental work breeds more dental work."

"That's a thought. Isn't there a pill I can take? What about penicillin?"

"Sorry, but having a root canal's the only answer. I'll take an X-ray to be sure, but everything's pointing that way."

"If that's the case, can you start it now? I've got too much to do to be distracted by a toothache."

"Let me take the film. While it's being developed, I'll make you numb. That will give you immediate relief. If you do need a root canal, I'll get it going."

Carly removed the yellow sheath covering the two-inch long, twenty-seven-gauge needle. The agent standing in the doorway started toward Carly. Behind him, a second agent drew closer, fingering his gun.

Knowing they would do this, Fromm held up his left hand to shoo them away.

With the Lidocaine spreading to his tongue and jaw, Fromm grew more relaxed. The pain was dissipating. The Air Technique automatic film developer spit the processed X-ray out. Carly slipped it into a black Adamount® holder, then held it to the cool white fluorescent light. There was no doubt.

"You do need a root canal. Before I start, I'm going to isolate the area with what we call a rubber dam. It's sort of like a raincoat. It keeps the area dry while I work and prevents any instruments from falling down your throat."

"Do what you have to do, Carly. I trust you."

Carly wanted to blurt out that he shouldn't trust her, that she hadn't done a root canal in four years. That wasn't exactly true, either. The director of the Bronx Zoo had called and asked her to do a root canal on a Siberian white tiger that had accidentally cracked its eye tooth off at the gum line. The tiger survived...and so did its tooth! No, Carly would not say a word about her being rusty; she was a fine dentist and would do a terrific job.

With the dam in place, Carly slipped a bur into the high-speed handpiece and tightened the chuck. She set about the task in workmanlike fashion. She first made an access hole to locate the orifices of each canal. There were the usual three: two mesial and one distal. Using barbed files, she extirpated the pulp tissue. She found healthy, bleeding nerves in both mesial canals, the distal canal had necrotic tissue.

Fromm couldn't speak with the rubber dam in place. So when Carly said, "One canal's already dead, the other two were on their way," Fromm widened his eyes to show he understood. Next, Carly irrigated the canals with 1% sodium hypochlorite before sealing them with a pledget of cotton and temporary cement. With a flick of the wrist, she removed the gray rubber dam that was now wet from saliva. He wiped his face with the patient bib and rinsed out.

"You've got a light touch. I'm grateful."

"I think you fell asleep in the middle of it." She pushed the bracket tray out of the way. "When you get back to Washington, it will take one or two more visits to finish. Then you'll be as good as new."

Fromm struggled to swing his legs onto the floor. He touched them. "You mean my tooth. The rest of me will never get back to the way I used to be."

"At least you're here to talk about it, Mr. President. Look what happened to the others."

Still sitting, he took her hand. "It's so easy to forget. Life goes on and yesterday's tragedies fade like a sunset. Thanks for reminding me." Carly was about to say something, when he added, "Damn I miss that Lute Aurum, don't you? I mean, without him, I wouldn't be here."

Now Carly didn't answer. She couldn't. How could she tell the president that his trusted advisor, Lute Aurum, was someone she despised? Although every fiber in her body cherished life, she was glad Aurum could no longer be counted among the living.

"I'm glad you came away from that accident okay, Mr. President. Now you won't forget to get that tooth finished, will you?"

"I'll see my dentist first chance I get back in Washington."

"Do you want me to send a report to Dr. Montgomery?"

President Fromm was surprised. "How do you know Elvin?"

"I met him at a forensics meeting. I understand he treats a lot of the Washington bigwigs. I took a shot that he might treat you."

Hearing Fromm say "Elvin" made the hairs on her neck prickle. She struggled to fix her stare on his glazed porcelain crowns, but Fromm's magnetic field drew hers away from his pale blue lips. Carly wanted to turn away, but she couldn't.

"Elvin *does* treat me. I'll let him know what a fine job you've done."

Fromm pushed off on the armrest and stood; Carly stepped back. When he lifted a foot toward the door, he stumbled. Carly leaned and caught him. Once their weights were in momentary balance, Carly raised herself—and Fromm—slowly, until both stood straight.

Fromm continued to hold onto her arms.

Carly tugged, he wouldn't let go.

She wanted to say something that would make him let go. She opened her mouth and was about to speak when Fromm's eyes began to glow. Or so she thought. *"Eye contact, eye contact."* Her mother was always telling her to look them straight in the eye. *"Appear confident and the world will respect you,"* she would say. But no matter what grades she got in school or what she accomplished on the volleyball court, Carly never gained the confidence to look squarely at people. She made it to their teeth and stopped. Now, seeing Fromm's eyes, terrified her. This was not the same man who helped her four years earlier.

Could power change him that much? Or was it the accident?

A Secret Serviceman knocked at the door. "You're late for your meeting, sir."

Fromm squeezed Carly's arms one last time. His fingertips, so light and gentle before, were talons now. "Be sure to visit me if you come to Washington, Carly. I'd like to give you the royal treatment. You're a credit to your profession."

Two Secret Servicemen entered the operatory and confiscated the mounted X-ray clipped to the fluorescent view box.

"Is this the only one?"

She nodded.

They left her surrounded by silence. As quickly as the tumult started, it had ended. Here she was, Carly Mason, treating the President of the United States. Only instead of being in awe of the man and glad for the experience, she felt empty. Alone. A God-awful feeling coagulated in the pit of her stomach. No matter how great the man, no matter how capable and talented, the office of the president transformed each inhabitant into an alien life form. Then for no reason, she let out a spine-tingling cry that if Willie were there would have declared loud enough to "wake the dead."

When the echoes receded, Carly returned to the closet housing the automatic developer. She retrieved the second X-ray resting in the plastic tray. She was glad the agents didn't know dental X-rays could come two-to-a-packet. Taking double films was hospital procedure. One went into the patient's chart; the other was used for insurance claims. Since there was no way the hospital would bill the White House, she slid the X-ray into its original white Kodak packet, and placed it in a manila coin envelope.

What harm was there in keeping a souvenir?

*   *   *

Carly plowed through the door.

"How'd it go?" Willie asked. He was making a Y-incision through the chest of a young man discovered in a footlocker on a Chinese freighter.

"He'll survive."

"The hopes and prayers of western civilization rest in your hands, and the best you can do is that 'he will survive?'"

"There was something about his eyes."

"Whose?"

"The President's. I've seen them before."

Willie cut through the sternum. "Who hasn't? Does it matter?"

"It might, if you saw what I saw. By the way, when you lost the Rock Center victims…?"

"They were *taken* from me."

"I couldn't resist. I still can't believe it happened."

"Believe it. So why are you reminding me of *that* unpleasant chapter of my life?"

"Because I just realized there should be duplicate X-rays in their charts."

"When the suits came they never asked for the charts, and I certainly wasn't offering. I locked them in my bottom desk drawer. You know where the key is."

Carly unlocked the file drawer, and slid it open.

"Find them?" Willie called out.

Carly kicked the drawer so hard, the cabinet banged up against the wall. The glass partition rattled.

Willie was cruising into the room by the time she got to the doorway. "Are you all right? It sounded like the whole world fell on your shoulders."

"All three charts are missing."

77

After identifying Slim's body, Jack remained in a stupor for two days. It got so bad Link made two runs without him. Jack lay in the bunk overcome by a flood of images. He saw the body he and Link found the day they entered Canada…that felt like eons ago. The locked fences, the guards taking *Ol' Betsy*, the way *Pinky's Place* grew quiet whenever the uniforms marched in. The day they opened the rig and cut into a dozen boxes. Billy. Slim.

He stared at the rough-hewn wood on the vaulted ceiling. A black fly buzzing in his ear was his only company. The room grew smaller. The thick air weighed heavy on his chest. He was suffocating in more ways than one. Tears trickled from his rheumy eyes. "Damn fools."

Jack did a slow spin and landed on his feet. Later, he would analyze what propelled him to Slim's bed. There was no thought process involved at the time. It just happened. Maybe he wanted to bond with Slim for old time's sake, before another stranger from Omaha, Butte, or Rapid City moved in and corrupted the memories?

The germ of an idea started crystallizing. He reached under Slim's mattress for Billy's letter. He rummaged through the cardboard box that held all of Slim's worldly possessions: a twenty-eight blade Swiss

Army knife, pictures of his parents, a brother, a sister, pictures of nieces and nephews, a rabbit's foot, and the Congressional Medal of Honor earned in the Persian Gulf War.

How come you never told us?

The letter was not hidden in an obvious place. Jack hunted for secreted nooks; he tapped for loose floorboards. In the end, when he was beside himself for not finding it, he pictured the day Slim followed Link into the john and stood on a chair.

"I won't let you down, Slim," Jack said, when his fingers touched the envelope that was tucked behind a tile.

*   *   *

General Gadol surveyed the corps of farmers Slim Armstrong used to belong to before he...and his tongue...were severed from the troops. The men were back from exhaustive field maneuvers. Some stood, most kneeled on one leg, a few lay flat on the grass. They poured water over their heads; streaks of dirt covered their faces.

Gadol mounted a makeshift platform. "You deserve to be congratulated. You have molded yourselves into a skilled group that any commander would be proud to lead."

"When can we get to farming?"

"Patience, my friend. Your assignments will come any day. For now, rest."

Now alone, Gadol stabbed the memory button on his cell phone. He heard a click.

There was no greeting, no salutation...only a whisper of inhaling and exhaling. Gadol was brief. There was no need to say more.

"They're ready." Soon, he would have the biggest payday of his career.

78

"There's a man to see you," announced the desk clerk. "He wouldn't give his name. Says you don't know him, anyway."

Henri Plumme was standing in front of a corkboard that ran the length of the wall, studying each crime scene with a magnifying glass. He put the polished glass in its brass holder and turned to the brown-painted door.

"My name's Jack Kincade. I need to talk to you about them murders."

The two men eyed each other. It was the sort of 'once-over' men do when they don't trust a soul in the world except themselves.

Plumme padded toward his armchair. "Have a seat."

The same high-backed leather chair accompanied Plumme to every assignment he ever had. Like a superstitious pitcher, Henri Plumme relied on his skills, his cunning, his abilities, and his lucky charms. His chair was one, the ceramic fish around his neck, the other.

Jack continued to stand. He tossed the stained white envelope onto Plumme's desk. "Read it, and then we'll talk."

"Do you want to tell me what this is about?"

Jack pointed to the corkboard. He reached out and touched two pictures. "It was addressed to him...from...him."

"Billy Squires to Monsieur Armstrong?"

Seeing the murder scenes up close, especially the enlargements with a forensic ruler next to the severed tongues, made Jack queasy. He edged into a chair.

Plumme read Billy's letter a second time. When he finished, he laid the letter on the desk and reached for a meerschaum pipe. He tapped the burnt shards into a green glass ashtray, and then filled the bowl with an aromatic blend. He struck a match before asking, "Do you mind?"

Jack reached into his pocket and drew out a cigarette.

Plumme leaned across the table. Jack cupped his right hand under the inspector's, and drew in. He blew a stream of smoke out the side of his mouth.

"Do you know who the killer is?" Plumme asked.

Jack drew in long and hard.

They studied each other.

Plumme waited for Jack to speak.

Jack picked his words. "I got me an idea how to find out."

79

Carly watched Willie sign the messenger's sheet while she waited for Dr. Montgomery to be paged. Willie held the eight-by-eleven envelope by a corner, and swung his crutches toward her.

"I need the biggest favor in the whole wide world, Dr. Montgomery." Carly explained how thankful she was that he located the X-ray. However, when she went to compare it to the bomb blast victim's, it was missing. In fact, both copies were lost. "I know this is irregular, but if you could tell me who your patient is, it may help us identify our victim."

Carly crossed her fingers. When her brow went up, and then she wrinkled her nose, Willie knew it was no-go.

"I understand. I'd do the same thing," she said to Dr. Montgomery. "By the way, you should be getting a call from President Fromm. He had a flare-up on tooth #30. I did a pulpectomy and medicated the canals. Can you arrange to have it finished?"

Carly spoke with Dr. Montgomery for another minute before saying, "Good-bye."

"What's wrong?" Willie handed her the envelope. "I knew he wouldn't divulge his patient's name."

"He said the president never had any dental fillings and was surprised he needed a root canal. When I reminded him of the accident and that he must have had a lot of broken teeth, it made sense to him."

"I can see something's troubling you."

"You know how you can tell when someone is holding back and not telling you everything?"

"Like our patients."

"Unlike our patients, Montgomery's holding something back. Our patients tell us everything we need to know."

"Most of the time," Willie added.

"So tell me what were our three Rock Center victims trying to tell us?" she asked. "What did we miss?"

"I'll keep an ear out for them if you promise to open that letter the messenger brought."

He handed her a scalpel. She cut open the flap. From inside, she pulled out a gold embossed invitation with her name in ornate calligraphy.

"Shit. Why does he wait until the last minute?"

"Is Prince Own-It-All inviting you to The Grand Ball?"

She shoved the invite in his face. His eyes widened.

"Impressive. Why are you still here?"

$$*\qquad\qquad *\qquad\qquad *$$

The intercom buzzed: her car was waiting. A final stroke of eyeliner, and then Carly stuffed her makeup into her purse. One last check in front of her full-length mirror. Black dress. Matching shoes. The image pleased.

She triple-locked the door. As the elevator went down, she pinched herself. Was this really happening to her?

"You could've given me a bit more notice," she said to Jeremy, sliding next to him.

"I found out the same time you did. It couldn't be helped."

She poked him in the ribs. "You're forgiven this time. Besides, how many times do I get to meet the Canadian Prime Minister?"

Jeremy added to her list of luminaries. "...And the president in the same week."

"That's right. President Fromm went to see you after me. How did he feel?"

"Seems you won him over," said Jeremy. "He thought you were terrific."

"Tell you the truth, I was more than disappointed. How well do you know him?"

The limousine cruised toward Teterboro Airport.

"The president? If you mean, are we bosom bodies? Not exactly. I have spent time with him. Always at the White House."

"Does he seem different to you? It's like I know him in some other way," Carly said. "It's spooky."

Jeremy dismissed her concerns. "Fromm's charismatic. He makes everyone feel that way the first time they meet him."

"It wasn't the first time we met," she answered. "It was at Lute Aurum's Institute. He was still governor then. My friend Conner Masterson said he saw you there."

"Your friend's delusional. How can he claim to have seen me when I've never been to Arizona?"

"That's what I told him. Conner was under a lot of pressure then. That's not the only thing he said that hasn't made sense."

They drove onto the Tarmac. Jeremy's plane was revved and ready to fly. Once they were in the air, Carly replayed the bit about Conner seeing Jeremy. She had every reason to believe Jeremy. What would he gain by lying to her? Conner, on the other hand, could be excused for seeing things. After all, having tarantulas crawl up your leg and snakes wrap around your neck can cause anyone to see more than double.

With their seat belts fastened, Jeremy leaned over and pecked her on her cheek.

She touched her skin. "What was that for?"

"For being wonderful. I know we're in New Jersey, but there's no law against being demonstrative here, is there?"

"Not in my book," she said, and kissed him back.

80

Each cushion in the two thousand-seat auditorium was occupied by a well-turned out man or woman bedecked in aristocratic attire. It wasn't lost on Carly that jewelry graduated to jewels, and baubles became heirlooms. Carly and Jeremy were seated dead center, first row, surrounded by heads of state and dignitaries from throughout the British Commonwealth. With the buzz behind her and with electricity befitting the Oscars, Carly wondered about all the secrecy surrounding the evening. She also wondered how quickly she could get used to this way of life.

Honey Fitzpatrick rapped the microphone; the mystery command performance was about to be explained. His first words were lost in the sea of tall gossip. Carly could only hear the last few words.

"...Her Royal Majesty, Queen Elizabeth II."

On cue, coronets tapped out a royal march, and the aged monarch marched gingerly to the podium with the help of a diamond-encrusted cane in one hand and an aide on the other. Mid-stage, Honey Fitzpatrick took over. He bowed deeply, all six-foot-eight inches of him, and then helped steady her at the podium.

She beamed at all the faces, found Jeremy in the first row, nodded, and then read from a TelePrompTer built into the lectern.

"Mr. Fitzpatrick, honored members of the Cabinet, distin-
guished leaders of Parliament, ladies and gentlemen. You have
been assembled here to honor a great man. This is not to be taken
lightly. For what we are about to do here this evening, is being
done for the first time in Canada's long and illustrious history.
Never before in modern times, has one man single-handedly
shaped a country. Never before has one man been responsible for
changing the lives of so many. Never before has one man been
able to grab the splendor and grandeur of the future, and turn it
into an everyday reality."

The Queen paused to sip water.

Carly saw Honey Fitzpatrick stand taller, beaming as the
Queen spoke.

Was this about him? Jeremy's friend?

The audience held its collective breath as the Queen continued.
"This man's vision of greatness has meant much to Canada and,
in turn, the British Commonwealth. As all of you know, Canada
has taken its rightful place among the industrial powers of the
world. She has done so not as a weak sister, but as a strong powerful leader. Today Canada feeds most people living in third world
countries. What's more, for the first time in history, she exports
grain to her long-time friend and neighbor to the south, the United
States of America."

Applause thundered.

"Canada not only has the highest per capita income of all countries in the world, but has eliminated poverty as we know it.
Ladies and gentlemen, no other country in the world can make
that claim."

Again, applause boomed through the room as if the sonic bar-
rier had been broken.

The Queen adjusted her glasses, and then looked at the audience for the first time.

"It is without further ado that I call before you the man who has single-handedly made Canada a beacon to the sisterhood of nations."

Honey Fitzpatrick beamed. If he was a volcano, the magma was about to explode. Queen Elizabeth looked at him, too. The audience was uncertain as to what would happen next.

The prime minister stepped toward her.

The Queen bowed her head in a royal curtsy. "Mr. Prime Minister, would you do me the honors?"

Everyone watched Honey Fitzpatrick glide past the Queen and march down four wooden steps. He stood on the auditorium floor, waiting for the Queen's next words.

"Mr. Jeremy Steel, would you please join me," she said, with a twinkle, "we have a surprise for you."

Jeremy grabbed Carly's arm, kissed her as if he just won the statuette for Best Actor, and then bound past the prime minister. As Jeremy mounted the stage, the curtain parted behind the Queen. Stewards dressed in stiff uniforms rolled a red velvet throne, lush with gold trim, to center stage. The regal chair was perched on a platform three feet off the ground. The aged monarch inched to the base of the throne and waited for the motorized seat to whir down. With a helping hand, she roosted into the chair and was raised to an exalted height.

Jeremy stood before her, head bowed. Three men in medieval uniforms appeared from the left, lifting six-foot long brass coronets to their lips. Short staccato notes blared from the ancient instruments, a battle hymn of bygone eons. Then, as four thousand eyes followed the proceedings in awe, a guard dressed in green satin draped with glittering buttons and golden tassels, marched to center stage.

The Queen sat tall, towering over the assemblage. The emerald-appointed attaché carried a large cushion that cradled a gold bejeweled sword. The ward bowed and waited for the Queen to lean and take the emerald-encrusted blade.

With a strength none thought she could possess at her ripe age, Queen Elizabeth II raised the sword over her head. All watched it quiver as she brought it down onto Jeremy's shoulder.

"Jeremy Steel, please kneel."

The audience watched with bated breath.

"As Queen of England and protector of this great land, for the millions you have housed and the millions you have created jobs for, and for the glory you have brought to Canada, I bestow upon you the title of 'Knight.' From this day forth, as God is my witness, you will be known as Sir Jeremy Steel, Knight of the Royal Order."

81

Aldous Fromm missed Jeremy's big night. He returned to Washington to tackle a backlog of presidential duties. Papers were signed, meetings held, and for the first time in ages—since the helicopter accident—he had a good night's sleep...his toothache a matter of the past, thanks to Carly Mason.

The following morning, Fromm was reviewing the day's agenda when Kip Greeley barged through the door. "How dare you shut me out of everything."

Fromm pushed back from his desk and crossed his legs. He rested his clasped hands on his belly. "You know, it occurs to me you're the only person in the country who enjoyed my prolonged recovery. It's painful to be stripped of power, isn't it, William? You know, I was wrong about you. Piss and vinegar do run through your veins, after all."

Greeley hated being called by his given name, and Fromm knew it. "What I am or how I've changed has no bearing on the fact that we've got to turn things around. Whether you realize it or not, this country's going to ruin."

Fromm unclasped his hands and sat straighter. "What is this 'we' business...William? Have you forgotten, I'm the president? You're here for the ride, and don't ever forget it. When I want

405

your opinion I'll ask for it. When I have a meeting that is *sup-posed* to include the vice-president, you'll be invited. Otherwise, stay where you belong, as far out of my sight as possible. Is that clear enough as to how 'we' are going to tackle problems?"

Kip Greeley was a changed person. It wasn't that sitting in the world's power seat went to his head; he realized how far removed Fromm had kept him from everything. The country was turning to shit; something had to be done.

Remember the issues.

It took all his willpower, but Kip Greeley stayed cool. "Farmers are walking the back roads of this country, sleeping in doorways, going to bed with empty bellies. Once we fed the world, now we can't even feed ourselves."

"What about the wheat deal I just signed with Canada?"

"Window dressing, and you know it."

"Amuse me, William. What have you learned in my absence."

"You arrogant sonofabitch. Any ten-year old can tell you the Greenhouse Effect is altering the world as we know it. Everything's gone topsy-turvy. Do you want to know how bad it is? I'll tell you. The day is coming when we'll see orchid's growing in the Arctic and snowflakes in the Sahara. America's soil is blowing away. Our best scientists are fleeing to Europe and Russia. Next year, India will pass us on the economic scale. Who's to blame for our planet becoming more inhospitable every day? Every year? A couple of centuries from now—if there are still people—they'll point to America. They'll say that we were the major catalyst, the country that poisoned the air and destroyed the ozone layer…all in the name of progress. If you don't get off your smug ass and start taking drastic measures, you will be left with one legacy: Aldous Fromm was the man who let it all happen. He could have done something about it, but he sat there picking his nose."

"Are you finished?"

Greeley slumped. "Now I am."

Fromm's silence spoke legions.

Greeley broke it. "It's just that since you've been back, Aldous, I've been *persona non grata*. In fact, you don't seem yourself. Not that we were ever close, but this is extreme."

"Now that you've had your taste, you should appreciate the challenges I face. Have you taken the time to consider I'm still healing? I'm not Superman. Falling out of the sky and being one step removed from a human pancake does have its drawbacks, you know."

"You've been through a great deal."

"You can't imagine."

Then Fromm stood and limped to the sidewall. He reached into a box and a white fur ball disappeared into his pocket. Next he lifted the glass top of the herpetterrarium and stroked Lute's viper. The snake pointed its head at Greeley and hissed. Fromm snagged the mouse and dangled it above the glass cage until the snake darted up and engulfed it—midair—in one mouthful.

Greeley's mouth turned dry. "Now that he's fed…"

"It's a she."

"How do you know?"

"Lute told me; they're more vicious."

"Aldous, you must have an agenda, plans you've been working on to get us out of this mess? What bills are you introducing? How can I help?"

"Bills? We're beyond bills. We're beyond mandates and restrictions, and reducing carbon emissions by pittances each year."

Greeley couldn't believe what he was hearing. "Then what are you talking about? Martial law? Are you going to militarize the country to follow an austerity program? Shove it down their throats? You can't pull that off. Not here."

Fromm chuckled and relaxed for the first time. "We've gotten too far from the democracy our forefathers envisioned, and there is a place for benevolent tyranny in this world. But no, that's not what I'm planning...nor could I. After all, my hands are tied as president. The power rests with both Houses."

"Then what are you going to do?"

"Address your concerns. The planet will be saved for the children."

"But how? What could you possibly do?"

Fromm didn't answer.

*   *   *

Kip Greeley left his meeting with Aldous Fromm confused, but with a lighter step. Power *had* changed him. While Fromm mended from his accident and surgeries, Greeley had matured into a force of his own. He was no longer a passive, ass-kissing VP like most of his predecessors had been. Fromm had made a one-eighty turnaround on ecological issues because he knew Kip Greeley would dog him every step of the way if he didn't. With the corner turned, Greeley would keep pushing Fromm until their priorities overlapped. While Fromm might be remembered as the president who put the brakes on America's—and the world's—slide into self-destruction, Greeley would end up getting the credit for its rebirth when he was at the helm.

This had been a good day for Kip Greeley.

It was ruined by the time he got to his office.

The white envelope was propped on his desk, postmarked "New York." He ripped open the flap, read the terse note, and then walked to the window. He stood there for some minutes, not wanting to believe a word of it.

The theory was absurd.

He scooted past his desk, grabbing a lighter the Boys Scouts had given him when they awarded him their "Man of the Year" award for advocating controlled burns of dead forest mass. He kneeled in front of the brick fireplace that had never been lit.

He reread the letter, and then ignited the corner. A spurt of black smoke curled upward. He watched the orange and yellow flames gobble the paper until he felt the heat. Then he tossed it into the unmarked grate and watched the last remnants turn into black ashes.

*   *   *

Aldous Fromm had little time to digest his exchange with Kip Greeley when Coulter Bell knocked.

"What did Greeley want?" Coulter asked.

"For starters, to tell me how to do my job."

"He's had a taste and the power's gone to his head," Coulter said.

"I don't blame him. From the outside, it does look like I'm ignoring the issues. If Greeley sees it, so does everyone else. Let's fix it."

Fromm outlined a media blitz for Coulter to sell to the public. It would go a long way to quelling his critics...including Kip Greeley. "We'll halt the Greenhouse Effect dead in its tracks. Tell them this administration is willing to pull out all the stops. We'll take a page from FDR's book. Federal works projects. Tax credits for companies willing to put their resources and energies into reclaiming the soil, like the Israelis did when they started from scratch in '48. We'll deploy everyone who's able to work. Start selling this to the papers, it will buy us time."

The president poured himself a glass of water. He gulped it down then added more. "And get this out, too. All the futuristic gurus have been predicting that wars will be waged over information. They claim that 'information' rules. Well, tell them they're wrong." He wagged the glass toward Coulter. "Potable water will reign supreme. It won't be any gigabits of data traveling in cyberspace. If we have water, we have food. If we have food, we rule the world."

"What should I tell them when they ask, 'Why the sudden change on domestic issues? What's Fromm up to?'"

"Tell them what they want to hear. Tell them that solving America's domestic issues is tantamount to curing what ails the world. Tell them to stop criticizing me. Tell them...Aldous Fromm is back."

Coulter's voice was peppered with both pride and awe. "You know, you're actually sounding like the old Aldous Fromm. That should buy us the time we need."

"Then go sell it...and who else am I supposed to sound like, damn it?"

Coulter did not have time to answer.

"Jeremy Steel is on your private line, Mr. President," the outside secretary announced over the intercom.

Aldous Fromm dismissed Coulter Bell before he pressed the blinking button. "Sir Jeremy, I presume? How does it feel?"

"It has a nice ring to it, don't you think?"

"From what I know, being a knight has its rewards."

"I've collected some already."

"At the hotel, I presume."

"What do you think?" said Jeremy.

"Nothing like one for old time's sake before lowering the boom. Eh?"

"Waste not, want not."

"I take it you and she have come to an understanding? We're too close to the end to take any chances. It would be a shame for Carly Mason to step in the way of our plans now."

"I took the liberty to insure that wouldn't happen, sir. If all went according to plan, we should be free and clear as we speak."

Fromm rubbed his hands together. "In that case, let the games begin."

98 More Die in Chicago As Heat Wave Continues

CHICAGO (UPI)-Ninety-eight more people died from the heat today, pushing heat-related deaths in Illinois to 225 for the month. The nation's heat-related fatalities are approaching battlefield numbers. One anonymous health official claims these numbers are low.

Chicago hit 103 degrees during the week, though cooling temperatures are expected over the weekend. Despite the break in the record heat, perennial Mayor Richard Daly urged residents to check that elderly friends and relatives are drinking enough water and are staying cool. Free fans are available at all precinct station houses.

The brutal heat has seized much of the nation. In a sad commentary as to how our elderly worry about day-to-day living, many heat-related fatalities occur in homes with air-conditioners that are not turned on in order to save on electric bills.

Triple digit temperatures have become the norm in most parts of the country. From Childress, Texas to Madison, Wisconsin, the heat is toppling people like trees in a storm.

In other related news, rare spring tornadoes are predicted for parts of Minnesota, Wyoming, and Montana. The Mid-Atlantic States are experiencing their worst drought since the summer of '99. If the drought continues much longer, bathing will be limited to every other day, for three minutes at a time. NYC's mayor plans to recommend communal showers.

82

For Carly, everything that happened after Jeremy's knighting ceremony turned into a gauzy blur. First there was the congratulatory hug when Jeremy returned from the stage with the banner of the Order of Knights draped across his tuxedo. From the moment he kissed her in front of the applauding throng to swirling under the crystal chandeliers at the champagne ball that followed, Carly lost all perspective of the word "normal." Flash bulbs followed her every step. In plain truth, she had become a media darling on the arm of one of the world's most powerful moguls.

Did she dare dream about becoming *Lady* Steel?

"You must be higher than a kite," Carly said as they danced a congratulatory spin in front of hundreds of watchful eyes.

"I should be...but it leaves me wanting."

She flicked his shoulder. "I can't think of a living American who's been knighted by the Queen of England, and you want more? What more could you want?"

"I can always hope, can't I?"

"For what?" She thought a moment. "Oh I get it. You're thinking of running against Aldous Fromm in the next election. Is that it?"

He kissed her on the forehead. "I knew I couldn't fool you."

First Lady?

After a round of good-byes, Jeremy whisked her to the penthouse suite in the Four Seasons Hotel. What could have been romantic lovemaking turned into "Mechanical Intercourse for Beginners."

Jeremy popped out of bed the second *he* climaxed, leaving her to clutch the pillow instead of him. She watched him trek to the bathroom. "That was great," he called out.

For whom?

The water ran longer than necessary. Instead of seeing him naked with a dangling member she might coax back to life for "her" pleasure, he emerged fully clothed. Carly sprung upright. The duvet fell to reveal her breasts. When he leaned to kiss her nipple, she batted his hand away.

He stood and straightened his tie. "Sorry about that, but I knew I couldn't stay the night."

"So you graced me with a good-night fuck and an *adios?* Well *muchos gracias* to you."

Jeremy remained nonplussed. "The last thing I wanted to do was leave."

Her lips turned into a soft pout. "Then why are you?"

"Honey Fitzpatrick is expecting me. I can't turn the prime minister down, can I?"

"At this hour?"

"I know it's odd, but something's come up."

"You're a knight. Can't you make it tomorrow?"

"I'll be back as soon as I can."

Carly covered herself with the duvet. She scooted until her naked back hit the fabric-covered headboard.

"I'm glad you understand," he said.

In one move she whipped a pillow at him, catching Jeremy dead-on.

"I don't, you shit."

"Be realistic. I wanted to share the evening with you. I'll be back before you wake up."

She clutched the covers closer to her body. "Don't bother. I made arrangements to go to the University tomorrow. They're letting me examine the teeth of the Indian found in a cave by the Thompson Ice Fields. Afterwards, I'll take the shuttle…so you can have more meetings. I hope they're successful."

He sprung for the door. "They will be."

Anger kept her awake. She had been made a fool of yet one more time. When would she learn that pretty boys, no matter how much money they had and how sincere they sounded, should be treated like lepers? Get over Jeremy, she told herself, and pray that his body parts start dropping off…at an alarming rate.

Outside noises filtered into her room. Late-night revellers made a racket in the hallway. A tray of dirty dishes rattled outside a door. Music wafted through the thin air.

An hour later, maybe two, she was cruising through Never-Never Land, hurtling toward her recurrent nightmare. In it, her mouth was contorted wide open, her teeth as big as piano keys. Then one-by-one they started to crumble, like wet chalk starting to flake apart. The incisors were the first to go, then the laterals. She screamed in her dream, but no one heard her. If she didn't make up soon, she'd be toothless. Castrated. The shrinks called women dreaming about losing their teeth, "Penis envy." Carly called it, "Fear of flying solo the rest of her life."

In her dream, the molars were just crumbling when she heard a click.

Her body lurched up from the mattress, her skin was soaking wet.

The door squeaked open. The hall light silhouetted a figure entering her room.

Carly groped for the lamp switch. "I told you not to come back."

Carly shrieked when the light went on. A man was standing there, dressed as a cleric in a black robe and white collar. He was of medium build. He had sandy brown hair streaked with gray. In the dim light, she could see that his colorless eyes were ice cold, but his voice was soft.

"Were you expecting someone?" He didn't move toward her, nor did he make a threatening gesture.

Carly reached for the phone.

"Don't."

Her heart was beating a cacophony of fear. A chill swept over her. "Give me one reason why I shouldn't."

"Because I asked you not to. Please. It'll only get in the way."

She lowered the headset into the cradle.

When he spoke again his tone was soothing, the tone a Sunday school teacher might have used to tell a story. He moved to a high-backed upholstered club chair. "I only want to talk with you. If you won't try anything foolish, I'll sit down, say what I have to say, and leave you alone. How's that?"

"Do I have a choice?"

He wasn't particularly muscular but he was in good shape. He might have been thirty years her senior. She thought about springing off the bed. If her birthday suit dazzled him long enough, she could make the door. Bad idea.

"No," he answered.

Carly continued to stare. Watching. Waiting. Her pulse slowed to a trot. The next move was his.

"They sent me to kill you."

She tucked her legs closer to her chest. Her knuckles were pure white. Her jaws clamped so hard together her teeth grated in a screech. She drew in a deep breath.

"What did I do?"

Why did she blow Conner off? He warned her!

"You've gotten some pretty important people pissed off, young lady."

Not priest talk. She noted that his skin was weather beaten. This *padre* had seen his share of the sun. His hands were large and powerful, disproportionate to his body size. His fingers were calloused. He rested them on the chair arms without as much as a twitch. He was in such control she had no doubt he meant every word he said.

The stranger read her face. "You don't have a clue what you did, do you?"

A plan was developing. "Enlighten me."

"Actually, they never tell me why. I get my orders, and someone disappears. I rarely know their names. Sometimes it's only a picture or a house number. This time they told me your name."

"So you kill without a reason?"

"There's always a reason. I just don't know what it is. I think of myself more like a doctor. I fix things."

"Killing people is senseless. Life is precious."

"It's problem solving. Like cleaning out the attic or depositing used clothing in the Good Will receptacles at the shopping malls. Besides, it's a living."

"You kill people because it's your job?"

How much longer could she keep him talking?

Carly's legs cramped. She sneezed. "You look familiar."

"I have one of those faces." He stood. "Maybe it's my cologne."

Carly braced herself.

He caught her staring for the bulge of a gun or knife he would use. He tapped his sides then opened his palms in a gesture of peace. "I told you, I wanted to talk."

"Is this a confessional for you?"

"You could say that."

She grew bolder. "Let me get this straight. You barge into my room, threaten my life, then leave. Is that how you get your jollies?"

He didn't answer. Instead, he gazed intently at her, absorbing her every detail.

Carly wrapped the duvet toga-style and stood. She still didn't know what to do. If he stopped her from using the phone this time she could hurl it at him, or at least take a shot at defending herself. Bolting for the door still didn't seem like a good idea.

The man made the choice for her.

He gave a mock salute, turned the doorknob, and was gone.

She sneezed again.

83

While Carly tangled with the assassin/priest, Jack and Link stole a dangerous course of their own. They had returned from their latest run—Steel Villages—and were hunkered down in the bunk. Jack was lying with his feet crossed, a smoke cloud floating above his head. Link was twanging the strings of a guitar.

"I still don't know why you bought that thing. You can't play a lick."

Link had felt sorry for an American they had come across at the last truck stop. The man was peddling everything he owned to get enough money to return home.

Link twanged on. "What's wrong with you? He came here looking for job, can't find a thing, and hears his mother's heart's giving out. I had to help'm."

Jack used his cigarette to light another. "Just not that charitable, I guess."

Link plucked more discordant notes. "You thinking what I'm thinking?"

"Can't say that I haven't."

"It's been two days." Link moved his fingers down the bridge, the squeal rose to a higher pitch.

"The inspector said it would take time."

"Time enough for someone else to get killed."

"What are you saying? You want to go out there and see for yourself?"

"That's what I'm thinking."

Jack smacked his lips and squashed the half-smoked cigarette out on the wooden floor. "They're going to be calling you Curious George pretty soon."

*   *   *

There was a full moon. The countryside was bathed in a silver sheen the way old black-and-white movies radiated crisp details in the dark. They hugged the tree line in case a car or truck came along. None did. They talked in whispers.

"Bet Billy had as clear a night as this," Link said.

"I wish we had clouds. We're too easy to see."

"Who's gonna see us out here? Even if they do, we have a right to be here."

"I hope we don't have to explain nothing to nobody."

What Jack said and what he thought were two different things. It was fresh on his mind that both Billy and Slim must have felt confident being out in the woods the nights they were killed. No one ever thinks disaster will come their way; bad things happen to other people.

Except for an owl hooting and bats flapping past, all was still.

They came to the silo. They mounted the rungs of an outside ladder one step at a time. Neither said it, but their hearts were stampeding in their chests. When they got to the top and peered through the opening, all they could see was hay scattered across a wooden floor. They climbed into the loft and waited for something to happen.

An hour passed and Jack was jumpy for a deep nicotine drag. He figured it wouldn't hurt to poke his head out the opening, and sneak a few drags. He shifted his weight getting ready to move when the silo doors hummed to life. Jack dove down before anyone could see him. The electronic buzzing sound was followed by the grating noise of metal-rolling-against-metal. The doors rolled open.

"Goddamn," Link said under his breath.

The flatbed truck backed into the silo. Steel doors hidden under the floor opened, sending a shower of dirt to the sides.

Link jabbed Jack. "Do you see that?"

They gaped, stunned at what they were witnessing.

Jack stirred first. "I've seen enough. Let's get out of here."

"Are you kidding? This is more fun than a month of Super Bowl Sundays. You go. I want to see what happens."

"Whatever's happening here is none of our business. Slim and Billy got killed for doing what we're doing."

Link waved him off. "Stop your worrying. You scoot and get an iced cold one ready for me. I'll be back before the frost melts off."

"Suit yourself, you big fool. Just be careful."

*   *   *

"I'm telling you, Jeremy Steel's behind this," Jack said when Plumme found him the next day. Jack was leaning against a tree behind the bunk.

"How can you be sure?"

Jack topped off a pyramid of cigarette butts. He lit another.

Plumme tapped burnt tobacco bits from his favorite meerschaum pipe, and then filled it from a brown leather pouch. He cupped his hand around the flame Jack held for him.

"Feel it in my gut."

When Jack awoke that morning and found Link's bed empty, he didn't rush to look for him. He knew. It was just a question of where they dumped the body.

"We need proof," said the inspector.

"Link makes fifteen killed. Every one worked for Steel. That's proof enough for me."

"There's talk of a sixteenth. An airline mechanic in Boston. At first they thought a homeless man killed him, but when they read about our series, they called."

"Don't tell me. He worked for Steel Airlines and his tongue was missing. Ain't that telling you something?"

Plumme eyed Jack. "You seem to have all the answers, *Monsieur* Kincade. Maybe you're the killer? It happens. The killer comes to the police with evidence. He says he's a concerned citizen who wants to help the police catch the killer."

"Why would anyone do that?"

"To satisfy a craving. To be part of the game. To feel important. To be loved."

"That's movie twaddle. This here's real life, inspector. Billy, Slim, and Link were my friends. Why would I want to kill them?"

"Precisely."

Jack squashed his cigarette. His steady eyes searched Plumme's for a hint of what the man was thinking.

"You're not serious, are you?"

"I wanted to see how you'd react."

"I resent that."

"You should."

"I guess you had to?"

Plumme nodded.

Silence ticked between them.

"I seen some Israelis here. Slim said they were training them to be soldiers. What's that all about?"

"A volunteer militia, perhaps?"

"We had them back in Kansas. They're assholes. This here was different. These farmers were combat-ready."

"Then it's one more mystery, *Monsieur* Kincade."

"Same as that fish you're wearing around your neck."

"Your point is?"

Jack lit another cigarette. Aiming the lit end said, "Creating some kind of hidden army has got to be linked to what I seen in that silo. Put it together and you'll know who is behind us Americans getting knocked off. Until then, more will die."

84

As soon as the mystery man had gone, there was a knock on Carly's door. It wasn't the priest/killer because he could bypass the electronic lock. Maybe it was the ever-thoughtful Jeremy who didn't want to scare her. If that was his plan, he was too late; she was plenty scared.

She yanked open the door.

The man hugged back.

Carly sniffed; he was different.

She stepped back. "How'd *you* find me?"

"Can we go inside?"

"Why should I let you in? Whatever you have to say, you can say out here."

Conner didn't answer. There wasn't time for a Talmudic debate. With a gentle nudge, he pushed her back, closed the door, and threw the bolt. Then he checked the room to see that she was alone. Lastly, he jerked the curtains closed.

Carly turned the knob on a table lamp. "Okay, no one can see us now. Care to tell me what this is about?"

She was sitting in the club chair facing the bed; it was still warm from the killer's visit. In the most bizarre way, it gave her comfort.

Before answering, Conner stepped to the window, pulled back the closed shade, and checked the street below. "Remember when I told you that you were in danger? I heard from this green-shirt who came for exit-counseling that someone's on his way. You're in real danger. It took me a day to find you."

"That's touching. Why didn't you call Willie?"

"He wouldn't tell me."

"He's a good boy."

"Good boy my ass. He almost got you killed. Lucky for you, Steel's secretary listened to reason."

"Which was?"

"That I'm your ex-boyfriend about to marry a woman I don't love. I told her I still hold a torch for you and have to find out, once and for all, if you'll take me back. My wedding's this weekend and I'm desperate to find you. Ergo, I'm here."

"She bought that? What about Jeremy?"

"She's a sucker for unrequited love. Besides, here's a flash: Jeremy's engaged to some leggy model, not-to-mention that his secretary's been carrying a torch for him for fifteen years."

Carly turned green. "Why don't you punch me in the stomach or something? How do I get myself into these situations all the time?" She looked at him. "And what is the truth? Are you really getting married Sunday?"

Conner boiled. "Is that the thanks I get for busting my ass to find you? I could've called you know. Doesn't that tell you something?"

"Why *did* you come?"

"I knew you wouldn't believe me over the phone."

"You're right about that."

"So I was right for coming. And if you must know, I'm not getting married this or any other Sunday in the near future."

She walked toward him and touched his shoulder. "Conner, I needed to be sure whose side you were on. I'm so confused about who I can trust. As for coming in person, I'm glad you did. It means a lot to me. Sorry I'm a bit blasé about the danger part, but you're too late. My killer left a few minutes ago. As a matter of fact, we had a lovely chat. Seems he preferred to look rather than kill me."

Conner craned forward in disbelief. "You don't know how lucky you are. They sent the best."

"He seemed like a nice man."

"Al Capone kissed babies, too."

"Was escaping from that Institute such a big deal?"

"That's not it. It has something to do with the bombing at Rockefeller Center."

"But we never found out who they were?"

"Don't you get it? They don't want you to, either."

Carly paced the room. She stopped in front of Conner.

"Who are they? Jeremy's asked about the bomb victims more than once. Come to think of it, Jeremy grilled me about Fromm's tooth and if the president's Washington dentist ever sent me any X-rays." Carly turned pale hearing what she was saying. "I told him everything. I mean I was dating the guy, why not? I even told him what Inspector Plumme knew about the serial killings. Am I an asshole or what?"

"You're a beautiful asshole."

"After all this?"

"Don't get mushy on me." He rubbed his chin. "I remember your right hook."

"So what's next?"

"Call Willie. Tell him to be on the lookout. They might send someone else."

"Didn't you hear me? The guy left. He didn't do anything to me? Whatever danger you're worried about, it's not happening."

"You don't understand."

"Then explain it to me."

"For whatever the reason, the man they sent couldn't kill you."

"You mean 'wouldn't' kill me."

"Don't get semantic on me. Maybe killing women wasn't his thing. If they want you out of the picture, they'll find a way. Call Willie."

Carly dialed the Medical Examiner's number. She counted the seconds until she heard Willie's warm, reassuring voice. Carly's heart sank when she learned Willie had gone to Delaware, to Dover Air Force Base for a site visit of their morgue and ancillary facilities.

Now what?

Willie was away, Jeremy was whale shit, and she was in a hotel room with Conner Masterson. "Make love to me."

85

Willie lagged behind the rest of the inspection team that made the triennial tour of military mortuary vaults. Dover Air Force Base, in Delaware, was the national clearinghouse for soldiers who died in their country's service. From mass disasters to cargo crashes to the maimed of the Persian Gulf War, soldiers were identified and body parts reassembled at Dover before being returned to their loved ones. It was the government's policy for a civilian review board to check the military's facilities to make certain the government's morgues were beyond reproach. The last thing the federal government wanted to do was to bury one more unknown soldier.

The investigating team scrutinized every aspect of the Dover facilities from the way bodies were received to where they were stored. They checked the autopsy room and reviewed the charts. Only a white glove test at Windsor Castle could compare to this sort of scrutiny.

"What's that room for?" Willie asked a military liaison, "it's not marked." Every other room in the vast complex had a sign identifying the contents behind the door.

"Nothing important."

Willie stopped so short he nearly toppled over. "Open it, please."

The man shrugged. "They're bodies left over from a carrier fire. We haven't been able to identify them yet. Maybe you have an idea to help us?"

"What about dental records?"

"They were lost."

The soldier unlocked the door. "See? Like I told you. Three bodies."

Willie swung his crutches toward the stainless steel gurneys. A blast of cold air hit his face. He swung inside.

Three bodies lay there. A rubber sheet covered their torsos and faces.

"I thought there were DNA samples of everyone in the military?"

"And everyone who works for the government, too. Guess you were never in the military, were you, sir?"

Willie tapped his polio-withered legs. "Too busy running marathons."

"Well if you had been, you would've known that no matter how tight a ship we run, a few things slip through the cracks. You're looking at three now. Not only did we lose their dental records, but also there's no way of matching their DNA until we have a clue as to who they are. Our programs can't identify DNA in the reverse."

"That's too bad." Willie knew that closure was necessary in every case. Families needed it, cops needed, and medical examiners needed it, too.

He passed the last gurney to leave when something caught his eye. It was the toe tag. Willie whipped around. "Son, take me to the base head this second, or I'm calling the FBI."

86

Honey Fitzpatrick stormed into the Oval Office prepared to extract an apology. Who did the American president think he was, ordering him to appear at the White House? He came to an abrupt halt.

Steel was sipping a red drink. "I recommend the Cosmopolitan. It has quite the kick."

Jeremy had returned to New York on his way back from Canada, signed some contracts, made a deal to build a speed car racetrack in Long Island, and then flew to DC. When he failed to reach Carly, he had his secretary send flowers.

Fitzpatrick was turning shades of pink. "Aldous, what the hell's going on here? You know how busy I am. That's what phones are for."

Fromm didn't answer, but rose from behind his desk. He turned to Jeremy. "You've earned the right. Straighten this bozo out."

Fitzpatrick started to protest but froze when Fromm put his index fingers to his lips and made a shushing sound. Jeremy pulled up a chair and sat knee-to-knee with Fitzpatrick.

"Simply put, we're asking for Canada's unconditional surrender," Jeremy said.

Honey Fitzpatrick looked from Steel to Fromm and back again, and then burst out laughing. He slapped his meaty thighs so hard it brought tears to his eyes. He struggled to gain control of his breathing. "You guys break me up. It was worth the flight down here just for that."

Fromm and Steel remained stone-faced. The PM wore a Cheshire grin.

"What's it going to take? Another permit? More land? What do you need this time?"

Jeremy circled Fitzpatrick's chair until he was behind him.

Honey twisted and turned, trying to see through Steel's mask.

Jeremy spoke. "Honey, I want...."

Fromm cut him off. "We want."

Steel bowed toward Fromm. "*We* want Canada. We've invested time and money into making your country a leading industrial nation. It's pay back time."

"You're serious!" Fitzpatrick stood to leave.

Fromm rapped the table with his knuckles. "Down."

Fitzpatrick dropped into the chair, his shoulders sinking with his spirits.

Fromm continued. "We already control your country. Millions of adults live in cities built by Jeremy. They live better than Americans do these days."

"What's your point?"

Jeremy piped in. "Canadian Broadcasting is housed in my complexes, so we control your communications networks. With the help of Israeli mercenaries, I've turned thousands of farmers into first-class soldiers. Think of it, an occupying army is already within your borders...courtesy of yours truly."

"We knew Gadol was big trouble."

"On top of that, you handed us the plane routes."

"After all the good you've done us, you deserved them...or so I thought."

"We counted on your soft spot. What you didn't know was that every plane was retrofitted with implosive bombs. We can render you helpless within minutes and America won't have to lift a finger."

"Have you two lost your minds?"

"Let's adjourn to the map room, gentlemen."

Fitzpatrick glared at the president. "I don't need any lessons from you, Aldous. I was educated here, remember?"

"Humor me."

In the famous room, they confronted a series of maps beginning with the thirteen American colonies. Each successive map showed an expanding country. The Louisiana Purchase. The Gadsden Purchase. The Mexican-American War. Seward's Alaskan Folly. The Spanish-American War. Islands gained from the World Wars. The newest map—soon to be distributed to American school children—depicted Canada as a territory governed by the United States.

Fromm was proud. "I'm going to be the Mark McGuire of American statehood. With one swing, we go from fifty to sixty states. Now that's what I call a fucking home run."

"With all due respect to your fantastic egos and misplaced sense of history, I'm not handing my country over to you. In fact, I'm not spending an extra second here."

Jeremy put his hand on Honey's shoulder; Honey wheeled and leveled Jeremy with a right hook. Jeremy twisted onto one knee. Blood dripped from the corner of his mouth.

Still on one knee, Jeremy dabbed his lip on his sleeve. "It's frustrating as hell when you don't have choices, isn't it...Honey?"

Fitzpatrick lowered his shoulder at Fromm, who was now blocking the door.

"Don't be a fool. Accept the inevitable," said the president.

"I'll take this to the United Nations."

"Like that would do any good. Get smart. We already own Canada. Make it official and sign the friggin' papers."

"Over my dead body." But Honey Fitzpatrick didn't have the strength to leave; he knew he was licked. What he didn't know, was that the knockout punch was about to be delivered.

87

At that moment, air traffic controllers in Toronto, Montreal, and Ottawa were confronted with dozens of unidentified planes flying in winged unison toward their designated cities. Chaos froze them into statues. By the time they cleared the air space of scheduled commercial flights and scrambled Canadian Air Force jets to get a better look, bombs had been dropped into Lac St. Jean, Lake Nipigon, and Lake Winnipeg. There was no loss of life, but millions of dead fish floated in the waters.

Masked terrorists seized hydro-Quebec. Power outages erupted across the country. Emergency generators were needed to power hospital operating rooms. The rest of the country was bathed in the darkness.

Traffic in and out of Canada was at a standstill.

Static and fuzz replaced radio and television broadcasts.

*   *   *

The phone rang in the Oval Office.

Fromm handed the receiver to the PM. "It's for you."

As if the air was molasses, Honey Fitzpatrick struggled to bring the headset to his ear. He listened and collapsed back into the chair. The receiver slipped onto the floor.

"Why are you doing this? What did we ever do to you?"

Ashen-faced, the prime minister capitulated without another word.

Fromm placed his hand on the prime minister's shoulder. "In a few days, invite me to Ottawa. We'll sign the necessary papers. Then each province will petition Congress to become a state."

"Leave the Inuits out of it."

"Who wants them? Sign this for now. It's a letter of intent, in case you change your mind."

With one flourish, Honey Fitzpatrick would sign away his country's freedom. He rubbed his fingers across the print, as if to search for some hidden message, some way to extricate himself from the morass he and his countrymen faced.

"Sign," barked Fromm.

The Prime Minister did. But when Honey Fitzpatrick stood to leave, he spit in Aldous Fromm's face.

President's Dentist
Has Heart Attack
Jogging in Tidal Basin

WASHINGTON, DC. General Elvin Montgomery, age 57, a career dentist in the US Navy, was found dead of an apparent heart attack yesterday by joggers in the Tidal Basin area of the national park. An accomplished marathoner and world-class rock climber, General Montgomery had turned to sports when his father died prematurely at age thirty-nine. His wife of twenty-seven years, Anabelle, said that her husband pushed himself because he had a congenital heart condition and didn't know how long he would live. Besides his wife, General Montgomery leaves two daughters, ages twelve and fifteen.

88

When power was restored, complaints streamed into the authorities about bombs exploding and dead fish floating in their lakes. No injuries were reported. Airports were back on schedule; life in Canada returned to its normal pace.

*   *   *

While Conner showered, Carly—not wearing anything—cracked open the room door leading to the hallway, and snagged the newspaper without being seen. On a back page, she caught the small article describing Dr. Montgomery's sudden heart attack.

Conner came out of the bathroom, toweling himself dry.

Carly wagged the paper in front of him. "I was supposed to meet this guy in New York tomorrow. It had to do with the Rock Center blast."

"What did I tell you? They're killing everyone off."

"Who's everyone? No one killed Dr. Montgomery. He died of a heart attack."

"*Conveniently* died of a heart attack. Do you remember the boat explosion a little while back? The doctor taking care of Fromm after the helicopter crash was killed."

"What I remember is that he had just gotten a full tank of gas."

438

"And the doctor's brother-in-law mysteriously disappeared at the same time. They found the body in the woods. Seems a hunter mistook him for a deer."

"Bad luck."

"Are we forgetting his brother-in-law made Fromm's caps? Don't you see? Everyone connected with Fromm's recovery has conveniently been neutralized."

"I fixed his tooth. Does that mean I'm going to die?"

He held his thumb and index finger an inch apart. "You were this close, except you're too dense to admit it."

"Slow down. You're seeing a conspiracy when there isn't any. You're the only one who said Montgomery didn't die of natural causes."

The more Carly denied that events were related, the more agitated Conner became. "Let me try again. Everything we've been talking about is connected. It's like that chaos theory, where seemingly random events are strung together in a meaningful way. In this case, the Rockefeller Center blast and the president's helicopter crash are linked at the hip. Figure out the name of the man in San Martini's chair and you'll have the key to the entire mystery."

She swallowed hard, reached for his shirt, feeling its weight.

"It means this is another Kennedy conspiracy." She waited for him to disagree, to tell her she was wrong. When he didn't, Carly tossed him the shirt. "Get dressed. We've got to reach Inspector Plumme."

"I thought you wanted to go to the University to examine the teeth of that Indian they found in the block of ice."

"After five hundred years, he can wait another day for his dental checkup."

    *   *   *

Events happened lightning-quick.

Carly found Plumme in his office. She explained that Conner was listening in on a second phone in the bathroom. Introductions made, Carly then described her priest-clad visitor from the night before.

"I doubt this man had anything to do with the murders," Plumme said.

"Then why was he in my room?"

"Surprising as it may seem, people get killed here who don't work for Jeremy Steel. Consider it a gift that he left you alone. He's probably a lonely man who wanted company."

"Don't discount him, inspector," Conner said. "Aurum's people are out to get Carly. This man had to be sent by them. You've got to find out who he is."

"That still doesn't put him at the scene of the other murders. Besides, one of the workers in Steel City thinks he knows how to trap the killer. I'm on my way there, now."

Plumme promised to call Carly if he discovered any new clues in the Pembina River murders.

Carly next called the anthropologist at the University. She apologized for canceling at the last minute, but wrangled an invite next time she was in town.

*   *   *

Plumme was expected at dusk. He entered the work compound and headed straight for Jack Kincade's bunk. He hauled himself up the steps, half-expecting Jack to barge through the door to greet him. It didn't happen. Plumme glided inside the room and stopped. It wasn't the darkness that bothered him. Plumme had a feeling that something was wrong. He waited for his eyes to adjust, his ear keen for the slightest sound. Certain he was alone, he flicked on the wall switch.

Nothing was askew.

The overhead bulb sprayed lengthening shadows on the back wall. The bathroom door was ajar. Plumme took a step then picked up his pace.

"*Merde!*"

Jack Kincade lay there, eyes shut, blood caking his lips together. A pool of blood oozed onto the tiles like a Rorschach blot.

Plumme felt a faint carotid pulse on Jack's neck. "Don't let go, Jack. I'm getting help."

Jack grabbed Plumme's arm. His eyes fluttered open for a moment. Jack blinked a rhythm. It wasn't Morse code, but Plumme knew what it meant. He trailed Jack's gaze to the opposite wall. There, slumped on the floor with a knife in his chest, lay another field hand. Bubbles gurgled from the man's mouth, painting a red sash down his chin and spilling onto his checkered shirt. Plumme went over to check the man's pulse. It was too faint to feel.

Plumme returned and cradled Jack's head in his arms. "Who is he, Jack? What's his name?"

Jack's lips moved; nothing came out.

Plumme leaned closer. He thought he heard the word "Incas." He put his ear right on Jack's lips. He waited for Jack to speak again.

He didn't.

89

Carly and Conner never made it out of the Ottawa Airport. A squall grounded all planes; LaGuardia Airport would be hit by midday. Anxious to get to New York, Carly and Conner rented a car. There was a familiar comfort in their trip until they passed Albany.

"I still think you should go to the authorities," Conner said. "Speak to your friend, LeShana. Tell her everything we know."

"What do we know? That three doctors who treated Fromm are dead? That there's a contract out on my life? We can't prove any of it. I told you what I'm going to do."

"You're asking for trouble."

"It can't be worse than the mess I'm in already."

Seeing Carly's mind set, Conner reached across and took her hand. "You didn't tell me you were this stubborn."

"You didn't ask."

*   *   *

They hit the Big Apple at two in the morning. Conner stayed at her apartment. Neither slept. At dawn's first light, Carly bolted out of bed to find Conner already showered and dressed.

"Where are you going at this hour?"

442

"Washington. If you're going through with this, I need to make certain you're safe."

"Can't you call?"

"If I see his face, I'll know if he's telling the truth."

"Aren't you being a bit overprotective?"

He grabbed her shoulders. "I didn't come all this way to lose you by taking something for granted. Ottawa proved they're out to get you. Only by the grace of God, did that man let you live. I know them. They won't stop. That's why I have to go to Washington."

She frowned.

"It's only for a day," he said. He pulled her into him.

"Promise?"

"Try and keep me away."

*   *   *

Carly showered. Half-moons rung her eyes. Her face was drawn and blotched. She blotted on a pound of foundation so she wouldn't scare babies and old ladies, tossed on a pea-green tee shirt and khaki shorts, and looked into the mirror. No. No approval today.

By the time she cabbed across town, the Starbuck's super-jolting Grande coffee kicked her into high gear. She found Willie at his desk. "Have I got a story for you," she said.

He grabbed his crutches and swung toward her, giving her a big bear hug. "I'm certain it pales compared to mine."

"I almost got killed," she said, "you, too?"

"That's about the one thing that could top my story. Glad you didn't."

"Die or top your story?"

Carly recounted everything that happened in Canada from the moment Jeremy left the hotel room to the moment Conner showed up.

"And where is the fair-haired boy now?"

"Washington. He's got a contact who should know what else is in store for me."

"If you're the fourth doctor to treat Fromm, shouldn't we be calling in the FBI? LeShana will know what to do."

"Fromm must have something to do with this. Let's leave the Fibbies out of it for now. I'm better off taking my chances alone."

"Sounds to me like you're in deep water already."

"You know I can swim with the best of them."

"Even so...."

Carly pretended a "ho-hum" yawn, which was her way of letting Willie know there was no use pursuing this line of talk. It would get him nowhere. She thumbed through her mail and did not hear what he said.

"Are you paying attention? Put that down and read this."

He handed her a paper with three sets of numbers on it.

"What's the big deal? They're morgue numbers."

"Recognize them?"

"It's the way we record bodies: consecutive numbers followed by the year. So?"

"Anything strike you about *these* specific numbers?"

She studied the sequence again, and then shot an all-knowing look. "Sure. They're the blast victims. Do I pass?"

"Now that you know the *what*, we still need to find out the *who* and *why* of it."

"Are you forgetting the *where*?"

"Try the Dover Air Force Base. In cold storage. They were passing them off as victims of a ship fire. I nearly missed them."

She pulled up a chair. "Tell me, tell me."

"It was the end of the day, I was dog tired. My escort tried to get me to skip the room, but something drew me to it. That's when I found them."

"The three were next to each other?"

"Like kissing cousins. Now we have to figure out *why* they were there."

"I think I know."

"Where're you going?"

Seconds later she marched back twirling a pen in the air.

"What's a pen got to do with anything?"

"Everything. Now stop wasting time, we've got work to do."

90

That evening, a sleepy soldier got the shock of his life.

"Super Eagle, this is Backscatter One. Do you copy, Super Eagle?"

"This is Super Eagle, Backscatter One. What's on your mind?" asked the dispatcher the same way he did for all routine broadcasts night after night.

"Super Eagle, three squadrons of unidentified planes are heading due east toward Alberta, Edmonton, and Calgary. Do you copy, Super Eagle One?"

"What have you been smoking, Backscatter One? Who'd schedule a training mission at this hour? Check again. Over."

"Roger, Super Eagle. Will confirm. Over."

"That's better," Sergeant First Class Melvin Seymour said to himself. It was three in the morning and the last thing he wanted to do was wake a commanding officer because some jerk in the Alaskan boonies was getting cabin fever seeing blips on a screen. Probably hit the sauce and they were fireflies that got through the screen door.

He was trying to forget Backscatter One ever called when the microphone hummed to life again. Sgt. Seymour flicked a switch. "I better hear the right words from you, Backscatter One, or

446

you'll be scrubbing the insides of cargo ships for the rest of your life. Now give it to me, good and slow."

It was a different voice. "Super Eagle, Super Eagle, this is Backscatter Two. Are you there?"

Melvin Seymour stabbed the "Respond" button. "Yes, Backscatter Two, this is Super Eagle. What have *you* got, tonight?"

"Unidentified planes heading toward Ottawa and Montreal. They'll be off my screen in five minutes. Better pick them up. Do you copy, Super Eagle?"

For two years Melvin Seymour worked the radar detail without a worry or concern. Every report was routine; the skies always clear. Now he had received two alarms in the span of seconds. He looked at the black screen with the map of the northern hemisphere outlined in moon-glo green. Yellow blips from all directions were moving toward every major city in Canada.

He fingered the red plastic phone, picked up the headset, studied the speed dial, and then pounced on it. How could they blame him for doing his job?

"Sorry to be calling this time of morning, Colonel, but Fairbanks, Alaska and Moscow, Maine picked up five squadrons of unidentified planes heading toward major Canadian targets. I've double-checked. They're not our planes. They're not Canadian. That's all I know."

"How about GPS and the satellites?"

Wasn't he ever cool and collected?

"Roger on that, sir. The Global Position System is jammed, that's why we're getting it on the Over-The-Horizon radar. As for the satellites, the pictures won't be ready until tomorrow."

"Are you thinking terrorists?"

"They're not headed our way, sir. They're on course to intercept with Ottawa, Montreal, Toronto, Calgary, Alberta, Vancouver, Quebec...all of them."

"God help us if you're wrong, son."

Melvin Seymour crossed his fingers; he was thinking the same thing.

"They are on my screen as we speak."

"Call in a Code Red. Inform NORAD, then report back to me."

*   *   *

At 3:30 AM, Buster Jorgenson drummed his fingers on the marble tabletop waiting until he heard the familiar voice on the other end. "Sorry to wake you, sir, but we have verified reports from Backscatters One and Two. Squadrons of unidentified planes are flying toward every major Canadian city."

President Fromm rubbed his eyes. "Tell me straight up, Buster, what does it mean?"

"It means that we picked up a shit load of planes that aren't supposed to be there. They might be cruising over Canadian air space to divert us from the real target."

"Are we in danger?"

"Depends on who they are and what they're carrying. If they're from Uzbekistan or any other Mickey Mouse country that has nuclear capabilities, then we're toast."

"Your assessment?"

"Unlikely. They could have fired their ICBMs earlier. My best guess? It's a Canadian matter."

"Then next time, talk to me at a more civilized hour."

The phone went cold dead in Buster Jorgenson's hand.

91

Carly couldn't sleep. In four days, she lived a lifetime. Jeremy's gala celebration; Prince Charming changing into the kissing cousin of a proto-human; a mysterious midnight caller dressed as a cleric, hired to kill her; and the real Prince, Conner Masterson, showing up to warn that her life was in danger. Talk about excitement, disappointment, danger, and timing in ninety-six hours!

Now Carly performed the final tests to determine the identity of the patient who died in Dr. San Martini's chair. Like most elements of forensic sciences these days, it boiled down to bits of DNA.

Who could sleep?

*   *   *

Bubbling with the prospect of solving the blast victim's ID, Carly dragged herself to the east side. She knew it was too early to get the lab results, but like an expectant father waiting for the stork to show up, Carly needed to be closer to the source.

She dropped a copy of the Times on a table in the hospital cafeteria and grabbed a sesame bagel with a smear and a large black coffee. She nibbled mindlessly at the stale bagel, thinking about Conner, then Jeremy Steel, and then Conner again.

Her first instincts about Conner had proved right. They clicked from the moment she laid eyes on him at the downtown Marriott West. Regardless of why he was brought to the Institute when she was there, he was in her corner...then and now. Without him, she never would have escaped. She still felt guilty about the horrific punishment he had to endure for helping her.

Jeremy was another matter. He came out of nowhere. His interest in her—though she wished it were genuine—was never right. With the benefit of hindsight, it was clear he struck up a relationship for the sole purpose of learning what he could about the Rock Center blast victims. What was so important that he dropped everything he had been doing in order to court her? What was he after?

Then Conner swooped back in her life after a four-year hiatus, and the same heat was back. Hope against hope, could she forge something meaningful with him? She was long overdue for a chance.

                  *   *   *

With a second cup of coffee in hand, she headed for the office. Four posts were waiting, two more coming in. It would be hectic.

The phone rang.

"Did you get my message?"

She recognized the accent. "Henri? Is that you?"

"Who else talks this way?"

She giggled, rummaging through the yellow Post-its.

"Here it is. I must have missed it, yesterday. What did you find out?"

"For starters, Jack Kincade led us to the killer. He worked for Steel."

"Worked, as in past tense?"

"That's the bad news. He died moments after I got there. Jack set a trap thinking he could catch the man, but the killer was too smart. Jack must've put up quite a fight. By the time I got there, Jack was drowning in his own blood. He was able to say one word. 'Incas.' Strange, isn't it?"

Carly thought for a moment. "Henri, do you still wear that silly fish?"

"The Lines of Nasca? *Naturalement.*"

"Think about it. Jack was giving you a clue only you would understand."

"For what reason? He killed the murderer."

"There's more to it, I just don't know what."

"I'll give it some thought, but I need your help," Plumme said. "Are you on-line at the office?"

"We can't live without the Internet."

"I am going to e-mail you a picture of the killer. One of the other workers identified him as Johnny Ray Mabe, but no one knows much about him. He had no ID. When I checked, his employment records were missing."

"What do you want me to do with his picture?"

"I've been thinking about the man in your hotel room. Maybe I was too quick to say it couldn't be him."

A victory smile creased her face. Plumme was finally coming around. Ten minutes later, Carly opened the jpeg: Johnny Ray Mabe was her assassin/priest. The more she studied his picture, the more familiar he looked.

Where had she seen him before...before that night in the hotel room?

When Carly had hunches, she knew not to let them rest. For one thing, she had no faith in coincidences. Coincidences described the unknown, not the unknowable. She made a list.

—Aurum shows up the day Jonah dies.

—A man wearing a raincoat and hat is standing in front of her apartment.

—Her door was unlocked.

—Conner left a message that she never got it.

Then it dawned on her: the cologne. She sneezed when the assassin/priest was in the hotel room; she sneezed that time when she came across the man in the hallway. Johnny Ray Mabe was the one who broke into her apartment. The more she thought of that day, the more she was convinced Johnny Ray Mabe must have killed Jonah. She wouldn't be surprised if Johnny Ray Mabe killed Artie Montefusco, too.

Who was Johnny Ray Mabe? She reviewed what she knew about him. Assuming he was the one who broke into her apartment, he took nothing except a passport photo. It stood to reason that he listened to the messages on her answering machine, and that's why she never got Conner's. True, this happened shortly after she escaped the Institute and after Willie tried to reach Conner for her. The green-shirt on the plane promised to "get" her in New York; was this how they made good on his threat? From what Carly learned about Humanetics and the way Aurum operated, sending Johnny Ray Mabe to her apartment was too benign to be a message. Something else was at stake and she wanted to know what it was.

92

Henri read Carly's reply. He was left with more questions than answers. What did Mabe want with Carly? She was a female and did not work for Steel. True, she knew Steel, but that was the only thread connecting her to the string of Pembina River murders.

Before sending a copy of Mabe's fingerprints to the FBI, he studied the whorls of ink.

"Talk to me," he said out loud.

Why Mason? Did mercy play a role in letting her live, or was it something else?

Then there was the matter of the word "Inca." What was Jack trying to tell him?

The more he thought about everything, the more an idea began to gel. *Mais oui!* Jack was right. The answer was right in front of Henri Plumme's big proboscis. He had to get to Ottawa.

*   *   *

"Good thing you put an end to those murders, inspector. We can rest a lot easier now," Honey Fitzpatrick said the next day when Plumme came to see him.

Plumme plunged his hands in his pocket. "Thank Jack Kincade."

"Modest as ever, eh Plumme?"

"Just truthful, sir. He's the real hero."

"You said you had something to tell me."

The prime minister motioned him to take a seat.

"I'll get right to the point, sir. Something's come up. I don't want to believe it, but the evidence is overwhelming."

Fitzpatrick muttered something under his breath that Henri couldn't catch.

"*Pardon?*" asked the inspector.

Fitzpatrick cleared his throat. "I said it's not always easy to do the right thing. What do you have?"

"Unless we stop him, you can expect the killings to continue."

"What are you talking about, man? You caught the killer."

"Johnny Ray Mabe was not a serial killer. He was hired to commit those murders, to make them look like the work of a madman. It was meant to throw us off."

"Who would do such a thing?"

Plumme told him.

93

Conner called from Washington. "They intend on getting you this time; they're sending their killer back. Call LeShana. Get a bodyguard."

"You're a day late." First she described what Plumme told her, and then what she discovered from the DNA tests. "It's over."

"There's no mistake?"

"Once we knew who we were looking for, it was easy. We got his military records and triple-checked it against the DNA fragments."

"Now what?"

"Willie has made the necessary arrangements. It'll be over soon."

"You're coming to Washington? I'll wait."

"The opposite. They'll be in Canada this afternoon. Something about a treaty. I'm meeting him there."

Conner's voice showed disappointment. "Wish I could join you."

"You are. Arrangements have been made. I'll see you there."

                    *   *   *

Inside the Langevin Block, Henri Plumme described his theory to the PM.

"What did Kincade say again?"

"'Incas,' then he died." Plumme fingered the medallion hanging around his neck. "At first, I thought he was referring to this."

Plumme held the emblem out for the PM to study.

"I'm not a bad fly fisherman, myself."

The only two people who ever recognized that symbol were Carly Mason and Jack Kincade. Only Jack Kincade understood what it meant.

"It's a copy of a gigantic icon the Incas created out of rocks. See the lines running through the fish. It's made of rocks high in the Andes. In Peru. They're called the Lines of Nasca."

"Didn't I read something about a landing site for alien space-ships?"

"Some think that. The practical answer is that farmers built it to show their thanks for their harvests. It had to be big enough for the gods to see."

Fitzpatrick fidgeted...President Fromm and his entourage were expected soon. There was much to do before ceding Canada to the Americans. What convinced him not to put up a fight was the unchallenged armada of planes that crossed Canada the other night. Resistance would have been futile.

"That's interesting, inspector. If that's all there is, I must excuse myself. The American president is coming to see me." He couldn't bear to utter Fromm's name.

Plumme nodded then blurted out the words he had rehearsed. "It was Jack Kincade's way of telling me who put Johnny Ray Mabe up to all those killings."

"Good Lord, man, stop dancing around. Who is it?"

"Jeremy Steel."

"I'd believe almost anything about Jeremy, but murder? I have to draw the line."

"That's what I thought, too. But once I figured what 'Incas' meant, it was easy to piece together the rest. We traced checks Mabe deposited to a dummy corporation owned by Steel."

"He's got a ton of businesses."

"I imagine most of them are legitimate. Not this one. It was Murder, Inc. We found cancelled checks made out to Mabe, one for each murder. By the way, the pay was handsome."

"How can that be? Two murders happened virtually at the same time."

"As the potential list of victims grew, Mabe needed help. He trained two accomplices to make the murders look the same. Mabe was one smart cookie. He meant to confuse. We caught one of his associates in Edmonton this morning. When we confronted him, he was quick to confess. We're looking for the third man now."

"Is the killing spree over?"

"From what we can tell. There's still a chance we'll find more victims."

The intercom buzzed. Fitzpatrick listened without comment. "Tell them to wait. A few more minutes won't make any difference." He leaned back. "You still haven't convinced me."

Plumme grew flustered. He wasn't good at this one-on-one speaking. Give him a challenge, and he was in his glory. Make him speak to a dignitary, and he bumbled. "That's where Kincade comes in. I got to thinking: what does he know that I don't? Then it dawned on me. It was simple."

"I don't follow."

"The Incas never let any group of workers complete a task. Never. They brought slaves from different parts of the empire to work on projects. Group after group was brought in for specific tasks. Once they finished, they returned to their homes. Some worked the quarries, others shaped the stones. Still others hoisted the rocks up steep mountains using an intricate system that's been lost to us. They built aqueducts and complex drainage systems. In the end, workers who never saw a master plan or who knew anything but the specific task they were given, built entire cities. Without a written language, everything was controlled by the leaders."

"That tells me skilled labor has been around for a long time. What does this have to do with Jeremy Steel?"

"Don't you see, they're one and the same? Inca workers were kept ignorant on purpose. Pizzarro knew that once he killed their leaders, the Incas were powerless to fight the Spanish. That's how one empire was destroyed and how Steel is building his."

"So you're saying one hand never knew what the other was doing?"

"Jack Kincade realized this. He knew that the truckers didn't know what they were hauling, and the contractors didn't know what they're building. When someone did figure it out, Johnny Ray Mabe—or his henchmen—killed them."

"And the tongues?"

"A signature to make us think a serial killer was on the loose, that it was not part of some master plan. At the same time, the tongues sent a message for the others to keep their mouths shut. It bought Steel time to execute his plan."

The intercom buzzed again. Fitzpatrick stood, signaling the end of the meeting. "That's quite a story. Even if I did buy it, what could I do?"

"Steel hired Mabe to do all the killings. Have him arrested."

"On what grounds? That he follows the Inca blueprints for building cities? Come on, Inspector, did you really think I'd fall for that?"

"You have the power to stop him."

"Not anymore. Now if you'll excuse me, I've kept my guests waiting too long."

        *   *   *

Honey Fitzpatrick headed toward the mahogany-paneled meeting room. Over the years, Steel received every permit and concession he wanted. There was Steel City, Steel Metropolis, Steel Villages, and Steel Communications Centre, not to mention Steel Airlines. There was that messy thing about the planes the other night. If Steel had anything to do with the murders—which the PM thought far-fetched—it would soon be the American's problem...not his.

The prime minister approached the carved double door and halted. Once inside the room there would be no turning back. America and Canada would be merged in a union that would better compete with the European Common Market. The world's balance of power would be changed forever.

Though not of his own design, Honey recognized its value. His bitter pill was that, in the name of progress, Honey Fitzpatrick's name would be forever linked to Benedict Arnold's.

94

Henri Plumme saw a motorcade of black cars pull up in front of Langevin Block. Kip Greeley emerged from the first limousine, surrounded by a coterie of Secret Servicemen. To his right, Carly Mason dashed to embrace Conner Masterson popping out of the rear car.

When Plumme caught Greeley's eye, he waved.

Greeley nodded back.

*   *   *

Fromm sat at the head of a rectangular table, Steel to his left. Neither rose to greet the prime minister.

"Well, well," Jeremy Steel said seeing the prime minister enter the room, "the cast of characters is complete."

"We *are* doing this in stages like we agreed, aren't we?" Fitzpatrick asked after taking a seat opposite the president. Steel was to the right.

"It's been accelerated by a few years. Why prolong the agony?" Fromm answered.

An aide handed Fitzpatrick a thick-paged document; the PM tossed it aside without cracking the cover.

"The St. Lawrence venture has to remain the same, or I'm not signing."

Fromm smiled at Jeremy before answering. "That's been changed, too. Why give any percentage of the oil away, when we can keep it all for ourselves? You don't have the capacity to deliver it, we do."

Blue veins erupted on Honey Fitzpatrick's face, a road map of rage.

Steel spoke. "And we're diverting water to the Midwest."

Fitzpatrick sputtered. "We agreed to a loose federation. There's precedence for that. Syria and Egypt were once joined that way. There's no way I'm signing anything else."

Aldous Fromm leaned forward. "Of course you can...and you will. Need I remind you how fast we can destroy your country?"

Honey pushed away from the table. "I've changed my mind."

For all Fromm's recent medical problems, he leapt like an agile panther. "You're not going anywhere until you sign this."

"Come to think of it, I don't have the authority to hand the country over to you. It's not legal and would never be recognized by any other nation, let alone my people. You want to declare war, go ahead."

On cue, a phone rang. An aide handed it to the prime minister. His long face grew longer.

"ICBM's are pointed at Parliament Hill at this moment. They've been activated," he announced to the room. He slipped the phone into its cradle and eased into a chair. No one stirred. "I see you weren't taking any chances."

This time, Fromm looked just as grim, his voice weak. "That's not part of the plan. What missiles are you talking about?" Then he turned to Jeremy.

"Maybe I can enlighten you gentlemen." Jeremy circled behind Fromm, stopping halfway toward Fitzpatrick. "You see, gentlemen, the missiles are mine."

"I trusted you, Jeremy. Gave you everything you asked for," Fitzpatrick said.

"Including silos to hide my missiles. You were quite accommodating."

Fromm blistered. "Have you gone mad?"

"On the contrary, Aldous, I've never been saner. If you both stay calm, there's enough for all of us. As king I will make certain Canada will use its vast resources to help our sister nation to the south. I'll make each of you ministers...without portfolios, of course."

"King!" Honey and Aldous spoke in unison.

"That's right. Getting anointed by the Queen gave me some ideas I thought rather appealing. Russia has its monarchy back, Canada should have one, too."

"Naming buildings and cities after yourself should have quenched your ego," Honey said.

"Let's say I've graduated to a higher level." He glared at Fromm. "What would Lute Aurum call this? Becoming a *Clear*?"

Jeremy gathered the original documents Fromm intended Fitzpatrick to sign and extracted three sets of papers from his attaché case. "Don't bother to read them, Mr. PM. Just sign on the dotted line."

"And if I don't?"

Jeremy inspected his watch. "You have ninety seconds before Toronto and Quebec are destroyed. Ninety seconds after that you'll lose Vancouver. Ninety seconds after, Calgary. Then Edmonton and Montreal. Get the picture?"

Fitzpatrick plumbed Fromm's face to see if he would yield.

The American president made no move to help.

The seconds ticked away.

Honey Fitzpatrick needed to know how crazy Jeremy Steel really was.

95

Honey Fitzpatrick ripped the document in half.

Jeremy opened his case and took out another. "I've got plenty."

Fitzpatrick refused to take it.

"This was not part of our agreement, Jeremy," Fromm said, his voice laced with more than a mild concern.

"You've led a golden life, up until now. This is probably the first time anyone's ever stood up to you. You'll get over it."

The phone rang.

An aide handed it to Fromm, who looked from Fitzpatrick to Steel. Steel was bemused.

"Let me prepare you," Steel said, "New York, Chicago, and Los Angeles, for starters. Then Atlanta and San Francisco. The rest afterwards."

Fromm listened then hung up. He turned to the Canadian PM. "Looks like we're both in the same boat."

"Two love birds," Jeremy said. "Now sign or sayonara to your cities."

*   *   *

Before pen hit paper, the doors swung open. A score of Royal Mounted Police in red uniforms with gold braids marched into the room. Carly, Conner, and Kip Greeley followed. They were with a bevy of Secret Servicemen.

Steel ignored them. "You're almost out of time."

Honey Fitzpatrick threw down his pen. "Then we all lose."

An ancient grandfather clock metered the seconds.

For all his scheming and calculating, Jeremy had never considered an illogical response from either Honey Fitzpatrick or the president. He ran to Fromm's side. "You're going to let Washington be blown to smithereens?"

Fromm shrugged. "It fits into *my* plans. I'll make Ottawa the capitol of this new federation."

Jeremy screamed. "There won't be an Ottawa. Can't you get that through your reconstructed skull? The missiles are in the air as we speak."

Fitzpatrick rose to his full measure and nodded to the head Mounty. "We've had enough of your insanity, Steel."

Jeremy was livid. "You don't understand. It's your sorry ass that's in the sling, Honey dear. No one's arresting King Jeremy."

Four Mounties surrounded Jeremy. He looked to Fromm for help, Fromm looked away. As they led Jeremy out of the room, he called over his shoulder.

"You'll never sleep again, Fitzpatrick, knowing you sent millions to an early grave."

Kip Greeley raised his hand for the Mounties to wait long enough for him to explain.

"On the contrary, Jeremy, you're the only one who will lose any sleep here. Your bombs were neutralized with Scud missiles even *you* couldn't buy on the open market. Once we knew where to look, sensors did all the work. If I'm not mistaken, you own stock in the company that developed the tracers. Poetic how your own company put you out of commission."

Steel looked at Fromm one last time.

Fromm waved. "See you."

"That was a brilliant piece of work, Kip. Wait until the world hears about this. Now Honey, it's been quite the exciting day, but it's time to get back to the business at hand. I don't know how Jeremy thought he could pull that stunt off. Rest assured, he'll get what he deserves."

Carly stepped forward. "So will you."

"If this is a checkup appointment, I'm rather busy at the moment, Dr. Mason."

"The charade's over. We know who you are."

Kip Greeley put his hands on Carly's shoulders. "Tell them how you figured it out."

Here she was, a girl from Queens, about to topple the president of the United States. And keep Canada independent.

Carly reminded everyone that the president's helicopter crashed at the same time the bomb went off in Rockefeller Center. All efforts to identify three bodies found in Dr. San Martini's office failed. These same bodies were whisked out of the ME's office by government agents. Stymied, but by no means about to give up, she projected an X-ray from one of the victim's at a forensic meeting.

"...so after I showed the anomalous X-ray on the screen, Dr. Elvin Montgomery, from Washington, contacted me. He had a patient with the same genetic quirk. He searched his files and mailed me a copy. When I went to compare it to the one taken from the victim, the original X-ray was stolen from my apartment. It was in a slide carousel. There was a duplicate in the chart, so I wasn't worried...or so I thought. By the time I got back to the office, the chart was missing from the chart room. Then Dr. Montgomery died jogging at the Tidal Basin."

The president stood. "What's the point of this fairy tale? Or should I say *sob* story? I admit we're all touched."

Carly ignored him. "What were the odds of you seeing me for a toothache?"

"The agent took the X-ray when I left."

Carly showed him a black mount that held a single X-ray. "Not the duplicate; there were two originals. The agent also should have thought to ask for the X-ray's outer sleeve. The packet had your saliva on it."

The president sunk back in his chair.

Honey interrupted. "Did I miss something? What are you trying to say?"

Kip Greeley chirped in. "It's complicated."

"Let me tie it together," said Carly. Greeley stepped back as Carly explained. "You see my boss, Willie Robinson, found the missing bodies at Dover Air Force Base."

"What bodies?" By now, Fitzpatrick was exasperated.

"It will be clear in a few minutes. Maybe this will help you understand." Carly marched up to Fromm. "Mr. President, do you have a pen I can borrow?"

Fromm extracted a slick black pen embossed with the gold presidential seal from his inside jacket pocket.

Carly waved it like a stage magician. "Do you remember giving me one as a souvenir?"

"I probably did. I've given scores out. Why?"

"What you didn't know—since *you* skipped orientation week at the White House two years ago—was that each president's DNA is encoded in the ink. This guarantees that their signatures can never be forged...unless the forger has one of these pens with the president's DNA in it."

"So? What does that prove?"

"It proves that you didn't kill Dr. Montgomery soon enough."

Fitzpatrick threw up his hands. "Will someone tell me what's going on?"

"Montgomery had a heart attack," Fromm said coolly. "It was in the papers."

"That diagnosis changed after we exhumed the body this morning. Toxicology reported that it was an overdose of digitalis. Lucky for us, Dr. Montgomery's wife kept his water bottle as a memento. There was enough residue in it to kill a horse."

"So he met an unfortunate death," Fromm said. "Washington's a dangerous place."

Carly was gaining momentum. "You realized when your tooth started to ache and I was the one treating you, it was only a matter of time before I discovered you were a fraud."

Fitzpatrick swiveled toward Fromm, relishing his anguish.

"You had an agent take your X-ray from me, and afterwards, arranged to have the corresponding X-ray from the blast victim stolen from my apartment. Then you had the victims' charts lifted from the Medical Examiner's. By the time I received Dr. Montgomery's X-ray, I had nothing to compare it to, and Montgomery was dead."

Fromm remained passive.

"What you didn't know—couldn't know—was that a second letter arrived from Montgomery telling me that the name attached to his anomalous tooth belonged to President Fromm. Montgomery must have sensed it was a match, and knew that the Rock Center victim was the president."

"Are you finished with this fantastic tale?" asked Fromm.

"Not quite. We were able to match the DNA from the blast victim found in Dr. San Martini's chair to the DNA in the pen you gave me. Ergo, he was Aldous Fromm...and you aren't. Once we knew the blast victim was the president, we identified the two Secret Servicemen who you sent deep undercover. Their assignment had them incommunicado for weeks; you made certain no one would be looking for them."

Fitzpatrick pointed. "Then who's he?"

"You can't prove any of this," growled Fromm.

Greeley stepped forward. "That's where you're wrong. Carly not only proved it to me, she proved it to the Chief Justice's satisfaction, as well."

"It goes back to the dental X-ray I took when you had your emergency. I kept the packet sleeve as a souvenir. We recovered trace amounts of DNA from the dried saliva on it. The amount of DNA was too little to use for comparison, so it was amplified using the PCR technique. The polymerized chain reaction technique replicates little bits of DNA until there's enough to use for comparison. In your case, we retrieved DNA from your old Navy records. The two DNA profiles matched."

"You sound like O.J. Simpson's lawyers bamboozling the jury with all their DNA crap. Anyone can see I'm the President of the United States."

"You may look like Aldous Fromm," Carly said in triumph, "but we know that you're not."

"Then who am I?" he said smugly.

"Lute Aurum."

96

Honey Fitzpatrick stuttered, "That can't be. Aurum died in the helicopter crash."

"On the contrary," Greeley said, "Aurum wasn't on the chopper. Neither was Fromm. Every president has two or three impersonators. This way the president can sneak away every once in awhile without the media being on his tail. Lute arranged for one of Fromm's decoys to be seen boarding the helicopter. Aurum had his own decoy on the chopper, too. So the helicopter takes off with the Fromm and Aurum imposters. Then the tragedy unfolds. The onboard computer is programmed to have a total electrical failure in mid-air. It goes down in a remote area close to Camp David. It crashes and burns, with a President Fromm look-alike as the lone survivor. At the same time this is happening, the real Fromm is sitting in San Martini's chair being drilled for a cosmetic overhaul."

"But how could Aurum be sure there would be a survivor? And how did he know who would it be? Come to think of it, how was it that no one questioned the identities of the others killed in the crash?" Honey Fitzpatrick asked.

"I can answer that." Conner stepped forward. "I worked for Aurum. I know how he operates. He's a planner. He won't take any chances unless forced to, and that's not very often. That means a ground crew knew where the helicopter would crash. They were in position to cordon off and sanitize the area before the local authorities got to the site. Depending upon how bad the crash was, if there were flames, and if anyone survived, they were prepared to create burn damage to all the victims so that none could be recognized. There were IDs for any contingency."

"Okay, I'll buy the fact that a score of brain-washed groupies followed Aurum's orders. I'll even accept the notion that they controlled the crash site," said Fitzpatrick. "None of that explains how they arranged to have a lone survivor, and that survivor just happened to have been the Fromm look-alike."

Conner gave him a knowing smile. "It was theater at its best."

"So how did they do it?"

"Simple," explained Conner. "Aurum's henchmen added the body *after* the helicopter went down. As for the others, their faces were burned beyond recognition. They used body types to figure out who they were, along with wallets, driver's licenses, wedding rings, etc. By the time Coulter Bell gave the manifest with the names of those onboard to the press, all the crash victims had the IDs Aurum needed them to have. There were no loose ends, once they removed Fromm's double."

Fitzpatrick scratched his head. "Then who was the survivor?"

"A second Fromm look-alike," Conner answered. "Knowing Aurum, they manhandled and burned the poor guy to within an inch of his life. His face was barely recognizable and he couldn't talk. The goons placed him at the crash site and waited for Vernon Barlow to stumble by."

Carly took over. "Aurum's people handpicked Barlow because he was a trained fireman and knew that Labatelli's clinic was the only chance the survivor had."

"What if he didn't drive past at the right moment?" Fitzpatrick asked.

"It was all orchestrated. If Barlow didn't finish his job on time to be on intercept with the helicopter, he would've been beeped about an emergency with his mother at the assisted care facility. The roads were blocked to guide him past the crash site. As soon as Barlow was on his way, Aurum's people kept any other cars off the road so there was no one Barlow could ask for help coming from either direction. They counted on him being the Good Samaritan that he was."

"So no matter what shape this Barlow fellow found the Fromm look-alike, he would bring him to Labatelli's clinic...where Aurum was prepped and ready to be surgically transformed to look like the president? Is that what you're saying?" asked Fitzpatrick. "What happened to the man Barlow brought in?"

"His name was Mead Roberts...one of the presidential look-alikes. We found him buried in the local cemetery and confirmed his identity through DNA and dental records," Carly answered.

"What I don't get," Fitzpatrick continued asking his questions, "is what was in it for Labatelli?"

Kip Greeley answered. "Labatelli was mortgaged to the hilt; he was about to lose everything he owned. He'd been day trading. Not only lost his cash, pension, and IRA, but his employees' pension, too. The good doctor tried to make it all back playing the options market."

"That's a fool's game," Honey said.

Greeley continued. "By the time Aurum came along, Labatelli was about to lose his clinic. Lucky for Aurum he was a better surgeon than a stock picker."

"If you are finished now, I have something to say." Everyone turned to Fromm/Aurum as he spoke, each noting how hollow and weak his words now sounded.

"I'm not finished, Lute," Greeley said his name with disdain. "You needed to alter your teeth to avoid future identification. To make it work, you convinced Fromm to get a remake of his. That's how he ended up in San Martini's office, accompanied by the two agents. You thought of everything, including the off-chance that if someone thought Fromm was one of the blast victims, his teeth would be whittled down and hard to identify. You used the crash as an excuse to change your teeth, so no one could compare your smile to past photos."

Fromm/Aurum stood. "This is getting more preposterous by the minute."

"Sit down, Lute." Greeley took a stride closer. "Don't bother denying it. Once we confronted Coulter Bell, he was only too willing to sell you out. He corroborated everything I'm saying. The only thing that never made any sense to him was why you were willing to go under the knife to look like Fromm? He felt you were the one with all the power before you ever started scheming."

"He always was a fool. What none of you realize is that I am who I want to be. I've been others before this...now I'm Aldous Fromm."

Greeley continued. "We know how you eliminated Labatelli and his brother-in-law after your surgeries healed. When you heard Dr. Montgomery was working with Carly, you had him killed, too. The only one left to dispose of was Carly."

"Does your fairytale have a happy ending, Kip? Because mine does," Fromm/Aurum said.

"Your happy ending vanished when Johnny Ray Mabe got cold feet about killing Carly. Still there are four thousand dentists in New York. You could've asked for anyone of them and avoided Carly. Why didn't you? The shrinks would say you wanted to get caught."

Then a change occurred in the room. Everyone felt it. Fromm/Aurum found an inner strength that, moments before, had all but disappeared. He looked different. Bigger. Stronger. More like his old persona.

"Kip, I can't believe you're buying into all of this. After all we've been through!"

Greeley didn't cower under Fromm/Aurum's change. "I admit you had me fooled. But, remind me, what have *we* been through?"

Then the musty, stifling air turned crystal cold. Fromm/Aurum stood and leaned over the table, tenting all ten fingers on the polished tabletop.

"You *are* a fool. You're all fools. I'm Aldous Fromm, and everyone in this room knows the truth." Then he shoved the original treaty document in front of Fitzpatrick. "Now if all the fun and games are over, let's get down to business. We can still forge a union the likes of which the world has never seen. Think of what I'm offering you, Honey. Wealth. Fame. Christ, I'm giving you fucking immortality. Sign this and our countries will be linked forever. Don't sign it, and everyone in this room is doomed."

All eyes were on the Canadian prime minister.

Fitzpatrick squirmed in his chair. He rolled his lower lip over his teeth and squeezed so hard, his lips turned pale blue. He glanced at everyone, not making eye contact until he got to Kip Greeley.

Greeley's body flexed, like he wanted to run to the PM and shake sense into him.

It wouldn't have mattered.

"Sorry," Honey Fitzpatrick whispered. Then he signed the treaty.

Kip Greeley threw up his arms to protest. "You can't do that."

"I just did."

Carly cried out. "You can't let him get away with it! I showed you the DNA. It's irrefutable. Aldous Fromm is dead. This is Lute Aurum."

Fitzpatrick handed the signed treaty back.

Fromm/Aurum slipped it into his case and said to Honey, "You won't regret this."

"Ah, but you will." Honey Fitzpatrick pointed to the Secret Servicemen behind Greeley. "Isn't there a law against impersonating a president?"

The Secret Servicemen held fast. They were confused.

Kip Greeley broke into a big smile, waving his Secret Servicemen forward. "I assume you'll waive extradition and let me take him back to the States?"

"He's all yours," answered the PM.

The Secret Service surrounded Fromm/Aurum.

"Take your hands off me, I'm the President of the United States," he said, still clutching the treaty as the Secret Servicemen led him away.

Outside the room, a wail exploded from Fromm/Aurum.

"What was that?" Carly asked.

Fitzpatrick giggled.

*   *   *

A Secret Service agent bent down and picked up the last page of the treaty Fromm/Aurum had ripped apart. Underneath Aldous Fromm's signature that Lute Aurum imitated so well, Honey Fitzpatrick had signed as his name: Manifest Destiny.

97

After Aurum was taken away, Honey Fitzpatrick ordered champagne for everyone. Corks were popped and bubbly was sprayed.

Honey proposed the first toast. "To meteors."

"What's that supposed to mean?" Carly asked. "When Willie called you, he said you were already onto both Fromm's and Steel's scheme."

Greeley gestured to Fitzpatrick. "In truth, we caught on quicker to Steel than Fromm."

Honey Fitzpatrick explained. "Steel enlisted Israeli mercenaries, headed by a man named Gadol, to turn farmers into quasi-soldiers. Your satellites picked up what appeared to be troop movements in peculiar places. In his arrogance, Gadol communicated with Steel via normal satellite links. We intercepted his messages and began to piece together that Jeremy Steel was up to something. We just didn't know what."

Greeley took over. "Before we had a chance to figure out what they were planning, Fromm returned to office and I was out of the loop, again."

"Couldn't you tell he wasn't Fromm?" asked Conner. "Everything about Aurum is different."

"I had no reason to think he wasn't Fromm. He had mastered Fromm's mannerisms to a tee. He looked like him, talked like him, even picked his nose the same way. He had me fooled."

"Didn't he make your skin crawl?" Carly asked. "He did when I treated him. That's when I first suspected it wasn't Fromm."

"Something clicked for me when he returned and went right to the snake. I should've known why Coulter Bell was keeping it alive."

Fitzpatrick cleared his throat. "You asked how we communicated? We did it by sending messages off the electrical tails of meteors. We've had the technology since the 1920's. It wasn't practical until high-speed electronic switches and advanced computers made it possible to respond to instantaneous changes when the comets were near by."

Greeley grinned. "We had messages bouncing off meteors like they were Ping-Pong balls."

"So you were running a clandestine operation out of the White House, without the president knowing?" Carly asked.

"So was he," answered Greeley. "I guess you could say, it was politics as usual."

"One last question." Everyone turned to Honey Fitzpatrick. "Did Aurum really think he could pull it off?"

Conner answered. "He was warped from the start. He thought he was immortal, that he was the next messiah. For him, killing people was problem solving. So yes, in his arrogance and as grand a scheme as it was, Lute Aurum thought he could pull it off."

Greeley put his arm around Carly. "The sick thing is, he almost did. Now if all of you will excuse us, I need to speak with Carly...alone."

98

Henri Plumme was waiting at the foot of Parliament Hill.

"What are you still doing here?" Carly asked. "I thought you would have left by now."

Plumme looked at Greeley to explain.

"I asked him to stay. That's not exactly true. I relayed a message to PM Fitzpatrick; he asked Inspector Plumme to wait for us."

"What's this about? You're scaring me."

Plumme handed her a piece of paper. The FBI insignia aroused her curiosity. Her eyes ran across the page. Then she faltered. Plumme grabbed her arm and Greeley supported her back. They guided her to bench.

"Why didn't you tell me right away?"

"I needed your help in there. You were the only who could explain the stuff about the teeth and the number of roots molars have. And you deserved to see his face when he heard that you compared the DNA on the X-ray packet to the DNA in the president's pen...and didn't get a match. That was ingenious. So I'm sorry if you feel used, but the truth is, I couldn't take a chance on how you'd react."

"You have my regrets, too, Carly," Plumme said.

"I saw him twice in twenty-five years, and didn't even know who he was. Wouldn't you know it, he was sitting right there, talking to me, and I thought he was some lunatic who liked dressing up like a priest."

"He was a professional," the inspector said, "always in disguise."

"Still, I should have known. All my life, I've been playing over and over in my head, asking what made him leave, what made him abandon me? Was I bad? Did I do something wrong? Was he ashamed of my mother and me? I had so many questions bottled up inside me. I couldn't wait for the day when he'd walk back in my life so I could ask them. Now I'll never know the answers."

Greeley touched her arm. "Sometimes it's better if things are left unsaid. That way, you can imagine the answers without ever knowing the truth. In the end, it's kinder."

"Why? Because the truth hurts? I've had enough hurtful truths in my lifetime to fill an ocean."

Carly leaned into Kip Greeley and started to weep.

Greeley stroked her hair until she quieted down. She sat straight, wiping the tears from her eyes with the back of her hand. She started to speak.

"Don't say anything," said Greeley. "You had to get it out of you."

"I should have done it a long time ago. Grieving for my father the way I have, wondering what I did to cause him to leave, has held me back my whole life." She found a used Kleenex in her purse and blew. "It's time."

She turned from President Greeley, and took Henri Plumme's hand. "Does anyone have to know about this?"

Plumme put his index finger to his lips, sealing her secret forever.

"Mr. President?"

"No one in the entire world has to know that your father, Hack Mason, was Johnny Ray Mabe."

99

Carly and Conner stayed in Canada overnight. The next morning they visited the University laboratory that was studying the five-hundred-year-old body of the Indian exposed by the receding glacier. Carly had developed an interest in forensic anthropology from her years of examining teeth and bones uncovered during excavations for new buildings or those found in locked trunks, hidden behind plaster walls, or recovered from exhumed bodies.

"Do you have a cause of death?" Carly asked the scientist in charge of the autopsy.

Professor Jean-Paul Lemieux was unequivocal. "He died of asphyxiation. When we matched gases found in his lungs to core samples taken from the surrounding fields, we were able to link it to a nearby volcanic eruption. We estimate he was about thirty. Can you get a better handle on his age from his teeth?"

Carly leaned for a closer look; frigid air radiated from the gurney.

"The wear patterns would make him ancient by our standards. A detergent diet would account for the flattened cusps. Have you checked his sternum for the percentage of red marrow? That's always a way to tell his age."

"That technique is more accurate for women. What can you tell from his teeth? They're pretty worn down from chewing dried meat and softening leather with them."

She picked up the Indian's dental X-rays and held them to the light. "His wisdom teeth are fully formed, he has alveolar bone loss in the molars, no decay. I'd say he's around thirty. Does he have any medical conditions?"

"The poor bastard must've had chronic diarrhea and pain in his stomach. His colon was full of whipworm eggs, which accounts for his low iron count. Look." Lemieux pointed to a large nut tied to a leather thong. "See this? He didn't have to call Prescriptions.com when he was feeling poorly. He carried his own pharmacy with him. This nut comes from the chenopod shrub. Its oil is added to natural laxatives found in the wild, and the mixture helps expel the worms and their eggs."

"So this is a case of man using the environment to help prolong his life," Carly said.

"Quite the opposite of what we're doing these days, eh?" the professor said.

Carly showed Conner how to use the digital Olympus camera she had brought with her. The camera's close-up lens allowed for detailed intraoral pictures that could then be computer enhanced. While she and Conner were engrossed in examining the oral tissues, teeth, and taking a complete set of photos, they missed the day's historic news.

Fromm Resigns: Brain Surgery Today, Greeley sworn in 2nd Time as President

DETROIT (FREE PRESS). After a brief comeback from his near-fatal helicopter crash, President Aldous Fromm will step down from office at noon today. Ever since his return to office, the president has been complaining of pain and headaches. An MRI taken early this morning found an expanding vessel leaking fluids into the president's brain. Doctors say this condition is a walking time bomb, and that the president must have immediate surgery. They expect the lesion to be removed without ill aftereffects.

When VP Greeley was notified of Aldous Fromm's medical crisis, he was in Detroit, touring a GM factory that had been converted into manufacturing battery-operated cars.

Due to the day's rapid turn of events, Chief Justice Goldstein was dispatched to Detroit to administer the oath of office to

Kip Greeley. Perhaps it was fitting that the swearing-in of the new president occurred on the floor of an automotive plant that once produced cars that helped deplete the ozone layer.

Reporters asked what his first priority of business would be, and the new president did not hesitate. "The environment, no questions asked. We owe it to our children and our children's children, to clean up the mess we've made. The planet will go on long after we're gone. My goal will be to make certain there are people here to enjoy it. That is why I am creating a task force to determine how best to change our society from petroleum-based to one that uses farm products, crop wastes, and trees to power our country. Black gold is out, green gold is our future."

President Greeley boarded Air Force One with the huzzahs from the UAW workers ringing in his ears when he promised, "The sacrifices we make for a cleaner environment will leave a legacy for every child who walks the earth."

100

It was mid-afternoon when Carly and Conner left the University and Professor Lemieux.

Conner put his arm around Carly. "Think Willie can live without you one more day?"

"Not if he's backlogged." She turned and faced him, putting her hands around his waist. "What were you thinking?"

"I was thinking we need a night to ourselves."

"They have 'nights' in New York. We could catch the Shuttle and be in town for a late dinner."

"Somehow, that's not what I had in mind." He pressed her into him. "I was thinking more on the order of losing ourselves in each other until we dropped from exhaustion. Truth is, I don't want to waste any time."

Her kiss was all the answer he needed.

*   *   *

Back in their hotel room Carly ran her hand through Conner's hair, tracing a delicate pattern down his neck and under his shirt. Their lips met. Her eyes fluttered open to catch Conner glancing at the TV in the opened armoire. Carly snatched the remote and clicked off the screen as a goddess-of-an-announcer introduced a fast-breaking news on CNN.

"This is not a good omen," she said, ignoring the news bulletin.

"You better know now, I'm a news junkie. If I don't get my fix, I get irritable."

She nodded toward the bed. "If I don't get *my* fix, *I* get irritable…and that's something you don't want to do. Remember, I can make bodies disappear."

"…and save countries and bring down presidents and…"

"…and this." She took his hand and placed it under her blouse.

Conner grabbed the remote with his free hand. "Please don't get mad, but I'm having withdrawal symptoms."

She bounced on the bed, and the box spring groaned. "So am I."

He hit the red "power" button and the tube crackled to life.

             *   *   *

At the same time, prisoners in the common area of the Ottawa prison had their favorite television show—*Baywatch*—interrupted by a news bulletin.

             *   *   *

"My fellow Canadians," began Honey Fitzpatrick, "I am now able to report to you about a crisis that threatened the security of our government, as well as that of our great neighbor to the south, the United States. Before I do, I want to extend my heartfelt wishes to President Greeley, and a speedy recovery to ex-president Aldous Fromm, on the surgery he had this afternoon."

             *   *   *

Omitting few details, the prime minister described the events of the last few months in chronological order. He extolled the virtues of Jeremy Steel and all the good he had done for the Canadian people, yet he apologized for trusting Jeremy as much as he had. The PM described the Israeli mercenaries, the bombs that imploded killing millions of fish, and the unscheduled flights that crossed Canada one evening. He explained how the US government destroyed the missile silos and ended with Jeremy Steel's arrest. Then he segued to another big news item.

*   *   *

Carly and Conner were lying in bed, still clothed. He stroked her hair. "Aren't you glad I turned it back on?"

"It's nice to see Honey, but we know everything he's talking about." She curled her hand under his shirt, and ran a finger across his chest. "Turn it off."

"In a sec. I can't believe how blasé you are about this. You discover the president's been murdered, you topple the sitting president, help install the vice-president into the Oval Office, and meet your father after twenty-five years."

She rolled her lower lip under her upper teeth, squeezed hard to hold back the tears, and then turned up the volume.

She'd trade it all in for…

*   *   *

The prisoners clamored to get Fitzpatrick off the screen. They had to wait.

*   *   *

"As of today, all properties owned by foreigners—including those of our American cousins—have been nationalized. The owners will receive the fair market value for their possessions. Never again will foreigners be able to control Canadian soil.

"In addition a treaty was signed late this afternoon with the United States. Our nations will create a joint venture to explore for oil in the St. Lawrence Sound. All discoveries will be the property of Canada, with royalties given to the US for their assistance.

"Furthermore, I am pleased to announce that President Greeley has committed the resources of the United States to exceed the reductions in Greenhouse emissions targeted in the Kyoto II Protocol. He will do so without buying 'Pollution Permits' from poorer countries. This is unprecedented. It demonstrates the courage and leadership needed from the world's biggest producer of Greenhouse gases. I applaud the new president for wanting to correct the ills his nation has so long ignored."

*   *   *

The remainder of the prime minister's speech was drowned out by the jeering prisoners.

"Who gives a flying fuck. Bring back the Baywatch babes."

"How much property do you own?" one inmate asked another.

"Four apartment houses. You should see the fistfuls I collect the first of every month."

The two broke into hysterics at the thought of owning any-thing. They could care less about politics or politicians. Pollution controls meant as much to them as the Pythagorean Theory.

Metal cups strafed across bars, some banged wooden stools on the hard floor.

One convict yelled to the new prisoner in the last cell. "Hey Steel, did you hear that? You're going be minus a few holdings after today."

"Poor Jeremy's lost his cities. My, my, 'tis a pity."

Another jailbird hooted above the ruckus. "What's the matter, Jeremy? Cat got your tongue?"

Hearing that, the inmates roared until tears streamed down their stubbled cheeks.

"Jeremy's lost his cities. Jeremy's lost his cities."

Jeremy Steel, inmate #142690, sat at the edge of his cot, hud-dled in his blue denim prison garb. When he heard Honey Fitzpatrick announce the new law, he wept in silence.

"Jeremy's lost his cities. Jeremy's lost his cities," they chorused

"Su...uh," he screamed back at them, only to have them whoop louder.

Jeremy tried to make himself heard a second, then a third time, but he never managed to make himself any clearer. "Su...up," he said. "Su...up."

The speech therapist told him it would take time.

When? he wanted to know.

Time, was all she answered.

Jeremy Steel was used to getting his way. All he could do now was glare as they continued to taunt him. He covered his ears with his hands; tears cascaded down his cheeks. In his worst night-mares, Jeremy never dreamed these indignities could be inflicted on him.

"Jeremy's lost his cities. Jeremy's lost his cities."

In a blink Jeremy Steel went from out-conning Lute Aurum and grabbing Canada for himself to unmitigated ruin. There was God's covenant to fulfill. He was their Moses. His divine mission was to make Canada the new Promised Land. He was a *Clear*, and would reign forever.

He had played it out over and over in his mind. Every detail was in place. Destiny was his...until Miss Tooth Sleuth came on the scene.

"Jeremy's lost his cities. Jeremy's lost his cities."

Jeremy had always fancied himself as the supreme communicator. He had the gift of gab. Was there a person alive who didn't believe Jeremy Steel had a silver tongue? Jeremy Steel could sell anything to anybody. He was the master builder. A world builder.

Jail was a temporary setback.

He would be back and when he was, watch out!

"Su...up," he yelled at the other prisoners. "Su...up."

Then he reached for a spoon and twisted it until he saw his face reflected.

He ran his fingers over his cheek, and then his nose.

The scratches would heal.

When he opened his mouth, he grimaced.

How could he make a comeback without a tongue?

101

Lute Aurum exited Canada dazed. He had entered expecting to unite two countries and end up ruling the greatest empire since Napoleon. He left stripped of power and title.

The return flight aboard Air Force One would be his last. Greeley sat next to him.

"You know you'll never get away with this," Aurum said, still not conceding defeat. "The people love me."

"You're mistaken. They loved Aldous Fromm, and he's dead."

"And I've taken his place. Who really cares? Do the people ever know who their leaders are? Who ran the country when Woodrow Wilson had a stroke? When Ike had his heart attacks? Was it really FDR crippled in that wheelchair, or had he died earlier? I've been to Yalta, you know."

"Now I know you're delusional."

"Eternal, is more like it. What do you plan to do with me?"

"The press will be told you resigned due to a medical crisis. I'll take over the presidency. You'll retire to Arizona and the Secret Service will watch you twenty-four hours a day. If you so much as fart at the wrong time, I'll know about it. Behave yourself, and you can live in dignity the rest of your life."

"Dignity?"

"Otherwise, you'll end up like Artie Montefusco."

*   *   *

When the plane landed, Aurum was taken to Walter Reade Medical Center where he was made to endure a fake battery of tests and stay over night. Nothing organically was wrong with him, but that's not what the rest of the world was told.

*   *   *

Greeley flew to Detroit where he met with the CEO of GM, and leaders of the UAW. Chief Justice Goldstein flew there for the swearing-in ceremony.

The following day, Aurum was released long enough to return to the Oval Office to retrieve what few personal belongings he wanted to take with him.

There was really nothing to take.

When he sat in the leather chair behind the big polished desk, he thought about what could have been. He clicked on the television. With the sound muted, he viewed Honey Fitzpatrick's face.

*   *   *

He

Only another Iotan could find him limned against the cool stone. If only there *was* another Iotan. *He* was lonely. The time had come.

He entered their corporeal world. *He* needed more.

He became a serpent. A viper. A snake. *He* needed more.

He created the forbidden fruit. *He* needed more.

He created chaos...and saw that it was good.
He would return.

*   *   *

There was a knock on the door.
Aurum ignored it.
"We've come for you, sir."
"One more second, son," Aurum said to the military attaché.
Alone, Aurum rose. In the center of the room he stopped for one last look...then he smiled. He almost forgot to say good-bye to his friend. He lifted the glass top and petted the snake that had traveled with him through the years.
The viper turned a lazy eye toward him.
Aurum lifted it from the cage.
The snake wrapped around his neck.
Aurum stroked the snake as he turned up the TV volume to hear Honey say,

*   *   *

"...extend my heartfelt congratulations to President Greeley. On a personal note, I want ex-president Aldous Fromm to know that every man, woman, and child in Canada wishes him a speedy recovery from this afternoon's surgery."

*   *   *

"What surgery? Those lying, thieving, motherfucking bas-tards." Then he hurled the snake at the television. The viper hit the screen, barely touched the floor and lunged for Aurum.

*   *   *

When the attaché entered to take Aurum away, he found the viper curled on Aurum's chest. Geysers of blood spurted from the two fang marks that had severed Aurum's left jugular artery.

Try as they may, expert carpet cleaners could not remove the bloodstains; the presidential seal in the center of the Oval Office carpet was ruined.

Epilogue

"How did the lecture go?"

Willie was reflecting the scalp of a newborn baby immersed in a water basin. He needed to determine if the one-week old had died of natural causes or had met foul play at the hands of its sixteen-year old mother. By removing the brain under water, there was less risk of damaging the fragile tissues. In this way, poor technique could not be mistaken for inflicted trauma.

"I think I'm reaching them," answered Carly.

She was returning from her weekly child abuse lecture.

"Here's one you didn't reach," said Willie.

Carly leaned over and stared at the brain. "Looks like hamburger."

Willie groaned. "How could anyone do this to a child? I am so sick of seeing child after child murdered by parents no better than animals."

"Animals wouldn't do this to their young. This mother should be sterilized. No two ways about it."

"Did you see him outside?" Willie asked, when she returned from checking her message box.

"Who?"

"Some guy. Said it was personal."

"I came the back way. Was it Conner? He's supposed to be at Boston. Back at school."

"I know what pretty boy looks like. This was an accountant-type. He might have been here before."

If it were another reporter, she'd scream. It was a week after returning from Canada and reporters wouldn't leave her alone. Even the ladies room wasn't safe!

                    *   *   *

"Remember me?" The man sported a blue-and-white seer-sucker suit. He stood in front of the plate glass window wiping his brow.

"Mr. Prescott. You had me sign some papers."

"I've got more for you to sign. Won't take but a moment."

Lex Prescott pulled a yellowed folder from his cracked-leather briefcase.

Inside the packet, Carly saw a red sticker with an arrow pointing the places to sign.

Carly took the fake emerald-green Mont Blanc pen. "What are these for?"

"I read your father died. My condolences."

"So?"

"You're the heir. The estate's yours. Remember the trust?"

She put the pen down. "I don't deserve anything from him. It's not like he was a father to me."

She might have believed that once, but not any more. Ever since Johnny Ray Mabe spared her, she began to think otherwise.

"That's all well and good, but it doesn't get the papers signed." He picked up the pen and handed it to her again. "Now if you don't mind, please sign by the red markers. Be certain not to miss any."

"Is there any harm in signing?"

"Finger cramps."

When she was finished, Prescott reached into his breast pocket and unfolded a paper. He adjusted his glasses.

"I was instructed to tell you once you signed this, that your father was very proud of you. He was sorry for the trouble and pain he caused you. Also, he wanted you to know that he was at your graduation from Duke, and sat in the back of the auditorium when you graduated from dental school. He even saw you in Central Park when you hit a home run against the emergency room physicians."

"That was last year."

Tears streamed down Carly's face.

Prescott handed her his sweaty handkerchief without missing a beat.

"He also came here, to the Medical Examiner's once, pretending to be a lab technician. He was able to watch you until someone realized he didn't belong there. He said that Willie Robinson was a good man."

This was too much to bear. Carly struggled her whole life, blaming herself for causing her father to leave. No matter how much her mother tried to correct this misguided idea, that adults caused their own problems, Carly believed something she could have said or done would have made her mother's life easier, and reversed her fatherless years.

When Hack Mason left home, Carly was forced to stand on her own two feet. Rather than hide in a bud at age ten and stay there until it was too late, Carly blossomed into a fine student/athlete. Sports taught her the meaning of winning, of striving to be the best. Academics were another form of being the best, and a means to an end. The end, in this case, was a way to grab some of life's riches that a poor girl from Queens didn't always have a chance to hold.

On paper, it was a good choice. Except dentistry—like her father—abandoned her. The glory of being a doctor was there, but the rewards remained elusive.

Though time lessened the childhood hurts she carried with her, she was never able to find a comfortable spot for her father...not in her mind, and certainly not in her heart. Recent experiences only served to confuse. Learning that her father was alive and a hired gun left her cold. Of course she cared that he was a murderer, but he was a stranger to her. Except for half her chromosomes, what connected them? The better genes came from her mother, anyway. The fact that he had reentered her life, even if it was to "save" it, didn't change her thinking.

Just when her emotions were finally sorted out, just when she came to believe that grieving for Hack Mason was a waste of time, Lex Prescott muddled everything.

In his own way, Hack Mason loved her. In his own way, Hack Mason had always loved her.

The lawyer fetched a last piece of paper from his case.

"What's that?" she asked.

"I want to meet you in my office next week. By then, I'll be able to give you a full accounting of what's in the estate. There will be taxes to pay and more papers to sign."

She wiped her eyes then returned his soiled handkerchief. She took the paper.

"Aren't you going to read it?"

"You just gave me the best news I could ever have. Who cares what's on the paper?"

He nudged it toward her.

"I think you ought to look."

Her eyes scanned words, but nothing registered.

"Well?"

"I don't know what you mean?"

"It's your father's portfolio. It describes the number of shares and what they are worth as of last year."

Carly centered on the page. There were hundreds of shares of dozens of companies. Microsoft, Cisco, Dell, Sun Microsystems, Intel, GE, IBM, AT&T, Pfizer, Merck, WalMart, and Genetech. Many were familiar; some were not.

"When did he buy these?"

"Most after the '87 crash. Never sold a one, either. He got all the splits. Look at the total."

Her eyes fought the dates and symbols and share amounts until she located the bottom number.

"Five hundred thousand dollars! I can't even imagine that much."

Prescott wiggled his skinny index finger. "Carly, you forgot something. Look again."

She looked at the bottom number again.

"I forgot a zero, didn't I? It's five *million* dollars!"

"As of last year."

"Whose is it?"

"All yours."

She sat tall. Sober. "No, it's not. I don't want it."

"That's ridiculous." Prescott put the signed papers in his leather case. "You have to take it."

"Mr. Prescott, I don't have to do anything I don't want to do." Carly was momentarily distracted by the moving traffic up First Avenue. She stood and walked to the plate glass window, pressing her face against the warm surface. Then she wheeled. "If it's mine, then I can give it away. Right?"

He saw she was determined. "When the transfers are done and everything's in your name, you can buy a penthouse apartment, travel around the world, or give it all away. The choice is yours."

"Then will you help me give it to the Shelter for Battered Women?"

"Don't you want to take some time and think about this? That's an awful lot of money to give away. I'm sure you can use some of it."

"My father earned it killing people, Mr. Prescott. I can't keep any of it. The least I can do is give it to those who really need it."

Carly wasn't kidding.

"If you insist." He reached inside his case and handed her an envelope. "Here's the last of it. He wanted you to have this."

It was a photograph of Carly and her father. Hack Mason was handsome then. He sported a banana-yellow blue rodeo shirt and worn riding chaps. Carly was no more than three or four years old, and was sitting on a palomino horse. She had a turquoise cowboy hat dangling on her back, held around her neck by a braided cord. She wore a tasseled buckskin shirt embroidered with different colored beads, and matching pants that dissolved into tiny plastic cowboy boots. In the picture she was leaning down from the saddle, with her arms around Hack Mason, planting a big kiss on her father's cheek.

There was love in her eyes.

Carly fingered the worn edges of the photograph and drifted to a time gone by, a time she had all but forgotten.

She looked at Lex Prescott and placed the photo against her lips. "Thank you for giving my father back to me."

THE END

About the Author

Alan A. Winter was born in Newark, New Jersey. He graduated from Rutgers University, New Brunswick, NJ, with a degree in history, and attended NYU and Columbia dental schools. He is a trained forensic dentist and a board-certified periodontist who maintains a private practice—Park Avenue Periodontal Associates—in New York City. He founded and edited a dental journal for ten years and is the author of 11 scientific articles.

His first novel, "Someone Else's Son," was a McNaughton Selection and is available through www.backinprint.com or through his web site.

Alan A. Winter is married, has five sons, and lives in New Jersey. His hobbies include traveling, mountain biking, and white-water rafting. He is currently working on a screenplay and a new novel. He can be reached at: www.alanwinter.net